CLAIMED

CLAIMED

REBECCA ZANETTI

BRAVA

KENSINGTON PUBLISHING CORP.

www.kensingtonbooks.com

BRAVA BOOKS are published by

Kensington Publishing Corp.
119 West 40th Street
New York, NY 10018

All Kensington titles, imprints, and distributed lines are available at special quantity discounts for bulk purchases for sales promotion, premiums, fund-raising, educational, or institutional use.

Special book excerpts or customized printings can also be created to fit specific needs. For details, write or phone the office of the Kensington Special Sales Manager. Attn.: Special Sales Department, Kensington Publishing Corp., 119 West 40th Street, New York, NY 10018. Phone: 1-800-221-2647.

Brava and the B logo are Reg. U.S. Pat. & TM Off.

ISBN-13: 978-0-7582-5925-7
ISBN-10: 0-7582-5925-5

First Kensington Trade Paperback Printing: November 2011

10 9 8 7 6 5 4 3 2 1

Printed in the United States of America

To my mom, Gail Cornell English, who has always been the go-to mom for us all—from being room mom, to coaching softball to helping us sew pillows for Home Ec. when we didn't have a clue. She also managed to raise three girls without going stark raving mad when we were all teenagers at the same time. Though as her grandchildren approach their teenage years, she has a funny smile on her face . . .

To my father, Jim English, who taught me three basic things. First, a sense of humor will get you through anything in life, while making it all the more enjoyable. Second, it is a colossal mistake to take golf lessons from your own father. And third, Dads are there for you no matter what.

I love you both.

And as always to big Toné—I love you.

ACKNOWLEDGMENTS

There are so many wonderful people to thank when a book actually makes it to print.

Thank you to my terrific editor, Megan Records, whose good humor and support always brighten my day, and whose excellent advice I could not do without—and thanks to the entire team at Kensington for the incredible support.

Thank you to my amazing agent, Caitlin Blasdell, who spent much appreciated time working on character arcs, plot devices, and pacing with me.

Thank you to my excellent critique partner, Jennifer Dorough, whose help and friendship make this whole journey all the more wonderful.

Thank you to the very talented Cynthia Eden and Kate Douglas for their kindness, support, and advice.

And thank you to my amazing, always present, and supportive family.

Chapter 1

She'd die if she jumped.

Probably with a great deal of pain first. The rotating hum of the helicopter blades echoed through the confined space of the aircraft as Emma Paulsen calculated her odds of a quick death—she'd likely hit a tree or two before slamming into the earth. Hmm. Not good.

Keeping her eyes closed, she lay curled on her side in the center of the beast, rocking back and forth from the movement of hurtling through the air. Dust littered the Black Hawk's floor, but she forced herself to breathe. Was it called a floor? Was it really a Black Hawk? If so, they'd modified the crap out of it. With a mental shrug, she cleared her mind.

Nothing.

No whispers from the future.

No glimpses of how this ordeal would end.

Damn. Maybe the drugs they'd injected into her arm accomplished more than simple sedation. She'd relied on her psychic ability her whole life, and now it was gone.

Her abductors, two living horrors, sat up front as pilot and copilot—she'd have to take them out last. Two other Kurjan soldiers escorting her to their Canadian leader sat in the rear of the chopper, arguing about football scores. Seriously? Undead monsters afraid of the sun talked about the Seahawks?

Their conversation slid around her unhampered by the wind rushing outside. The restructured walls denied sun and sound from filtering inside.

She centered herself. She'd have to kill them.

The odds of being successful calculated inside her head with a nearly audible click. The result: not good.

Nausea rose in her belly, and gray murk swam across her vision until she zoned out again. Damn drugs.

She floated in the place between dreams and reality, a place she visited often. Where was he? For so long she'd been afraid of meeting *him*, now she feared it would never happen.

Like an antenna had been angled, a large room swam into hazy focus. A massive fire crackled beneath a stone mantel, the walls rock, the floor dirt. There he was—Dage, King of the Realm. He stood near the wall, his jaw hard, his eyes molten silver of fury.

What century was she visiting? An early one—he held a broadsword in one hand, his legs encased in coverings reminiscent of an old warrior movie she'd seen as a teenager.

He stood shoulder to shoulder with a man who had eyes the color of gold coins. Talen, his brother. Three other men, boys actually, faced them. Similar bone structure, similar stances. All huge. The oldest tightened his grip on a deadly sword. "They killed our parents."

"Aye," Dage agreed. "So we killed them—and their parents. Enough." He dropped his sword to the ground. "We're done with the killing—with the war. Right now we strive for peace."

"I donna take orders from you, brother," the youngest lad said, his eyes a deep burnished copper.

"Maybe not from your brother Jase, but you'll obey your king."

The boy shifted his stance, his eyes narrowing. "Is that who you are now?"

"Aye. Until they cut off my head, I'm your king."

Emma started herself back into the current century, coughing out dust. Relief filled her that she could still connect with her silver-eyed savior in *his* past, if not her future. Her visions always predicted the future unless Dage was in them. Then she saw the trials of his long life. A highlight film of war, honor and hope.

"She's awake," came a hoarse voice from behind her. "Should we inject her again?"

"No," the Seahawk fan replied. "What can she do?"

Indeed. Emma pushed to a sitting position, scooting until her back rested on the inside wall and across from the door. "I could kill you with a simple thought." The metal chilled through her jeans and she fought to control her body. Shivering would show fear.

Their purple eyes widened in their inhuman white faces. Devils, Kurjans, the evil vampire race to be sure. One flipped his red, black-tipped hair over a shoulder. "You could not." His tensed shoulders belied his words.

Of course she couldn't. Dumbass. "Sure. You already know Franco wants me because of my psychic abilities. They include frying brains." Okay, the frying part may have been too much.

The pasty-faced bloodsuckers remained silent, bizarre gazes on her. How was it possible these freaks lived among humans without being noticed? They must hide really well during the day. In fact, what genetic mutation created these guys? The urge to study their physiology nearly overpowered the urge to end their lives. Nearly.

She glanced at the door, wondering how heavy it was. The sun blazed across a blue fall sky outside—beautiful and damn deadly to the Kurjan creeps safely ensconced in the helicopter. If she opened the door, would the sun angle in the right direction?

She rapidly considered wind speed, the sun's position, and their location. Nope. She needed the Kurjans to move.

Forcing fear down deep, forcing concern for her sister Cara down even deeper, Emma formulated a plan. Once she escaped she'd get back to Cara and rescue her from Franco's cousin, the Kurjan soldier who'd kidnapped them both yesterday.

Emma's plan was to lunge for the door, hoping at least one of the Kurjans went for her. If the sun hit him he'd fry like bacon. She tensed, ready to move . . .

And didn't get the chance.

Something hard slammed into the thick metal. The door creaked, the hinges twisted and peeled away. In the next second the door was gone, ripped away from the helicopter to sail through the air. A broad hand reached in, grabbed the nearest Kurjan, and sent him spiraling into the blue day. The soldier's high-pitched scream echoed in the distance as the sun ate him alive.

In a blur of motion, a huge male form dodged inside, ducked a punch from the Seahawk fan and shot an elbow into his nose, splashing blood across the wall. The monster dropped his weapon, hands going to his face before he too was sent hurtling out the door. The Kurjan's loud screams followed the helicopter for several moments before dying out.

Her rescuer didn't need to turn for her to recognize him.

Dage.

Could she still be dreaming?

His silver gaze ran over her before a sharp burst of green light ripped into his collarbone, throwing him back into the rushing air.

"No," Emma shouted as he fell, his large body half outside the helicopter. The massive bird teetered for a moment, then regained its course. She lunged forward, grasping his arms.

Or tried to; his biceps were too big. Her nails bit into his flesh as she wrapped both hands around his left arm and pulled.

The Kurjan in the copilot's seat stopped firing his weapon, probably afraid to injure her. She was the prize, after all.

Dage eased back inside, attempting to shield her with his body.

She pushed at his uninjured shoulder, leaning down to yell in his ear. "Get behind me."

His eyes flashed fire even while his upper lip quirked. "You get behind *me*."

She gave a sharp shake of her head and shoved at him again. The wind screamed a warning outside, waiting for its next victim. Dage didn't budge. He grabbed the gun off the floor, pointed it at the copilot, and fired.

The Kurjan ducked, but the light green bullets ripped through the front windshield, allowing pure rays of sunshine to cascade inside. He screamed a shrill protest, throwing his hands up. The helicopter swerved and the pilot regained control, edging his body away from the sun and toward the side of the craft, his trembling fingers clenching the controls.

The copilot continued to scream in pain. The smell of burned hair and sizzling flesh filled the small space, and Emma fought the urge to vomit.

Like a rat fleeing a tomcat, the copilot scrambled over his seat, landing with a hard thud on the floor. His pasty-white skin melted down his face. Raw red blisters sprang up across abused flesh. Sharp yellow fangs protruded from his wide open mouth, while the rushing wind stole any sound he made.

Quick as a whip, Dage reached forward and grabbed him around the neck, tossing him toward the gaping hole. The Kurjan hit the side of the hatch, the impact rocking the small craft. Clutching both long-clawed hands into the floor, he tried to inch way away from the deadly opening. Dage shot one large flak boot into the Kurjan's battered face, and the copilot fell into the sun. Then Dage shifted, pointing the gun at the pilot's head.

The pilot aimed his purple gaze over his shoulder, sharp canines flashing in a dare. Kill him, and they would all die.

Dage grabbed Emma close and fired, striking the Kurjan in the head. He fell forward onto the stick, the metal bird spun, and shot for the earth.

Emma clutched Dage's shoulders, and then . . . nothing.

It was as if they traveled through a vacuum—no sound, sight, smells—just . . . nothing. Except the vague sense of Dage. Power and safety but shrouded.

Reality crashed back followed by Dage's hiss of pain. He released her to fall onto spongy grass, and she shut her eyes against the glare of the sun. The smell of wet pine and moist earth filled her nose.

The world spun. She opened her eyes, and the world spun more. Dage stood with his knees bent, held upright by . . . a tree limb? A protruding snag from an old tree stump emerged from Dage's left shoulder, his silver eyes pissed, his blood a deep red.

His right hand patted the shards of wood emerging from his body. "Not my best landing, love. Sorry about that."

Emma shook her head to clear it. Her knees popped when she rose and stumbled toward the king. He'd impaled himself on an old limb. She peered around his back to find the gnarled trunk protruding from deep in the ground. *Damn it.* She needed some sort of chainsaw to cut him loose. And a medical team to remove the wood from his body.

An explosion over the next hill rent the air with an angry boom. She turned. Furious smoke billowed into the untouched sky. "The helicopter?"

"Yes."

"We didn't jump?"

"No. I can teleport. A bit, anyway." He readied his stance,

positioning both hands on his knees like a lineman waiting for the snap.

Teleport? How in the world was that possible? Something to do with dimensions or gravity? Possibly relativity theory. "What are you doing?" She hated the quake in her voice. The smell of copper scenting the air made her gag.

He gave a weary grin. "I thought I'd take out this splinter."

Panic rushed through her. "You can't. I mean, you'll bleed to death. You can't." She pressed a hand against the black cotton covering his good shoulder where muscles tightened in response.

His eyes darkened. "I've waited centuries for your touch, Emma." He hissed out a breath. "This isn't how I pictured it." Shutting his eyes, he drew a deep breath. "Now step out of the way, love."

"No. You can't do this."

Silver eyes pinned her. "Night will fall within three hours. The Kurjans will descend upon the last known location of their helicopter, and we need to be long gone from here."

"Where are we?" The forest pressed in with silence. No doctors nearby, that was for sure.

"Shoshone mountains in northern Idaho. I chose to intercept you here because there are old mining caves to hide in."

Forget hiding. He was going to bleed to death. "Can you teleport us to a hospital?"

Shaking his head, Dage drew another deep breath. Round bullet holes from the copilot's attack dotted his upper chest and neck near the wood splintering his body. His blood flowed freely and spoiled the fresh air—along with the strongest hint of sandalwood. His scent. "No. I usually can only teleport once, then need to recharge. I've done it three times today, and I'm wiped."

"Three times?" She pushed harder against his good side, trying to keep him in place.

"Yes." Amusement lit his eyes even through the raw pain swirling in the depths. "Once to the ground along your known flight path, then to the helicopter when you were in sight, then to right here."

"How did you know my flight path?" Damn. He shouldn't remove the wood without a surgical unit on the ready.

"We raided the Kurjan facility in Montana right after they forced you to leave." Dage gasped in a deep breath. "One of the Kurjans kindly volunteered the information."

Emma raised an eyebrow. "Good thing you spotted the correct helicopter," she murmured, glancing at the stained branch. A warm tingle teased her heart. He'd come for her. Because his brother had married her sister? Or because he knew her as she'd known him all these years? Through visions. Of course, while she appreciated the rescue, she wouldn't have needed help if the vampires hadn't dragged her and her sister into their world. "So you were in time to rescue Cara?" Hope filled Emma. Please let her sister be safe.

"Yes. Talen should have his mate safely home by now."

Thank god. Emma exhaled. Vibrations from Dage's pain pounded toward her, and she concentrated on the situation at hand. Blood from his wounds flowed into each groove of the wood, resulting in the look of stained teak.

Dage groaned. "Step back, love."

Her trembling hand patted his shoulder before she stuck it in her pocket. "You're really a vampire?" She'd known of the vampire race for a couple of months since Cara had married Talen. Though this was the first time she'd actually been face to face with one. Apparently the sun didn't bother the good guys, only the Kurjans.

"Yes."

Emma took a step back. Vampires were immortal, right? "You'll survive this?"

"Yes. We can only be killed by beheading."

"Okay." She couldn't see an alternative. Her stomach pitched, and fear slithered down her spine. This had to work.

Dage sucked in air, then sprang forward. The tree branch ripped out of his flesh with a protesting snap. He landed on his knees in the crusty pine needles, emitting a string of Russian, Greek, or maybe Gaelic that sounded like curses. The earth rumbled and the wind picked up its strength around them. Winding down, he pushed to his feet. "Damn." His good arm grabbed the hem of his shirt and ripped it over his head, his back to her.

Emma gasped at the raw wound above his right shoulder blade. Sharp wooden splinters emerged from split bone, shredded muscles, and cut tissue next to the dangerous tattoo she knew so well. The breath caught in her throat when he pivoted and blood poured from his broad chest. "You're bleeding." She shook her head, her focus narrowing on the wicked tattoo of intricate markings along his left arm and over his shoulder to his back.

The design had haunted her dreams like a warning talisman.

He nodded, inhaling deeply, his metallic eyes unfocusing for a moment, his muscles visibly relaxing. The blood flow stemmed, leaving the bullet holes seeping. The wide gash crusted over. "That's the best I can do for now. It'll heal." He shoved the tail ends of his shirt into a back pocket and held out one large boned hand. "Come."

No. She wouldn't run into the woods. Not again. "Ah . . ."

Dage raised an eyebrow. "We need to get going, love."

How many nights had she run through the woods to escape her drunken father and his beefy fists? Those days were over. She'd thought she was done running from monsters.

Dage waited patiently, his gaze on her, his hand extended.

She hesitated, glancing at the tarnished limb still protruding from the ground and awaiting its next victim. In slow motion, she shifted her gaze to Dage and paused for the briefest of breaths before sliding her hand in his. A click echoed throughout her heart, throughout her head when his warm palm closed over hers. No. Wrong time to deal with this. "I need to get to Cara in case the Kurjans had time to infect her with the virus."

Dage tightened his grip and started to jog, tugging Emma to keep pace. "Cara is fine." Pine, sunshine and wildflowers commingled into a scent carried by the slightest breeze as the trees rushed past. "Talen made sure of it."

Thank God. "The Kurjans didn't get a chance to inject her with the virus?" Relief began to wind through the nerves still jumping in Emma's skin.

"No. Cara and the baby are safe."

Emma stumbled, then regained her footing with the king's help. "She told you about the baby?"

Dage flashed a grin, the sunlight dappling through branches high above to kiss his bronze skin. "No." He tightened his grip. "I sensed the babe's heartbeat when Talen carried Cara out of the Kurjan research facility earlier today. I take it she told you?"

"No." Emma grinned back. "Psychic here. Sometimes, anyway."

"Ah. I wondered if you were an empath like Cara. A psychic scientist, huh?" Not by one breath did Dage show he ran with blood streaming from his shoulder.

Reality crashed back like falling boulders. "Yes. A scientist who helped develop the virus that might kill all vampire mates, including my sister."

Dage shook his head, slowing his pace. "No. The Kurjans didn't design Virus-27 to kill our mates." He stopped, resting his back against the trunk of a lodgepole pine, blood weaving down a six-pack worthy of billboards. "I need to close these damn holes."

Emma tugged her hand free to bend at the waist to suck in air, her calves protesting the sudden stop. "You'd think with all the running I've been doing from the Kurjans I'd be in better shape." Her lungs ached. She'd been on the run from the bastards for five terror filled weeks when they'd finally caught her. She eyed the path she'd just run, adrenaline prickling goose bumps on her skin. Were the Kurjans behind them?

Wait a minute. "Virus-27?" She tilted her head. "What do you mean it doesn't kill?" She thought her lab had been working on a cure for cancer. Not a way to genetically alter vampire mates, like her sister.

"Well . . ." Those silver eyes probed her for a moment, bringing an unwelcomed skittering to Emma's abdomen. "What do you know about a vampire mating?"

The skittering turned into a full flush which traveled north to heat her face. "Just what Cara had time to tell me when we were locked in the room by the Kurjans earlier today. And she, um, showed me the brand on her ass." The design resembled the tattoo winding over Dage's shoulder.

Twin dimples flashed in Dage's strong face. "Yes, well. When we find our mates, a marking appears on our palm. It transfers to our mate during sex and changes the human to immortal."

Warmth heated Emma's face, and she struggled to focus on the genetics involved, stretching her calves during the moment of rest. "Your mates are always human?"

"Well, non-vampire anyway. Vampires are male only." He pushed off from the bark and her senses swam with sandalwood, leather, and amber. Power. "The marking changes a human from having twenty-three chromosomes to twenty-seven."

Emma's scientific mind reeled. "Vampires have twenty-seven chromosomes?"

"No. We and the Kurjans have thirty."

She shook her head. "So Cara now has twenty-seven chromosomes and is immortal?" Emma needed to get back and take some blood samples. She wouldn't have believed it had she not stolen lab results full of proof.

"Yes. And as a mate, she's safe from the touch of any other vampire or Kurjan. We call it the mating allergy." He closed his eyes, breathing deeply as the holes in his body reduced in size. "My brother Jase tried to kiss a mated woman a century or so ago and ended up in agony with raw blisters across his face." Dage smiled in remembrance.

"So my research to create a virus that mutates chromosomes was actually to change this mating allergy?" She'd hoped to combat non-Hodgkin's lymphoma by having a man-made virus attack and mutate the cancer cells.

"We think that was one of the goals. The virus initially attacks the twenty-seventh chromosome, thus my brother Kane named it Virus-27. We believe the twenty-seventh chromosome ties into the mating bond. The Kurjans want to steal our mates." Dage opened his eyes, dark gaze on her.

"Why? I mean, why don't they just find their own mates?"

"Ah. Well, mates are enhanced humans. Psychics, healers, empaths—and you're few and far between." He eyed the sun just beginning to lower in the west. "In fact, there's a pretty strong theory that enhanced humans are descendants of the fey people, cousins to the witches."

Witches? No way—she was a scientist, damn it. And his reference to her as a potential mate should not have set butterflies to flight in her stomach. The desire to explore a world where her psychic visions not only made sense but were accepted flirted with her need to protect a hard-earned, well-ordered life. Focus. She needed to focus. "So Cara and the baby are safe from the Kurjans, so long as they're protected from the virus?"

"Yes. They're safe from the Kurjans." Dage stretched his arms, his gaze sliding to the forest before them and clearly avoiding hers.

Unease wound down Emma's spine at his tone. Something

concerned the king. "Who isn't my sister safe from?" Good God. Was Talen dangerous? Or ... "Is something wrong with the baby?"

Dage sighed and rubbed his chin, sending a tendril of unease down her spine. "Probably not."

"Probably?" Not good enough. Not nearly good enough.

His silver gaze wandered her face, taking her measure until she lifted her chin in response. He sucked in air. "The speed of the pregnancy is unheard of in our people. Cara's physiology is still changing from human to immortal—no mate has ever reproduced so quickly. It usually takes decades or even centuries of trying for a successful conception."

Well. Nice of him not to sugarcoat it. "Successful conception?"

"Ah, yes. Apparently creating immortals isn't that easy." While he smiled at what appeared to be an understatement, concern filled his amazing eyes.

"But you have four brothers." How hard could it be?

Dage shrugged. "I know. It took three centuries of attempts and miscarriages for my parents to have me. Then my brothers came along quickly. I can't explain it."

She needed a lab and blood samples from all of them. There was a rational explanation for the scenario—the right research method was all that was needed. Science could explain anything, regardless of the species and genetics involved.

He reached out and grasped her hand. "Being a mate carries danger, Emma. You need to know that right now." Loping into a jog, he tugged her into a run.

She had no intention of being mated with a vampire, regardless of her dreams. "What's up with the primitive language? I mean, assuming the legends of vampires are true and you're fairly immortal, shouldn't you have progressed past the whole possessive 'my mate' language?"

He rasped out a chuckle. "Fairly immortal? We can be

killed by beheading, as can the Kurjans." His hand tightened on hers and trees rushed past. "Don't for a second think the possessive 'my mate' language is archaic terminology. It fits."

A warning tickled the back of her neck even as warmth spread through her limbs. A glance at the sky jerked her out of her thoughts. The sun angled lower toward the mountains. They were running out of time.

Chapter 2

Dust tickled Emma's nose and powdered her knees as she knelt next to Dage while the last rays of the day filtered inside the dank cave. They'd run for nearly two hours until reaching the hills and myriad of caves. A dripping somewhere down a small tunnel caused a shiver to run up her back, and she pushed away thoughts of bats. And spiders. She had real monsters to worry about.

She shifted her attention to Dage, who sat against the wall, blood running in rivulets down his broad chest to stain his jeans. He'd been sitting for nearly fifteen minutes attempting to close the holes in his body without success.

The sound of her throat clearing echoed around the rock walls of the cave. "You're hurt, you need to feed."

He raised an eyebrow, arrogant even in pain. "Feed? You watch too much television, love."

"You don't drink blood?"

"Sure. During extreme situations like battle or sex. But for dinner I prefer a nice steak with a vintage cabernet." His grin slid into a grimace.

"I'd say this is an extreme situation." The scent of his blood sent her instincts reeling. She may not have her sister's empathic abilities, but even Emma could feel vibrations from the king's pain. "You need blood."

His chin lifted, a challenge sparking though those dangerous eyes. "Do I?"

Frustration whispered through her. "Yes." Although she needed saving because of his people's war, he had mounted a battle against several monsters to save her, and she couldn't do less for him.

"Sure you can. You don't owe me anything." He closed his eyes and leaned his head against the rough rock wall. "And while the Kurjans dragged you into this mess by using your lab for research, you'll soon learn this is where you belong."

Damn it. "Listen vampire, you'll show me the respect of staying the hell out of my head." Great. That's all she needed. The guy who'd starred in her kinkiest fantasies since her teenage years reading her thoughts.

His full lips quirked up. "My apologies. I'm not at one hundred percent here—blocking takes effort."

"Try."

"I promise I'll try." He kept his eyes closed.

She fought to concentrate on anything but the king's pain. "How old are you, anyway?"

"Three and a half centuries or so."

Wow. "How long have you been king?"

"All but twenty-five of those years. Our parents were killed by the Kurjans and I had to step up." His breath hissed out on a note of pain. "We went to war for too long, and then we brokered peace. Until last month."

"When the Kurjans discovered me." Guilt slid down Emma's spine. She'd led the devils right to Cara and Janie, Cara's young daughter. Two more gifted females.

"Yes." Dage stretched the long column of his neck, sucking in air. "They discovered you when using your lab to conduct some of their research." A pained grin lifted his lips. "You must be very good at your job."

"Good enough to figure out I wasn't working on a cure for cancer." She'd never forget returning to the lab one night to discover two Kurjans meeting with her old boss. "I saw the

Kurjans and ran away." She'd mailed her flash drive to a friend, and she'd been on the run since.

"We're going to need you to recount what you remember from your research." Dage paled further.

"I know." She leaned forward, willing his bleeding to stop. Coppery fresh blood flowed down the hard planes of his chest. That tattoo whispered secrets and flared nerves to life along her skin. The Kayrs Marking. A quick glance at his collarbone and neck revealed bullet holes oozing blood. Smaller than before, but still bleeding.

These were the first actual bullet holes she'd ever seen. Her father had shot toward her with a shotgun during his drunken rages, but he'd always missed. "The green flash from the Kurjan's gun looked like lasers. Why are there bullet holes in your neck?"

"The burst of light is a laser which hardens into bullets when meeting flesh."

Weapons to injure immortals. God knows what damage such devices would inflict upon humans. She sighed. "Do you think the Kurjans are near?"

He shook his head without opening his eyes. "No. I don't sense evil anywhere near us. We're probably safe for a couple hours, then we should move again."

A couple hours? Damn. She needed him in fighting shape. "Will drinking my blood help heal you?"

His lids flipped open, revealing those silver eyes that had haunted her dreams for fifteen years. Hunger, raw and pure, filled them. "Yes."

Emma gulped in air. The husky timber of his voice caressed nerves she didn't want to own. "I won't become a vampire?"

His dimples winked at her. "No. Vampires are born, not made."

Fear and her damn curiosity blended until she could only whisper. "Okay." She held out her wrist and shut her eyes. And waited. The breeze picked up outside the cave, rustling pine needles and leaves inside the small entrance, and she shivered. Finally, she opened her eyes in exasperation. "What?"

Reaching out with his good arm, he lifted her chin with one knuckle, waiting until her gaze met his. "I want your neck."

Low and rough, his voice skittered need through her midriff. Talk about direct. "Um, well, why?" Her mind reeled and she fought the urge to drop her gaze to his mouth. She lost the fight. He ran a tongue along those full lips. Need rippled through her. How did he do that?

He waited again until she focused on him, her eyes widening on the pure confidence shining in his. "I've been waiting to taste you for centuries—I don't want you extending your wrist to me and looking the other way."

"What do you want?" She shouldn't have asked that.

For answer, he reached out with his healthy arm and lifted her until she straddled his lap. She should've protested, but the easy strength and warm hand on her hip caught the breath in her throat. Fascinating. Such true, raw power. She pressed both hands against the undamaged muscles of his chest, balancing herself. His erection lay thick and hard beneath her, and she fought the urge to clench her thighs against his legs.

He stared at her through half-lidded eyes, his hands going to unbutton her cotton shirt.

"What are you doing?" she breathed.

"I don't want to get blood on your shirt." His gaze dropped to the swell of her breasts over the plain white bra. Fire flared within those silver depths and she fought a moan.

"That's enough." She covered his hands with hers.

With a nod, he gently placed her hands on his thighs before clasping the shirt and drawing it down both arms. The lower buttons remained engaged, and the material trapped her arms at her sides.

He pinned her with a gaze so full of hunger she couldn't speak. "You'll give your blood?"

Emma nodded, her focus narrowing to the man before her.

Sharp fangs emerged from his canines and he growled, reaching one arm around to cup her head and pull it to the side. Her neck stretched and vulnerability battled with arousal down her length. Every muscle in her body tensed to flee. His other hand gasped her hip, flexed, then slid up to her bare shoulder, entrapping her.

There was no escaping him.

Tugging her closer, he buried his head in the hollow between her neck and shoulder. She tensed, waiting for the pain. Instead, he pressed one tender kiss to her rapidly beating pulse. She felt it to her core.

He inhaled, running his mouth along her collarbone and up to her ear, where he nipped. "You smell like spiced rum and peaches." He breathed against her skin, his hands holding her firmly in place. "Some dreams I could smell you, but not this strongly. Never this fully." He rose up, drawing in a deep breath. "Never so much I'd do anything to have you."

Quick as a whip, he struck.

His fangs pierced her skin. Emma cried out, shutting her eyes.

Her blood boiled.

Raw need flared her flesh to life and a hum began deep in her core. Without caring enough to stop and think, she pressed against him, so hard, so full. His mouth pulled harder, and her nipples pebbled into pinpoints of need. Something contracted in her womb, begging for him. He drank more, and she exploded into a thousand pieces. The room sheeted white as an orgasm tore through her with the force of a furious tornado. She went limp, held upright only by his hands.

Sealing the wound, his tongue lashed across her skin and she shivered, nearly dazed. He held her in place and lifted his head away from her, his gaze piercing on her heated face.

She should be embarrassed, but a warm haze clouded her vision, her brain.

"Emma?"

She lifted heavy lids to focus.

His eyes burned hotter than molten steel. "I want you."

"I know." She sat on the proof of his desire. Hard and throbbing. "But we just met." Hours ago.

His hands slid down to cup her hips, pulling her closer along his rigid length. "Have you dreamed about me?"

"Yes." She fought a groan at the warm strength grasping her even as desire began to heat again.

His gaze dropped to her needy breasts, and his hands flexed before he looked back up. "For how long?"

She glanced away, evading his question to see the bullet holes close into healthy flesh and the large wound from the tree stitch together until disappearing. His chest appeared as if never injured. "You're all right."

"Yes. I asked you a question."

She'd say the arrogance returned with his healing, but really, had it ever disappeared? "I'm aware of that, Dage." The breathiness coating her voice ruined the sarcasm.

He released her to grab his discarded shirt and wipe the remaining blood from his skin. "Then answer me."

She shrugged. "Fifteen years or so." Since she'd hit puberty.

Pleasure filtered across his strong features, and he tossed the shirt away. "I've dreamed about you for two hundred years. I'd say we've known each other for quite a bit of time."

She grinned. "Is this your way of making a move?"

His eyes darkened to zinc. "No. This is." One large hand covered her breast and flexed.

She gasped, fighting the absolutely insane urge to rub against him.

Desire and intent filled his eyes. His free hand clasped her hair and pushed her mouth to his. Pure raging fire slid through her veins as the immortal made his move.

Sweeping his tongue inside her mouth, he tasted at his

leisure, pressing her further into him. Her mind spun, her breasts ached. Almost as if he knew her thoughts, he swept one callused thumb inside her bra, sliding across a turgid nipple. She moaned into his mouth, both hands clutching his strong shoulders closer.

He deserted her lips, trailing hot kisses along her jawline to her neck, where he nipped. Leaning back, he slid her shirt down farther, his clever hand flicking open the front clasp of her bra and sliding the sides apart. His eyes flared hot and hungry before his head dropped and he drew one hard nipple into his blazing mouth.

She moaned, her hands clenching his hair, drawing him closer. Oh God. Pure wanton need shot through every nerve, clamoring together in a craving only he could satisfy. He suckled, sliding his hand around her waist to plunge into her jeans and cup her ass. Rough and warm, he kneaded.

Wait, something tickled the back of her mind. Something there . . . "Dage!" She pulled back, her breast leaving his mouth with a soft pop.

"What?" he growled, clearly disgruntled, moving back toward her chest.

She tightened her grip and yanked on his hair.

He stilled, danger flashing through his eyes. "What?"

"Your hand." She gulped in air, trying to focus, trying to dispel some of the need. "Your hand."

"What about it?" He pulled free to glance at it.

For answer, she released his hair, grabbed his hand and flipped it over, curling the fingers of her hands around the edges. A raised crest, intricate and black spread across his palm. Lines crossed and swirled, and a thick K rose through the design. A smaller version of his tattoo.

"The marking," he said, his voice deepening to a rumble.

"The marking," she affirmed. They needed to get a couple of things straight right now. Her visions never lied, and she had to protect them both. "I'll not be branded, Dage." She swallowed rapidly, trying to clear her head.

He raised an eyebrow. "The marking only appears when we touch our mates, love. I drank your blood, and it appeared." His jaw firmed. "You will be marked."

Her temper stirred to war with desire. "No."

His full lips quirked. "I should've known the Queen of the Realm would be a pain in my ass."

The queen? She cleared her throat. "I'm no one's queen, Dage. Not a chance." She shifted against him, her eyes nearly rolling out of her head at the delicious friction.

Reaching out, he placed one warm fingertip against her chin and traced a path straight down, inch by slow inch until coming to a stop above her left breast. His hand flattened, pressing against her heart. "You sure about that, love?"

The traitorous little organ gave one hard thump against his palm. "Yes."

He wet his lips. "Well then, how about tonight is just about tonight?"

"Tonight?" She rocked against him. "What about the Kurjans?"

"They're nowhere near us right now." He lifted his head and inhaled as if seeking answers from the universe. "With any luck they searched toward the eastern mountain range, which is why we made a beeline to the south. We have a couple of hours before we need to move. So, tonight?"

Tonight sounded good, and the added thrill of danger caused shivers down her spine. Dage had haunted her dreams for years, she deserved one night. Just one. "All right. But no marking or invading my thoughts." He could never know what her visions had revealed.

What might have been.

Grasping her sagging blouse with both hands, he tugged. The remaining buttons scattered across hard-packed earth. She gasped, forgetting all about the future.

Only the present mattered.

He slid her shirt off followed by the straps of her bra. "I

think I can entertain us both without marking or invading—at least for tonight." His hands went to her breasts, molding, exploring, appreciating. "You're so pretty, love."

A pure flush of desire rose from those breasts to her face. She ran her palms down the hard muscles of his chest to his tight abs. Finally. She was finally touching him. So much strength—truly worthy of a king.

She yanked free the button of his pants, and her gaze met his while she released his zipper. Her breath came in short bursts. She was more than a match for the leader, as he would soon see. Emma leaned forward to nibble on the sizzling skin she'd dreamed about. The reality tasted even better. Smooth, salty man tantalized her when she nipped at his collarbone. Then bit.

He growled low, hands going to her waist to tug her to the ground. She opened her senses to him. His heartbeat echoed throughout her own head, and then . . . he stilled.

His head lifted and he scented the air. Slamming his metallic eyes shut, he swore. He grabbed her shirt and yanked it up her arms, holding tight to the front.

"What is it?" Her stomach dropped in fear. "Did the Kurjans find us?"

"Worse." Dage shifted her to the side and stood, lending a hand to help her up.

Two men crowded the entrance to the cave—the men from her dreams. "Your brothers?"

"Yes."

Her mind spun. A hollowness echoed throughout her body that might never be filled. "How is that worse?" She took his hand, holding her shirt together with trembling fingers.

"Because I can't kill them," Dage said grimly, pulling her forward. He nodded at the green-eyed brother in the lead. "It's nice to know you followed orders and went to secure the facilities as needed." He shifted his focus to the copper-eyed brother. "One word Jase, and I'll rip out your jugular."

Jase wisely kept silent, though the twinkle in those eyes laughed hard enough to make sound.

The first man threw caution to the wind. "Hi Emma. I'm Conn." He clapped Dage on the back. "We couldn't let the king miss the ball, now could we?"

Ball? What ball?

Chapter 3

Dage tugged on his onyx cuff links as he dressed in the family quarters, fury sliding under his skin. To be so close as to actually taste her . . .

"Conn and Jase have made themselves scarce somewhere in this damn hotel," his brother Talen noted, yanking on a black bow tie.

Dage couldn't help but smile. Forcing Talen into a tuxedo was like making a leopard wear a tutu. His brother was made for flak jackets and combat boots. "You look *pretty* in a tux, brother. Your mate will sigh with joy."

The good natured punch from Talen would've killed a human. "Shut up. By the way, that's a lovely marking on your palm."

The marking ached like a raw tooth and had since appearing the previous night. It needed to find a home on Emma's flesh. Now. "She doesn't want to be marked." The words hurt to say. He hadn't seen her since handing her off to Cara for much needed rest because he'd been swamped with Realm business all day.

Talen grinned. "Can't blame her. Branding is archaic, neanderthalic, and absurd."

"Neanderthalic? Cara makes up her own words, I see." Damn but Dage adored his sister-in-law. He clasped his long dark hair at his nape, then straightened his black jacket, his gaze sweeping the plush executive suite with its thick carpet and rounded beige chairs. The hotel smell of lemon cleanser began to irritate him.

"Yeah, I know." Talen snorted in amusement. "But the marking is necessary for their protection—to give them our defenses as well as immortality. There's no other way—and there's no other choice."

Dage chuckled. "Life is so black and white for you, isn't it? You plan, fight, conquer, and go home." His brother was perfect for his position as head of security for the entire Realm.

"Yes." Talen double-checked the weapon stored at the small of his back. "You're a fine king and well suited for the crown." Golden eyes flared. "But in this instance, at this time, diplomacy be damned. Find your woman and mark her as your own."

While his brother was as subtle as a ten point earthquake, Dage hoped to entice his mate rather than conquer. As a first resort anyway. But whatever the means, the end result would be the same. He'd finally touched his queen. Finishing off his grape energy drink, he rolled his shoulders, his own weapon in place. "We haven't had to arm ourselves for the colloquium in centuries."

"*You* haven't. I've always been armed." Talen tucked a knife against his shin. The family quarters were well guarded, but once inside the grand ballroom there would be too many guests to be certain of safety. Vampires, shape-shifters, and witches galore. All of the leaders throughout the Realm—a symposium equal to that of the United Nations. Talen snapped another knife in place up his left sleeve. "You need to stop drinking that stuff."

"Why?" Immortality had some benefits. "I'm allowed one vice."

Talen grinned. "That's a stupid vice. At least at the damn colloquium we get scotch."

Dage shrugged. "I know you wanted me to cancel the colloquium, but we couldn't with us having gone to war with the Kurjans. Diplomacy is at a must right now."

"I know. Portland was a good choice of location this year. Easy to travel from if necessary." Talen returned to his main topic. "Are you going to mark Emma or not?"

Dage fought a growl. "Of course." His pretty blue-eyed scientist would damn well wear his mark—sooner rather than later. He'd waited centuries to find her.

The wait had ended.

"Ah, I have news." Talen shifted his feet in shiny new loafers, no doubt wishing for combat boots. "Cara's with child."

Dage threw an arm around his brother's thick shoulders. "Congratulations. You'll have a fine son."

"Are you sure? I mean, have you seen my son in your head?" Talen's eyes held a never before seen uncertainty.

Dage forced a smile. "No—which means there's nothing to worry about." He hoped. He cleared his throat and sought the right words. "In fact, I'd like you to concentrate on strategy and security for the next while." His brother was a strategic genius, a talent that would more than serve the Realm.

Talen stilled. "Is that so?"

His brother was also known for a deadly temper. "Yes. We're at war and need to focus on making plans with the shifting nations as well as covens. We need to organize."

"I'm not sitting on the sidelines." A muscle began to tick in Talen's jaw, a sure sign punches would soon follow.

Dage readied his stance. He'd hate to have to kick his brother's ass right before the ball. Damn but it'd be a good fight if they both let loose. "You know as well as I that planning for the battle is more important than shooting a gun."

Golden eyes flashed. "You know as well as I that no battle strategy goes according to plan. I'm as good as Conn on the ground."

Together the two men were unbeatable. "I know."

Talen sighed. "Dage, I appreciate it, I really do. But my job is my job and I need to do it right, whether or not my mate's with child."

"I know. But with Janie and now the new baby, you have a lot to think about."

"Yes, and if something happens to me, I know you'll take care of Cara, Janie, and the baby. We're at war, Dage." Talen clapped him across the shoulders. "We can't turn our backs on duty, no matter the reason." He grinned. "Now let's go find our mates."

Several suites down, Emma bit her lip as she tugged her skirt into place. One minute she was running for her life through a dark forest with the evil undead on her tail, and the next day she stood in the loveliest blue and silver ball gown imaginable. They'd arrived at the Portland hotel in the wee hours of morning, and she'd even had time to sleep before being reunited with her sister. Now she was pretending to be Cinderella.

She looked down at the pretty fabric and sighed. The corset top pushed her breasts up while the waist cinched in before the skirt flared out. The three-inch silver heels made her feel like a princess. She tried to bring reality back to her mind. "I need to call Henry at the lab and see what's going on."

Cara glanced up from her perch against the sofa, looking beyond beautiful in a light golden gown that brought out the highlights in her auburn hair. "Why? Dage is having a research lab built. I'd assumed you'd want to work there."

"My life is in Boston, Cara." At least it was. "Henry is a good friend and an excellent lab partner. I'm sure he had no idea what Davis was up to."

"Yeah, good old Davis, your creepy boss." Cara rolled her eyes. "Great plan hooking up with the Kurjans to conduct research. What could go wrong?"

"I need to find out what's happening at the lab, and no

phones would call out from the hotel today. I don't like being kept here like this." Armed guards lined the halls of the family quarters. Dage had supposedly been conducting business all day and had yet to make an appearance. She'd met her hulking new brother-in-law earlier when Talen had dropped by for an introduction. The guy was dangerous, no question about it. Just like his older brother.

"I know." Cara smoothed back her hair. "But we're in danger and I guess security has to be tight. Can't you just enjoy the ball tonight?" She flashed an impish grin. "With your black hair pulled up and those blue eyes, you look like Sleeping Beauty."

Emma rolled her eyes. "At least the dress fits." In fact, an entire wardrobe had been provided for her. The vampires had some clout. She sighed. "It's just that, I feel trapped like when we were kids. Yesterday, running through the woods, I thought of all the times . . ." Pain clenched her stomach.

Cara nodded, losing her smile. "I know. All the times we ran from Daddy and his latest beating. What a prick." She straightened her shoulders. "But we survived. We're here now."

Emma nodded. "Yes. This is where you want to be, right?" She focused on her younger sister, trying to open up any psychic power she may own. Was the baby all right?

Cara laughed, fingering an intricate golden cuff winding up her arm. "Yes, Emma. We don't need to plan a big Lucy and Ethel type of escape. I love Talen and want to stay with him."

Relief washed through Emma. Good. No matter what happened to her, Cara and Janie would be taken care of.

"So." Cara raised an eyebrow. "Such a strong sense of relief you're experiencing. Making plans of escape yourself?"

Damn empath. "Get out of my emotions, sis. I don't need any plans to walk out the door. They can't keep me here." She had work to do back home.

Cara straightened her skirt. "Besides relief I'm sensing concern. What has you in knots?"

Emma cleared her throat. If Cara wasn't worried about her pregnancy, no way was Emma going to plant that seed of doubt. "Knots? Seriously? All of a sudden everything we know about genetics, intelligent species on this planet, and reality has been challenged. I mean, vampires *exist.*"

Cara laughed. "Science has always evolved with new discoveries, Em. This is no different."

Well, that was true. Emma nodded. "I want to take your blood and sequence map your DNA."

"Now you sound like a vampire geneticist." Cara snorted. "So, vampires. What about Dage? You've been dreaming about him forever and now he's here. You going to walk away from him?"

No. She'd run. Emma opened her mouth to answer, shifting her attention as her niece skipped into the dressing room wearing a frilly white dress with sparkly shoes. "You look beautiful, Janie."

The four-year-old clapped her hands together and gave a happy hop, her brown curls bopping and her iris blue eyes sparkling. "I wish my friend Zane could see me."

Emma gave Cara a reassuring smile, knowing full well her sister was concerned about the friend who only visited Janie in her dreams. Sometimes psychic abilities were more of a curse than a gift. "I'm sure we'll all meet Zane someday, Janie girl."

Janie grinned. "I know a secret."

Cara glided toward her daughter, a smile on her face. "What kind of secret?" She turned a questioning glance in Emma's direction, who shrugged.

The giggle Janie gave echoed with fun. "I'm not 'posed to tell."

Putting her hands on her hips, Cara set her face in a mock glare. "Says who? Talen?" Her voice warmed even as she rolled his consonants.

Janie clapped her hands over her mouth. "Uh huh."

"Spill it, kid," Emma said.

A tiny frown appeared between Janie's eyes as she pondered. Then she gave a happy giggle. "Okay. He changed the center . . . center . . . um . . . center . . ."

"Centerpieces?" Cara guessed.

"Yep."

Emma frowned. "What were the centerpieces?"

The silk dress shimmered when Janie shrugged. "Some crystal thingies."

"What are they now?" Cara tugged one of Janie's curls into place and then smoothed down the little girl's skirt.

"Pretty plants with little flowers." Janie skipped over to Emma.

"Oh," Cara said, her cheeks pinkening and her eyes glowing.

Emma smiled. A plant physiologist, Cara was most comfortable with live plants or flowers nearby. "Talen's got a sweet side."

The door swept open. "I most certainly do not." Talen, his dark hair loose around his shoulders, strode inside and reached for Janie to envelop her in a hug. "It was a *secret*." He smacked a noisy kiss on the little girl's cheek, setting her on her feet. "You look stunning, little one." Janie preened and smiled. Talen zeroed in on his wife.

Emma glanced to his side and fought to keep her mouth from hanging open. Dage stood in the doorway dressed in a black tux—all powerful male animal. The sharp angles of his face enhanced those amazing eyes. Even in the civilized garb, something not quite tame emanated from him.

His gaze swept her head to toe. "You're wearing my colors, love." He stalked forward and leaned down to brush her cheek with a kiss. "Soon you'll be wearing me," he whispered for her ears only.

Desire blasted into her even as she stepped back. She liked

things organized, nicely lined up in test tubes. There was nothing nice about Dage, and she sure as hell couldn't predict him. And any outcome she'd envisioned ended with the king destroyed—because of her. She shook her head. "No." Damn but that sounded breathy and unsure.

His eyes hardened but he didn't get a chance to respond because Janie threw herself into his arms. "Uncle Dage. Do you like my dress?"

An astonishing change came over the king. His face softened and his eyes glowed as he caught the little girl and stood her on a cherry wood end table. "You're beautiful, Janie." His smile crinkled the corners of his mouth.

"Like a princess?" the little girl whispered.

Dage held her tiny hand with a delicate touch Emma would have to be blind to miss. "You are a princess, sweetheart."

The smile bursting across her niece's face reached Emma's heart. An odd relief eased her mind. Janie's safety wasn't only on her shoulders anymore. Dage and Talen were more than equipped to keep the little girl safe should the worst happen. In case she failed to find a way to cheat death.

Talen cleared his throat. "Maybe we shouldn't go to the dinner tonight. I'm armed, but . . ."

Cara shook her head. "Oh no, I am so going. I'm starving." She tucked her arm through his and held out a hand to Janie. "Come on, sweetheart."

Dage set the little girl on the floor. "We'll be right behind you." His gaze dared Emma to refuse.

Cara gave her a lopsided grin and tugged her family out the door. "See you at the ball."

Emma inched toward the door. "Let's go to the dinner, Dage."

He shifted his weight, effectively blocking her way. "I thought we'd get a couple of things clear, love."

Butterflies took flight in her stomach. "Like what?" She lifted her chin. Damn but that sandalwood scent made her want to tackle him to the floor and shred clothing until she reached his flesh.

His callused finger traced a path along her jaw and she had to quell the warmth in her core. "First, you need to understand it's well-known you're a probable mate—my mate."

She drew breath in, counting slowly to five, fighting the urge to tap her pretty shoe on the plush maroon carpet. The idea of his naked skin slowly wafted away as temper slid in. "I choose my own destiny, Dage. Period."

He nodded. "Of course. Tonight you're going to choose to finish what we started in the cave." Clasping her chin between his thumb and forefinger, he leaned down to brush her mouth with his. Once, twice, and then a third time.

She tightened her shoulders, fighting the need to grab him. Desire beat against her independence. Her mind ruled her body, not the other way around. Yet her hands drifted up his jacket, the soft fabric tickling her palms. Her knees trembled and she clutched his lapels, yanking him closer and taking his mouth. She slid her tongue in and explored. Mint and male exploded on her taste buds.

Independence be damned.

With a low rumble in his throat, Dage stepped in and deepened the kiss, one hand curving to cup her ass and tug her against a rock hard erection. He took control of the kiss smoothly, naturally. So easily. Bending her slightly, his tongue explored her mouth, his lips turning firm and demanding. She softened, accepting him. Her need to meet his passion, her need to please him was one she'd dissect and deal with later. For now she allowed desire to fill her mind, to fizzle her thoughts. Her hands slid to the buttons on his shirt and were instantly captured by his.

He released her mouth, raising his head. "Duty calls, love. We need to table this for later."

She stared for a moment at his stunning face before taking an awkward step back. What in the hell was she thinking? Her knees trembled while her breath panted out.

He held out his arm and she took it still in a daze, shaking her head as he escorted her through the door and down the hallway. Tall, dangerous looking guards stood at attention every few yards against the oak paneling.

She fought to control her raging thoughts. "Dage, I don't understand why you're having this ball and symposium when you just went to war."

He shortened his stride, eyeing her high heels. "We have the colloquium every ten years without fail so we can update each other, consolidate, and know our allies. We also need a Realm show of force—an in-your-face type of thing for the Kurjans."

"What exactly is the Realm?" As she walked beside him her feet already ached in the three-inch designer heels—but they were so worth the pain.

"We're like your United Nations. Several vampire nations, shape-shifters, and witches all belong."

"You're the King of the Realm?"

"Well, king of the vampires. We run the Realm, though I don't have a say in individual shape-shifting clans or covens."

"So you're at war just because the Kurjans have been working on a virus for the mating gene?"

"That and Janie. They've prophesized our niece's future with a psychotic little Kurjan named Kalin—and I won't let that happen. Ever." Dage paused to lean against the wall, tugging Emma to face him. "The virus also affects shifters."

"Shifters?" Emma teetered on her heels before finding her balance. "Like Katie and Jordan?" Cara and Talen had stayed with the lion shifters when running from the Kurjans.

"Yes." Dage's eyebrow rose. "Have you met Katie yet?"

"No. But I spoke with her on the phone when Cara stayed with them." Katie had done her best to explain the hierarchy of her lion shifting clans, but the organization was still a jumble in Emma's head.

"Ah. Wasn't that when you ran cross-country with the

Kurjans on your tail?" A vein stood out in the king's neck and the air shifted around him. Anger.

"Er. Yes." She needed to retrieve her research in Montana. "I didn't want to put Cara in any more danger, so . . ."

"And once she told you about us?"

"About your family or the vampire race at large?" Emma had been shocked to discover the Kurjans, and then thankful beyond belief to find out the white-faced mutants had enemies strong enough to take them on. She thanked the fates every day Talen had found Cara and Janie before the Kurjans did.

"Both." Dage's grip on her arm tightened.

"Then I figured Cara was safe and I should continue to Montana."

Dage pivoted, pinning Emma against the raised wallpaper. "I'm hoping you learned your lesson."

Considering the blood-sucking bastards had captured her and nearly taken her to Canada to mate with their leader, then yeah. "I need to hide better next time." She bit her lip against a grin.

Dage's large hand ran down her back to cup her ass and gave a gentle squeeze, tugging her into male hardness.

Heat rushed through her. She fought to keep her voice calm. "You know, for a king, you're rather improper sometimes."

"You've never met the king, love." He nipped her ear and her knees began to tremble. "It's the man who has you."

Heat pooled in her abdomen even as she shoved both hands into his hard abs and pushed. Neither of them moved an inch. "You said something about the virus affecting shifters as well as vampire mates?" Damn, she needed to get her hormones under control.

Dage inhaled, his shoulders moving with the effort. "Er, yes. We think the twenty-seventh chromosome of a shifter controls the shift or mandates the type of shifter." He spoke against the column of her neck, his breath warm on her skin. "To be honest, we don't know anything for sure."

"Type of shifter?" Emma struggled for a moment to accept this new reality. "I don't understand."

Dage lifted his head. "Shifters are either canine, feline, or multi."

Emma fought a shiver of pleasure when he grasped her hand. She shook off the sensation. For the love of Pete, she was holding hands with a *vampire*—another species on this earth, one far stronger than humans. True danger in a seriously sexy package. Focus. She needed to focus. "Multi?"

He wound his fingers through hers, instantly warming her palm. "Yes. Multi-shifters can change into any animal except for feline or canines."

Geez. How was it possible for humans to have missed this? Emma's rational mind began to organize the information. "What does the virus do to shifters?"

Dage shrugged. "We think the virus attacks the gene to change the shifter into a werewolf."

Emma chewed her lip for a moment. "A werewolf?"

"Yes. Werewolves are pure animals who crave feeding and killing. They're bound to a master with a single spell, no rational thought, no humanity."

Well, that sucked. "How does one become a werewolf?"

"Humans become weres by being bitten by a werewolf. Before the virus, shifters were immune to such a bite."

Emma shook her head. "I don't understand. Why go to the trouble of creating a virus to turn shifters into werewolves? Why not just bite a bunch of humans?"

"Because human werewolves don't live long—a year at the very most. Shifters are much stronger." Dage pushed away from the wall. "We think the Kurjans truly had no idea the scope of this virus when they began their research."

So the Kurjans were attempting to create an immortal slave class. It made sense from a psychotic world-domination type of viewpoint.

Dage drew Emma's arm through his to ease down the hallway again. "My brother Kane has had men creating a lab for us. I was hoping you'd agree to do some research."

Wariness warred with an uneasy interest within Emma. No doubt the vampire's lab would be state of the art. "I have a lab, Dage." Unless the Kurjans still controlled it.

Dage paused and cleared his throat. "Ah. No, you don't."

Emma swung around to face him, halting him in his tracks. "Excuse me?" He was so not telling her what to do.

His gaze met hers head-on. "We blew the building up."

Her mouth gaped open. "You did not." Her good Manolos were in her locker, damn it. As well as her passion pink Newton lipstick that had been discontinued. She couldn't even find it on eBay.

"Sure we did." Not by one tiny tick did the king appear anything but factual and at ease with the truth.

"Why?" she gasped.

He shrugged. "The Kurjans controlled your facility. All data there had to be destroyed, so we did a complete job of it."

"What about the people who worked there?" The vampires wouldn't have killed anyone, would they? Fear began to tremble down her legs.

"We're keeping dossiers on all of them. So far, only your boss Frank Davis seems to have known about the Kurjans." Dage rubbed a hand down her arm. "He's disappeared, but probably to another Kurjan facility."

Goose bumps rose in response. "What about Henry Duvall?"

"We can check the data later if you want." Dage's eyes narrowed. "Why? Who's Duvall?"

"My lab partner." Emma lifted her chin. "And a good friend."

"Ah." Dage's eyes lightened in understanding. "That's right. I remember that name. He protested when we moved your belongings to storage and put your house on the market."

Shock made her voice tremble. "You did what?"

Dage lifted an eyebrow. "Love, the Kurjans are after you. You certainly can't go back to your old life." He clasped her hand again. "We had to send Duvall a couple of letters from you insisting there was a family matter and you'd gone on vacation with your sister. He finally quieted down." The king's tone implied Henry had made a wise choice in doing so. "Were you, ah . . ."

"What?" Emma stumbled. "No. Of course not. We were just friends." Good friends, considering they had the same taste in men.

"Good to know."

They'd put her house up for sale. Unbelievable. She'd spent hours choosing just the right paint color for each room. It had taken over a week to sand and refinish the hardwood floors—with Cara and Janie pitching in to help. The garden was a work of art with its pansies and hydrangeas. Emma loved that house. She sputtered for a moment, her mind reeling as Dage turned and began leading her down the hallway again. She gritted her teeth together until her jaw ached. "We'll discuss this later." When she could form a coherent thought without wanting to kill him.

"Of course." Dage reached a large double door and tucked Emma's arm more securely in his. "You stick close tonight to either me or one of my brothers."

She nodded, then barely suppressed a gasp as he swept the doors open to reveal a ballroom rivaling anything royalty had devised through the years. About two hundred people had already taken seats around blue covered tables set for eight with fine china and crystal. The scent of roasted chicken wafted through the air. Dage led her through the room, nodding to several dignitaries until reaching the head table where Talen, Cara, and Janie sat with another couple.

Dage grasped her hand. "Emma, this is Jordan Pride and Katie Smith."

Jordan stood and held out a large hand. Ah—the mountain lion shifter. A myriad of brown, black, and blond streaked hair reached his broad shoulders. Tawny eyes twinkled at her. "My pleasure."

She shook his hand, realizing she hadn't quite believed in the existence of shifters until right that moment. An odd electric power shot up her arm from his touch. Weird. "Nice to meet you." He released her and she took the seat Dage pulled out.

Katie grinned, her golden eyes alight. "It's nice to finally meet you in person."

Emma returned the smile. She'd enjoyed her phone conversations with the lioness while Talen and Cara had stayed with the shifters.

Katie leaned forward, her blond curls pinned up in an elegant chignon. "I'm still incredibly impressed you were able to outmaneuver not only the Kurjans but the vampires chasing you." She shot a teasing glance toward Dage.

Emma shrugged. "I didn't see an alternative. I had to keep traveling northwest until I could reach my friend's place in Montana." She'd almost made it, too. One second she'd been gassing up her car at a Texaco just outside Bozeman and the next lying in the back of a Kurjan van, half drugged out of her mind. She still didn't know how they'd found her. Unless Davis had somehow figured out her plan, which was more than possible.

"Where's your friend now?" Katie asked.

"Working abroad."

Jordan leaned forward. "Where is the data now?"

Dread pooled in Emma's stomach. "The Kurjans said they found the cabin, and my flashdrive in the car. It has probably been destroyed, though I have a fairly good memory of most of the lab results." Her kidnapping had led to Cara's kidnapping by the Kurjans. Was it only yesterday she and Cara had been locked in the Kurjan facility? Cara patted her knee under the table, no doubt sharing her sister's feelings at the moment. Damn empath.

Waiters poured wine. Cara raised her eyebrows at the herbal tea placed in front of her.

"You can't have wine, Cara," Talen said, smiling when the waiter put a Shirley temple in front of Janie.

Cara rolled her eyes. "I probably could, but since my stomach is a bit pitchy, I think I'd rather have the tea."

Katie covered her wineglass with one hand. "I've been fighting a cold and would like tea as well." The waiter immediately fetched her a cup.

Emma smiled, suspecting Katie of claiming a cold just to keep Cara company. Apparently her sister had found a good friend. A friend who could shift into a mountain lion. What an odd world she'd just entered.

Dage leaned over and brushed a curl off Emma's face, sending a shaft of pure need through her body. His unique scent of leather and sandalwood wafted her way and she fought a shiver.

"I'm going for the wine." She took a deep sip, hoping to cool her desire. Yeah right. That would work.

Chapter 4

Several hours after dinner, Dage stood near the bar and tipped back a bourbon on the rocks, half listening to Jordan's good-natured recap of his speech. The tables had been cleared from the floor to make space for dancing. He nodded at his friend while his gaze remained on the woman across the room. Emma. So close. Finally.

The chandelier cascaded light down to create shimmers of movement in dark hair she'd pinned up in an intricate knot, leaving her delectable shoulders bare. Even with the distance between them, her heartbeat echoed within his own chest. Her eyes a sapphire blue, her skin the purest of marbles, even without knowing her as he did, he'd be interested. But he did know her. A fierce intellect pounded behind that pretty face, outmatched only by the spirit of fire held within her breast.

His mate.

She tossed her head, laughing at something Katie said next to her. Then Katie gave a nod and wandered toward another bar in the far corner.

A man approached Emma and Dage fought the urge to growl. A vampire, a young one. Tall, blond, and from somewhere in the eastern district. What the hell was his name?

The young vampire took her hand and leaned over to brush a kiss on it.

Dage let a snarl loose.

Emma laughed and tugged her hand away, smoothing her hair back before speaking to the interloper.

Dage would kill him. The bastard had touched his mate.

Setting the glass on the bar behind him, Dage shifted his stance and set his feet, his gaze focused on his prey. All sound receded into the background.

The young vampire turned and Dage caught his eye. A slow smile slid over the king's face, menace tinged with a promise of pain. For a brief moment he let a hint of his power glint in his eyes and glow from his skin. He'd have the young buck fearing his own shadow by the end of the night.

Blood drained from the vampire's face until his lips turned purple, his eyes wide. He stumbled away from Emma, sweeping his hands out in a placating gesture. With a bow of his head toward his king, he backed away several feet before turning on his heel and dashing for the nearest exit.

Emma fought to keep her balance, the abrupt departure of her companion startling her. Suspicion filtered in and she turned to look where Dage stood across the room. His dimples flashed when he grinned at her, pure innocence shining in his deep eyes. Next to him Jordan struggled to contain his laughter, studying the floor.

The king was up to something. He existed as his own force and she had to consciously fight the urge to gravitate toward him, to let that heat and power surround her. To think she'd almost had sex with him in the cave. Need still rumbled in her blood and her breasts ached for his mouth. She gave him a quelling look which he met with a raised eyebrow.

Two men sought his attention, and he turned toward them, flashing her a look containing a promise she could feel under her skin.

Relief filled her when his gaze released her. Tipping back her champagne, she emptied the glass, raising an eyebrow at the stunning dark haired vision coming her way. Woman's intuition had whispered the porcelain skinned goddess in the flowing crimson gown would stop eyeing her across the room and make a move.

The low hum of voices across the ballroom dimmed as the woman reached Emma's side in a cloud of rose scented perfume. "Rumor has it you're the king's mate." Sharp gray eyes narrowed and crimson nails sharpened to dangerous points tightened around a champagne glass.

Emma tilted her head. "Emma Paulson."

"Simone Brightston." An odd energy containing more than mere female anger pulsed around the woman. Shifter? Witch? "Former lover to the king."

Well damn. Emma had known the guy couldn't have lived as a monk for centuries, but still, the truth slid between her ribs like a knife. She forced a slow smile. "Former? You mustn't have been very good at it."

A rustle of silk announced Cara's arrival. "Good at what?" The curious tone belied the sharp gaze. Nothing like an overprotective sister to make things interesting.

An odd humming set up in Emma's ears while an electric current cascaded through her flesh. Power—at home and comfortable within her body. She cut her eyes to the king who remained absorbed in his discussion. The energy came from inside her. Interesting. One day in his presence and her physiology had already altered. She'd have to watch that.

Emma inclined her head. "Cara Kayrs, meet Simone Brightston. Former lover to the king."

Cara's smile belonged in a toothpaste advertisement. "How indiscrete." She turned to run her gaze across Dage where he stood speaking to the group of men. "Why in the world would you let a man like that go?" She pursed her lips. "Oh. He let you go. Sorry about that." Honey would've melted in her mouth.

Simone sniffed. "Such a pity when a royal vamp slums it with humans." The glacial eyes slit into luminous orbs as she eyed Emma up and down. "Of course, you've not actually mated. Maybe there's hope for the monarchy yet."

Emma had no plans to mate with Dage, but this woman needed a smack down. Emma scented the air. "What in the world is that smell?"

Cara tilted her head. "Brimstone. Yes, I believe it's brimstone."

"You're a waste of my time." Simone gave a short huff and pivoted on her heel to glide across the room, her hips swaying in tune with the orchestra.

Emma bit back a chuckle. "Brimstone? Seriously?"

Cara grinned. "I was inspired. What a bitch, huh?" She tilted her head. "I'm getting the oddest feeling from you right now."

"How so?" The energy ebbed to a soft pulse within her.

"I don't know. Not psychic or anything. Just different." Cara paled. "We've certainly entered another world, haven't we?"

Emma huffed out a laugh. "Yes. Vampires, shifters, and witches. Who knew?"

Cara wobbled on her heels, her hand going to her stomach. "Oh crap."

Oh no. Emma knew that look. Not good timing. She grabbed Cara's arm and hustled her out the door. Emma nearly tripped in her heels, her arm around Cara's shoulders as they all but ran for Talen's suite.

Cara had a hand clasped to her mouth, her eyes a panicked hue in her too pale face. "Hurry."

The guards lining the way let them pass, more than one instantly tapping an earpiece to relay information. Cara threw open her door, kicked off her ruby heels and hustled past a surprised vampire to the bathroom where she fell to her knees. Emma barely made it in time to pull back her sister's hair before the vomiting began.

The vampire, Max, had been babysitting Janie since she'd left the party after dinner. He immediately tapped his ear communicator.

Cara purged her stomach and Emma flushed the toilet, releasing the auburn curls to run a washcloth under water. She handed it to her sister, who wiped her mouth and sat back against the flowered wall. "Well, shit."

Emma smoothed Cara's hair back from her face, concern pooling in her stomach. "The ball was lovely."

Cara's lips trembled as she tried to grin. "Yeah. Dage's speech was awesome. Very rah-rah, go Realm." Her gold dress pooled on the marble floor, which matched her pasty face.

Emma grabbed her embellished skirt, jumping out of the way to avoid being run over by Talen.

"Cara?" His eyes widened in panic as he reached for her, lifting her in his arms. "Dage, get the car. We're going to the hospital."

Dage slid to a stop right behind his brother, his gaze fierce, his jaw set hard.

"Jesus." Cara put her hand to her head, her gown spread over Talen's arm like a princess in a fairy tale. "Stop freakin' moving me, damn it."

Emma slapped one palm on the vibrating muscle in his arm. "Put her back down, Talen. It's okay. She was like this with Janie." It was just morning sickness. It had to be.

Cara began to gag again and Talen dropped to his knees, still holding her over the bowl. Emma leaned in to tug her sister's hair out of the way until she finished heaving.

Talen turned his molten gaze on Emma. "What should we do?"

"Put me the fuck down," Cara muttered, grabbing the washcloth and wiping her face again.

"No." Talen shifted, sliding down until he sat with his back against the wall, his love in his arms, his face pale. Being helpless clearly pissed him off.

Emma turned toward Dage and Max. "Order some herbal tea from room service. Orange Zing if they have it."

Talen met his brother's gaze. "I want the doctor here. Now."

Dage nodded, his gaze concerned as it slid to Cara. "He's on his way." Max hurried off to call room service.

Cara rolled her eyes. "I don't need a doctor. This is normal morning sickness for the love of Pete."

Talen's jaw firmed. "It's not morning."

Emma tried to fight a grin. Her poor sister had puked for three solid months while pregnant with Janie. If Talen reacted like this every time, the doctor might as well be on retainer. She cleared her throat. "Why don't I help Cara out of her dress before the doctor gets here?"

Talen's jaw hardened until it looked like granite. "No. We're not moving until the doctor arrives."

Emma gave her disgruntled sister a sympathetic smile, trying not to laugh. A knock on the door heralded the doctor.

Dage grasped her arm. "Emma and I will be in the gathering room next door awaiting the doctor's prognosis." He tugged her through the suite, giving a curt nod to a round man with bottle thick glasses before turning to the vampire guard. "Max, please wait in the living area until Talen has his head on straight."

Max nodded, grabbing a book off the sofa table. "Probably take nine months," he muttered.

Emma didn't have time to protest before Dage whisked her through the door into a well-appointed gathering room complete with fireplace, stocked bar, and deep sofas. He poured them each a brandy, flipped on the fire, and handed her a glass. "Cheers."

"Cheers." She tipped back her drink and took a healthy swallow. "Cara is fine, Dage." A niggle of doubt tickled the base of Emma's neck. What if the pregnancy had happened too soon and Cara's physiology hadn't adapted enough for her to carry a vampire baby? She shrugged the fear off, forcing a smile.

"Then the doctor shouldn't be there much longer." Dage's own smile appeared forced. "Talen is going to drive us all crazy for the next several months, isn't he?"

Apparently. "Let's just say that when Cara was pregnant with Janie, I ended up running to the store for peppermint ice cream at midnight more than once." Emma cleared her throat. She needed to conduct some tests on her sister.

Dage nodded. "I understand Janie's father died in a car accident before she was born."

Emma grasped the subject with relief. "Yes. Simon worked as a plant biologist for the same company where Cara worked." He was a good man and a great friend to her sister. Certainly not the love of her life. Like Talen.

"So you took care of them. Like always." The king's eyes warmed.

Emma fought arousal from his lowered tone and shuffled her sore feet. They'd hit the point of dull ache in the heels until receding into numbness. She struggled to focus on anything else, not wanting to step out of the shoes. She needed all the height she could muster to face the king. Not that he didn't have a foot on her, even with the heels. "Earlier I met someone named Prophet Milner." The guy had parchment wrinkled skin over a bony face.

"Ah, yes. The prophets are our spiritual rulers—Milner is a couple thousand years old." Dage swirled the amber liquid in his glass. "He considers me a young upstart." Those damn dimples flashed and made her nipples harden.

Emma lifted a shoulder, taking a moment to control her libido by admiring the authentic C.M. Russell oil paintings. She loved western art. "You can go back to the ball if you want."

"I don't. Conn and Jase can deal with anything going on for the rest of the evening." Dage glanced at a wall clock. "I mean morning."

"Are you sure Jase and Conn are on the job? Jase was all over some cute young redhead." Emma would bet almost anything Jase and the little shifter had headed off to get to know each other better.

Dage shrugged. "Maybe. But Conn's mate is across the ocean, so his focus is pure."

"Conn is mated?"

The muscles in Dage's neck rippled as he swallowed some brandy. "Yes. He accidentally mated a witch about a century ago in northern Ireland."

"Accidentally?" Emma bit back a laugh. "You mean he had a one night stand and ended up marking some girl?"

"Yep. And I think he's coming to the end of his very impressive patience. I believe my brother is about to reclaim his mate, whether she's ready or not." Dage's eyes heated.

Was there a warning in those words? The topic echoing around in Emma's head shot to the surface. "I met Simone Brightstone. Shifter?" Emma swirled her own drink.

Dage narrowed his gaze. "Witch. In more ways than one."

"Yet you dated her."

"I was young and stupid. It lasted less than a month."

"Really? That's interesting, considering she's about my age. You haven't been young and stupid for quite some time, King." Did he think she was a moron?

Dage grinned. "She's a few centuries old, love. True witches—not those just practicing a religion—true witches are another species on earth. Immortal."

Well, crap. "There's no way to kill them?" How had humans missed this?

He laughed out loud. "Beheading or burning. Both methods will take care of a witch." His eyes softened. "Again, I was young . . . we weren't a good match."

Emma could understand that.

Dage eyed Emma's blue and silver gown like a hungry tiger who'd spotted dinner. "I have to say, my taste has certainly improved through the years."

The phone buzzed and Emma placed her drink on the sofa table, moving in a rustle of silk to the desk. "Yes? Okay. Tomorrow, then." She replaced the receiver, pivoting to face Dage. "The doctor said Cara has morning sickness and to drink some tea before getting a good night's sleep. He'll check her in the morning." The doctor would know, right? "Though, I'd like to conduct my own tests as soon as possible." That sense of unease whirled in her brain. She couldn't think rationally about her own sister. Cara had to be okay.

"Of course. Our lab will be ready soon." Dage's gaze warmed and wandered down her form and back up again.

Emma shifted her stance, an awareness beginning to weigh down the oxygen in the room. She fought to breathe normally and returned for her drink, her gaze on the king.

Firelight danced over the hard planes of his face like a lover in heat. Kissing, melting, landing. Silver eyes melted to liquid while he tracked her progress across the dusky room, his deceptively calm stance belying the vibration of muscle and power beneath his skin.

Stillness echoed around him as he stood near the daunting stone hearth; it was as if the air held its breath. For what she didn't know. Wasn't sure she wanted to know. She reacted to the tension, and lifted her chin in instinctive defiance.

Sharper gray flecks appeared in his eyes in response, and she wondered what ran through his mind. She stared back at him unblinkingly, her heart speeding up to knock uncomfortably against her ribs. Power blanketed him like the thickest of mantles even in the comfortable room. A wicked shiver of awareness wound leisurely down her spine.

He straightened and nodded toward the chair.

She didn't move, continuing her perusal of him. His black hair was unbound and free about his massive shoulders. He'd tossed his jacket aside, his hard chest outlined nicely by the soft shirt. Through his slacks, his thick legs showed power in the bunched muscles. She tried not to notice the obvious bulge in the center of his groin; an impressive erection he did nothing to hide.

"Emma, we need to talk." His voice was a low growl.

Even with that spectacular body, his face commanded the most attention. Sharp planes threw deep hollows into dangerous darkness, the square jaw hinting at determination and the full lips promising the heated depths of wicked sensuality. The dark slashes of his brows and the irrationally long lashes unapologetically contrasted with the burning silver of his eyes.

"I know." A breathiness coated her voice and she fought the urge to clear her throat. It wouldn't help.

"Sit down." This time he didn't nod toward the chair.

She didn't want to sit, needing to be on her feet to face the masculine power swirling around the room. "No."

A simple word Dage hadn't truly heard in over three hundred years.

Three feelings slammed into him simultaneously; the first was surprise, the second a grudging admiration, and the third was need. The need to dominate. It flashed through his blood with raw claws and struck harshly at his groin. Yet he deliberately turned and placed his brandy on the mantel before facing her squarely.

He reminded himself that he was a king, and control was his responsibility. But as his eyes slowly wandered down the deep shimmering gown that hugged her lush figure and brought out her incredible blue eyes, he knew with a man's certainty control was merely a hopeful thought taught by those who knew better.

"Not used to the word *no*?" she asked with a hint of sarcasm.

He narrowed his gaze. "Most people wouldn't dare." The fact that she'd dared made him harder than he'd been in his long life. The urge to teach her the result of tempting his beast was one he'd satisfy. Without question.

"I would think most kings aren't. However, you are not my king, either by birth or fealty." Her eyes flashed with too much challenge for him to ignore.

He cocked his head to the side. She knew exactly the temptation she presented.

What the hell was she doing? Emma fought the urge to

take a step back, knowing she might as well be shaking a red flag in front a raging bull. She couldn't seem to help herself. "And I won't take orders from you."

The smile he flashed her was not kind, even with the flirtatious dimple winking for just a second. It was knowing, wicked, carnal. "Oh love, you misunderstand. It wasn't the king demanding your obedience." His muscles bunched like a predator before springing. "It was the man."

"There's a difference?" The urge to run spiked through her blood.

"Absolutely. The king has rules." He moved faster than she could track and hauled her off the ground, easily holding her an inch from his mouth. Her legs dangled uselessly as her hands reached to protest against his chest. "The man doesn't."

His mouth plundered hers. Gone was the sweet kiss of seduction he'd used in the cave or the teasing exploration of his tongue from earlier in the evening. Masculine need, demanding and strong, surrounded her as he swept inside her mouth, taking what he wanted.

Her world spun, and her mind swam. A sharp longing spiraled through her body to pinpoint in one vulnerable spot. She had to get away from him. She kicked out, not connecting well enough to do any damage.

He lifted his head. "You promised me a night, Emma. I'm collecting now."

She slapped both hands against his chest, jerking her head back. "That was in the cave. This is different."

"Is it?" He raised an eyebrow. "I can smell your desire right now. You want me, and you want this."

True. She might've been able to fight the desire rushing through her nerves, but the curiosity was something else entirely. Would it be as good as in her dreams? Would *he* be as good as in her dreams?

"Better." He lowered her until her stilettos met the floor. "This first time I take you, love, I'd rather it not be in a living room."

She took a step back, her body trembling with need. God, she wanted this. Just one night. She could enjoy one night without becoming too attached. Or giving him false hope of a future. "The same rules apply. No marking and stay the hell out of my head."

He sighed. "As you wish." Grasping her hand in his, he led her to the door—where they smacked into Conn. "What the . . ."

Conn glanced from Dage to Emma and back again. "Er, sorry bro. Prophet Milner wishes to speak with you."

Dage pushed his brother out of the way, tugging Emma down the hallway to the staircase. "Tell him no."

She had to practically run to keep up with him until they landed safely inside a plush bedroom complete with an extra large bed covered in shimmering silk. Dage snapped the lock into place, its click echoing around the room.

Emma took a step away from him. What in the hell had she been thinking?

He took a step forward, reaching to release his cuff links, a dark flush across his cheeks, his eyes heated silver and trained on her. His cuff links slid out and he unfastened each button with sure hands, striding forward until he stood but a breath away. The shirt cascaded to pool on the plush carpet, revealing that wicked sharp tattoo and hard tanned muscle.

The scent of sandalwood and male whispered over her skin until her nerves tingled with need.

His heated hands encircled her biceps, and he gently turned her to face the shaded window. She shivered. The release of the corset's hidden zipper pierced the silence. The breath caught in her throat when he slid the material off her, his immortal body so big and strong behind her.

Gentle hands released the pins from her hair. Curls tumbled down to cover her shoulders.

Dage stepped in, winding one arm around her bare waist, pressing his heated chest to her bare back. Her body melted right into his, as if issuing one big sigh. His other hand swept her hair to the side, and his mouth descended to run along her shoulder. The moist warmth sent shivers through her body and she tilted her head to grant him greater access. His teeth scraped her jugular as he traveled so slowly up her neck to her jaw.

He flattened a hand against her bare midriff, just under the nipples all but crying for his attention. What was he doing to her? She couldn't move if someone firebombed the hotel.

The room spun when he turned her, his mouth dropping to hers, his tongue sliding in to explore. To taste. Tempt. Take.

Fire rushed through her. She stepped further into him, both hands tracing his abs up to his chest, appreciating the raw strength the king covered by diplomacy and design. She'd waited so long for him, to feel him. Just this once.

He clutched her hair, tilting her head so he could go deeper, a growl emitting from his throat that somehow caused liquid need to coat her thighs. Prickles of erotic pain cascaded across her scalp. She fumbled with his belt buckle, releasing a sigh of relief when it unclasped. Sliding the zipper down, she took him in her hand. Part of him, anyway. Hot. Hard. Male.

He released her mouth to concentrate on her skirt, releasing the side zipper until the material dropped to the floor. His eyes flared at her silk thong just before he snapped it in two. The tiny scrap of material joined the skirt.

Kicking off his pants, he lifted her in a move of such casual strength she had to fight a purr. He paused next to the bed. "Are you certain about the marking, love?" Desire and need swirled deep sky through those incredible eyes.

Temptation. To belong with him for all time. But the visions told the truth—the king might be destroyed by her if she didn't beat fate. "I'm sure." Her voice waivered. She didn't sound sure. She needed to retain at least part of her sanity. It'd be too easy to get lost in the king's plans.

Regret filled his eyes for a moment before he lay her down, following her to take one nipple into his mouth. He rumbled a sound of pure contentment, then his clever fingers found her.

She almost shot off the bed. He inserted one finger, then two in her—criss-crossing until she clutched her hands in his thick hair, moving against him. "Dage, now."

He chuckled against her skin, his mouth tracing a liquid path around each breast to kiss her nipples, her navel, and finally down to her core. His broad hands slid up her thighs to tug them apart and his mouth went to work.

She arched off the bed as he favored her with slow licks, humming in pure appreciation, the vibrations nearly sending her over the edge. Nothing could've kept her from glancing toward his dark head as he feasted. Deep silver eyes met her gaze, and with a lopsided grin, he closed his entire mouth over her clit. And sucked.

The world exploded. She cried out, pressing into his mouth, stars exploding behind her eyes. Her entire body short-circuited. The only thought in her head was his name. She rode out the waves and slowly lowered back to the bed. Her heart thundered so loud it echoed through her ears.

Dage maneuvered up until he hovered, poised at her entrance, his inhuman gaze piercing hers. Her thighs grasped his hips, pressing inward. More. She needed more.

His hand clasped her hip. "You're mine, Emma. The sooner you accept that the better." Heat engulfed her mouth as his lips devoured her, and he drove inside her with a force that shook the bed. Maybe the room.

She locked her ankles around his truly suburb ass, one hand fisting in his hair, the other digging into his hip as he started to move, his mouth busy on hers.

Sensations ripped through her—the fire at her mouth, the heat at her core. She met him thrust for thrust, so many feelings crashing into her that her mind shut down. Raw hunger had her returning his kiss, sweeping inside his mouth to duel with his tongue. She *took*.

Spikes of fire whipped inside her, bearing down an orgasm that rippled through her entire body until her ears rang. She rode it out, clutching to Dage, all sanity gone. He caught her cry in his mouth, his fingers bruising her flesh as he growled his release against her skin.

Her thighs released his damp hips as the ripples slowly subsided. Dage shortened his thrusts until he remained motionless inside her. For one brief moment, his heartbeat echoed throughout her body, so full of emotion she had to blink away tears.

He rolled to the side, spooning her into his large body and grabbing the bedspread to cover them. "Are you all right, love?"

She stretched like a satisfied cat, forcing all emotion into a box. "Fantastic." A tingling set up through her veins as if carbonation mixed with her blood. Nerves flared to life in her extremities.

No. Anger and dread pooled near her solar plexus. "Did you mark me?"

He stiffened behind her. "Of course not. I said I wouldn't." Thick arms tightened their hold around her waist and his breath stirred her hair. "Tonight, anyway."

She ignored the not-so-veiled threat as well as the renewed desire beginning to hum throughout her pores. "I feel different. Powerful." What the hell had he done to her?

He shrugged. "You're my mate, love. Your body knows that, even if you don't. The marking is only one part of the process."

The mattress dipped and she found herself on her back, her gaze held captive by his. "I told you I won't be forced into this by fate."

He nodded and his lips whispered against her. "Yes, you did. But I'm not fate." Slowly sliding inside her, he nipped her lip. "I'll give you time, Emma. But if you think I'm letting you go, you've misread me." His polite, matter of fact tone did nothing to hide the determination in each word.

A chill wound down her spine even as a warm hum set up in her core. Her eyes rolled back in her head as he started to thrust. Gently at first, then with a strength that had her nails digging into his skin.

She'd argue the point with him later.

Chapter 5

Controlling his irritation with the two feuding leaders, Dage finished his third meeting of the day. How in the hell had these assholes become leaders? He rested his elbows on the small conference table and nodded to Felix, the head witch of the New Jersey coven who sat to his right. "You'll agree to the new boundaries?"

The young witch flashed black painted nails and bit his lip, his bloodshot gaze sliding to where Conn leaned against the door of the makeshift office, a muscle ticking in his large jaw. Dage fought a grin. Conn hated diplomatic shit and would probably solve the problem by shooting both jackasses.

Dage stamped down on his own basic need to do just that, forcing diplomacy to the surface once again. He took a drink of his grape energy drink, rolled his shoulders against the feeling of being trapped in a cage, and pierced the witch with a hard gaze.

"Um, yes." Felix shifted back to face Dage. "We'll agree to the new boundaries."

Ignoring the hotel's lemon cleanser scent, Dage turned toward Niles, the shit-kicking cowboy vampire who'd been trying to retake land lost by his uncle centuries ago. "Niles?" The dumbass had sat with his back to Conn and the door. Not smart.

Niles perched his battered Stetson farther back on his head, his dilated eyes narrowing. "Ah, I guess."

What a couple of morons. Dage stood. "The papers will be ready for signature after the tea today. Gentlemen"—he allowed his canines to drop—"if either of you break this contract, I'll come after you myself."

Both men made a hasty exit and Conn slammed the door shut. "I hate this shit."

Dage ignored the shredding pain in his hand from the unused marking. "I know. But Talen's with Cara who isn't feeling well, Jase disappeared with some redhead, and Kane is on a jet heading this way."

Conn's eyes narrowed. "Cara's still sick?"

Dage shrugged. "I guess she had morning sickness with Janie, so she isn't concerned. Though Talen . . ."

Conn grimaced. "I'll keep my distance."

"Good plan." Dage stood and straightened his dark suit coat before striding toward the door. "We need to get to the tea. You're sitting with the prophets."

Conn hissed out a breath. "Seriously? Damn it. Milner's on me to retrieve Moira and procreate. I can't stand that guy."

Dage paused. "I have a feeling you're preparing to do just that."

Conn nodded. "I am. I've waited long enough. She's a full witch now and it's time—after we get things settled here." He yanked open the door. "But why do I have to sit with him?"

Dage stalked into the hallway. "It's either the prophets or the Bane's Council. Considering we're keeping something from them, I thought I'd face that challenge."

"Maggie," Conn breathed.

Yeah, Maggie. A young wolf shifter who'd been infected with the virus, and was hiding in Dage's Colorado headquarters. Hiding from the Bane's Council, whose job it was to hunt down and kill werewolves. "During the full moon, Maggie managed to turn into a wolf and not the werewolf trying to get out of her. Hopefully the virus will run its course and fail."

Conn nodded. "The virus will fail. If the Kurjans were able to turn immortal creatures into werewolf slaves, well . . ."

It would be a disaster. Dage paused in the middle of the hallway. "Do you think the law requires us to inform the Bane's Council about Maggie?"

Conn shook his head. "No. I think you were right. The law requires notification if we suspect a werewolf so the council can investigate and destroy. Maggie isn't a werewolf. She's a wolf shifter."

Who might become a werewolf. Dage started walking again. "Besides, Jordan has put her under the protection of his pride. All I need is his going to war with the council."

"We stick with Jordan." Conn threw open the double doors to the ballroom, nicely set with floral tea cups. "Whose fucking idea was it to throw a tea every ten years at the symposium?"

Dage shrugged, waving a hand to Terent Vilks, the head of the Bane's Council. Time to dance.

Exchanging pleasantries as he maneuvered between tables, Dage's gaze kept returning to the dark haired beauty chatting with Jordan at the head table. His mate—whether she liked it or not. A polite smile slid across Dage's face as he gave a nod to Jordan. "Where's Katie?" While the young lioness and Jordan weren't a couple, she usually accompanied him on business issues.

Jordan cleared his throat. "She's not feeling well, and Terent dropped by to bring her some special tea."

Terent rolled his eyes. "It's lavender tea—guaranteed to cure the common cold. I was not hitting on your woman, cat."

Jordan's eyebrow rose. "We're just friends. You know that."

Terent quirked his lip but remained silent. Dage bit back his own smile, taking his seat next to Emma, brushing a kiss to her cheek as he did so. She might as well get used to belonging to him. "Kate did say she was fighting a cold last night."

Terent flashed strong canines in a bronze face. "Well . . . cats." The wolf shifter gave a mock sympathetic shudder of his shoulders.

Jordan grinned. "Listen, pup. I believe the last time we played one on one, I schooled you."

Reaching for a roll, Terent shrugged massive shoulders under a gray jacket that brought out matching streaks in his deep eyes. "You cheated." He spread butter across the pastry. "You had Katie trip me, and it was either fall on and flatten the poor girl or release the ball." He pushed the roll basket toward Emma. "I'm sorry Katie's not feeling well."

Dage cleared his throat. "Where's the rest of the council?"

"The other two members are hunting down rogue werewolves," Terent said.

Dage made a pretense of sipping his water, wondering again if he should notify his friend about Maggie. If the council had any idea Maggie might possibly be a werewolf, all hell would break loose. Emma's hand on his knee jerked his attention to her.

"How were your morning meetings?" she asked with a lift of one finely arched eyebrow.

"Productive." He flattened his hand over hers, more than liking the feeling of having her near. "Sorry to leave so early."

A pretty flush colored her high cheekbones. She nodded her thanks to a waiter who placed a scone on her plate while another began pouring tea. "I stopped by to see Cara on the way to this tea." A frown marred Emma's face. "Talen's going to drive her up the wall."

Dage grinned. "We take centuries to find our mates, love. He can be excused for being a bit overprotective."

Terent grabbed his cup and pushed back from the table. "Why do I always have to give the council update during the friggin' tea?" he muttered for his table alone to hear.

Jordan chuckled. "That's my favorite part of this whole damn week."

During the tea, anger began to roll in Dage's gut while Terent gave the statistics for how many werewolves had been created the last ten years. Most had been captured and destroyed by the council.

Terent returned to his seat with the applause still dying down. "I'm good for ten years, my friends."

Emma cleared her throat. "You didn't let any of the werewolves live?" She pursed her pink lips as if calculating scientific formulas in her intelligent head.

Terent frowned. "Of course not. When humans are bitten by a werewolf, they turn into one—pure animal wanting to eat and kill. They don't live for long, even if they're bound by a master with a spell."

Dage patted her hand, knowing she'd keep quiet about Maggie. He had seen the spell performed once in his youth. The werewolf stood shackled in silver while an incantation was read by the new master. Dage leaned toward Terent. "Your numbers were extremely high this time."

Terent's gaze narrowed. "Yes. Someone is purposefully trying to create slaves. Short term, anyway. We're on it." He raised an eyebrow at Dage. "We need your data on the virus and the goal to impact shifters, though frankly I don't see it happening."

"Kane will be here tomorrow and has cleared his schedule to work with you," Dage said. His brother would share most of the data, anyway. Everything but the fact that one little wolf shifter had already been infected. Damn but he hated lying to his friend. The fact that Dage made a good king, could lie easily for the sake of diplomacy and the common good truly served to show what a bastard he'd become.

Emma placed a hand over his and he stilled, swiveling his gaze to her soft eyes—understanding eyes complimenting a small smile. She gave him a reassuring pat.

Damn. How had she read him so easily? His shoulders relaxed from her comforting gesture even as his mind spun. His mate.

The tea over, Emma placed her napkin on her empty plate and stood. "I think I'll go check on Cara."

The rest of the table stood, and Dage grasped her arm, taken aback for a moment by the fragility of the bones beneath his hands. Fate had created her for him, and he'd be damned if his world would cause her harm. "I'll accompany you." He smiled at his friends. "See you at the general meeting in a few hours."

They had almost made it to the door when Prophet Milner sidled up. "Well now, isn't this a grand sight?" His beady dark eyes sparked with approval, then his hooked nose sniffed the air. "Wait a minute. You haven't marked her yet?" Bony hands went to bony hips.

Dage forced a half smile. "My private life is private, Prophet." The ability to couch a warning as polite conversation had been taught in his infancy.

"You have a destiny to fulfill." Parchment thin skin stretched over sharp bones, giving Milner the look of a buzzard. The man wouldn't know a warning if it bit him on his nonexistent ass.

Emma shifted. "I will not be marked, Prophet. Get that through your head, now."

Milner chuckled, his pale hands clasping together. "Of course you will, my dear. Our people need a queen."

"No. I will not be your queen." Emma's lips firmed and sparks of fire lit her pretty blue eyes. "I'm heading home as soon as my sister is settled in."

Rage shot through the king like he'd never known. She'd denied their future to another person. It was one thing to need a little persuading, quite another to publicly reject him. The woman had another think coming if she thought to pat his hand, offering the supporting comfort of a mate and then take it away. He tightened his grip on her arm and nodded to Milner. "See you at the meeting."

It took every ounce of Dage's formidable control to continue escorting his brat of a mate out of the room without
tossing her stubborn ass over his shoulder. Anger and need
flared through him in equal measure. Damn but she made his
blood boil.

She jerked her arm back. Unwise move. His hand tightened even further. "I strongly suggest you refrain from speaking until we reach privacy, love."

"Let me go, damn it," she hissed out of the corner of her
mouth.

Now she kept things between them.

He didn't answer her, just yanked her into the hall and to
the family quarters where he nodded at the two guards. "If
anyone tries to get past you, shoot them. We will not be dis-
turbed." Ignoring her protests, he tugged Emma down the
passageway to the gathering room. It was time to get some
fucking things straight.

Emma stumbled into the room, finally yanking her arm
from Dage. What the hell was his problem? She hadn't lied to
him. Even so, she backed away from what appeared to be a
furious vampire. "You've no right to be angry."

He took three long strides, leaned against the cherry wood
desk, and crossed his ankles. A red flush slid across his face,
and his normally silver eyes swirled with a dangerous blue.
Gone was the diplomat, leaving pure, pissed-off male in its
place. "You denied who we are. That will never happen
again." An animalistic growl rode every word.

She gazed at him, her nostrils flaring as the truth of the matter struck her dead center. "You only pretend that smoothness."

He raised an eyebrow, his massive shoulders tensing. "Excuse me?"

How could one simple phrase sound like a threat? "The
diplomatic suit you don—it's bullshit."

He raised his head and slowly lowered his lids to half
mast, his bluish-silver eyes focusing on her like a wolf with a

trapped doe. "I don't believe the Queen of the Realm should use such base language."

The low rumble of his voice, the inherent danger threading through each word, nearly distracted her from the fact they were talking about *him*. "I don't give a shit."

Every tiny movement, every royal thought focused with incredible precision in those metallic eyes as they focused on her. Completely and absolutely. He didn't move. He appeared to barely breathe. Yet the strength of that focus kept her rooted firmly in place. How could so much power come from one gaze?

She lifted her chin—the potent energy swirling around the room belonged to both of them.

Then he grinned, and she lost her breath for a moment. Okay, maybe more of the power was his. For now.

At the realization, her temper spiked. "Do you really think I failed to see you coming?"

He cocked his head to the side, a glimmer of challenge sparking his eyes to flint. "Do tell."

The pure arrogance of his stance, the full cockiness of his words forced a rushing sound to fill her ears. "I saw you. In visions." She slapped her hands down on her hips. "I'm ready, Dage. I know what you can do"—she showed her teeth, lowering her voice—"and I prepared for it."

He pushed away from the desk, standing to his full height. She locked her knees to keep from stepping back; even so, her legs trembled with the need to retreat.

His eyebrow lifted and his lips tipped in the slightest amusement as if he enjoyed her struggle. "You have no idea what I can do." Silky and dark, his voice slid over her skin, raising goose bumps and need.

Damn him. She hadn't backed down from a challenge her entire life. "Try me."

Surprise flashed across his hard face before blue completely banished the silver of his eyes. "As you wish." He flicked a glance at the top button of her sweater, and it flew through the room to ping against a Russell painting. The second hit the doorknob and the third a window. A dark flush played over his high cheekbones. "Shall I continue?"

She kept her hands on her hips, refusing to make the obvious move and clasp her sweater together. It lay open to just below her bra, and a small part of her enjoyed the heat filling his eyes when the cool air brushed across her breasts, pebbling her nipples through the sheer satin.

He'd moved quicker than she'd expected, but now she was ready. "Kiss my ass."

His head jerked up and he took a step toward her. The air changed, heated, stilled. He dropped his gaze to the next button, and she threw up a shield. Imagining shards of ice between her sweater and his eyes, she pushed.

The button remained closed, and Dage lifted his chin, then tilted his head to the side. "Indeed." Wonder filled his eyes, even as a muscle began to tick in his jaw. "I very much would like to avoid breaking you, mate."

His words sent a chill down her spine, rivaling the imaginary ice protecting her clothing. "I don't believe you could." The words came unbidden. She knew better than to challenge him, yet some things couldn't be helped.

He inhaled deeply as if stealing control from the oxygen around them. "You forget, Emma. Your new trick is here because we've begun the mating process. Your power comes from me." He gave a slight mental push against her shield, as though testing her strength.

She pressed back, relieved when her block held firm. "Maybe." Of course this power came from him—it certainly wasn't human. "But it's mine now." And it was—sheer intelligence had prepared her to take, adapt, and learn. The king fooled himself if he thought her anything but a worthy adversary.

"Is that what you are?" he asked, his gaze traveling up the cashmere to her eyes. "Are you sure that's what you *want* to be?"

She faltered and he snatched the fourth button out of the air as it zinged by his ear.

"Stay out of my head, Dage."

He raised an eyebrow. "I believe all bets are off, sweetheart." Flipping the button through the air, he caught it in his other hand. "Two buttons left, then the clasp of your bra." He slid the tiny disc into his pocket. "Then your skirt." His hands went to the buttons of his silk shirt, slowly undoing each one until the material hung open to reveal a broad chest. "Then those satin panties that match your pretty bra."

Then what? She gulped in an uneasy breath and eyed the door.

A sharp click of the lock snapping into place provided her first clue. She focused back on Dage.

He smiled slow and dangerous. "Then what? Well . . . then I'm going to bend you over this desk and fuck you until you scream my name." With a shrug of his strong shoulders, the silk shirt dropped to the floor, revealing tanned, hard muscle. "I guess you were right. The smoothness is bullshit."

Chapter 6

Emma's knees trembled in earnest. But it wasn't with fear—not even close. Want and need slammed so hard through her she wondered how she didn't combust right then and there in the well-appointed gathering room. She cut her eyes to the desk, then back to the King of the Realm.

His hands went to his belt, drawing out the motion of releasing the buckle and pulling the leather through the loops. She waited for him to drop it to the floor with his shirt and lost her breath as he tightened his grip on the belt instead.

He raised an eyebrow. "I'm going to give you one chance here, Emma."

The woman in her wanted to either kick him in the balls or rip his pants off and take him hard and fast. "What would that be, Dage?" Pride filled her at the steadiness of her voice.

"Drop the shield, remove the rest of your clothing, and . . . come here." His voice rumbled down to smooth silk at the end.

Her rational side warred with her emotional side as the air beat around them with a tension of its own. Desire, raw and pure, fought with the pride she'd held on to her entire life. "Bite me." Apparently pride won out.

Dage placed the belt next to him on the desk without breaking eye contact. "I plan to, mate. Never fear. Probably right after I mark you as I should've done last night."

She took a step back. "But you promised."

"I promised I wouldn't mark you last night, love. And I didn't." His gaze traveled down her form and up again, leaving a tingle of awareness along every nerve ending. "You've lost the right to bargain with me now."

Bargain? Bargain? The man wanted to brand her and he thought this a negotiation? The flush burning her face actually hurt.

And then . . . he waited. A powerful being, one who could've struck fast and hard, he waited. Eyes dark, muscles tense, hands at his sides. For the love of God, why didn't he just toss her over the desk?

The uncertainty, plus the unfairness of the fact that he had three hundred years as well as advanced biology on her, spiked a fury through her that filled her bones. Or maybe the basic need clawing beneath her skin did that. Either way, she channeled every bit of that energy into fortifying her shields. To keeping him out.

"You'll never keep me out, Highness," he said, soft and slow.

"You want to bet?" she snapped out, readying her stance. She'd learn to block her thoughts.

The smile sliding across his face could never be considered kind. "Bet? You already threw down the gauntlet, Emma. The battle has continued this length of time only because I've allowed it—to grant you a chance to retreat, as you know you should."

Retreat? Not a fucking chance in hell. Pure strength of will had her slamming imaginary mental shields around her brain. She nearly jumped at the sound of them clicking into place.

He lifted his head, true appreciation flashing through his eyes. "Nicely done, love. Very nicely done."

His approval unnerved her as nothing else could have. He should be furious. Dread pooled to mix with the desire in her stomach—his confidence was real and probably earned.

Keeping his predatory gaze focused on her eyes, he mentally tapped against the shield covering her body. Just a bit at first, then with more force.

She held firm, every muscle she owned tightening in response.

He shoved harder, looking for all the world like a guy preparing to take a casual stroll. The effort cost him nothing, yet a fine bead of sweat emerged on her forehead. Then her upper lip. Her shoulders started to tremble with the effort it took to block him.

Sighing, he gave a sharp push and her shields crumbled to the ground, the sound of shattering ice echoing throughout her ears. Damn. He'd been playing with her.

Her final two buttons dropped to the floor with soft pings and a gust of air ripped the sweater off her body.

She tilted her head to the side. Even with the raw need cascading through her, the scientist's mind wondered how he'd get the skirt off. Pencil thin, tight, she'd need to step out of it.

She wouldn't.

He showed his teeth, and the sound of shredding fabric rent the air. The skirt split down the middle to pool onto the floor. He'd ripped her skirt! She hissed low, she'd liked that skirt.

"Then you should've removed it when I told you to do so." His gaze cut to her bra. As if an imaginary knife slashed through the air, the straps on her shoulders sprang free and the center clasp released. The bra sailed across the room to hang drunkenly from a curtain rod.

Her breasts hung heavy and full, needing something.

Someone.

Him.

She ached, standing vulnerable in her panties and three-inch heels. She lifted her head, pure stubbornness forcing her to face him.

Her panties snapped in two.

"You may keep on the heels, love," he drawled. His gaze

ran over her nude form, the silver returning to blend with the blue in his eyes and deepen to a color not even close to human. "I can smell your heat, Emma. Sugared peaches, saucy rum, feminine. For me."

"I can smell yours too, Dage," she snapped back. If power had a smell it was Dage. Raw, sandalwood with amber, dangerous. For her.

"Come here, Emma." He straightened, the intricate ink webbing over his shoulder and down his arm standing out against the bronze of his skin. A wicked, sharp tattoo.

She told herself she didn't take orders from him. In truth, she balked. A cold slap of air pushed at her from behind, propelling her forward. Damn it. He controlled the air, too?

"Sometimes," he acknowledged. "The elements are Jase's forte, but I have some talent as well."

Talent, her ass. It was a weapon and he knew it. She forgot how to breathe as she came to rest before the king. Not a force existed on earth that could've kept her from lifting her chin and squarely meeting his eyes.

He gave a short nod of appreciation. "You are truly fit to be a queen." Placing a large hand to rest against her neck, he drew her forward and dropped his mouth to hers.

Roaring fire lanced through her and she groaned, trembling from need. Her hands went to the hot skin of his abs to trace the ridges of hard muscle even as he deepened the kiss. His tongue swept inside her mouth, claiming, yet a gentle restraint echoed throughout his entire body.

As if he waited.

He lifted his head, showing his teeth in the smile of a wolf. "I told you how I wanted you, Emma."

She dropped her hands, her gaze sliding to the desk and back again. He was crazy if he thought—

"Not crazy," he murmured, apparently still in her head. The hand at her neck slid down between her breasts. "You waged war, love." Tracing a path down to her stomach, he leaned even closer. "You lost." The rough timbre of his voice encouraged the trembling deep inside her womb. Was it possible to orgasm just from a voice? "Now you surrender." He reached his final destination and cupped her core.

Her knees buckled. There was no other explanation for it. His other hand went to her waist, keeping her upright. Nearly dazed, she glanced at the exit. His gaze followed hers, and the lock disengaged with an audible click, the door moving slightly ajar.

He straightened, removing both hands. Cold and emptiness rushed over her and she shivered. "You want to run, Emma, do so now."

There was no way her pride would allow her to run, and they both knew it.

His muscles began to vibrate with a need she felt in her own womb. "Make your choice, Emma. The desk or the door."

Pride was a dangerous animal. They both knew he could have her on the desk in seconds should he choose. He was bigger and most certainly stronger. Yet the king had pride, too. No way would it allow him to make this easy on her.

She'd challenged him—and she'd lost.

Keeping her head high, she shifted to the side, placing both hands on the cold, smooth wood of the desk. Her gaze failed to acknowledge the beautiful oil painting before her, every ounce of focus she owned stayed on the man behind her—the vampire she could no longer see. She stubbornly refused to turn her head to track him.

He didn't make her wait. One palm spread out between her shoulder blades. She jumped. "Ah, Emma. You make it so easy to forget." He traced a line down her spine, his callused finger caressing each vertebra, his voice low and soft. She shivered in need, no longer able to hide even that. "So much spirit, nearly larger than life." He reached her tailbone and went lower. "I forget how very small, how very fragile you are."

Cupping her ass, he caressed to the apex between her legs.

She gave an audible gasp, pushing back against his hand until he slid one, then two fingers inside her. She was wet and ready, and pretty much certain she was going to kill him if he waited any longer.

The release of his zipper coincided with his deep chuckle at her ear. Heat surrounded her from behind as he removed his hand and the rustle of clothing sounded.

He gave a gentle nudge to her ankles above the high heels and she widened her stance, eyes crossing as he pressed himself against her—hot, hard, and male. His hand returned, warm and heavy, to her shoulder blades, guiding her down until her cheek rested on the cool wood of the desk. Oh God.

Grasping her hips with both hands, he drove into her.

The cry she gave was for him and him alone. She lifted up to her elbows, pushing back and encouraging him to increase his speed. He accommodated her, thrusting hard and fast until a spiraling tickle of awareness began to hum deep inside her. Then he slowed.

"Hey—" she protested, clenching around him.

"Say my name, Emma." Animalistic need rode every word.

Jesus, she'd recite the Gettysburg address if he'd hurry up. "Dage."

"You'll scream it." Releasing her hips, he gathered all of her hair into one broad hand, tilting her head to the side. Her flesh rippled around him.

He was going to bite her again.

He increased the strength of his thrusts, his hand clenching in her hair, his heat filling her. Her muscles tightened, a trembling beginning to echo somewhere deep inside her.

Harder.

Faster.

More.

Flesh slapped against flesh. He hit a spot she hadn't known existed. Stars sparked behind her eyes. Then his other hand clasped her shoulder. A piercing pain shot through her bliss followed by a burst of reality. Of shocked awareness.

He'd branded her. On her upper right shoulder—for the world to see.

Fury blast through her even as the hum returned to her womb. Even as she pushed back against him. Pressing his entire length against her back, increasing his thrusts past what was humanly possible, he yanked her head farther to the side and struck. His fangs pierced her skin, and her orgasm slammed home.

And she did, indeed, scream his name.

Chapter 7

He'd *branded* her.

Fury cut through Emma until she feared a brain embolism as she yanked on jeans in *their* room. The arrogant ass had had her clothes moved that morning while she'd sipped tea. She clasped her shaking hands together, facing Dage. "What just happened changes nothing."

The rasp of a zipper filled the space when he donned his jeans. "That's a stupid thing to say, love." His jaw could've been made from rock and his eyes from slate. "I strongly suggest you don't mess with me."

Awareness slid through Emma at the declaration that lacked a qualifier. Most people warned not to mess with them "right now." Not Dage. His was a blanket statement for all time. The king epitomized absolute control and flame-filled promise. As if Sister June from her Catholic school cautioned her against touching him, Emma wanted nothing more than to step forward and get burned.

She shook her head to concentrate. "I need to get to work, Dage." Her data and recent results needed to be combed through for a solution to the virus problem.

"I know." He yanked a dark shirt over his head. "The best lab for you will be the one Kane's designing, and you know it."

Yeah. Considering they'd blown up her last lab. "I'm sure many labs are adequately equipped for me to continue my research." A weak argument at best.

"Right. About a virus most humans have never heard of. You're staying with us, love." His gaze narrowed on her. "Are you all right? I mean, does the mark hurt?"

She pushed appreciation for his concern out of her heart. "No. My shoulder burns and bubbles are popping in my veins as my physiology alters." As she changed from human to immortal. The urge to study her own blood tempted her to make use of the vampire's laboratory. "So far the process isn't painful."

His gaze cleared. "Good. If it becomes so, we do have dampening pills—though they're usually taken before the marking."

"Dampening pills?" She frowned, her mind reeling.

"Yes, ah"—he cleared his throat—"sometimes the marking is a bit intense, and since many of our unions are pre-arranged, we have pills to counter the effect." He grinned. "I assume it's like drinking a bottle of malted scotch—kind of eases the experience the first time, though I believe it also has a pain inhibitor as a key ingredient."

She may be pissed from being branded, but she'd never have wanted to be numb and miss out on the excellent sex she'd just had. "I'll keep that in mind if my shoulder begins to really hurt."

"Excellent. I'm truly not sure how long the process takes." He leaned over and yanked open a drawer, his hand emerging with an intricate gold cuff.

"That looks like the cuff Cara wore on her arm last night."

Dage grinned. "It's very similar. Our mother had them created by an alchemist to keep track of us." He extended the jewelry toward her. "Only a member of the Kayrs family can keep this on. You'll wear it now."

Emma took a step back. "No." This was temporary.

The door burst open and Dage dropped into a fighting stance, shielding Emma. He slowly straightened. "Jase?"

The youngest brother gulped in air, his eyes a wild copper. "Cara's ill. Talen sent me."

Emma broke into a run several steps behind the men as they ran toward Talen's suite. Her bare feet burned across the hotel carpet and her stomach pitched. Nothing could be wrong with Cara. Her sister was safe surrounded by deadly vampires who'd give their lives for her. But what about the baby?

There had been so much stress, so much danger lately. Maybe Cara was too worn down. Damn it. Emma should've made her stay in bed and not go to the ball last night. What was she thinking?

Fury and fear not her own whipped into her from the king as he cleared the path. It was weird to feel his feelings. They passed vampires standing guard every few yards as well as hotel tables overflowing with flowered lilies. The sweet smell nearly made her gag.

Dage threw open the door to find Talen holding the doctor by the neck at least three feet off the ground, clunking his head against the bedroom door frame. "What do you mean you don't know?" Talen growled, his face an inch from the doctor's rapidly reddening one.

"Talen, damn it, put him down," Cara hissed from the bedroom.

The doctor's thick eyeglasses went askew, giving him a cartoon-like appearance. "I'll figure this out, I will."

Talen dropped the doctor.

The man quickly sidled toward the hallway and glanced at Dage. "We've taken blood, your majesty."

"What's your best hypothesis?" Dage asked, his gaze hard on the doctor.

The doctor shrugged. "A pregnancy this early in the mating process is unheard of, sir. I just don't know, though there are indications this could be viral."

Fear exploded in Emma's gut. No way. It was just morning sickness. She ran for the bedroom, pushing open the door and running smack into another man in a white coat. Lab technician or additional doctor? Talen smashed into her from behind and for a moment she was sandwiched between both men. She scooted to freedom and reached for Cara's hand, then sat on the bed.

Cara had paled until even her lips lacked color while a fine dot of perspiration lined her brow. Tears filled her eyes. "The marking has faded. Almost completely." The low whispered pain in her voice caused Emma's eyes to instantly fill. "I feel . . . *different.*"

Shit. Emma turned toward the second man and nearly knocked over the pot of bright geraniums on the bed table. "How long will it take to test her blood for the virus?"

He patted his bag. "We have a plane waiting to send the sample to Kane." His concerned brown eyes cut to Talen and he inched his way past the furious vampire toward the door.

Emma's gaze met Dage's. "We need a lab. Here. Now."

He nodded and grabbed a cell phone out of his pocket. Barking orders, he stalked out of the room.

Emma brushed Cara's hair back from her face. "You'll be okay, Car. I promise. I'll fix this."

A slow tear wound its way down Cara's pale face and her golden cuff fell off her arm to rest on the bedspread. Her eyes widened. "Em, you can't fix everything." She bit back a sob. "What will the virus do to the baby?"

Talen growled low and sprawled on the bed, pulling Cara into his arms, where she began to cry softly. "We don't know it's the virus, mate. It could just be a difficult pregnancy." His eyes held a dangerous hue that glittered with frustration. This was an enemy he couldn't fight.

Emma fought her own sob. She had to *think*. Cara's marking had faded—it had to be the virus. Not a time for emotion. She was a geneticist. "The baby's strong, as are you. We'll fix this."

The carpet sank under her bare feet when she dodged into the other room where Dage growled into his phone. "Tell Kane we'll land in two hours. And get the blood work on Maggie from last month, as well as all current data." He slapped the cell shut, pivoting toward her, anger bracketing the lines near his mouth. "How is she?"

Emma shook her head. "I don't know."

Dage turned toward Jase, whose large body hovered by the door. "Find Conn. You two discover how the Kurjans could've infected her, if this is the virus." He shifted his attention to Emma. "We're leaving for Colorado in fifteen minutes—go pack."

"Colorado?" Emma's mind spun.

"Yes. Kane has had men building a state of the art research facility on the outskirts of Boulder. He's been flying most of the day from Europe to get here—I just had him diverted to Colorado. He'll beat us there by minutes." Dage lifted her chin, his gaze searching. "How are you feeling?"

"Me?" Emma frowned. "Why?"

"Because you've been with your sister the entire time you've been here. If she was infected . . ."

Emma's stomach swirled. "I don't know. I feel nauseous, but that could be fear." Damn.

Dage's jaw clenched shut before he gave her a gentle push toward the door. "Find Janie and pack for both of you. I need to talk to Talen."

Emma turned on her heel toward the door and a blinding flash filled her skull. Pain radiated out her ears. She moaned, swaying in her bare feet. Both hands pressed into her temples to keep her brain from oozing out. Darkness wavered over her eyes, and she began to drop into nothingness.

Strong arms caught her, pausing for a moment before lifting her into the air. A hard chest cradled her face and she centered herself with the rhythm of an ancient heartbeat. Dage. He tucked his chin around her head, drawing her nearer, protecting her from the world, his body rigid, his breathing even.

Sure movements had her on the couch, the king kneeling next to her, still shielding. "Love? Let me recall the doctors."

She opened her eyes. Her vision cleared and pools of concerned silver met her gaze. "Ouch."

Dage frowned. "I'll be right back."

"No." She tried to sit up, but one large hand pressed against her shoulder and kept her in place. "I'm all right. I had a vision."

He lifted his eyebrows. "Does this happen every time you have a vision?"

Hell no. She shook her head and winced as pain fired from her neurons. "No. Usually I only have visions while dreaming. Never when I'm awake. Why now?" She put a hand to her still aching temple.

Sandalwood and spice tickled her nose when the king leaned back on his haunches, thoughts scattering across his face. Finally, he sighed. "The marking. Your abilities have increased, melded with mine, and you're not used to the power. Your gift will someday develop to match mine." He brushed a curl off her cheek. "I'll help you control the ability so it doesn't hurt."

Freakin' terrific. She had a brand on her shoulder, could feel what he felt, and would now get visions that made her want to cut off her head. "This is just great."

He grinned, reaching out to knead her shoulders. "It'll be okay, I promise. What did you see in your vision?"

"Katie. Frightened and running alone through an alley in some type of city." Emma bit her lip, her gaze on Talen as he entered the room. "I couldn't recognize any of the buildings."

Dage helped her to a seated position.

Talen tapped the communicator at his ear. "Find Jordan Pride." Golden eyes shifted to pin Emma. "Any idea the time of year?"

Emma shrugged. "Light rain was falling, and there was no snow or ice on the ground." She needed more information.

Dage tugged her to her feet. "We'll figure this out, sweetheart. Don't worry."

"I know. I'll have the vision again. Hopefully next time I'll get more details." Emma glanced toward the bedroom.

Talen followed her gaze. "Cara fell asleep. Do we have a lab set up?"

Dage shook his head. "We need to fly to Colorado—Kane's lab is the best we've got. The best there is."

"Is it ready?" Talen asked.

"The facility is almost ready. But we still have humans there."

"They'll just have to stay out of our way," Talen said, a grim set to his jaw. "I want the jet—Cara can sleep in the small bedroom."

Dage nodded. "I'm leaving Conn and Jase here to finish running the colloquium with Terent. The rest of us will leave in ten minutes." He clapped his brother on the shoulder. "Your mate will be all right, Talen."

Talen's eyes flashed a hellish fire. "She damn well better be. Or the Kurjan nation will cease to exist."

Several rooms down, Katie paced by the window, using every ounce of willpower she had to force nausea down. Now she had the freakin' flu. Wasn't it bad enough to watch Jordan play the diplomat yesterday and flirt with that fucking witch from the big apple? No wonder Katie had been puking for hours.

She hated the flu. Spasms ripped through her stomach and she clutched her ribs, biting her lip to keep from crying out. She needed to shift. She'd heal faster in animal form.

Groaning, she glanced around the room. She'd probably bust up some of the furniture with the energy released during the shift, but at least no one would get hurt.

Her bathrobe swished to the carpet before she dropped to the floor. Pain sparked through her skin. Damn, she was sick. She straightened her hands, searching for her other half—for the animal inside.

She sought the connection to the wild, the amazing energy bubbling beneath her skin to allow her a primitive release into true nature. She searched for the feeling of freedom as muscles tightened, focus centered, and humanity fell to the side. She awaited the sense of being one with the earth and her creatures, a lost binding she mourned when in human form. She delved deep, and . . .

Nothing.

Odd. She hadn't had to concentrate to shift into a lioness in, well, forever. A buzzing set up between her ears and she shook her head to dispel it. Then she slowed her breathing, focused and . . .

Nothing.

Panic blasted through her system, heating her blood. She couldn't shift. She tried again. Only pain met her attempt. Yanking on her bathrobe, she ran to the door, tripping over the belt in her haste. The carpet burned her knees when she fell.

Sobbing, she scrambled to her feet to throw open the door and run down the hall to Cara's room. She stumbled inside, relieved to see Jordan standing with Dage and Talen.

Jordan rushed toward her, his tawny eyes alight with concern. "Katie?"

She tripped into his arms, her breath coming in short bursts, words tripping over themselves.

He gave her a slight shake. "Slow down. I can't understand you."

She sucked in air, gulped down the pain, and met his gaze. "I can't shift." The buzzing exploded into stars and she fell into the comfort of blackness.

Chapter 8

Emma clasped her bag to her chest while leading Janie across the rough asphalt. The scent of night jasmine wafted on a slight breeze. They'd made haste driving in dark SUVs to the private airport, and she was sure she'd forgotten more than one pair of shoes back at the hotel. Dage assured her his men would go through all the rooms to double check.

A dark rumble of clouds toppled across the dusky sky and the wind bit her skin. She shivered, tugging Janie into a jog across the tarmac where the silver jet waited at the end, engines running. For some reason she felt like a thief scurrying away to safety. Displeasure rumbled toward her from Dage as he ran on her right. The king wanted to stay and fight and only made this move to protect her. Damn but being the king must suck sometimes.

Her ears began to ring. How in the hell had she gotten caught up in this war? She was a geneticist. Cara studied plants. Janie should be in bed early so she could go to preschool tomorrow. While Emma's world had never seemed safe, at least she'd understood the rules. Vampires and shifters were supposed to be make-believe. Not real.

Talen jogged ahead of her with Cara in his arms, Jordan carried Katie, while Max hurried along next to them. Kate had yet to regain consciousness, and the fierce curling of Jordan's lip bespoke pain for whoever had infected the lioness.

Several vampire and shifter soldiers surrounded the group.

It had been less than twenty minutes since Katie had shown up with her announcement. Emma's mind spun. Cara and Katie drank tea instead of champagne last night. Jesus. Was it that easy to get to them?

Dage kept up his pace next to her. "Can a virus be taken orally?"

Emma's eyes filled with tears. "Yes. Easily. In fact, many of the new cancer treatments involve drinking a virus that'll mutate cancer cells." It had always stunned her that there were people with scientific knowledge who would use the information as a way to harm. Science helped humans survive—to triumph over death—not act as foot soldiers for the grim reaper.

"Damn it." Dage tapped his earpiece. "Leave word for Kane that he might have three subjects, Cara, Katie, and Maggie. Maggie will arrive at the facility shortly." A raw rumble of anger rode his words, a cold plan to get Emma to safety so he could fight. While he may be king, Emma could hear the soldier's need to draw blood in his deep tone. She wondered how often he tamped down his nature to fulfill his duties as king.

"Good. I need to conduct research on Maggie's blood." Emma breathed deep. Would the wolf shifter's DNA resemble a human's?

"I'll double-check her arrival time." Dage had no sooner retapped his earpiece than a burst of green light rocked into his leg, dropping him to the ground.

"Dage!" Emma screamed, halting and turning toward him. Ozone and blood scented the air. Several more bursts of light filled the night, and the soldiers around them scrambled into position.

Dage yanked her and Janie to the ground, shielding them behind his broad back as he shifted and returned fire. Emma rolled over Janie, covering the child with her body. Something banged into her shoulder and she fought a groan.

The scent of burned ozone filled her nostrils. Asphalt scraped her flesh as she cuddled Janie's head into her chest. Oh God. How could she keep her niece safe? How badly hurt was Dage? The child's fear made her tremble against the pavement, while Dage's rage popped the air around them.

The bursts of light came from the top of a hanger to the left, and the soldiers around them began to return fire. Green lasers ripped through the air with deadly force to bounce off buildings and shatter windows. Once in awhile a grunt of pain echoed from the men surrounding her and from the ones on the roof of a building trying to end her life.

Dage cursed low, and pain radiated toward her. He'd been hit again.

Emma tightened her hold on Janie, trusting the trained warriors to keep them safe. Helplessness shot through her, and she flashed back to childhood when there were no warriors to protect her. She needed to fight—to protect Janie. She lifted her head.

"Stay down," Dage ordered, flipping around, one broad hand cupping her head and forcing her down. She struggled for a moment, then stopped, reality filtering in.

The jet engaged and slid into position between them and the shooters. Loud pops rent the air as bullets tore into its side.

Strong hands ripped Janie away from Emma and she yelled, struggling until she realized Max had lifted Janie and jumped inside the craft. Dage picked Emma up and followed, setting her down in a plush seat, yanking the shifters inside, then bellowing furious orders for the soldiers to find the shooters and keep them alive if possible.

He shut the hatch and the jet turned before increasing speed and lifting into the air.

So much for visions. Emma hadn't seen the attack coming.

Fear had her head spinning until she glanced at Janie across the aisle. "Janie!" Jumping out of her chair, Emma tugged on the little girl's sleeve. Blood welled between a large tear in the pink material. "Janie. Oh God." Emma began to breathe heavily. Wide blue eyes filled with tears and met hers. She lifted her head to Dage. "She's been shot."

Shock crossed his face chased by absolute fury. He gently pushed Emma out of the way and ripped Janie's sleeve off. He wiped her arm with the softest of touches, somehow catching Cara with one arm as she rushed for her child. "She's okay, Cara. The bullet merely burned her."

Crying, Cara ran her hands over Janie's tearful face.

"I'm okay, Mama." The four-year-old wiped away tears. "But my arm hurts."

Jordan threw a first aid kit at Talen, who caught it and dropped to his haunches. "Hey there, little one. We should put a bandage on that, huh?"

Emma leaned over and took a good look at the wound. It looked like a deep scrape. Red and puffy, but not a hole filled with a bullet. She pressed a hand to her clamoring heart and dropped back into her seat. "Thank God. What in the hell just happened?" she whispered to Dage.

As Talen bandaged the wound, Dage stood, a gaping hole in his pant leg showing the impact of a bullet. A bullet popped out of his neck to bounce on the ground and the skin slid together like melted butter. "We were attacked." He cut his gaze to Jordan several seats up. "How in the hell did they know where we'd be? Only a few people knew we were leaving, and we didn't tell anybody our route or which small airport."

Jordan growled, his tawny eyes blazing with a lion's fury. "I don't know. How the hell did anyone get close enough to infect Cara and Katie?"

The plane leveled off and Talen finished bandaging his daughter. "The Kurjans have someone on the inside. Someone close to us." He spoke quietly, calmly. Probably for Janie's benefit.

Emma swallowed several times to dispel the churning of her stomach, a dull ache setting up in her temples. Great. A traitor who knew their every move. One who had access to the virus threatening them all. She fought to concentrate and understand the other weapons involved so she could counter them. "The green laser bursts turn into bullets the second they touch flesh, even human. Right?"

Dage kept his gaze on Janie, a furious muscle working in his jaw. "Yes." His anger filled Emma's nostrils and she struggled to breathe past her mate's fury.

Wonderful. Special, flesh seeking bullets. Freakin' great. Emma fought the bile rising in her throat. She needed pure oxygen.

Talen bent and lifted Janie into his arms. "Cara and Janie are going to use the back bedroom for the two-hour trip." He turned and helped his mate up.

Janie scrunched her nose in a frown, tiny tear tracks adding frailty to her small face. "Auntie Emma? You're bleeding."

Dage knelt next to her in an instant, his hands moving to unbutton her shirt. "*Na pari i eychi.*"

"What?" Emma looked down at her chest in slow motion, a numbness setting into her limbs. "How many languages do you speak, anyway?"

"All of them." He peeled off her shirt and the amount of red made her gasp. A buzzing set up in her ears. "You're in shock, love." He wiped her flesh with the fabric to reveal a hole in her upper left arm. Tugging her forward, he glanced at her back, grimaced, then released her. "She'll be fine. Talen, take your family to the bedroom, please."

Cara protested but Talen grabbed her arm and gave her no choice but to move.

Dage waited until the back door clicked shut before pinning Emma with a hard gaze. "You're losing too much blood for my taste, Emma."

"Won't I heal like you now?" Geez. The man had branded her. Shouldn't that come with some immortal benefits? She wished the odd buzzing sound would stop. Grayness fell across her vision.

Dage gave her a little shake. "You'll heal faster, but we've only been mated since last night. The talent takes some time to develop."

Her mind spun. "This isn't how I die, Dage." Sure there was fire and pain in her vision. But no bullets.

He paled. "Of course not, damn it."

Jordan cleared his throat. "If you don't need me for this, I'll get Katie settled into a lounger in the front row." The shifter glanced at Emma's bleeding wound, then graced her with a sympathetic smile. "It'll be okay, Highness."

Max turned, his gaze on Emma's injury. "I'll move." The stoic vampire crept up the aisle toward Jordan.

Emma tried to focus on the plush gray seats of the private jet. "Um. Why is everyone squirming? Am I dying?" She lacked the ability to focus. Shock was good. She should be in a lot of pain.

Dage brushed her curls back. "No love, you're not dying. But you might not like my solution." His voice softened, while his eyes hardened with purpose.

She tried to roll her eyes, but even that slight movement tugged her stomach into a nauseous swirl. "I am not having sex with you right now, Dage."

A snort sounded from a few rows up.

Dage grinned, slow and sexy. "Turnabout's fair play, love."

"Turnabout?" Why did her head feel so heavy?

"Yes." A flash of silver sparked. Dage slit the vein in his left wrist. He cupped her head and brought his arm toward her mouth.

"No." Emma yanked to the side, squirming to get away from him. Oh God, no way. Clarity came with a flash, as did a shrieking pain in her arm.

He held her still, his hand firm. The bloody wrist came at her relentlessly. The wet skin met her lips and she fought a gag, clutching both hands into his arm to push it away. Dage pressed harder, forcing the liquid into her mouth. "Drink Emma, or I'll plug your nose until you do."

The king's strength easily outmatched hers. She opened her mouth to scream, and he took full advantage, shoving more of his wrist inside until her teeth had no choice but to clamp on. Blood dripped down her throat and burned. The thick liquid sizzled like carbonated hot coffee.

A craving for more lit her on fire.

Moaning deep, she sucked with great pulls, her mind spinning with the greatest high imaginable. It was . . . heaven. Beyond heaven. Against her will, her jaw slackened. Her body became too heavy to move and her eyelids dropped. She stopped fighting.

Her heartbeat slowed and she barely registered when Dage removed his arm, brushing a gentle kiss to her cheek. "Sleep now, love. You'll be all better when you awaken." A soft blanket swished over her, and she snuggled down with a whispered sigh.

She dreamed in color—bright flashes of inspiration and beauty through tunnels of expectation, of history, of the future. Visions flashed into her brain with a rapid staccato—some new, some old.

There was nowhere to hide from one vision that caused her heart to shatter, her mind to scream, her soul to thunder in fury. She'd been asleep for several hours, knowing full well she needed to awaken to keep it from happening. But the darkness won, as always.

The vision opened on a summer dawn, pure sky, a slight tulip-scented breeze with Dage striding toward a white metal building where she worked, a lab of some sorts. She knew without question she was inside. Shadows walked with him, probably his brothers. But this plan, this glimpse into the future was about the king. He looked strong, a smile on his face, those dangerous dimples flashing. Safe.

He nodded, saying something to a shadow as a flash of fire reflected in his eyes. The earth trembled. A cloud of black billowed into the sky where the building had stood.

Death danced around the destruction, and the king fell to his knees. Raw agony ripped across his face, and it was as if Emma could actually see his heart harden and disappear. Gone. Destroyed. His head dropped to his chest.

She came awake with a start, her mouth opened to scream.

"Shh, love, it's okay." Dage settled himself more securely around her, his breath whispering against her hair.

Air shot into her lungs and she gulped, trying to quell the rapid beating of her heart. Darkness met her gaze. "Where am I?"

"Colorado. In a residence facility outside Boulder." He ran a gentle hand over her arm. Her *healed* arm.

"I slept the whole way? Even from the plane to here?" Her mind spun as she stretched against him. Her body felt *fantastic*. "Your blood provides a serious whammy." Too bad her heart ached from the vision.

"Thank you." He flattened a hand against her tummy. "Tell me about your dream."

Dread flushed through her. "I don't remember it."

"Liar." The room tilted and she ended up under a vampire. He dropped a gentle kiss on her mouth. "I want to know what frightens you so, love."

She couldn't tell him. He'd made no secret of his intent to love and protect her, a path that might destroy him. Past failures already haunted her, and she was a woman who learned from her mistakes. *This* vision she'd heed. "How is everyone else?"

"Fine." He settled himself more comfortably at the apex of her legs, and she fought a whimper.

A sudden thought occurred to her. "Why aren't you reading my mind?"

He lowered his head to run his heated mouth along her neck to nibble on her ear. "You have shields up. Even when you're asleep."

Her hands crept down his back to clench his tight ass on their own volition. "Couldn't you breach my shields?" He'd won their last psychic contest of wills hands down.

"Yes." His palm spread over a breast before he rolled the nipple between his fingers.

She arched into him, her mind spinning for a moment. "So why didn't you?"

He pinched and she fought a moan. Then he grasped the back of her thigh and pushed her leg up, opening her for him. "Because I respect your privacy?" His heated palm reached around to clench her hip.

Oh God. "Is that why?"

His hand slid under her ass to squeeze. "No." He nipped at her jaw until reaching her mouth, sliding his tongue between her lips to tempt her with pure male.

Her head spun when he deepened the kiss and it took a moment to refocus as he began to wander that mouth down to her breasts. "No? What do you mean, no?"

He sighed, raising up until his silver gaze slid through the darkness to pin her in place. "I didn't breach your mental shields because you're too fragile right now."

Fragile? Bullshit. "I'm not fragile." He needed to learn she was strong enough to protect him, maybe even stand beside him someday. She tried to lower her leg, but his broad hand clasped her thigh and held it in place.

"Yes, you are. You've recently been marked and now you've been shot. I could damage you if I ripped open your shields." He sighed. "Though I'd hoped at some point you'd trust me enough to take them down."

The damn king had a sweetness to him he'd certainly deny. One that she was going to miss. "I'm done talking, Dage." She reached for him, so full and hard.

He growled low when she took him in hand and began to lightly run her fingernails along his length.

She smiled. "So. Are you going to use this or what?"

Grabbing her hand, he manacled both wrists above her head. "Nice distraction, love. Though I've had enough of this bullshit."

The crass language from the king sent an alert through her system. "Ah, doesn't duty call? Shouldn't we get to work?" She tried a tiny struggle, not surprised when he held her in place.

He settled his erection against her core. "The king's life is about duty, love. You belong to the man." The nip to her lip nearly stung. "And the man wants to know why you deny what he can feel in your heart."

She rolled her eyes, fighting the urge to rub against him like a cat in heat. "Talking about yourself in third person is a bad sign, Dage. Nutsville."

He grinned. "True. Not letting me help is crazy as well. Tell me what you're running from."

She couldn't. Well, she could, but there was no way Dage would allow the visions to alter his life. For once, someone would have to protect the king. And the man.

Determination filled his eyes. "Is it about your child-hood?"

She froze. "What do you know about that?" Her hands loosened their hold on his butt.

A ticking set up in his jaw. "Cara told me your father was a mean drunk who liked to hit."

Cara had told him that? Interesting. "She never talks about that time in our lives. I'm surprised she said anything."

Dage planted a soft kiss on the underside of Emma's jaw. "I think she was trying to explain why you'd be a pain in my ass. She told me about the times you purposefully put yourself in his path so she wouldn't get hurt."

Loyalty welled up in Emma's heart. "Cara saved me more than once. She even bit him so he'd drop a knife. She was so brave, Dage."

A broad hand that would never hit brushed Emma's curls off her forehead. "You were both brave."

She sighed. "I wasn't sorry when he died. Something in me should've been, but . . ." The guilt from letting her mother die, too, would forever eat at her, but she couldn't tell Dage about that.

"I don't blame you. But times have changed, your life has changed. As has your role." A firmness entered the king's tone to replace the kindness.

"My role?" Emma tensed.

"Yes. You're no longer a shield, love. That's my job."

Her mind began to spin. "I don't understand." Hoping to distract him, she wrapped both legs around his heated hips. Damn but he felt amazing against her. Power hummed through her veins from the blood he'd given her, and she wanted to take it for a spin—with his incredible body.

"You understand. Use that gigantic brain and click the facts into place. Why did you think you needed to protect your sister and mother?" Desire turned his voice to a raspy timbre that made her shiver.

She struggled to focus on the thread of conversation. "Because I could. I'm stronger—harder to hurt." Physically and emotionally. Cara's gift as an empath came from the heart, while Emma's psychic ability was all mental.

"Are you stronger than me?" He lifted his eyebrows as if in a dare.

Come on. The guy was twice her size as well as being a

vampire. "Pain doesn't have to be physical, Dage." Emotional scars cut much deeper than a backhand from a drunk. And the king had his own ghosts. She wouldn't become one of them. She'd never haunt him, so long as their relationship ended quickly.

"Listen." He swept a kiss across her mouth, his gaze pinning hers. "I may not be inside your head right now, but I can feel enough to know you're protecting me. It's beginning to piss me off."

Too bad. For too long the king had single-handedly shouldered the world, and she'd be damned if she'd allow him to lump her in with the rest of those he needed to shield. "I don't know what you're talking about." The brand on her shoulder began to burn. An ache deep inside her wanted him to fill her. *Now.*

"Yes you do. I don't want your protection. I want your trust." And your love. The unspoken word hung in the air.

Enough of this. "You need to listen to me. I don't want this life—I'm not staying." Her heart sliced into pieces as she said the words. She'd loved him since the first time she'd shared his past in a vision. "After we find a cure for Cara, I'm moving on." She needed him prepared just in case she didn't beat death, so she tensed, waiting for the explosion.

A smile flirted with Dage's lips until spreading into a full grin. He began to chuckle, his eyes filling with amusement. "You're adorable."

Fury instantly burst into her. "Don't you even think about being condescending with me." She was a top-rated geneticist for God's sakes. People with brains took her seriously. The king better follow suit, especially since power now pumped through her blood.

He shrugged, grasping one of her hips and plunging inside her with one powerful stroke.

She gasped, digging her nails into his skin. Fire lanced

through her and nerves jumped to life as he filled her. Completely.

Dropping his forehead to hers, he tightened his grip. "Then stop being silly." His fangs flared in the dim light. One strong hand tugged her head to the side, revealing her neck. "Mine."

Quick as a flash, he struck.

Chapter 9

Several hours later Dage threw a stack of papers down on the glass table in a conference room. Shades let in the soft light of dawn from the two wide windows and he fought a growl at how exposed his people were in that place. They should be underground at headquarters.

He glanced at Kane. "So we've confirmed Cara, Maggie, and Katie have been infected." His mate might as well have a target on her back.

The Kurjans would be coming for her.

A burning lit along his spine to explode at the base of his neck, the beast inside him clawing to be free—to protect and avenge. Quelling the creature took him several deep breaths as well as a formidable will unmatched by human or immortal beings. As his mind took control, he flirted with the thought of passing the reins to Talen or Kane. But he couldn't do that to his brothers.

"I've double-checked the results using a direct fluorescent antibody stain similar to the H1N1 flu test—only takes thirty minutes. The virus is alive and duplicating itself within the cells of Cara, Maggie, and Kate." Kane leaned against a wall papered in an executive green and maroon stripe, his intelligent eyes trained on Dage. "Preliminary tests show that Emma hasn't been exposed."

"How good are the tests?"

Kane shrugged. "The Kurjans have been mapping DNA for the last century and thanks to Talen's raiding last month, we have all their research. Of course, we're double-checking and confirming the data as fast as possible."

Dage rubbed a hand across his eyes. "I hate this. Bringing in the human researchers might be the decision that takes the Kayrs family down for good." Though then he wouldn't have to play king any more.

"I know. But we need fast results and the humans have the necessary bodies to get it done. Since I've separated them into small labs, they have no idea what they're working on." Kane sighed. "I should've been concentrating the last century on genetics and not on weaponry."

"No." Dage shook his head. "We knew our peace with the Kurjans would end and advanced weapons would be crucial." He'd never thought a biological weapon would threaten his people. The failure here was his. "So what happens now? I mean with the virus?"

Kane shrugged. "Viruses are either progressive or the host fights them off and wins, like with the common cold."

Dage's shoulders tightened to rock. "Progressive? Explain."

"I will. But first I need to read the latest information from Talen's raid as well as review the blood samples from the women. The most helpful at this time are Maggie's. Since we've had her blood for a few weeks we can trace the development of the virus."

"For shifters. Humans may be different."

Kane nodded. "Yes."

Dage stood and tossed his empty grape drink bottle into the trash. "I'll awaken Emma as soon as the lab is ready." He began to pace, an odd pit in his gut giving him pause. Fear? The realization sent fury bubbling to the surface.

Kane cleared his throat. "Any headway on discovering how the Kurjans found you on the tarmac?"

"No. Our soldiers killed the shooters before being able to interrogate them. We don't know how they discovered our plan to leave." The damn Kurjans could've been covering every airport just in case. Dage's boots made a dull clomping noise on the industrial tiles.

Kane straightened. "We'll figure this out, Dage."

"Figure this out?" Dage rounded on his brother. "Are you fucking kidding me? They shot *my mate*." His arm swept the table and papers spun toward the floor and cascaded across sparkling tile. A dark haze covered his vision with the need for violence, nearly blinding him. "And Janie. God, Janie . . ." Shock filled him as he realized his hands trembled. *Trembled.* "They caused her to bleed. For that alone, they'll all die."

Calm, serious, always thinking, Kane didn't flinch. The man had taken a full grown grizzly down once while seriously wounded, but even then reason had directed his moves. "It's time for science, not warfare, brother."

"Ah yes, science. Your god, right Kane?"

Silver sparks shot through Kane's violet eyes and his jaw snapped shut. "*My* god? They're using science—my life, our future—to harm my family. You're fucking crazy if you think I'll allow this to continue."

Dage sighed. "I'm sorry."

"No. Get it out so you can think." Kane rubbed a hand along a clean shaven jaw. Square and hard, just like their father's had been. Though his clear, intellectual mind came from their brilliant mother.

"You're the thinker." Dage dropped into a chair, his body weary, his soul pissed.

Kane gave a slight tip of his lip in what amounted to a full grin for him. "No. You're the thinker, Talen's the planner, Conn's the soldier, and I'm the scientist."

"And Jase?" Dage lifted an eyebrow. "What about our youngest brother?"

Kane gave a half nod. "Well, that's the question, now isn't it? Jase has more power in his little finger than the rest of us put together. Maybe the time has come to use him." Kane cleared his throat, his gaze firm. "Maybe it's time to forgive yourself and stop protecting him."

Dage shot to his feet. "What the hell are you talking about?"

Kane sighed. "We're at war. We need Jase to fight."

Son of a bitch. Kane spent a little time overseas and became a damn psychologist? "Jase will fight. I took him on the raid to rescue Katie and Maggie from the Kurjan facility a couple weeks ago." The two shifters had been kidnapped by the Kurjans as experimental subjects for the Kurjan virus. While he was too late to protect Maggie, Dage had arrived in time to prevent Katie from being infected at that time.

The room echoed with Kane's low chuckle. "Don't tell me. You positioned Jase behind Conn, the greatest soldier we've ever had? Wow. Dangerous, King."

"I turned Jase into a killer while he was still a child." The weight of that failure, his first as king, still ripped holes in any soul he may own. Memories of seeing his youngest brother bloodied and bruised, charging forward to kill the enemy often plagued the king's dreams. Nightmares based in a reality he'd created.

Kane shook his head. "Jase was fifteen. The Kurjans had slaughtered our parents and we were at war." A broad hand clasped Dage's shoulder when Kane moved forward. "Letting Jase fight wounded *you*. If you'd denied him the right to avenge his parents, you would've destroyed *him*. You made the only possible decision."

Jase's carefree attitude rarely dropped, but when it did the killer Dage had created showed its face. Cold and merciless, it shaped a teenager into a dangerous warrior. Not the fun-loving brother most of the Realm thought they knew. "Why hasn't he said anything?"

Kane shrugged. "We've been at peace for several centuries, and it's not like you've kept him from training. And he's Jase. You're his brother and you're still hurting about this. He won't push it until he needs to."

Man, Dage had missed Kane. Talk about putting things into perspective. "Do you really think he's that powerful? I mean, the whole little finger comment?"

Kane grinned. "Yeah. But don't tell him that."

"No way in hell." A beep sounded in Dage's communicator and he gave Kane a nod. "The lab is ready. Keep in mind I don't want Emma anywhere near the basement level."

"No worries. I won't tell her we've secured a werewolf if you don't want her to know."

Dage nodded. "She can know, just not go near it. I'm assuming the Bane's Council hasn't been informed?"

"No." Kane sighed. "We captured the werewolf outside Paris without informing the council. Not knowing is probably safer for them at this time—no difficult moral choices to make."

"Terent won't view the situation in such a way."

"No. Terent will want to draw blood." Kane grinned. "Yours or mine."

Dage hoped his friendship with the wolf would survive the next few years. "True." He stood. "Who captured the werewolf, Kane?"

Kane raised an eyebrow. "I did."

Dage had already known the answer. "By yourself?"

"Sure."

Most people believed royalty did nothing but attend parties and write laws. "How scientific is that, Kane?"

His brother grinned. "Jase isn't the only one you trained. The need to fight pumps through all our veins."

Not a sentiment Dage could fault. "I'll go get Emma."

"Can't wait to meet your mate, Dage." Kane blinked twice and the scattered papers rose from the floor to settle into neat piles on the table. "I'll see you at the lab." He gave a curt nod and strode out of the room.

On the other side of the large building, Janie clutched her stuffed bear in her arms and snuggled down under her new comforter with running unicorns chasing butterflies on it. She liked the residence place but not as much as her house on the lake. Talen's house. Her new daddy. He was scared for Janie's mama, and she didn't know how to help. She counted lilies in her head until finally slipping into her favorest dream world.

Trees made out of chocolate swayed in a breeze smelling of strawberries. She bit her lip. Even in her dream, her arm hurt. She'd told Mama it was okay, but the bullet burn really ached. She needed to be brave for when Zane arrived.

She sensed him a couple seconds before he jogged out of the trees, his dark hair loose around his big shoulders. He'd just turned eleven and cool muscles had started showing up in his arms. Steeling her shoulders, she instantly burst into tears.

Zane ran across the meadow in seconds, dropping to his knees next to her. "Janie Belle?" He'd given her the name the first time they met, declaring Janet Isabella too grown up for his new pal.

Sobbing, she moved into him, her head resting under his chin. He let her cry it out, patting her back, making soothing sounds like a big bear. She gave a final hiccup. "I got shot."

Zane gently pulled back, his green eyes turning almost black. "Someone shot you?" His gaze flashed to the large bandage on her arm. "The king let you get hurt?" The bumpy muscles still holding her shook like they were chilly.

"It wasn't Uncle Dage's fault." Janie wiped her nose on her sleeve with its pretty pink butterflies. "The bullet just burned me."

A really cool vein popped out in Zane's neck and began to pound. He was mad.

"Don't be mad. I'm okay, Zane." She sniffed.

The vein froze when Zane shifted his focus to the tree line. He released her and stood up. "Let him in."

"Who?" Janie opened her eyes wide. Zane was getting better at feeling their visitor. For so long she had been the one to keep him out of her dreams. Kalin.

"You know who. He's trying to get in." Zane put his hands on his hips. "Let him. Now."

Her lip trembled. "You're only eleven, Zane. You're not a grown-up." He couldn't boss her around, even if they were bestest of friends.

"You're only four. That makes me in charge." He didn't turn back to her.

"I'll be five next week." She lifted her chin, pleased she'd been able to remind him of her birthday without just saying it. Six years difference wasn't a whole lot.

He looked down. "Please, Janie Belle? I need to see him."

The soft tone had her nodding, and the sweet nickname had her wanting to make him happy. "Okay. But I need help to get him out."

Zane nodded. "Stand behind me."

She stood, mentally opening a door on the other side of the forest, then held her breath. A teenager soon walked into the meadow. Well, kind of a teenager. He had pasty white skin, purple eyes, and black hair with pointy red tips opposite of the other Kurjans she'd dreamed about. "Wow."

He flashed sharp teeth in a smile. "You must be Janet." The breeze lifted his thick hair when he bowed. "I'm Kalin."

She knew that was his name. So this is what the Kurjan people looked like up close. She wondered who cut his hair.

Zane gave a low rumble. "Your people shot at her?"

Kalin gave a heavy sigh. "A miscommunication, I believe." Sharp green flecks swirled through his deep eyes. "I'll deal with the person who gave the orders." His gaze traveled over Zane's form. "I've sensed you."

"I've sensed you, too."

The Kurjan sniffed the air, his gaze sharpening. "You know one of us will kill the other, right?"

Zane gave a short nod. "Yes."

Janie stepped out from behind Zane. "Why? I mean, why does anybody have to die?"

Zane grasped her good arm and tugged her behind him again.

Kalin laughed, the low rumbling sound making birds take flight high above in a big flapping of wings. "Oh Janie. It's going to be so difficult waiting until you're of age." He shifted his gaze to Zane. "I don't suppose you and I could meet up before then?"

Zane cocked his head to the side. "Name the time and place."

Janie took in the two boys. Kalin was obviously older, but Zane nearly stood head to head with him. An oiliness skirted around the Kurjan—they'd never be friends. She sighed. "We could fix things. The three of us." Every window into the future that opened up in her head had different endings. They could make this right.

Kalin made a fist and covered it with his other hand, sending a smacking sound across the distance. "I think we may have different ideas of what fixing this would mean, Janie." His tone was matter of fact, almost like a grown-up's.

Next to her, Zane's body began to vibrate. "I want to kill you, but Janie's right. We could end the war. So many people are going to die. Is there any part of you that would like to do the right thing?"

Kalin lifted his pale face to the dreamlike sun. "In the real world, I can't feel this. No sun. I won't give up the chance to walk outside in daylight."

Zane shook his head. "You wouldn't have to. We could find a peace that would allow you to continue research to combat the sun."

"You know about our research?" Surprise made Kalin's voice rise to a higher tone.

"I know more about you than I'd ever want." Zane widened his stance like a cowboy in a movie. "We could end this right now."

Swirling purple eyes glinted for a moment as Kalin glanced at Janie. "What about her? Our oracles have declared that one day she'll align with my people." He took a step toward Zane, his gaze slashing to the younger boy. "Is peace worth your people losing her? To save the world? Are you willing to make that sacrifice?"

"No." Zane took his own step forward.

Janie peered around Zane's much larger back. What was the creepy boy talking about?

"Does she even know what you are?" Odd red glints began to spark through the weird colors in Kalin's eyes.

Zane made a low growling noise that reminded her of Talen. "No. Neither do you."

Kalin hissed out a breath. "Don't I? Well. If the choice were actually hers, who do you think she'd pick? I mean, who's the biggest monster here?"

A sharp breeze shot through the meadow, making Janie shiver.

Zane shook his head. "The choice has been made. It's time for you to leave."

What the heck were they talking about? Janie shut her eyes and concentrated to push the wind away. Silence settled again and birds began to chirp.

A flash of teeth in Kalin's too pale face provided warning. "If I refuse?"

Zane tensed and dropped into a fighting stance.

Janie grabbed his arm, digging her feet into soft grass. "Now isn't the time, Zane." She wasn't sure about the rules in the dream world. Could somebody get hurt? Maybe.

Kalin threw back his head and laughed a chuckle much too deep for a teenage boy. "True. Now isn't the time." He began to back toward the tree line. "I may drop by a time or two to check in." He winked.

Zane tugged her fingers off his arm to hold her hand. "I hope you'll come looking for me soon."

Kalin gave a salute like a soldier on television. "You can count on it." Then he was gone.

Zane turned and tugged her down to the ground until they both sat with their knees almost touching. "Teach me how to open and shut that door, Janie."

"No." Zane would open it without her to fight Kalin. She just knew it. "What did he mean?"

Zane shrugged. "I don't know."

"Yes you do. What are you, Zane?"

Dimples flashed when he smiled. "I'm your best friend, Janie. I thought you already knew that."

"That's not what Kalin meant." She studied her friend, his handsome face and pretty green eyes. "What are you?"

Zane took her hands in his. "I'm just me, Janie. He was probably talking about the future, about the fighter I'm to become. It probably won't be nice." A shadow crossed Zane's young face and Janie shivered. "Now please tell me how to control that door. I need to know."

She sighed. "All right." Besides, she'd seen the future in her head. The fight didn't occur in a dream. Unfortunately.

Chapter 10

Emma's mind clicked plans into order as she followed Dage through the residence facility, passing wing upon wing set up for family, friends, and soldiers. First she'd review the new data and then begin experimenting with the isolated virus. She needed to cure Cara before heading home. Or rather, before finding a new home—though pure male temptation with a superb ass strode in front of her.

The sun nearly blinded her as the door slid open and they walked into the warm day. She blinked against the dazzling light, wishing for sunglasses and the ability to control her libido. "I guess summer has arrived."

Dage slowed his steps on the new concrete and took her hand. "The lab is only a few yards from the residence facility, though I wanted it underground in our main headquarters, which is up in the mountains to the north of here."

"Underground?" She took in the surrounding trees, summer full and quiet in the nonexistent breeze, following him on the new path. His hand surrounded hers with warmth and a tempting offer of safety.

"Yes. But Kane insisted on special return air vents, so . . ."

That made sense. They might end up working with some fairly interesting chemicals, so being underground wouldn't work. "Yeah, he's right."

Dage slowed. "Ah, I'd like you to wear my cuff, love. I'll give it to you tonight." He turned suddenly and she walked smack into his chest.

Heat roared in her ears. Desire slid through her veins. Only the most stubborn of souls could've stepped back. Good thing she was Irish.

He mirrored her retreating step, and one broad hand slid to the small of her back to tug her farther into male hardness.

She had to tilt her head back, way back, to meet his gaze. "What's this? Your new approach to gaining my cooperation?"

He raised one eyebrow. "Is it working?"

Hell yes. She'd agree to almost anything if he'd quench this desperate fire he'd lit. "No. Of course not."

He breathed in deep and flashed a smile. "Liar." His hand slid down to cup her buttocks.

Her knees trembled. "I appreciate the jewelry gift, but I'm not ready for it." Even if she decided to stay with him, she doubted wearing a large cuff would suit her style. Besides, her mind rebelled against his being able to find her at his whim.

A dangerously warm mouth nipped her earlobe and tracked down to the pulse beating in her neck. She reached up and clutched both hands into his strong chest, tilting her head to grant him better access.

His mouth enclosed part of her collarbone, then he released her, stepping back. "I don't need the cuff to know where you are any time of night or day."

The damn marking. Probably better than any beacon. She narrowed her eyes and clenched her fists to keep from stepping into him again. It couldn't be healthy to want this badly. "No cuff." Desire limited her vocabulary to one syllable words.

He sighed. "All right. For now."

Retaking her hand, he pivoted and tugged her down the

path. They turned a corner. She nearly dropped to her knees. Fear hammered into her stomach. A loud gasp of air escaped her and she stopped dead in her tracks.

Dage stilled. "What?"

Emma gulped. "Ah, nothing." The white building shimmering in the strong sun had starred in her greatest nightmares for over ten years. She looked around frantically—the forest looked different than it did in her nightmares. Angling her head, she took in the expanse of concrete on the other side of the building. That was where the king would slam to the ground in pain.

"Emma." Dage leaned down, his concerned gaze running over her face. "What's wrong?"

Wrong? This was beyond wrong. She straightened her shoulders. "Nothing." The cure for her sister lay inside that damn building. Emma had understood her time was limited, but to be face to face with the place she was supposed to die, well . . .

His hands tightened on her arms. "Tell me." A warning tone slid into his voice that did nothing but warm her blood further.

She shook her head. "I'm worried about Cara and need to get to work." Her tennis shoes slapped against the smooth concrete as she yanked Dage into motion. Her time to find a cure for her sister was limited. Besides, she had no intention of actually dying in the laboratory. Fate had given her a warning she'd heed. Destiny be damned.

His boots clomped on the path. "Damn it, woman. Prepare yourself because your shields are about to be ripped to shreds."

"What about my fragile mental state?" She rolled her eyes, grabbing the doorknob to yank. The door refused to open and she fell back into Dage's arms.

He tightened his grip on her, his mouth at her ear. "I'll take my chances, love. You have one day to lower them. This time tomorrow I invade." His teeth closed over her ear and sent a hard shaft of need through her body.

She trembled—whether in fear or desire, she wasn't sure. There was no way she could keep the king out of her head if he decided to plunder.

Dage flipped open a thick cover to reveal a keypad, quickly punching in a code. The door released with a soft click.

For a wisp of a moment, Emma thought about running— back to safety, away from the lab. But if death wanted her, death would get her. That much she knew. Maybe being able to know the place, if not the time, would be to her advantage. The scent of tulips and fresh earth always foreshadowed the explosion, so she had until next spring when they emerged from the ground. She'd spent plenty of time researching tulips; they only poked out of the earth in early spring.

Was she smart enough to cheat death?

She grabbed the doorknob and opened the door. Dage grasped her hand and tugged her inside a square entryway with freshly painted walls where two armed guards stood to attention. The farthest wall held a maroon metal door next to another keypad.

Dage nodded to the guards, punched in the code, leaning his face toward a small window. "Kayrs24256." He lifted his head. "We'll get you set with an iris and voice match today."

The door slid open to reveal another Kayrs brother. "Hi." He held out a hand. "I'm Kane."

Emma took his hand, tilting her head back for a better view of the scientific brother. Intelligent violet eyes set in a square face studied her. Deep brown hair fell to his shoulders and was held back in a clip. He had the Kayrs size. He pulled her into a hallway lined with intriguing posters of amoebas and viruses.

"Pretty artwork," she said, traipsing along. The climate controlled environment settled her nerves. She was back home. In a lab.

"Yeah. I thought so." He grinned, then lowered his head to whisper in a mocking tone, "Though some of the images gross out the king."

"Really?" Emma slanted a glance back.

Dage rolled his eyes. "A picture of a creepy crawly is just icky."

Did the King of the Realm just say icky? Emma stifled a laugh as Kane directed her into a large room. Then she sucked in air as they entered a large lab equipped with genetic analyzers, computers, printers, and high-tech equipment that must've cost a fortune. "Is that an ABI Prism 3100 analyzer with ninety-six capillaries?" The one at her previous lab had only forty-eight capillaries.

"No." Kane followed her into the room. "This Prism has four hundred eight capillaries."

Impossible. Emma shook her head, the truth of the matter sitting before her, waiting for her to push the buttons. "That's incredible." The vampires had some serious clout, money, or designers. Even the printer sitting peacefully in the corner was an array printer she'd only dreamed about.

"It will do." Kane tugged her over to a round table overflowing with papers. "Okay. This is our private lab—only members of the Kayrs family are allowed here. I'll give you a schematic of the rest of the building. We have four clean rooms sealed by vacuums and you have access to them all. There are fifty researchers on the other side. They have access only to the first clean room as well as the twenty labs on the other side."

"Humans?" Emma asked, her mind spinning.

"Yes."

She turned, pinning him with her gaze. "Do they have any idea what they're researching?"

"No," Dage answered from behind her.

She pivoted, both hands going to her waist. "Just like the Kurjans. You're treating humans just like the Kurjans treated the researchers at my lab. Like they treated me."

Dage shrugged. "I don't give a shit."

Angry breath caught in her throat as temper had her eyes widening on his. "Excuse me?"

Dage lowered his chin, his gaze hard. "The words were clear, love. We're paying the researchers plenty for their help and they may even cure some human genetic diseases on the side. But under no circumstances are they allowed to know about us."

She sucked in air to keep from kicking him in the shin. "Listen here, buddy. It's impossible to conduct research without a complete picture of the matter at hand."

"Too bad. It's your job—and Kane's—to put all the data together in one complete place. The humans are workers only. Period."

She saw red. Plain and simple. "I'm not saying we announce to the world that vampires exist, Dage. But breaking all of the research into small sections isn't the best way." They were talking about a biological weapon with unknown implications and final results. As many good brains as possible needed to be solely focused on saving mates. On saving Cara.

Kane chuckled low. "Much as I enjoy a good marital spat, I've had my ten top researchers working on their individual projects for several months now before moving them here. As a process, I'm pleased with the results, which I'm happy to go over with you right now, Emma."

"No marital spat. We're not married," Emma hissed, stalking around the table and dropping into a thick orange chair.

"Yet," Dage said with a hard glare, which he turned on his brother. "I don't like these ten people having access to the residence, Kane."

"I know. But they need a place to live until we buy them houses, Dage." Kane's calm façade didn't waiver.

Emma shook her head. "Where do the other forty people live?"

Kane shrugged. "Somewhere in Boulder. We bought out Colorado Labs last month and put their geneticists to work for us. They already lived here."

"I want the humans out of our residence facility within a week, Kane." The king strode toward the door. "I have some calls to make from Kane's office, and we'll meet again in two hours to discuss our options with Talen."

Emma gave him a glare while Kane nodded, glancing back and forth between them with a small grin. "Sounds good. See you then."

A pounding set up at the base of Emma's skull a couple hours later. She sat between Kane and Dage on one side of a large oak conference table facing Cara, Talen, Maggie, and Katie. Jordan paced behind Katie, the muscles vibrating along his forearms, a vein standing out on his forehead.

Emma tried to be inconspicuous in her survey of Maggie, who looked like the girl next door with curly brown hair and deep chocolate eyes. How could this pale woman change into an actual wolf?

"So"—Cara leaned forward, hope filling her eyes—"what did you find out?" The shades behind her allowed in enough light to bathe her in silhouette, turning her into an angel.

Emma shook off the fanciful thought and twirled her key card in her hands. The card that granted her access to every half-painted lab in the building. Labs with a myriad of test tubes, centrifuges, incubators, and autoclaves. Top of the line. "Well, we already knew Virus-27 attacks the twenty-seventh chromosome of mates and shifters." Every single twenty-seventh chromosomal pair in every single cell of the body.

"But definitely not vampires," Kane said. His broad hand tapped papers together before him.

Talen raised an eyebrow. "How do we know that for sure?"

Emma turned toward Kane. They didn't know that for sure. Did they?

Kane shifted, his gaze going to the papers he shuffled. Silence pounded around the room.

Dage pushed back from the table, his jaw clenching shut as he stared at his younger brother over Emma's head. "You dumb bastard. You did not." Disbelief combined with anger in his voice.

Emma frowned and realization dawned. "You didn't." She'd just spent two hours with the man going over her results, and he hadn't even mentioned the risk he took.

Kane shrugged. "It was the only way to make sure. I mean, it's not like we own animal test subjects who have twenty-seven chromosomes."

Katie frowned. "I don't understand."

Dage's eyes blazed a hard silver. "My dumbass brother infected himself with the virus to see if the bug impacts vampires. He used himself as a *lab rat*."

"Jesus." Talen shook his head. "You're supposed to be the smart one, Kane. How could you?" His hand covered Cara's on the table.

Kane met his gaze squarely. "Like I said, there was no alternative. Once I heard your mate was infected . . ."

Cara paled even further, her skin a complete contrast to the black sweater covering her shoulders. "You did this for me? But . . ."

"Damn it." Talen's gaze went from Kane to his mate and back to his brother again. "Kane, you only found out last night. You wouldn't even know if the virus has taken hold in you yet."

"I feel fine. We'll monitor my blood and will know for absolute certainty in twenty-four hours." Kane reached for a pencil to tap against his papers. "But so far everyone infected has shown symptoms within hours. I'm fine." He rubbed his square jaw. "Emma and I put our research together and discovered the Kurjans have been able to pare the virus down to two injections. But only the first one is truly necessary."

"Yes." Emma rolled closer to the table. "The heart-breaking

films you told me about where the infected Kurjan mates went crazy from injection led to the Kurjans creating two separate injections. The first is the virus, which attacks the chromosomes, the second is a catalyst, which speeds up the process."

Jordan stopped pacing. "Catalyst?" His eyes shifted to catlike gold, then back to brown.

"Yes." Emma leaned forward. She'd love to see him shift into a cougar. "Look at it like radiation combined with chemotherapy to treat cancer. The two combined often get the best results."

Kane nodded. "Similarly, while the virus itself is engineered to eventually reach the desired goal, we think this catalyst speeds up the process—so the Kurjans would acquire their werewolf slave class much faster. So far Maggie is the only person who has had two injections."

Maggie blew out air, having arrived the night before with her test results in hand. "Yippee for me." She watched her hand tremble on the table as if not quite sure the appendage belonged to her.

Emma reached for the applicable file, her gaze concentrated on the pale brunette. "The virus immediately attacked the twenty-seventh chromosome, which affects your shifting ability. The catalyst made the virus attack the twenty-sixth and twenty-fifth chromosomes, taking you down to twenty-four—or to the genetic makeup of a werewolf." The protein binding the virus to the chromosomes held like glue, and they needed to find an unraveling agent. They also needed to run another battery of tests on the wolf shifter.

"But I shifted into a wolf instead." Maggie bit her lip.

"Exactly." Kane nodded. "The virus is new and hopefully not as strong as we feared. So far your natural defenses are fighting the illness, and your chromosomes are struggling to repair themselves." He cleared his throat. "You've beaten one full moon so I'm greatly encouraged you'll beat this bug."

Emma nodded. Apparently when humans were bitten by a werewolf, the human went through changes during three full moons, remaining in full werewolf form for the rest of its short life after the third change.

Katie's gaze slid to the table's surface. "What about me? I can't shift."

"Right." Emma shifted her focus to the lioness. "You were just infected. You're sick right now, for a lack of a better term. Your body is fighting the virus—and we don't know the cycle. Without the catalyst in your blood, you may even beat the virus faster than Maggie is." They hoped. The wolf shifter had been kidnapped by the Kurjans and kept at a hospital for an unknown amount of time and had no memory of the experience, or of her life before the capture, so they were just guessing at possible experimentations.

"So I'll be able to shift again?" Hope filled Katie's dazzling brown eyes.

Emma couldn't promise that. "I hope so."

Jordan took up position behind Katie's chair and clasped both her shoulders with his broad hands. "You'll shift again, Kate. I promise."

The young woman paled further and remained silent.

Dage frowned. "So if a feline shifter doesn't fight off the virus, will she turn into a werewolf?" He sent a sympathetic smile toward Katie.

"We think that's the goal," Kane affirmed. "But again, we don't know if it actually *works* that way."

Talen stretched an arm across Cara's shoulder. "And mates?"

Kane sighed. "The virus initially takes away the individual mating aspects." His gaze softened as he glanced at Cara. "So you're immortal right now but not tied to any particular vampire." He grinned. "In fact, you could choose a different brother if you wanted."

Cara smiled, rubbing her bare wrist where the cuff had been clasped. "I'll keep that in mind." She pursed her lips.

"But I can only mate with a vampire? I mean, I couldn't be mated with a Kurjan after this short time. Right?"

Talen stiffed next to her, a semblance of a snarl curling his lips. Emma crossed her legs under the table, fighting unease. Damn but her new brother-in-law looked deadly. Was Cara safe with him? From him? She'd need to get her sister alone for a discussion and soon.

Kane nodded. "Yes. The virus immediately removed, er, the bond with Talen." He cast a sympathetic glance at this brother. "A long term progression of the virus is designed to turn you back into a human at twenty-three chromosomes. So you could be mated by a Kurjan."

Talen's long fingers played in his wife's hair, and relief filled Emma. The guy may be able to kill on demand, but he adored Cara. Emma wondered for a moment if he had any idea how affectionate he was toward Cara. The big dangerous vampire was touchy-feely. Emma fought a grin.

He tilted his head in response. "So worst case scenario is that Cara ends up human again?"

Dread pooled in Emma's abdomen. She so didn't want to have this discussion. "Um, we really don't know yet."

"Excuse me?" Talen's eyes hardened to gilded coins.

Emma focused on Cara. "The virus is designed to reduce the amount of chromosomes in your body from immortal to human, we think."

Cara paled. "Ah. So what's to stop the virus from continuing the reduction?"

Talen frowned. "I don't understand."

Cara bit her lip. "The Kurjans are creating an unknown virus. What if they screwed it up? Why would the little bug stop attacking at the twenty-third chromosomal pair? Why not keep reducing chromosomal pairs past human? To animal? To single cell organisms? To nothing?"

Talen slashed his gaze to Kane. "Is that possible?"

Kane stared at his brother before glancing at Cara, his

gaze softening. "We don't know. None of the data from the Kurjans includes final results. They're still conducting tests. We're conducting tests now, but if nothing else we've discovered that the virus reacts differently in a test tube than it does in a human body."

"So my mate is a guinea pig?" Talen roared, his face flushing with pure danger.

Cara flinched next to him before reaching out and patting his arm. "Knock it off."

He turned his focus on her. "What did you say?" Deadly softness coated his words. Emma began to stand, pausing only when Cara flicked her a warning glance.

"I said to knock it off." Cara's chin hardened in an expression Emma knew well. "We're all doing our best here and getting pissed won't solve anything."

Talen sucked in air, a hint of a smile threatening on his full lips as his shoulders visibly relaxed. "But I like getting pissed."

Cara grinned. "I know. But you're scaring my sister and I just can't have that."

Talen caught Emma in his golden gaze. "Sorry."

Emma frowned. What an odd interplay. "Okay." She studied her sister. "Kane has designed a new software program that greatly reduces the time needed to map DNA and chromosomal differences. We should be able to keep track of the changes and know if you begin to go too far." Maybe. Maybe not. The virus could continue deleting chromosomal pairs. Or just create single chromosomes, thus creating an aneuploidy, which would open Cara up to genetic diseases.

Talen threw an arm around Cara's shoulders. "So the solution here would be to remate my mate and her chromosomes would start increasing again?" Interest and something darker wove through the words.

Cara blushed to the roots of her hair.

Kane huffed out a laugh. "Well maybe. Unfortunately, we

don't know enough about this virus. Since the bug is still in her very pregnant system, you may do more damage than good. I'd advise against it at this time."

Maggie frowned. "Wait a minute. If my chromosomes keep deraveling, I could become human?"

Kane sucked in air. "We've been mapping your DNA for the past month, Maggie. Your twenty-seventh through twenty-fifth chromosomes have been attacked. The virus is progressing and we just don't know where it will end."

Talen frowned. Not what the strategic leader wanted to hear. "So what do we do now?"

Emma stood. "Now we try to find a way to assist their bodies in dealing with the virus." Maybe some of the new HIV antivirals would be of some assistance. One little bound protein was not going to ruin her sister's life.

Cara tilted her head to the side. "Are you going to contact Rachel?"

Blowing out a breath, Emma shifted her gaze to Kane. "We argued about Rachel earlier."

"Who's Rachel?" Dage asked.

"My friend from Montana. She's the foremost expert on genetic research in the world right now," Emma said.

"Let's go get her." Talen stood.

"Wait." Emma held out a hand. "She's in Europe on tour, lecturing at top hospitals on new cancer treatments. She won't leave in the middle of the tour."

"I won't give her a choice." Talen tugged Cara to her feet.

"Rachel will be missed." Dage stood. "We don't want that type of attention right now." He pinned his brother with a gaze. "How about we have Emma contact her and lay the groundwork while she and Kane continue their work?" While he phrased the suggestion as a question, the note of kingly command tinged each word.

Talen nodded. "You have one week."

Dage fought the urge to beat the crap out of his brother. Two brothers, actually. What in the hell had Kane been thinking injecting himself? Smoothing on his diplomatic smile, he gave Emma a kiss on the cheek. "I need to fly back to Portland and meet with the prophets. Stay with Kane and I'll return later tonight."

His mate lifted her pretty blue eyes to his. "Did something happen? I mean, you've been on the phone all afternoon."

He paused. "I'm sorry. Have I been ignoring you, love?" Women needed attention. He knew that.

She smiled, her arched eyebrow rising. "I can entertain myself, Dage. I was concerned about the frown between your eyes." Her tone lightened to teasing yet her gaze wandered his face, studying him.

The frown between his eyes? He made an effort to smooth it out, his heart thumping hard. He was the king. People asked him about the Realm, about war, about laws. No one asked about the man. Her concern warmed him throughout, from his toes to his ears—and he'd had no idea he'd been cold. The little scientist cared about him, the man and not the leader. He hadn't realized how much he needed someone to see the man. "Everything's fine, Emma." Better than fine. He'd found his mate.

"Are you sure?" Now she frowned.

He wanted to laugh at the pure delight he'd just found. He should be worried; the woman held the power to destroy him. Yet only pure contentment slid through his veins. "Yes. A plan has come together quite unexpectedly and I need to meet with the prophets. Nothing to worry about." Right. He may be preparing to tear the Realm in two. He had the strangest urge to confide in her—to ask her opinion. But the woman had enough on her plate dealing with the virus.

"Okay." She dropped her focus to the papers before her, frowning and beginning to scribble furiously in the margin.

He ran his hand down her long length of hair, impressed by the scholarly side of her. He'd worry about her power over him later. For the moment, he wanted to bask in it. But duty called. "Talen, escort me out, would you?" No one who knew him even remotely would mistake his question as any-thing but a clear order.

Talen flashed a full grin in response. "It'd be my pleasure." He settled Cara back into her chair. "Stay with your sister, mate. This shouldn't take long."

Kane rolled his eyes. "Do you need a level head at the meeting with the prophets?"

Dage gestured for Talen to precede him out the door. "No. I need you to deal with this damn virus before it reduces our women to single cell organisms." He stalked out of the room, following Talen down the hallway and into the summer day, neither man speaking to the guards posted at duty. Sighing, Dage squinted into the sun. "Three hundred years ago I of-fered you the crown, and you hit me in the face."

Talen shifted so the sun stood to the side. "I know. But we're talking about my mate. What would you do?"

Choose Emma over the Realm. No question. "I'd stop and think. Kidnapping a well-known human would bring more trouble down on us than we need." He reached out and placed his hand on his brother's shoulder. "But if it comes down to it, we'll take her. I promise."

Talen gave a short nod. "I know." His jaw tightened. "I should be with you at the meeting today with the prophets."

"No." Talen on edge would be disastrous. A mated vam-pire was the most dangerous being in existence if his mate was threatened. "Your place is with your mate right now. And with mine. I need you to protect them both." Dage stepped back. "Keep an eye on our asshole brother. I can't believe Kane did that."

Shards of emotional green shot through Talen's golden eyes. "He did it for my mate. Eating a virus that might kill him. For my mate." A pebble skipped across the cement when Talen kicked it. "I don't know whether to hug him or punch him in the face."

Dage grinned. "Hell. It's Kane. Do both."

Talen returned the grin, then quickly sobered. "Do you know what you're doing today?"

The air crackled for a moment as energy shifted around the king. "Hell no. Bringing Caleb back into the Realm may be the biggest mistake I've ever made."

"I agree we could use him and his allies." Talen squinted toward the white building. "The prophets won't like it."

"Half the Realm won't like it." Dage tapped a signal on his watch to let the pilot know he was ready. "Caleb may tell me to go to hell." In fact, that was probably a guarantee.

"True. When will you be able to transport again?" Talen raised an eyebrow.

Dage shrugged. "I could do so now." The time had come to be smart, not convenient. "I'm holding on to the strength just in case." So he had a two-hour plane ride to think about strategy.

"Smart move." Talen clapped him on the back. "Good luck."

Dage nodded and began to jog for the airplane hangar on the other side of the lab. He'd need it.

Chapter 11

The two-hour plane ride had been a strategic waste of time. Striding down the hotel hallway lined with bouquets of fresh lilies as if directing a wedding procession—or a funeral—Dage wasn't any closer to a solution. He shook his head at his youngest brother. "What do you mean Caleb isn't here yet?"

Jase shrugged. "Conn went to fetch him at the airfield and he's late."

Not good news. "Caleb said he'd be here, so he'll show up sometime. We'll go ahead as planned." Dage had wanted to meet with Caleb before meeting with the prophets. If his old friend told him to go to hell, there was no reason to piss everyone off with his plan.

"Good." Jase grabbed Dage's arm and pulled him to a stop. "I, ah, I've been working on something."

"Really? What?" Dage shifted to meet his brother's gaze.

"You know how I can heal some wounds with my thoughts?"

"Sure." A handy talent to be sure.

Jase cleared his throat. "I think I can yank the virus out of the women."

Shock bashed into Dage for a moment. Reality soon filtered through. "What would happen to the virus?"

Jase shrugged. "If I could get it out of their chromosome, which to be honest, I'm not sure I could, then I might need to attach the bug to mine. Who the hell knows?"

Dread and pride filled the king in equal measure. "Sacrificing yourself isn't a solution, Jase." His brothers were truly men of honor.

"We protect mates at all costs, Dage."

He gave a short nod. "We're not to that point yet, but I appreciate your willingness." Damn. Now Jase as well as Kane had to be kept from sacrificing themselves. That was his job. Dage pivoted, stalking down the hallway until reaching a thick double door manned by two armed vampires with the prophecy signet on their lapels showing their ranking as guards to the prophets. One opened the door.

He crossed the threshold, his spirits lifting as a cloud of wild strawberries rushed toward him and a small woman graced both of his cheeks with a kiss. "Dage." Kind eyes the color of midnight twinkled before a grape energy drink was thrust into his hand. "For you."

He grinned. "Prophet Sotheby, you're as lovely as ever." Gazing closer, he fought a frown. Dark circles marred the pale skin of the prophet's stunning face. Her golden hair had been pulled up into an intricate knot but her perfect makeup failed to provide camouflage. The prophecy marking on the back of her neck stood out in deep blue.

She returned the smile. "My friends call me Lily, and you mustn't look so concerned. I took a bet from a multi-shifter last night involving a dart game and tequila. I lost."

"Lily. Multies claim incredibly fast metabolisms. You didn't stand a chance." He tugged her arm through his and led her to a plush chair near a crackling fire. Her hand trembled slightly against his forearm. Poor thing. A hangover and now her day was about to get worse. He settled her down.

He shifted his attention to Milner, who appeared regal in a

deep velvet waistcoat. "Prophet." Who in the hell wore waistcoats these days?

Milner shook his hand, taking the chair next to Lily's. "King. I hope you don't mind, but Prophet Sotheby suggested we meet in here by the fire instead of yet another cold conference room."

Lily nodded next to him. "Yes. I do love a nice gathering by a warm fire."

Milner nodded toward Jase, who had taken up position next to the door. "Prince."

Jase returned the nod, then smiled at Lily.

Dage hid the concern for Lily from his eyes. "Thank you, Lily. This setting is much nicer than usual." He turned and took the next extended hand. "Prophet Guiles."

"We appreciate the chance to speak with you, King." Guiles gave a short shake and took the chair opposite Lily. His long brown hair cascaded down his strong back. He had to be, what? Maybe a hundred years older than Dage's three and a half centuries? The fates designated him a prophet the same day Dage became king. War and death had created the openings for them both.

Prophet Milner cleared his throat. As the oldest person in the room, the meeting would be run by him—for a while, anyway. "First, let me say how pleased we are that two of the royal family have mated. We'd like the rest to follow suit." He shot a glance at Jase, who grinned in response.

Lily clapped her hands together. "Yes. I spent some time with both Emma and Cara at the ball. Wonderful women. I'm so happy for you, Dage."

Dage smiled. So far so good.

Milner continued, "We reviewed the information you provided regarding the Kurjan virus. Has there been any luck finding a cure?"

"Not yet." Dage might have a duty to inform the prophets about Cara and Katie being infected. Probably. "We finished setting up the lab and are hard at work." Nah. The less the prophets knew the better. He took a drink.

Lily leaned forward. "Has the wolf shifter had any other episodes?"

"No." Dage had hoped to avoid this issue. The doctor who'd diagnosed Maggie had copied the reports for the prophets. "In fact, there's a good chance the virus will run its course with her, leaving her healthy."

Milner shook his bony head. "We must report her existence to the Bane's Council."

Dage bit back a sharp retort. "All due respect, Prophet, but you are a spiritual leader of the vampire race only. I lead the Realm."

Guiles set his drink down. "We're all members of the Realm and are subject to the same laws, Kayrs."

"True. But as King of the Realm as well as the vampire people, I decided it is unnecessary to contact the council at this point." Damn but he hated to pull rank. He needed the meeting to go smoothly.

Lily gave a delicate cough. "Well then. I guess that's settled." She fluffed her pale yellow skirt around her legs. "So, what's next on the agenda?"

Dage wondered once again what the fates were thinking to make this fragile woman a prophet on the day her mate died. Her mate, Miles Sotheby, had been a prophet and a good one. Sympathy for the woman charged through him.

"Dage?" Lily raised an eyebrow.

Milner leaned forward. "Now we talk about humans being given access to our DNA." His beady eyes narrowed.

"Meaning?" Dage kept his voice low and controlled.

"Meaning it has come to our attention that you've allowed *humans* to be a part of the research team investigating the virus. Do you have any idea how many laws this breaks?" Milner swept his hands out, his jaw clenching.

Dage didn't twitch a muscle. Apparently he had a leak.

"I've broken no law, prophet. The human scientists believe they're studying cancer treatments for humans. They have no access to any data regarding Realm species."

"You can't guarantee that," Guiles said, shaking his head. "This could put your kingship in jeopardy. Don't you know that?"

The temptation to step away from the kingship nearly overwhelmed him. "My family has led the Realm for centuries." They'd *protected* the Realm for centuries.

"True." Milner sat back in his chair. "But only because there's been no reason to remove you as the ruling family."

Dage narrowed his gaze and lowered his voice. "You threatening me, Prophet?"

Milner shrugged. "The council has a duty to make sure the ruling family is doing its job. If it isn't, the council must take steps to replace the current monarchy."

Steps that would entail Dage's head being removed from his body.

Lily slapped her hands together. "Enough of this nonsense. Dage is a fine king and the Kayrs family is doing an excellent job." She glared at Milner. "We're at war and the last thing we need is an internal battle. One I don't think *you* would win."

If Dage had had any question as to where Lily's loyalty lay, he now had the answer. He gave her a short nod. "I appreciate the support, Prophet. And I assure you, the humans are not aware of our existence—nor will they be."

"Good." She took a sip of tea, carefully setting the cup back down. "So, what's next on the agenda?"

He might as well hit them with all of it. "Ah. Well, it's time to bring Caleb Donovan back into the fold."

Lily gasped, Milner paled and clutched his chest, while Guiles jumped to his feet. "You must be jesting."

"Nope." In Dage's peripheral vision he could see Jase settle into a readied stance with his knees bent and his concentration focused on the door.

Milner swept a brown speckled hand toward Lily. "Caleb killed the prophet. Her husband. How can you think—"

"No he didn't." Dage stood as well. "The Kurjans killed Sotheby. You know that."

An ugly red crept up Milner's withered face to make his eyes bug out. "You truly are trying to end the Kayrs monarchy. Caleb was responsible. The Kurjans said they'd let Sotheby go if Caleb stopped his search. He didn't."

Lily put a shaking hand to her head. "He was avenging his sister's death. You can't begrudge him that." She chewed on her lip for a moment. "The Kurjans would never have released Miles. We all know it."

"You disloyal witch." A dark vein popped out of Guiles's neck.

Dage pinned him to the wall in a heartbeat, forearm against the bastard's neck. "I strongly suggest you apologize, Prophet."

A soft hand on his arm kept Dage from pressing any harder. "Dage. Let him go. I'm not a witch, darn it." Lily cleared her throat. "If I were, he'd be croaking as a toad right now."

Dage started in surprise at the humor but kept his gaze on Guiles's blue eyes. "I'm waiting."

The door banged open and the two prophecy guards dodged inside, guns at ready. Dage pivoted toward the entry as Jase took one guard down to the floor and the cocking of a gun stopped the other. Caleb flashed a grin, his weapon pressed into the second guard's neck. "Well now. I can see not much has changed with the Realm." His booming voice echoed around the room.

Dage tightened his hold against the prophet's jugular. Shit. He couldn't exactly kill a prophet today. "Now."

Guiles cleared his throat. "I apologize."

Lily nodded, dropping into her chair.

Dage threw Guiles back into his seat and gestured for the guards to leave. Jase tossed one out on his ass while the other backed away.

"Caleb. Thanks for coming." Dage extended a hand.

Caleb shook it, his multi-colored gaze encompassing the entire room. "So. Invited to speak with the Realm after a century and a half of being exiled. Hell has frozen over, huh?" He sprawled into a chair next to Lily, turning toward her. "Before we start, I'd like to say how sorry I am the Kurjans killed your mate. I'd have prevented his death if possible."

She nodded, her hand going to her throat. Dage frowned. She appeared paler than before. Maybe this was a bad idea.

The red in Milner's face flushed darker until his skin matched his waistcoat, though he held his tongue.

Conn entered the room and stood at the other side of the door from Jase. Dage gave him a short nod of acknowledgment. "We're at war. The Kurjans have allies and are prepared, scientifically as well as strategically. The smart move is to reunite our allies."

"Allies?" Guiles sat forward, biting out the words. "Are you kidding me? Caleb and his crew turned their backs on us years ago."

"You exiled me, boyoh." Caleb leaned back, the chair protesting under his weight. He was as tall as Dage, and thick across the chest. A dark eyebrow rose. "In addition, you underestimated the number of my followers. Lost a bit of the Realm, did you?"

"You gave us no choice but to exile you," Milner hissed. "First you refused to stop your crusade, then you protected your brother."

"My brother didn't do anything wrong." Caleb relaxed back in his chair. He'd probably tied his blond hair back not in an attempt at fashion but as a prelude to a fight. Dage had done the same thing.

"Nothing wrong?" Guiles jumped to his feet again. "He mated with a wolf shifter who'd been betrothed."

Dage cleared his throat. "First, there's no law against vampires and shifters mating." The union was rare, but not unheard of. "Second, the woman chose him. The prophets do not need to get involved with such matters."

"She was betrothed to a ruling demon," Guiles spat. "We needed the demon nation as an ally."

Dage cleared his throat. "What's done is done. Now we need to consolidate for this war. Without question." He turned toward Caleb. "The prophets will confirm you are no longer exiled"—he put a deadly threat into his gaze as he eyed each member in turn before focusing back on Caleb— "or the royal family will denounce them." He hoped nobody would call his bluff. He couldn't go to war and denounce the prophets in the same fucking month.

Gasps filled the air. "You wouldn't," Milner muttered. His gaze darted around the room, obviously seeking to land somewhere away from the king. Grabbing a handkerchief out of his pocket, he wiped his ancient brow. "I'm not an enemy you want, King."

The prophets could certainly try to take him down. At the very least a fight with them would tear the Realm in two. Dage shook his head. "We're at war. You may want to remember the prophets need my protection right now more than ever." Weaselly little prick. Dage had had enough taking orders from spiritual leaders who had no clue of the means necessary to keep the Realm whole. As a soldier, as a leader, Caleb did, and Dage would choose his old friend over the prophets any day. Regardless of the outcome.

Caleb straightened. "Why would I want to rejoin the Realm? I don't need you."

Dage lifted an eyebrow. "Don't you? You've been fighting

three shifter clans because of your brother's mating. Not to mention the entire demon nation. Aren't you tired of feuding?"

The grin sliding across Caleb's face lacked any semblance of humor. "You going to broker peace for me, Kayrs?" His voice lowered. "If we unite, there's a better chance the demons will declare war on you."

Dage nodded. "I hope to keep that from happening. But even now our alliance with the demons is uneasy. They won't lift a finger in our war with the Kurjans." He glanced at Lily, then back to Caleb. "You will." With Caleb's soldiers, the balance would tip in the Realm's favor.

Caleb sighed, shifting his attention to Lily, challenge sparking his eyes. "What do you think, Prophet?"

She shot a gaze to Dage, then squared her shoulders and lifted her chin, focusing back on Caleb. "I think you do need us."

Dage stifled a grin. She may be dainty and old-fashioned, but the woman had grit.

Caleb winked at her. "If it's done, it's absolute. There's no tossing me out later once the war is over." He shifted his melded gaze toward the king.

"Agreed." Dage nodded.

Three muted *agreeds* filled the room. Silence beat around the room before first Lily, then the other two prophets made polite good-byes and hustled through the exit. Jase and Conn followed suit, leaving Dage and Caleb sitting in the loungers. The fire's peaceful crackle helped dissipate the irritation left in Milner's wake.

"Quite the bold move." Caleb reached for Lily's tea and downed the rest of the fragrant brew.

"Yes. Milner is no doubt on the phone planning to dethrone me." The weasel might succeed, but not during a time of war. Not right now. Dage grinned. "I've missed you, old friend."

"Ditto. I heard you found a mate. Congratulations."

"Thanks." Dage eyed the door. Something began to tingle at the base of his neck, an awareness of some sort.

"Has Lily been ill?" The casual question belied the sudden intensity sparking Caleb's colorful eyes.

"Rough night." Since when did Lily party the night away? "She was so young when her marriage to Sotheby was arranged. Maybe she's spreading her wings."

Caleb shook his head. "They were only married for two weeks before he disappeared." He quirked a lip. "Did you know I was courting her at the time?"

"Ah. Er, no." Dage lifted an eyebrow.

Caleb nodded. "Yeah. She chose duty over me." He shrugged. "Can't blame her."

Dage took another drink of grape energy. Caleb sounded like he blamed Lily. "Well, she has always been mindful of duty." Always. Awareness slammed into reality. She wouldn't have gotten drunk at a colloquium event. "Damn it." Dage leapt to his feet, three strides taking him through the doors.

Caleb followed on his heels. "Kayrs. What the hell?"

Dage all but ran through the hallway and up to the next floor, stopping to pound on the door he needed. "I hope I'm wrong." He should've paid better attention.

The door clicked open a couple of inches, the chain in place, the scent of strawberries wafting out. Lily's pale face filled the slot. "King? I'm sorry but I'm not feeling well right now. Could you come back later?"

"Open the door, Prophet." He placed his palm against the wood.

"No." The word trembled weakly from her mouth.

Caleb pushed him to the side. "Lily, open the door. Do you need a doctor?"

"I need the nosey vampires in this place to leave me to rest. Now I'll speak with you gentlemen later." She stepped back, and the sound of a small thud filled the silence.

Caleb threw a shoulder against the door and the chain snapped in two. Dage followed him inside to where he'd dropped to his knees to cradle Lily's limp body. Caleb lifted his gaze. "What's wrong with her?"

Dage shook his head. "We'll need to run some tests to make sure. But I think she's been infected." If he was right, the Kurjans would pay.

Chapter 12

Emma stepped out of the decontamination shower attached to Lab Four, dried off and entered the next chamber, hitting the button and shutting her eyes as the ultraviolet light moved over her skin. Any possible virus that clung to her would be killed. Shivering, she dodged into the next room and slid into a black jumpsuit, grabbing a clip off the counter to pin up her wet hair. She grabbed socks out of a cubby, yanked them on, then stepped into her tennis shoes, leaning over to stare into a glass plate next to the door. "Emma42249."

The door slid open.

She trudged down the hallway into another bright lab, not surprised to see a young man bent over the Transmission Electron Aberration-Corrected microscope. He sat alone in the chilled lab, row after row of test tubes lined up on the shelf before him. Machines whirred on either side of the room, calculating data. "Devon. Even Einstein took a break now and then." She loped over to a file cabinet to find a copy of Rachel's dissertation on proteins binding to cancer cells. They'd need to get Rachel's help soon, and there's no way the brilliant scientist would be fooled by the protocols set in place by Kane. She'd know they weren't studying cancer within minutes of reading the data—which is why Emma was currently working with doctoral students like Devon. He was highly intelligent, yet lacked the experience needed to see through the charade.

Devon straightened and pushed back his unruly brown hair, swiveling on his stool to flash a wide grin. "If Einstein had worked harder, maybe we'd have a better understanding of time travel right now."

Bleach and lemon cleanser tickled her nose. "Maybe. Or maybe he would've burned out and not discovered several theories that we do understand."

"Well, it's all relative," Devon snorted.

Man she loved lab geeks. Emma laughed, shaking her head, shutting the file cabinet and heading for the door.

Devon cleared his throat. "Dr. Paulsen? Is there any chance we'll be able to see the other labs?"

Unease swirled in Emma's stomach even as she schooled her face and paused to face him. She hated lying to her coworkers. "I don't think so, Devon. You know how delicate these governmental experiments can be." What a load of crap. She fought the urge to roll her eyes at herself.

"I know. And I know the dangers of a secured lab—so many pathogens. But I can't help but wonder . . ." He tugged a loose thread on his worn jeans.

"I know." Curiosity was a scientist's greatest asset. "I hope you know how much you are appreciated." He'd make an incredible geneticist someday.

He shrugged. "Thanks. I couldn't do half this work without Sandy." He blushed, his usually pale cheeks turning a bright pink.

Lab romances. Emma smiled again. "You're all invaluable. I'll see you tomorrow." At his nod, she hurried out of the room and down the hallway, using voice, hand, and eye recognition to get through three areas of security. She finally reached the private lab where the prophet perched on an examination table. Waiting. The scent of rubbing alcohol mixed with strawberries filled the large lab. Emma forced a smile, and pushed down her concern. "You've had quite the day. Dage said you were unconscious for most of the plane ride here."

Lily nodded, wiping a hand across her pale forehead. "Yes. My results are ready?"

"Yes. The direct fluorescent antibody stain test revealed you've been infected with the virus. Probably the night of the ball." A printer spit out the data she'd input in the vacuum sealed lab. Grabbing a chart, she made a quick notation. She'd need to compare these notes with Rachel's before doing more tests. The next test would measure the strength of the protein binding the virus to the prophet's chromosome. For some reason the prophet seemed more ill than Cara. Maybe the baby or the pregnancy hormones slowed the virus down in Cara. But how much time did the prophet have then? A sudden thought occurred to Emma. "Um, do you mind if I check your marking?"

With a frown, Lily turned her head to the side. An intricate Celtic knot in deep blue decorated the nape of her neck.

"That's beautiful," Emma breathed.

Lily turned back around. "Thank you. The prophesy mark appeared the day I was chosen by the fates. Hurt like a knife wound."

So far it was the only fact in the odd new world that Emma couldn't explain through science. Could fate really play a part in all their lives? She shook her head. There had to be a rational explanation for the appearance of the knot. "Do the other prophets wear this mark?"

"Yes." Lily smoothed her pale skirt over her legs.

Emma made another notation on the chart. One mystery at a time. "I meant your mark from your mate." She fought a flush.

Lily grinned even white teeth. "Um, only the royal family gets, er . . ."

"Branded?" Emma's cheeks filled until the blush burned.

"Yes. Something about the Kayrs lineage." Fathomless eyes sparkled fun for a moment. "Most vampires complete the sex act along with a good bite, thus mating for life." She pointed to very light twin marks in her neck—bite marks.

A wave of sympathy swept through Emma. "Your mate was killed by the Kurjans?" Dage had mentioned the fact to her earlier.

"Yes." Lily bit her lip. "We'd only been married for a couple of weeks—I barely knew the man." She sighed. "Arranged marriage."

"Ah. So, you, I mean haven't . . ." The barbaric custom of being tied to a dead spouse was unthinkable in today's society.

"No. Mating allergy." Lily sighed deep. "Though it's not like a prophet, a spiritual leader, can just go sleeping around. Unfortunately." She chuckled at the end before sobering. "You know, as part of my job, I often provide counsel."

"Counsel?" Emma reached for a blood pressure cuff to wrap around Lily's arm before pumping air.

"Yes. Take me as part nun, part psychologist, and part goodwill ambassador." Humor tipped the prophet's lips up.

"Okay." Lily's blood pressure numbers were good. Emma released the cuff and jotted down the information on the chart.

"Emma. Our people need a queen and our leader needs a mate. Both have embraced you." Lily rubbed her arm. "And you know it."

Emma snapped her head up. Warmth swirled around her heart and she ruthlessly pushed any sentiment down. "Fate does not get to dictate my life or future, regardless of a branding on my shoulder."

Lily rolled her eyes in a very unprophet-like manner. "Fate schmate. Forget destiny. The man loves you." She yanked the sleeve of her sweater down to cover the red flesh. "What you decide to do with such good fortune is up to you."

"Fate schmate?" Emma bit her lip. "Love is dangerous. My mama stayed with a man who beat us—because she loved him."

Lily's eyes softened. "So make your own decision. Stay with a good man who'll protect you because you love him." She reached forward and grasped Emma's arm. "I genuinely liked Miles. I may have been able to love him with passion someday." She shrugged. "Maybe not with the fireworks lighting the air when you and Dage are near each other, but with something."

Intrigued, Emma focused her gaze. "Fireworks?"

"Sure. I watched you at the ball. You're head over heels for him, too." Lily smiled even teeth in a wan face, dark circles standing at attention under her eyes. "I'd give anything for a chance at happiness like that. Instead of being tied to a legend who's long gone."

A chance at happiness? Emma had fought her entire life for what she wanted. First for survival, then for her career, now for what? She did love the man, no question. Had since she'd learned all about him in visions of his past. Death had lost to her before, maybe she could win again, and keep Dage. The marking on her shoulder began to burn in agreement. She shook her head, focusing back on the prophet. "You're not tied to a legend anymore, Lily."

Lily frowned. "I don't understand."

"I'm not sure how you're going to feel about this, but the virus takes the individual mating marker away." The marks in Lily's neck would probably fade away.

Lily lifted an eyebrow. "Meaning?"

"Meaning you're free to, ah, well, you know." Emma eyed Lily's demure sweater atop yet another long, rustling skirt. The woman still dressed as if a lady from the eighteen hundreds and yet the style fit her.

"I can have sex?" Lily's eyes opened wide before she clapped a hand over her mouth. "Are you sure?"

Emma shrugged. "As sure as I can be about this virus right now. We're still conducting tests."

Lily's gaze shot to the door and her face filled with color when Caleb stalked inside. "Oh my."

He approached the bed, his thick hair tied at the nape, his long strides carrying him across the room in seconds. "So a prophet was infected at the Realm colloquium? Seriously?" Anger rode every word.

"Yes." Emma said. The man remained as pissed as he was earlier when he'd carried the prophet inside the lab. Did the guy ever loosen up?

"She's not mated anymore?" Caleb raised an eyebrow, his multi-colored gaze hard on Lily.

"That's none of your business." Lily lifted her chin.

"Is the tramp stamp gone?" he growled back.

Lily sucked in a breath, her eyes going wide. "You're calling the mark of the prophecy a tramp stamp? Infidel!"

He reached for her, yanking her head to the side. "I asked you a question, woman." He hissed out a breath at the deep marking. "You shouldn't be a prophet any longer."

Lily tossed her head away and shoved at Caleb's chest. "Bite me, Caleb."

He raised an eyebrow. "Apparently Lady Lily has entered this century. You use words like that, milady, and you'll get what you're asking for."

Emma reached for the phone. "Caleb, leave or I'm calling the guards." Either her patient needed to stay calm, or these two needed to find a freakin' room. The sexual tension in the lab sped up her own heart.

Need help? A deep voice whispered throughout her head. She instantly threw shields into place. When had they fallen? Her heart shot from a jog to a full-out gallop.

A sigh echoed from the doorway where Dage stood leaning against the side. "Not nice, love. Not nice at all."

"Stay out of my head," Emma hissed, her gaze raking him from head to toe. She told herself he didn't look wonderful in black slacks, a silver silk shirt, and thick boots. Liar.

His gaze sharpened. "I've given you until tomorrow morning. Lower those shields or I'll shred them."

Anger began to boil like acid in her stomach. She lifted her chin. "We'll see about that, King." He may be powerful, but they'd mated. His powers belonged to her now. "Please take Caleb out of here." If she decided to make a go of this, the vampire had some things to learn.

Dage glared at his friend and then at his woman. Both needed to be dealt with and soon. "Caleb? Talen's waiting to discuss strategy with you. Let's go." He'd handle his mate later.

Caleb gave a low growl and followed him from the room.

Dage didn't look back, choosing instead to keep striding toward the conference room. "Stop being an asshole."

"Me, an asshole? You just threatened brain damage on your own mate," Caleb shot back.

Dage rolled his eyes, stopping to gesture his friend inside the room. "She's got the strongest brain you could imagine. Stubborn woman."

Caleb grinned. "Your perfect match."

Damn straight. The little blue eyed scientist would admit it before the week was out. Dage was done with this crap. He needed his home life settled so he could concentrate on fixing the rest of the fucking world.

Talen glanced up from his seat at the table, the swirling colors of his golden eyes giving Dage pause. He'd forgotten. Talen had been so calm lately, usually in front of either Cara or Janie. The women were absent, and the vampire was pissed.

"Nice of you two to join me." Talen nodded to chairs. "A traitor is hiding in our safe little world."

Dage dropped into a chair. "Yes."

The table jumped when Talen pounded a fist into it. "We're doing a piss-poor job of protecting our women, now aren't we?"

"Yes." Much better for Dage to let Talen get this out of his system. Then that clear, rational, strategic mind would create a plan.

The gold fled Talen's eyes. "Are you envisioning anything?"

"No." Dage hadn't seen any of this coming. "Fate is being an asshole about visions. I see nothing right now." While Emma was having visions, they weren't focused on Talen's family, at least not yet. There was no way to control the visions of the future.

Caleb grabbed a chair and sat. "That's because nothing's set right now. Too much jockeying is going on." He blew out a breath. "I can't believe a prophet was infected at the Realm ball."

Anger ricocheted through Dage. He couldn't believe it either. "No. I failed to protect her."

"Nay, that's not what I meant." Caleb raised an eyebrow. "I meant, why at the ball? Was she unreachable before that? Did they want to show you how close they could get? Or was it the first opportunity?"

Talen nudged some papers their way. "Here's Lily's schedule for the last six months. If I were targeting her, I'd have chosen at least five easier times to infect her than at the colloquium." He grabbed a pencil and snapped the utensil in two. "Cara and Katie have been under wraps. It was the first opportunity to reach them."

Understanding dawned on Dage. "So it was the first opportunity to infect all three of them."

"Yes." Talen threw the pencil pieces toward a trash can.

Caleb cleared his throat. "I'm assuming there were other mates and shifters at the ball?"

"Yes," Talen said.

"Then it's safe to conclude those three women were specific targets."

"No," Dage said. "Cara and Katie drank herbal tea while most everyone else drank champagne or hard liquor. The tea ordered for Cara was spiked. Katie just happened to order that."

"Lily loves herbal tea," Caleb noted.

"Yes." Talen grabbed a fountain pen. "She confirmed she drank the tea. Why Cara though?"

Dage shrugged. "Revenge for Lorcan's death?" The Kurjan leader had deserved death after kidnapping Cara. "Or because of the baby?"

Talen growled low, danger all but sliding across his face. "I've asked if anyone else ordered the tea, insinuating the herbs caused the food problems, and so far no one has replied in the positive." The pen broke in two and he tossed it to the garbage. "Jase is tracking down the waiters from that night, and one is missing."

"He's dead," Caleb noted without expression.

"More than likely," Talen agreed. "We must find who he was working with from our end. My men are searching his apartment and going through his laptop."

Talen's cell buzzed and he lifted it to his ear. "Kayrs." He sat to attention. "When? How bad? Great." He snapped the phone shut and threw it across the room. The device hit the freshly painted wall and shattered into pieces. "Rachel Davis is dead."

Shock stormed into Dage's gut. "Emma's friend, the geneticist? How?" Another woman he'd failed to protect.

Talen yanked the band out of his hair. "They're calling it a botched robbery. Someone broke into her Paris hotel room last night and apparently she fought back, ending up with a broken neck."

"Kurjans. They probably wanted to kidnap her."

"More than likely." Talen jumped to his feet to pace. "We knew of her and should've assumed they knew of her as well. I'm so tired of being three steps behind these bastards."

"Me too." Dage's mind ran through likely scenarios. "Find out if she was working with anyone on her research. We won't make the same mistake twice."

The land line rang on the table and Talen exhaled, grabbing the handset and raising it to his ear. "What?" Metallic eyes rose to meet Dage's gaze. "Yes. He's right here." Talen dropped back into his chair, an incredulous look flashing across his hard face. "Are you kidding me? No?" He slammed the phone down, breaking the handset in two pieces.

The lab wasn't sturdy enough to withstand Talen's current mood. Dage steeled himself. "Who was that?"

"Conn. The demon nation just declared war on the Realm. Happy fucking Tuesday."

Chapter 13

The night filled with the loud hooting of a lonely owl outside the large lab, searching, calling for something in the darkness. For someone. The mournful demand slithered down Emma's spine as she straightened from her bent position over the charts, an ache setting up between her eyes. She'd spent half the day supervising Devon and the other geneticists in the all-access labs, the other half in a heavy, thick suit dealing with the virus in the private clean lab by herself—because humans weren't invited into that space. With a sigh, she put a hand to the small of her back and stretched, stifling a groan as her vertebra popped.

"Time for bed, love," came a deep voice from the doorway.

She jumped and pivoted toward the exit where Dage once again leaned against the doorjamb. Broad and packed hard, clothed casually in cargo pants and a cotton shirt, mere camouflage for the vampire lurking within. The temptation to cross to him and taste that dangerous flesh had her mind spinning with denial. "No. I'm not finished working."

He raised an arrogant eyebrow. "You've been working nearly fourteen hours. You need rest." The low rumble of his voice held a direct line to her core. Sandalwood and power wafted her way.

Fourteen hours? It seemed like more. She'd already been

deep into her research when Dage showed up in the late afternoon with the prophet. "I'm not leaving, Dage." Her multi-channeled pod buzzed and she turned to push a series of buttons. Time was running out for her sister and the shifters. She just knew it.

Strong arms grasped her hips and whirled her around, and she emitted a startled yelp. The king ducked. The world tilted as she was flung over his broad shoulder. Her stomach impacted solid muscle and the air whooshed out of her lungs. Man, he moved fast. Desire battled with irritation.

"Put me down."

"No." He strode past Kane typing busily in his office and past the guards into the star filled night. "I'm at war on three fronts, love. Ours gets settled tonight." He shifted and she found herself cradled in strong arms. She smacked her fists against his chest.

"That wasn't nice." The silver of his eyes glowed in the near darkness.

"I don't feel nice." She settled into his chest, eyes widening at the expanse of stars in the sky.

"Me either." Muscles vibrated around her with a tension she felt in her own body.

She cleared her throat. "I can feel what you're feeling."

Teeth flashed in the darkness. "I know. Probably not very comfortable right now."

"No." Anger, irritation, and a deadly determination filled the king, and Emma said a heartfelt thanks he wasn't mad at her. She shrugged and bounced off a rock hard chest. "What am I feeling?"

"Scared."

"No. I'm mad."

"No. You're scared to death."

Acceptance settled onto her shoulders. "Yeah. I'm scared this virus will speed up. I'm scared for Cara and her baby." And she was scared she might not be able to thwart death and save the king.

"I know." He nodded at the guards posted at the residence, stalking inside the hallway. "It's amazing. We're immortal and the strongest beings on earth. Yet a bug too small to see may take us down."

"No. I'll wipe the stupid thing out." Warmth began to hum throughout her blood. Tilting her head, she ran her tongue along the corded muscles of Dage's neck. "Salty." More than that. The king tasted of power and man combined.

He opened a door and began descending, his boots echoing against cement stairs. "Hold that thought."

They were going the wrong way. "Where are you taking me?"

He twisted a knob and kicked another metal door open to reveal a shimmering indoor pool. "For a swim." His voice echoed throughout the humid room. He dropped her to her feet and ripped her T-shirt over her head, reaching for his own.

A swim? Awesome. She toed off her tennis shoes and yanked her jeans to the ground. Her bra and panties followed suit. Turning, she dove into the deep end. Cool water washed over her and she broke the surface with an appreciative hum to swivel just as the king dove deep.

He gave a tug to her ankle before rising next to her. "You just jumped in." Water caressed down the hard planes of his face and chest, making her mouth go dry.

She cleared her throat, treading water. "Sure."

He shook his head, spraying droplets of water. "Scientists aren't the 'jump first and ask questions later' type. The water could've been freezing. Or just chlorinated. You didn't pause." He raised an eyebrow, liquid gaze warming. "Why do you suppose that is?"

Hmm. Because the water appeared so inviting? She sighed. "Because I trust you." She hadn't stopped to consider why. If the king brought her to swim, then swimming was safe. Vulnerability rushed through her.

Twin dimples flashed and he grasped her by the waist, jerking her to him. Heat cascaded off the vampire in direct contrast to the cool water. "Don't looked so pained." He kissed the top of her nose and leaned back, a serious glint lighting his eyes. "I'm sorry trusting a man is foreign to you."

She gave a short nod, her gaze dropping to his full lips. "I'm really strong, Dage."

He grinned. "Saying the words takes something away from their impact, love."

Laughter bubbled up. "So true." Her hands flattened against his chest and she wrapped her legs around his waist. "Don't let me fall." Her breath hitched as she said the words.

"Never." His hands dropped to cup her ass, tugging her closer. He gave a strong push and she ended up with an aroused male body pinning her to the side of the pool.

"We're not at war, Dage." Her voice pitched to a huskiness from the erection rubbing against her core. "I mean, you and me." She slid both arms around his neck.

He quirked a lip. "We're not?" His hands tightened. "Isn't this where you tell me you're leaving and not to get too attached?" The teasing words failed to mask the glint of challenge in his eyes.

An ache started to thrum to life somewhere in her chest. "I can't stay." Tears pricked her eyes and she forced them back. "You need to understand what I'm saying. Love and forever aren't for us." He needed to be prepared in case she wasn't able to outmaneuver fate. She wanted to stay. She wanted that life full of fireworks and love. Could he unbend enough to trust her to keep herself safe?

"I don't understand." He lowered his head closer. "And it's too late. You have my love and are my future."

She shook her head, pain crushing into her heart. The brand on her shoulder began to burn with need. "No." Grasping his hair, she yanked his mouth to hers.

He stilled, then plundered. No softness, no seduction, just pure, raw need. He tangled a hand in her curls and tilted her head to the side for better access, the hand on her ass clutching hard enough to bruise. One quick shift and he impaled her, driving in balls deep.

She cried out, arms tightening around his neck, her eyes opening wide. Ripples of pain slid into pleasure as her body softened and accepted his invasion.

He released her mouth, raising his head to pin her with a look so full of determination she forgot how to breathe. "Say it."

Her lungs kicked in and she expelled air. Say what? She reached into his mind and quickly shook her head. No. Her mind rebelled against the raw demand of need echoing throughout his heart. A heart that she could feel within her own chest.

He widened his stance on the concrete slope, fully embedded in her. Fangs elongated in slow motion, wicked and sharp. "Need proof, love?"

"No." She didn't require proof. She knew what she felt and telling him would solve nothing. "You may not bite me." The desire for him to sink those dangerous fangs into her neck was one she'd fight.

Too dangerous. For both of them.

Blue shards ripped through the silver of his eyes. "You're my mate." His voice lowered to a low rumble that almost had her orgasming. "I don't need permission to taste you." To prove his point, he kissed her neck, and slowly, so slowly sank those sharp points into her vein.

She exploded.

Lightning zapped through her. Stars imploded behind her eyelids and her entire body spasmed with something beyond an orgasm. Something that had her heart, body, and mind opening for him—for whatever he demanded. She plunged her own teeth into his flesh, biting until carbonated blood sizzled on her tongue, prolonging the crashing waves beating throughout her.

Releasing him, she threw her head back, her mouth opening on a silent scream as she rippled around the hard cock pulsing inside her. She slowly came down, her eyes wide on his dangerous face.

His gaze dropped to her mouth. "Jesus." A flick of his tongue licked blood off her lips. With a groan, he pressed her against the wall, spasms shooting through his muscles and his head dropping to the nape of her neck as he came. His orgasm threw her into another whirlstorm of cresting waves. She tightened her entire body around him, crying out his name.

Soon only the harsh sound of their combined breathing echoed throughout the secluded pool room. He sucked in air and lifted his head. "Say it."

Her heart fluttered. "I love you." The words held a promise she didn't intend to give, a promise that she'd fight fate to stay with him. A vow of trust in his ability to bend and accept her.

His smile rivaled the stars still sparking behind her eyelids. "I'll give you a bit of time, love. But the shields stay down."

Unease slithered beneath her skin. "Ah, no."

"Ah, yes." Leaning forward, he nipped her bottom lip. "I'm not asking."

"I'll consider it." She settled her hands over his shoulders. "Do I taste different? I mean, since we've mated?"

He huffed out a chuckle. "Forever the scientist, huh?" His thumb rubbed against the twin puncture wounds in her neck and she fought a sigh. "No. You taste just as wonderful as before I marked you—like passion fruit and vintage wine. Maybe a Shiraz."

The king had the heart of a poet. "So, are we still at war?"

"No. I'd say we've reached an uneasy alliance here."

She smoothed his dark hair back from his rugged face. "Until I roll over and drop all my problems in your lap to solve?"

His jaw relaxed. "Exactly."

Not in a million years. Love or not. The king had borne

the weight of ruling by himself for centuries and she couldn't allow it to continue. She shook her head, her thighs tightening against his hard hips. "You said you were at war on three fronts. Besides the Kurjans, who's gunning for us?"

With their connection she could feel his heart fill from her use of the word *us*. He smiled. "The demon nation declared war on us earlier today."

Shock rumbled through her. "Demon nation? *Demons* exist?"

"Sure."

"Are they minions from hell?"

Dage threw back his head and laughed. "Well, right now don't ask me that question." He dropped a quick kiss on her mouth. "Though, no. Demons are yet another species trying to survive on earth."

It couldn't be good to have demons mad at you. What kind of powers would a demon have? "Why are they mad at us?"

"Caleb has been at war with the demon nation for quite some time."

She knew the massive rebel would be trouble. Maybe she should warn Lily. "Oh. He became our friend and thus his enemies became our enemies?"

Dage nodded in approval. "Simply put, but yes. For now."

"Can you fix it?" She began to trail her fingers across his chest and down those amazing abs.

He stilled. "We'll see."

"Dage?"

"Yes, love?"

"You're still inside me."

"I'm well aware of that."

"So do something."

His cock jumped inside her. "I thought you'd never ask."

A couple of hours later Emma ran her foot down Dage's leg, her entire body loose and relaxed in the big bed.

"Knock it off. Unless of course, you'd like to go for round three." His low rumble pulsed around her.

She stifled a giggle. "Round five. I believe it would be round five."

He tucked her further into his warmth. "Go to sleep. You have a virus to demolish tomorrow and I have a demon nation to appease."

"If we both finish before lunch maybe we could go out." She grinned, wrapping her hands around the arm banded at her waist. Even his forearm was lined with muscle and strength.

"Funny." His breath brushed her hair.

Questions clicked through her in slow motion. "Do you ever go out? I mean, when you're not at war?"

He nipped her ear. "Sure. There's an Italian restaurant in Boulder I'd love to take you to. Sometime."

"What about jobs? I mean, have you guys had jobs through the years?"

His arm tugged her closer into his heat. "Being the king is mainly a full-time job. In peace and war." He sighed, his body relaxing behind her. "Talen has plotted strategy for centuries and Conn has trained our soldiers full-time. Though Kane has attended many schools to study science, biology, genetics . . ."

"Probably a good idea." She'd love to open up Kane's brain and suck all the knowledge into her own. "What about Jase?"

"Ah, the youngest brother. He's mastered all of the above."

"No kidding." He seemed so carefree and happy, though the sense of danger clung to him like a well-fitting jacket. She'd figured that was part of being a vampire. A predator.

"Yes. When he wasn't skydiving, working as an oceanographer, giving flying lessons . . ."

She fought a laugh. "So Jase has quite the résumé, huh?" Talk about a vampire of all trades.

"Yes. He wanted to be a race car driver for a while, but I had to veto that idea." Dage's voice rumbled with sleepiness.

"You didn't want Jase getting hurt?"

A masculine snort stirred her hair. "No. I figured he'd win and get his picture in the paper. We can't afford that."

"Oh." Jase probably would've wiped the track clean.

Dage yawned. "I forgot to ask. Does Kane's blood show any sign of the virus?"

"No." Her mind began to swim in lazy circles. "But if it shows up, we may have found the path to an antidote. Assuming he doesn't contract an illness." She yawned. "That was brave of him to ingest the virus for Cara."

Dage shrugged, his chest knocking against her head. "He's a good man. You do what you have to for family."

Hurt caught the breath in Emma's chest for a moment. For family. She hunkered down and began to count test tubes until sliding into an uneasy, dream-filled sleep.

Damn. She hated this dream

Fall had given up the fight to winter and its murky fog descended low. Eighteen years old, she sat on the chipped front steps of her home. The dirt road potted with holes stretched out before her. The trees spread naked limbs through the chilled air, allowing themselves to be swallowed by mist while dots of frost littered the brittle brush.

She shivered, the scent of nature's demise skittering across her skin. It was the saddest part of the day—dusk. The day ended and night had yet to provide the protection of darkness.

Yet she waited on the porch.

Cara hummed a quiet tune inside the house, working on a school project. Mama had gone to the library and Daddy . . . Well, Daddy was likely dead.

A low rumble echoed from down the road and soon the sheriff's battered squad car emerged from the murk. He'd left the lights off this time. No one was screaming or getting hit, so why hurry?

He rolled to a stop and stepped out of the vehicle, hitching his pants up over his big belly. "Hi Emma." A pronounced limp impeded his way as he moved toward her until Old Spice tickled her nose.

"Hi Sheriff." She stood to her feet, wiping her hands on ripped jeans. She needed to look surprised when he gave the news. "What are you doing here?"

His faded blue eyes softened. "I have bad news, sweetheart." The soft jowls in his neck jiggled as he spoke.

She nodded, sorry the sheriff had to feel anything for her father. The cop was a nice old man, one who'd tried to help more than once. "What is it?" He needed to tell her the bad news. Then she, Mama, and Cara could move on.

"There was a car accident. Your father's truck went over the embankment by Shilly's Hill."

Yep. She'd seen him crash to the bottom in a fiery explosion. Handy curse these visions. "Was he drunk?"

The sheriff widened his eyes for a moment and slowly nodded. "He left the tavern an hour or so before the wreck." Rubbing a hand across his thick white beard, the sheriff sighed. "You're eighteen, so there should be no problem for you to keep your sister with you."

Emma had celebrated her birthday a few weeks back. "Well, sure." A warning tingle set up at the base of her skull. "Mama should be home soon. I'll ask her to call you."

The sheriff paled. He extended his hand, then dropped it back down to his side, empty and useless. "Oh Emma. I thought you knew. They were together. Your mother was in the truck, too."

A decade later Emma's strangled cry had her sitting straight up in the bed.

Warmth instantly wrapped around her and she found herself cradled against a hard chest. "Oh, love. I'm so sorry."

She trembled, biting her lip until blood welled. "I'm all right."

"No, you're not. Let it out." Dage's warm breath brushed her forehead, the scent of sandalwood and power easing her muscles.

"No. I don't cry."

"Why the hell not?" His gentle tone softened the harsh words.

"Because it's weak."

He tugged her back down to snuggle against him. "Is not."

"Like you cry."

Large, gentle hands caressed her back from shoulder to tailbone, spreading warmth and reassurance. A guarantee of support and protection. "I promise I'll cry next time I'm upset. Okay?"

She laughed, tears instantly filling her eyes and beginning to fall. "It was my fault."

"What was?"

"I saw his death. I knew a year before it happened that he'd die. But I didn't know Mama was with him, that he'd pick her up at the library on the way home." Tears of shame and guilt scalded her face, dropping onto Dage's warm chest. "I never said a word."

Dage's warm hand rubbed circles into her lower back. "What if you had?"

"What?" She hiccupped.

"What if you had told him? What would he have done?"

"Beat the ever living shit out of me." The crazy bastard had thought she and Cara were possessed by the devil who had given them their special abilities.

Dage's expelled breath stirred her hair. "Ah. So telling him wouldn't have changed a thing."

"I don't know for sure. He may have heeded my warning—even if he did beat me first." And Mama would've lived.

Dage's muscles tensed until they vibrated from within. "I wish I could've met your father. For just an hour."

Emma grinned through her tears. "Me too." She placed a soft kiss above Dage's heart. "Do you think it's possible to cheat death?"

"Cheat? No." He ran a hand down her hair. "But I think the future can be changed. The visions you and I share allow us to do so."

She had every intention of altering the future she'd seen in visions. Their future. "Yes. But every time you try to alter the future, the new path becomes unclear. Isn't it better to know sometimes?"

"Sometimes. If you like that future." He rolled her over and brushed a gentle hand across her wet cheeks. "Better now?"

"Yes." Safety surrounded her. A foreign feeling. The temptation to let go and hide behind the king rocked through her. But she was stronger and smarter than that. The king needed her whether he knew it or not.

"So, about round five . . ."

Chapter 14

Dage took a deep breath, waiting for the wall screen in his private conference room to clear. The vulnerability inherent in the aboveground lab weighed on him. His mate should be at the underground headquarters up in the mountains. Only the need to cure the virus kept her here. Her intelligence was a resource they needed, but he had no intention of failing when it came to her safety.

He'd left her sleeping peacefully in their bed a mere hour ago, and only the heavy mantle of duty kept him from returning to her side to cuddle her close in a way she'd been denied as a child. He channeled his fury at the dead man into a focused calm to deal with the matter at hand. While he wouldn't admit it to anyone, he hated diplomacy and would rather take the demons on hand-to-hand.

Chalton punched in keys next to him. A pop sounded and the screen filled with the image of a large man dressed in the black uniform of the demon military. "Suri."

"Dage." A base growl emerged from the demon due to an odd configuration of vocal cords. "You having any fun being king?" Shiny silver triangles decorated his left shoulder, showing his rank as leader. *The* leader.

"Shit, no." Dage forced a smile for his old friend. "You?"

"No." Suri's eyes flicked from green to yellow and then

back again. He'd cut his hair short for once. Preparing for war? "I heard you found your mate. Congratulations."

Irony ran through the demon's words and Dage raised an eyebrow. "Thank you. I take it you're still looking?"

Suri shook his head, silver hair shining under overhead lights. "You should know better, Kayrs. You just exposed your jugular." He stepped closer to the camera. "A mate is a weakness a military leader can't afford."

"A valid viewpoint, to be sure." Dage paused for a moment. The demon had better not be threatening his mate. "Of course, I just became all the more deadly. Something to protect and all that."

Suri nodded, the light glinting off his shiny decorations. "Yes. Rumor has it Franco wanted your mate, and yet he's still breathing."

Dage laughed. "Franco's currently the least of my worries."

Suri nodded. "Even so, I'm surprised your peace lasted this long."

"As am I." Dage met the demon's gaze squarely. "You and I were once great friends." They still were, as far as he was concerned.

"Yes. Until one of your highest ranking officers stole my brother's mate." Anger sizzled in those eyes.

Dage rubbed his chin. "Will that wound ever heal?" For the love of Pete, eons had passed.

"No." Suri gave a short shake of his head. "Not until Caleb Donovan's remains are providing the earth with fuel."

Exasperation swept through Dage but he kept his face bland. "You've been fighting Caleb's forces for a hundred years. We stayed out of the feud because you both asked us to remain neutral." Though at the moment he wished he would've locked the two stubborn men in a room and let them duke it out. For good.

Suri's eyes narrowed. "You are no longer neutral. You chose a side yesterday."

Dage lifted an eyebrow. "No. We are gathering our forces and putting our allies in place. Are you aware of the Kurjan virus?"

Suri lifted a shoulder. "I have heard rumors."

The guy knew more than rumors. He was as connected as Dage. "Have you considered how it would impact your mates? Your family? Your allies?"

Fire crackled along the demon's skin for a moment. "It would not impact us."

"You sure about that?" The demons had thirty-two chromosomes and their mates twenty-eight. How could their twenty-seventh chromosomes be safe? He made a mental note to speak with Emma. If Suri was right, maybe a cure or antidote existed within the demon mates.

"Yes." A red flush spread across Suri's broad face. "Although we've declared war, as a gesture of friendship, I'll give you one week to denounce Caleb and his forces as an ally, Kayrs."

"And then what?"

Suri smiled slowly. "We take you out."

The screen faded to black. Now Dage had to destroy one friend in order to keep another one. His diplomacy skills seemed rusty, though the damn demons loved a good fight, maybe even needed one, to keep their mental faculties focused.

He ran a rough hand through his hair, his gaze on the blank wall. A beep at the door had him nodding to Chalton.

Janie skipped inside, leaping for his lap. "Hi Uncle Dage." The scents of baby powder and innocence filled the room.

"Hi." He settled her into place, the need to protect her nearly overwhelming him for a moment.

She clasped a blue bear, known as Mr. Mullet, in her small hands. "This room is like the other communication room in the mountain."

"Yep." The mountain—where the little girl should probably be safely ensconced. The main fortress was impenetrable, unlike their current facilities.

"Who were you talkin' to?" Her deep blue eyes, so curious and trusting, focused on his.

"An old friend named Suri." One he may have to kill.

Janie scrunched her face in a frown. "Guy with yellow eyes? Sometimes?"

The king breathed deep, pushing down his concern. "Yes, that's him. Have you dreamed about Suri?" Dage could protect his niece from any outside force, but no shield existed for the visions.

"Yep." She patted Mr. Mullet's blue hair. "But it's always kinda foggy around him, like he's not sure which way to go. Were you trying to tell him which way to go?"

"Yes, I was." But the path the demon had chosen would lead to bloodshed for them all. So much for Dage's diplomatic training. He didn't think the demons would mount an attack on him, but Caleb's forces were fair game. Now he was honor bound to jump into the fray. "What are you doing wandering around, little one?"

She rolled her eyes in an expression so like her aunt's he had to grin. "I'm almost five, Uncle Dage."

Dage nodded. "Yes, I understand your birthday is coming up. I already gave you a pony. What are you fishing for here?"

"Fishing?" Eyes that reminded him of the clearest blue lake in the Himalaya Mountains widened on his. "What do you mean, fishing? I don't wanna go fishing."

"Right. Hinting. What are you hinting at? I mean, what do you want for your birthday?"

She pursed her tiny lips. "I want my baby brother to be okay."

Emotions commingled and swam through the king until he couldn't differentiate between fear, pain, and pride. "I want your baby brother to be okay, too." Dage paused, sorting to find the right words. "Have you seen anything in your head?"

"No." She buried her nose in the bear's fur, her voice becoming muffled. "He's kinda foggy, too."

Well, damn. That wasn't good. "Your mama and your brother are strong people, Janie. We have to trust in that."

She lifted her head, a delicate eyebrow arching. "No we don't. We have to make it right."

The little girl was more like Emma than he'd thought. "We're doing our best, sweetheart."

"No." She frowned. "I mean, who's Mowra?"

"Mowra? You mean Moira?"

Janie shrugged. "Yeah. Who is she?"

Dage sat to attention, a tingling snapping at his neck. "Ah, why?"

"I saw her in my dreams last night." Janie began to play with a button on Dage's silk shirt.

Why? Had yet another one of his brother's women been infected with the virus? What would the tiny bug do to a witch? He needed Conn to contact his mate. "Moira is . . . ah, she's married to Uncle Conn, honey." How was Dage going to explain that one in preschool language?

Janie blew out a bubble. "Why isn't she here?"

"Basically, she's been studying at a far away school." That should appease the child's curiosity.

"Studying what?"

"Well, magic." Cara couldn't be mad if he taught Janie about witches and magic, could she? He didn't want to tick one of the Paulsen women off, that was for sure.

"Oh, okay. Where?"

"Across the ocean in Ireland."

"Is she done?"

"Er, yes." So much for appeasing Janie's curiosity.

"Why isn't she with Uncle Conn, then?"

"Ah, well, you should really talk to Uncle Conn about that, sweetheart." There. Served his brother right.

A peal echoed in his earpiece. He tapped once. "Dage."

"There's a problem. I'll meet you in conference room two," Talen said.

"Two minutes." Dage threw Janie into the air, catching the giggling child and striding toward the door. He handed her off to Max, who stood just outside. "Take Giggles here to her mother, please."

Janie smiled and gave him a little wave. "I also want an Xbox, Uncle Dage."

Dage entered the conference room still chuckling at the little minx. He lost his grin as he took in the frowning faces around the table. The scent of wild strawberries lingered in the air. "Lily? You should be lying down."

"I'm feeling better." She gave a delicate shrug, appearing beyond fragile sandwiched between Conn and Talen.

Jase dodged inside right behind Dage. "What's going on?"

Talen pushed back from the table. "The Kurjans kidnapped Prophets Milner and Guiles. They've demanded an exchange for Lily."

Dage frowned, shifting his gaze to the prophet. "They contacted you directly?"

She nodded. "Prophet Milner sent me an e-mail through a secured server. Even he doesn't know where I am."

Modern technology at work. For a moment Dage longed for the good old days when he controlled the flow of any and all information. He turned toward Talen. "Did you trace the e-mail?"

"No." Talen pounded on a keyboard and a land map lit up one wall. "It's secured. But we traced Milner's movements and discovered he and Guiles were taken from Portland as they left the colloquium."

"Their guards?"

"All dead"—Talen tapped twice and the screen zoomed in to show a series of buildings sprawled over about a mile— "which is why we didn't know they were taken until an hour ago." He stood. "This is where I think they are in central Idaho."

"Why?"

"The Kurjans started preparing this facility about a year ago—I've had my eye on it. Just this weekend the number of guards quadrupled."

"Is Franco there?" Dage grabbed a band from his pocket, yanked his hair out of his face, and tied it back with the band. He needed the location of the current Kurjan ruler to take him out. The fiend had planned to mate with Emma, thus sealing his fate.

Talen shook his head. "I don't think so. Last my sources knew he was still in Canada."

Dage kept silent for a moment, ticking off scenarios in his head. "Think it's a trap?"

"Yep." Talen nodded. "More than likely."

Lily sat forward. "I don't understand."

Dage began cataloguing weapons in his head and turned toward her. "The Kurjans must know you're with us. They also know we wouldn't trade you." He frowned. "What were Prophet Milner's instructions?"

"He said to tell you I was going home and to call my guards to escort me." Lily drummed her fingertips on the table. "Do you think they know I've been infected?"

"Yes," Dage said. "The waiter would've watched to make sure you drank the tea." Of course the Kurjans wanted Lily. They'd want to study her reaction as well as trace the progression of the virus—until they injected her with the catalyst.

"But"—Lily's face drained what little color remained—"it's a good plan. I mean, if I ordered the prophet guards to take me home, you wouldn't stop me."

The hell he wouldn't. "Of course not," Dage said smoothly. "Okay. Talen, you have ten minutes to devise a plan. You, Jase, Conn, Caleb, and I are the only ones going from here. Everyone else remains on high alert."

Talen gave a short nod. "In case the trap is for us to leave."

"Yes. Find Caleb and ask how fast his men can get to the Idaho compound. The Kurjans won't be expecting them. Meet in the south armory in ten minutes." Dage pivoted on his heel and stalked out of the room, jogging back down the hall to his private conference room to play the game.

Chalton looked up, a question in his gaze.

"Contact Franco."

Without batting an eyelash, Chalton typed in a series of codes and waited for a moment before a dark figure slowly formed on the large screen. Amethyst eyes set in a stark white face glared across the distance. "What could you possibly want to discuss?"

Dage grinned. The prick was in Canada. "Hello Franco. Rumor has it you stepped up as ruler when my brother sliced Lorcan's head off." No reason to be cordial.

"Yes. My cousin will be sorely missed." Franco flicked fiery red hair tipped with black ends over his shoulder.

"I'm sure. He kidnapped the wrong woman." The moron had thought to mate with Cara, which had ensured his death by Talen's hand.

Franco shrugged. "You stole my mate from the helicopter, Kayrs. I guess that means I kill you." Blood swirled odd patterns in those bizarre eyes.

The urge to end the Kurjan ruler's life spiked through Dage's blood at the mention of Emma.

"I'll look forward to meeting up with you, as well as Kalin, if he doesn't kill you first. Apparently he's nuts."

Franco grinned sharp canines. "Yes. The boy is crazier than a rabid dog." True fondness colored the words. "He has such impressive plans for your niece."

Rage threatened Dage's clarity for a moment, and only by sheer force of will did he school his features into boredom. "He'll die first."

"Maybe, maybe not. Our oracles don't seem to think so." Franco nodded to someone off camera.

Nice try. Dage's equipment was the best—he wouldn't be located. "So, I thought I'd give you a chance to return my prophets. I doubt you want fate fucking with you."

Franco clicked his tongue against the roof of his mouth. "You've gone and lost your prophets? Not good, King." He shook his head, red hair flying. "Not good at all." Sharp nails flashed when he spread his fingers wide. "I don't have them."

Dage frowned. "Really. Then why ask for Prophet Sotheby to exchange herself for them?"

Franco's nostrils flared. "Prophet Sotheby?" A deep flush slid crimson under his pasty skin. "Can you imagine the prophet as a Kurjan mate?" He sucked in air, a pleasured humming emitting from his throat.

"No." What a pervert.

"Oh. Well, let me assure you I do not have your prophets." Franco moved closer to the camera, his gaze intent. "If I did, they'd already be dead." He shrugged. "After I'd tortured all of the information they possessed out of them, of course."

"Last chance." Dage would blow the Kurjan nation apart.

Franco smiled. "I've work to do, Kayrs. Bye." The screen went black.

"I can't wait to remove his head," Dage muttered to Chalton. But first he had to reclaim the prophets.

He stalked out of the room and down a flight of stairs to the armory where he donned a bulletproof vest. Several knives quickly disappeared into various pockets. He lifted his head as Emma rushed into the room.

"You are not going." She smacked her fists onto her hips, her voice shaking. Her anger increased the scent of spiced peaches always surrounding his mate.

He'd forgotten about his own shields. "I'll be fine." Grabbing a green gun off the table, he tucked it into his waist, his gaze remaining on her. She was entirely too pale.

"You think it's a trap." Fear filled her voice.

He *knew* it was a trap. "Probably not, love."

"I'm in your fucking head," she screamed, her pupils dilating to swallow the iris. "You know it's a trap."

Damn it. If he raised mental shields now he'd hurt her. Not physically, but even worse.

"Try it." She lifted her head, her entire body vibrating with fury.

True appreciation swept through him. Damn but his mate was magnificent. "I promise I'll return in one piece, Emma." Her love shimmered with anger toward him, and he fought a primitive need to be inside her.

"You're the king. You shouldn't fight."

She would try to use a human's logic in her argument.

Dage focused on her thoughts. Fear of losing him. Hearing her say she loved him the other night had warmed his heart, feeling it from inside her body blessed his soul. "*I am the king.* Thus I *must* fight." He took three steps forward to run a gentle finger down her smooth skin. "We're leaving most of our troops here to protect you. The Kurjans won't see Caleb's force coming at them in Idaho, so even though it's a trap, we'll spring the prophets." Her concern warmed him, but she needed to learn the risk of being Realm royalty. "I lead our troops, love. If they're in danger, I'm in danger." He dropped a fast kiss to her sweet mouth, raising his head to meet her gaze. "I promise, I'm damn good at my job."

She rolled her eyes. "I do understand the weight of responsibility and how the walls can close in on a person. You need to show leadership, but how much of you putting yourself on the front lines is really an effort to escape?"

He started, his gaze focusing on the stubborn set of her chin. Escape? She thought he put his ass on the line to escape the office? "You think I'm evading duty?"

Her pretty blue eyes sparked. "Hell no. But I do think that

in battle, when there's one single goal, you can focus that energy, focus that soldier's need for a moment, without having to take into account the entire world." A slow sardonic smile slid across her face. "There really isn't anyone else who could do the job as king, now is there?"

"No," he breathed, his mind spinning. The woman was perceptive, that was for damn sure. Intrigue swept through him along with desire. Raw and pure.

She sighed. "You're a great king. The fact that you'd rather be doing something else makes you even more impressive." Reaching up, she ran one slender finger down the side of his face, making him want to shut his eyes and just feel. But he didn't. He kept his gaze on his mate as she continued. "I'm just saying there may be a better way to escape strategy and diplomacy than letting the enemy shoot at you."

His gaze dropped to her pink lips. "Is that so? Any ideas, love?" Damn but he planned to keep her. For eternity.

Her tongue darted out and wet her lips, forcing a low growl in his throat. He raised his head, fully expecting to see a pretty blush covering her face. Instead, the color drained away, leaving her skin a fragile eggshell. "Emma?"

"I, uh, don't feel so well." She paled even further and her chest hitched when her breath caught. She swayed and dropped toward the floor.

He caught her, standing for a moment staring at his unconscious mate. She was out cold, a vulnerable vein pulsing in her fragile neck. How could she be so strong and so delicate at the same time? Anger and fear mixed together until his hands shook. Guns hit the floor when he swept the table clear to set her down. A quick shake had her groaning into the silence.

"Ouch." She lifted a shaking hand to her temple.

Dage inhaled through his nose, closed his eyes, and yanked the pain out of her head. The agony swirled in his skull for a moment before he tossed it away. "Better?"

She sat up. "Um, yeah." A sudden cough racked her body.

"I saw Prophet Milner in that place Talen showed you earlier."

Dage raised an eyebrow. "You sat through my briefing?" She could already see out of his eyes? Pride filled the king.

She grinned. "Yep."

He schooled his face into a frown. "Hmm. We'll discuss boundaries later. What else did you see?"

She glanced up, apparently remembering. "They're preparing for you to come. Guns, rockets, knives. So many weapons."

He already knew it was a trap. "And?"

Her pretty blue eyes focused back on his face, her gaze running over his skin. "The plan is to follow you back here to find us. You should check the prophets for bugs."

Dage nodded, his palms itching to touch every inch of her. "Already in the plans, love." Relief swept him that the trap was away from his mate. The Kurjans should know better than to lay a trap for him. His men would reverse it in a heartbeat, snapping the teeth of death around their enemy. He leaned down and captured Emma's mouth in a kiss. Then he helped her off the table. "Go kick the crap out of that virus. I'll be home tonight."

She faltered, then placed her hand against his arm. "I love you."

Heat filled his heart and for a moment he couldn't speak. "I love you, too." Pure, raw need for her ripped through him

Talen stomped inside, and with a small smile, Emma left.

Dage tossed a vest toward his brother. "Emma had a vision. The trap awaits us in Idaho and for now, our mates are safe here."

"Good. With Caleb's forces meeting us, the trap will be on the Kurjans," Talen said, shrugging into a vest.

Dage nodded and took a good look at his brother's bleeding mouth. "What the hell?"

Talen secured the sides of the vest. "I had to throw Kane into a wall."

"I take it he bounced back?"

Guns slammed into pockets as Talen nodded. "He hit me first actually. Wanted to go on the raid."

"Don't blame him. But I need him to deal with the virus." Kane was a fine fighter. Cold, precise, and deadly. Right now they needed the scientist. Plus, Dage felt better having one of his brothers nearby protecting his mate.

"Yeah. I had to say *please* to get him to back off."

Dage fought a smile. "Bet that hurt."

"Yep." Talen twirled a double edged knife in his hand before plunging the weapon into his cargo pants pocket. A trio of guns soon followed into various holders. "Ah, Cara's getting worse. Weaker."

Dage lifted his head. "That's not good."

"No." Fierce determination etched across Talen's face. His mask as a soldier. "Let's go kill us some Kurjans."

Now that was a plan.

Chapter 15

Emma leaned against the old pine tree and dug her shoes into the dirt, her gaze on the empty tarmac. The cement sparkled in the sun, returning waves of heat to the bleached white sky. The helicopters had lifted into the air with barely a swish of sound, taking Dage to war. To blood and death.

Her hands trembled and she sought her center. The cool forest behind her failed to provide the peace her sister always found in such depths. While Cara had sought safety from their father in the trees and bushes, Emma had often left a safe haven to put herself in front of the monster who'd raised them so he'd hit her instead of little Cara or their lost, beaten mother. Emma had sought counseling in college and understood her anger toward both parents was normal. But sometimes memories still clawed at her.

The door to the residence opened and Devon hustled out, his hands full of papers and his glasses askew on his face. With a wary glance at the huge soldier accompanying him, he hurried toward her. "Dr. Paulsen? Something's not right." He shoved a piece of paper in her hands.

"I'm sorry, Dr. Paulsen." The soldier's gravelly voice rumbled with irritation. "This guy insisted we find you."

"That's all right." She glanced down, quickly reading the paper. Damn it. Devon wasn't to have seen this. "What is this?'"

"I found it with the new cancer data." Devon shrugged. "There's a clear genetic profile of something with more than twenty-three chromosomes. There are thirty here."

She cocked her head to the side, attempting to settle her racing heart. Would the vampires harm a human who held too much knowledge? "Well, since that's impossible, what logical solution could there be?" She forced a grin.

Devon exhaled. "Seriously. Someone's playing a joke?"

"What else could it be?" She wrinkled her nose, shaking her head. "You totally fell for it."

"Dang it." He laughed, the sound filled with relief. "I did *not* fall for it. I was just afraid someone on my team royally screwed up. A joke, huh?" He rubbed his chin. "I'll bet it was Sandy. She's been working so hard on the proteins that I'm sure she needed a break." A blush filled his high cheekbones. "She's got such a great sense of humor."

"Yeah, she does." The scientist was in love, no doubt about that.

He glanced with resignation at the silent soldier. "All right. I'll head back to work."

Emma kept hold of the papers. "Sounds good. "I'll meet you in the lab later today." She didn't allow worry to cross her face until the soldier had escorted Devon around the building to the public side of the lab. She needed to be more careful with her data.

Her knees felt weighted. She sighed, her mind spinning. The residence door opened again and Janie skipped out, the formidable Max on her heels. Spotting Emma, he gave a short nod and pressed his back into the wooden siding.

Janie shouted in recognition and ran in new electric pink tennis shoes toward her aunt. Clouds of dust rose along the small path.

Emma tilted her head, stunned once again by the beauty of the little girl dashing through the sunshine. Blue eyes sparkled with a clarity that only came from a pure soul, and tiny patrician features lifted in joy. Light brown ringlets cascaded around her delicate shoulders. Shoulders that would one day carry the fate of the world. She smiled and tiny white baby teeth flashed.

Baby teeth.

Determination crashed through Emma with a strength that snapped her spine in place. She was here for a reason. To protect the child. And she would.

"Auntie Emma," Janie yelped, throwing both arms around her middle.

"Hi pretty girl," Emma murmured, returning the hug. Sweet powder wafted up.

The little girl leaned back. "Don't worry 'bout Uncle Dage. He's fine."

Was he, now? Emma slid down to sit, allowing the shade to cool her. A soft tug had Janie perching next to her. "Have a vision, did we?"

"Nope." Janie reached out and plucked a stick from the ground, drawing a happy face in the dirt. "Sometimes I just know stuff. Like . . ."

"Like what?" Emma brushed wild curls off her niece's face.

"Like you're about to have a vision, Auntie." The cheerful smile failed to match the serious adult glint in those otherworldly eyes.

"Really? Well, maybe we should go get some ice cream first." Ice cream sounded good. With chocolate syrup.

"Nah. Let's stay here." Janie patted her knee. "On the ground."

Emma smiled. "No, let's . . ." Nausea washed through her. The tree swayed behind her. "Hey—" Pain slashed into her brain, and she shut her eyes before they could shoot out of her head. An image of Janie came into focus—a Janie at least two decades older. Beautiful, feminine, and strong. A carved out hall, firelight, and groups of men. A symposium of sorts. A murmur of voices and then . . . an explosion. Fire.

She shook her head to escape the smell of burning flesh. Her eyes opened wide on her niece.

"It's okay. I get out." Janie reached up and wiped tears off Emma's face. "I'm pretty sure."

A dull ache set up in Emma's neck and she groaned.

Janie brushed two fingers across Emma's throat. The pain wafted away.

What the hell? Emma frowned, focusing on the little girl. "How did you make the pain go away?" Janie's eyes were clear and her color healthy—she didn't hurt.

Janie shrugged. "Dunno. Just did."

"Does your head hurt?"

"Nope." She grabbed her stick to scratch a puppy into the ground. "Did you see Zane in the vision? He sat across the fire from me."

"Zane? No, I don't think so." The puppy stared back at Emma with big eyes, providing no answers. "Are you sure you get out?"

"Yep. We all do." A cat began to take shape next to the dog. "Zane reminds me of Uncle Dage as a grown-up."

"Because he's big?" Her niece could do worse than the King of the Realm. Maybe Emma should try to track this mysterious Zane down.

"Yeah. The black glow around Uncle Dage's skin sometimes will try and swallow Zane when he's a grown-up." Janie tried to straighten the cat's triangular ears. She sighed. "I think I'm 'posta stop it."

Dark edge? "You mean their auras?" Did auras really exist? Emma needed to buy a book on those to keep up with Janie. And how the hell was Janie supposed to fight with dark glows?

The little girl shrugged. "Dunno. It's something I see sometimes."

"Do I have an edge?"

"Yep. Bright blue. Like Mama's."

"So you know that. And you knew I was about to have a vision." One that freakin' hurt. "But you don't know how you know."

"Nope."

The cat looked like a rabid mouse. "Okay. So, what else do you know?"

Janie pursed her lips, cocking her head to the side. She glanced back toward Max. "Katie's coming out and she needs a favor."

The door opened and the young lioness glided into the sun.

"Can you read minds, Janie?" Awareness tickled down Emma's spine.

The little girl wrinkled her nose. "Nope. Sometimes I just know stuff."

Katie strode forward, her petite form in tight faded jeans and a white hoodie. Dark circles appeared like bruises under her tawny eyes, and her flawless skin was so pale it reflected the sun. "Emma. I was looking for you."

Emma smiled and swept her hand toward the nearest tree. "Have a seat. We're just talking here."

Katie faltered and then shrugged, sliding down to sit. "So. What's going on?"

"Not much. Just enjoying the fall day," Emma said.

"Yeah," Janie chirped up. "Katie's mad at Jordan, Auntie Emma."

"Yes." Katie's nostrils flared and a trembling smile lifted her lips. "I've loved Jordan since I was four years old, and he's never even looked twice at me."

Emma frowned. That certainly wasn't true. She'd only been around the shifters a short time, but Jordan had it bad for Katie. "I think you're wrong."

"No." Katie shook her head and honey-blond hair flew. "I'm not. Now this has happened, now I can't shift, and he thinks we should mate. That I'll get my shifting abilities back if we do."

"Oh my." Emma glanced again at Janie's puppy, her mind spinning. "Well, that might work actually." Who the hell knew? The virus hadn't even been completely mapped yet.

"If it doesn't?" Katie's eyes darkened to deep brown. "The leader of our pride will have mated with someone who can't shift. Ever." She grabbed a rock and threw it across the path to land with a hard thunk against a tree. "Besides. I'd rather not be a pity fu—" She glanced at Janie and cleared her throat. "A pity marriage."

The door next to Max swung open, and Cara poked her head outside. "Janet Isabella? Come eat lunch and then we need a nap." She gave a wave to Emma and Katie, leaning back against the doorframe.

Emma waved back and hid her concern, helping Janie to stand. "Anything else I should know, little wise one?"

Janie grinned. "That's e'nuff for now." She hopped, skipped, and then ran for her mother, who enfolded her in a big hug before drawing her inside the building. Max nodded at Emma and followed them inside.

Katie chuckled, her gaze on the closed metal door. "It's a damn good thing she's on our side, now isn't it?"

A breeze filtered through the trees and pine needles rained down. Emma brushed one off her legs. "No question about that." The girl's abilities were astonishing. "You know, I just don't understand why your species hasn't allied with humans through the years. We could have so many more trained, medical minds working on this problem right now." Cara was getting sicker every day. They needed help.

Katie lifted both eyebrows. "Seriously? Remember your history? Through the years humans have hunted and destroyed any race they felt was more powerful. Even so called witches in Salem." She sighed. "If your government had any idea I existed right now, I'd be hooked up to machines and studied—against my will."

Emma shrugged against the unease tickling her nape. "We're not all like that, Katie."

"I know." She looked at Emma. "But even you have wondered about our abilities, if the science involved could be applied to cure human frailties. Human illnesses."

"Well sure. I want to ease pain and suffering as well as curing diseases."

"What then?" Katie grabbed another rock. "The planet isn't big enough for humans to be immortal too, Emma."

Emma shook her head, not wanting to debate the issue. "Okay. So Janie said you needed a favor?"

"Um, yes. You've isolated the catalyst, right?"

Shit. "Yes."

"I, uh, want you to infect me with the catalyst." Katie set her trembling lips in a firm line.

Emma huffed out a breath. "You're unwilling to let my government experiment on you, yet you want me to do it?"

Katie's eyes flashed topaz. "First of all, they're not your government any more. You're the Queen of the Realm, and your husband leads your new government. Second, you know I'm right. The virus takes away the shifter's ability to shift. We know from watching Maggie that the catalyst speeds up the virus so the shifter's body begins to fight."

"If the shifter's body loses, he or she might shift into a werewolf," Emma hissed. Oh God. Katie wasn't really asking her do to this, was she?

"But the virus doesn't work completely. So far Maggie has been able to shift back into her true wolf form instead, and the catalyst has given her the ability to do so."

Emma sucked in a deep breath. "We don't know that. In fact, we have no idea how long Maggie's been infected. Maybe the virus just reached a point, catalyst or not, where her body produced enough antibodies to fight it." Emma should start wearing a hat saying, WE JUST DON'T KNOW. She bit her lip. "And Katie, we have no idea how the catalyst would work on a lion shifter, and you in particular. You might turn into a werewolf. Or you might just die."

"I'm willing to take the chance."

The woman had a right to choose. "I understand. But it's way too early to take a chance like that." Emma held up a hand when Katie opened her mouth to protest. "I'm not saying *no*. There's a process to follow in this. First, we need to see if Maggie survives the next full moon. We also need to give your body time to start creating antibodies." She reached out and clasped Katie's arm. "You might be able to beat the illness without any more help. It's just a *virus*. There's a chance your body will heal itself."

Katie inhaled so deeply her shoulders lifted two inches. "I know."

Emma released her friend. "I already have been conducting experiments on your blood and the catalyst."

Katie quirked a lip. "You were a step ahead of me, huh?"

Emma shrugged. "We need all the knowledge we can get." She stretched her neck. "You have time. You don't need to make any costly mistakes."

"You don't know we have time. The progression of this thing could always speed up."

"You're right. Though the risk is too dangerous."

"I'll wait until after Maggie beats the third full moon before asking for the catalyst again. Afterward, if it doesn't work, I'll need your help getting away from Jordan."

Emma straightened up. "Are you in danger? I mean, are you afraid of Jordan?"

Katie shut her eyes, shaking her head. "No." Opening them, they filled with tears. "I can't stay." Her voice choked on each word. "Not like this." She gestured at her body.

The woman's pain echoed through the air. "How could I help if you decide to run?" Emma whispered.

Kate grabbed and threw another rock. "You're the queen. I'll need transportation and a head start."

Emma sighed. "You just said you loved the man. Shouldn't you fight for him?"

Kate shook her head. "Not like this. Not half of what I was. Half of what he could've loved but never did." She picked up the discarded stick and began to trace a fierce outline of a lion into the dirt. "Though, I did think, I mean, what the heck. How about one night, you know?"

Emma huffed out a laugh. "One night with Jordan? Before you leave?"

"Yeah. You know. Just a night of great sex—no mating. Something to keep me warm forever." A dark blush competed with the sleepless circles on Katie's face.

More laughter bubbled up and Emma let it loose. "That was my plan, too." She sucked in air and fought the tears of hilarity that welled up. "One time. Just one night with Dage." She wiped her eyes.

Katie pressed her head back against the tree. "I take it your plan didn't work out quite that way?"

"Um, no." Emma shook her head and sighed. "You let a guy like that under your skin, into your heart, and once is never enough." She kicked a pebble. "There's never enough." His blood flowed through her veins and her heart beat in tempo with his.

Dust billowed when Katie tossed the stick back down. "Yeah. You probably think I'm pretty stupid, huh?"

"No." Emma leaned back against her tree. "I think you're human. Lost and searching like the rest of us."

"That sucks. And . . . neither you nor I are human, Emma."

She hadn't truly let herself consider that fact. "Katie, what about my vision? I told you about seeing you running through some alley, angry and scared."

"Yeah, you did." Tawny eyes sparkled for a moment. "I'm not worried, Emma. Even without the ability to shift, I'm a hell of a fighter. If someone chooses to chase me through an alley, they're going to get hurt."

Emma smiled. "Katie, I need you here for now. I need your blood to keep an eye on the progression of the virus." She cleared her throat. "I also want to learn to fight—if you wouldn't mind giving me a few lessons." The karate classes she'd taken in college seemed so far in the past.

Katie sighed. "I'd be happy to teach you self-defense." She stood, brushing off her jeans. "Okay. I'll stay for a while, but when the time comes, I want the injection. And when I need to leave, I'm gone."

Emma nodded, pushing to her feet. "I'll help you, Katie. You know I will." God help them both.

Chapter 16

Sighing, Emma fought the urge to toss the computer print-out to the tiled floor of the small lab. Dage had been gone for hours and she'd thrown herself into the research to keep from thinking. Bleach and the odd scent of rubber filled the quiet space. "The AC21 sample does nothing to the virus." On paper, calculations showed the concoction would break down the proteins in the virus and demolish the little sucker. And it did in a test tube. But take the same virus attached to a chromosome and the little bastard seemed impenetrable. Damn it. If she had to put on the damn sterile rubber suit one more time today, she'd go nuts.

Kane rubbed a hand over his eyes, his charts spread across the table. "Did you try the sample on the virus or the cata-lyst?" He stood and stretched his back.

"Both." The sample was close to the new cancer treatment that infected chromosomes and defeated the cancer cells. "We're running out of samples of the catalyst. We'll need Maggie to give more blood." Of course, her blood could al-ready have transformed the virus into something unique to wolf shifters. Or werewolves.

Kane glanced at his watch, then back up. "Whose blood is in that vial?" He pointed to a sample set in a tray. "And why is it in this lab and not in the clean labs?"

"It's my blood and I'm not infected, so there's no need to

keep it in the clean lab." Emma frowned. She'd taken her own sample an hour ago, maybe she should draw another vial. She eyed the hammer sitting on the edge of the counter.

Kane raised an eyebrow and followed her gaze. "Er, okay. Are you afraid you've been infected?"

"What?" Emma turned to face him. "Oh, no. I've been taking samples since Dage marked me." A flush warmed her chest and slid like a river north to heat her cheeks.

"Oh. Forever the scientist, huh?" Kane grinned.

"Yes. Changing me from a human with twenty-three chromosomes to a near immortal with twenty-seven is amazing." Her mind still boggled when she considered the genetics involved. "I don't know where the science could lead us, but keeping accurate records of the process is vital."

Kane eyed the hammer. "And the weapon?"

Emma bit her lip and shuffled her feet. "I, er, well . . ."

Kane let loose with a chuckle. "Please tell me you weren't planning on harming yourself." He reached a large boned hand forward and grabbed the hammer to tap against his other palm. The handle disappeared in his large grasp.

"Well . . . it's just that, if I have Dage's healing abilities, I want to see how the process works." Man she felt like a dumbass. Her face burned hotter.

"No." Kane shook his head. "There's no guarantee you'll gain all of the same abilities as your mate, Emma." He tossed the hammer in a drawer where the iron clattered against wood. "Even if you do, it should take some time. Decades even."

Oh. Well crap. Good thing she'd chickened out before breaking her finger. "So if I broke a bone, it might take the usual amount of time to heal?"

"Yes." Kane's smile widened. "I can't wait to see your and Dage's sons blow up your kitchen in the name of scientific experimentation." With a low laugh, he turned back toward his research.

A low hum of pleasure slid through her skin at the thought.

Dage's kids—little silver eyed devils. She shook off the image. "Hey, I've been wondering. Why do vampires and Kurjans only procreate males?"

Kane turned back around. "Vamps and Kurjans have an X chromosome and a Z chromosome and only pass on the Z. So, it combines with one of the X chromosomes passed on by a woman, and you end up with an XZ baby, or a vampire. No matter what."

How odd to know if she and Dage had babies they'd all be little boys. "What about the demons? Are there female demons?"

"Yes there are female demons, but for some reason they're rare. Only one in five hundred babies born to demons are female."

Emma stiffened. "Is that on purpose?"

Kane raised both eyebrows. "No. Not at all. Female demon babies are celebrated as something rare and precious."

Well. That was as it should be. "What's the science involved?"

Kane rubbed his chin. "Demons have a D chromosome. Demon females have a DX combination and males have a DY, similar to humans." He grinned. "I wonder if your kids will be as curious about science as you are?"

She shrugged. The genetic implications from the different species truly fascinated her. Thinking of silver eyes, she closed her eyes and tried to reach out. *Dage? Can you hear me?*

Loud and clear, love.

Are you there yet?

"*Yes. Just waiting on Caleb's men before we go in. I need to concentrate now. Love you.* Shields rose like stalagmites to protect his thoughts.

"Humph." She frowned.

Kane laughed. "I take it the king shut you out?"

Emma swiveled on her chair. "Why do you do that?"

A Kayrs eyebrow rose. "Do what?"

"Call him *'the king.'* All of you use his title."

Kane rubbed his chin. "So we don't forget." Violet eyes swirled with wisdom. "Because Dage does forget. He jumps in front of each of us, an older brother needing to protect and defend."

"That's bad?"

"No. But he's the king. The figurehead of the entire monarchy. That means something." Kane shook his head. "The king needs to be protected. At almost all cost."

"Almost?"

Kane grinned. "After the queen, of course."

The idea of her being an actual queen made her want to laugh out loud. Emma rolled her eyes just as Janie and Cara strolled in.

Emma hugged her niece, letting the familiar scent of powder center her for a moment. "Why aren't you two resting?" Dark circles marred the too pale skin under Cara's bloodshot eyes. They had to fix this.

Cara sat wearily in a thick chair with a soft sigh. "Janie wouldn't take her nap until she talked to you." The bones in her neck protruded too much. While it was too early to show, Cara shouldn't be losing weight to this degree. To any degree, actually.

Emma knelt down and smoothed rioting brown curls off Janie's forehead. "What is it, sweetheart?" Oh please not the prelude to another painful vision. Not already.

Janie gulped in air. "You need to call Mowra. Right now. Call Mowra." She clutched Mr. Mullet with white hands. Emma had given the girl the bear with its odd blue mullet nearly two years ago. When life seemed normal. "Mowra can help fix my brother. Call Mowra."

Kane frowned and dropped to his haunches so he and Janie faced eye-to-eye. "How can Moira help, Janie?"

Blue eyes widened. "I dunno. But you need to call Mowra."

"Kane? Who's Moira?" Emma stood, her knees popping. Man, she needed to get back on a treadmill.

"Conn's mate. She's the seventh sister of the seventh sister." Kane picked Janie up to sit on a table.

Emma glanced at Cara, who gave a shrug. "Does that mean something?"

"Oh. Yes. Powerful witch. Very." Kane dug in a drawer for a lollipop, which he handed to Janie with flourish.

"Science is going to fix this, not magic." Emma peeked around Kane. How long had there been candy in the drawer?

Janie grabbed her hand, and Emma swung around to focus on her niece. The little girl scrunched her face in a tiny frown. "You said to trust what my head said. To trust what I hear and see."

Emma slowly nodded. "I did." Nobody would teach this little girl that her gifts were bad or something she shouldn't embrace. She'd made that vow the first day she'd discovered Janie had talent.

Wisdom swirled in those sapphire eyes. "So you trust me, Auntie Emma. Call Mowra."

The child was right. "Okay. Uncle Kane and I will call Mowra." Now she was agreeing to consult with witches. What was next?

"Moira," Kane corrected, tossing her a miniature candy bar. He reached out and assisted Cara to her feet. "You go take naps and we'll contact Conn's mate. I'm sure she'd love to hear from us." Teeth sparkled in a wise ass grin.

Emma held up a hand. "Um, just give us a second, okay?" She took Cara's arm and tugged her into the hall.

Cara leaned against the papered wall, an eyebrow raised. "What's up, Em?"

All right. What were the proper words here? "It's just, that . . . Well. I wanted you to fully understand you're no longer mated."

A frown settled between Cara's arched brows. "Yeah. I got that." She cocked her head to the side.

"It's just, well, I am going to destroy this virus. And you have choices."

A ghost of a smile played on Cara's lips. "Choices?"

Emma cleared her throat. "Yes." She sighed. Imaginary eggshells crunched under her feet. "I feel like fate didn't give you a chance. Or Talen didn't." Her brother-in-law seemed a force beyond nature. "You don't have to be mated to him."

A soft laugh breathed out of Cara. "I love you, Em."

What did that mean? "I love you, too."

Cara moistened her lips, pure delight shining in her eyes. "So please understand. That man is going to remate me if I have to stake him to the ground and land on his palm."

Relief made Emma's smile wide. "So you love him, huh?"

"With everything I am." Cara smiled. "I'm a big girl now, Emma. I know what I'm doing."

"Okay. I'm happy for you." Something warm settled around Emma's heart.

Cara grabbed her by the upper arms. "Time for you to fight for what you want."

Understanding and acceptance slid through Emma. "Dage."

"Yes. Dage."

"Yes. I am." She smiled at her sister. Death didn't stand a chance against the Paulsen women.

"Good." Cara leaned around the doorframe and called Janie, who hopped forward and took her hand. "We'll see you genetic geniuses later tonight." The two swept down the hall.

Emma crossed back into the lab, and Kane gave her a lopsided smile. The guy probably had super vampire hearing or something. She sighed. "We need to find an obstetrician and get an ultrasound machine."

He cleared his throat. "Talen has already contacted two obstetricians who will be here next week. But ultrasounds don't work on vampire babies."

"What? Why?"

Kane shrugged. "Let's just say the waves can't penetrate to see the baby—too much natural protection."

That might be good. Maybe the baby had some innate protection against the virus as well. Unlike Cara. "I'd like to study up on what to expect from a vampire birth." Emma had some work to do.

Kane nodded. "Of course." He tossed down his files. "I need to head into town for a few more supplies and we'll call Moira when I return. Want to come?"

"No thanks." Emma shifted back to her printouts. "I have a couple more thoughts with the AC21 sample I want to try while they're still fresh in my head."

"Okay." Kane left her to her work.

She studied the colorful chart. They'd combined the cancer treatment with a werewolf's blood—from the werewolf contained two floors down. And nothing. An idea began to tingle at the base of her neck. What if she combined the treatment with werewolf and vampire blood?

Excitement rushed through her. The protein would cling to the chromosome and perhaps antibodies from both werewolf and vampire would then attack.

A sudden, blaring alarm cut through the silence. She punched in keys on the nearest laptop, brought up the fourth clean lab, and gasped. Devon Jones lay on the floor surrounded by broken vials. What the heck had happened? And what the hell was he doing in Lab Four? Only she and Kane had access.

With her heart beating against her ribs, she ran down the hall and punched the code into the wall pad, leaning forward for the iris scan and giving her code. The door opened and she hustled inside, following the same procedure in both the ultraviolet room and the showers—overriding the computer's warnings that she hadn't followed the guidelines. Visions of Devon's goofy jokes and blushing face as he talked about Sandy Newcomb ran through her mind. She had to help him.

Finally she dashed into the lab, throwing the door closed behind her, only to slide across liquid and fall to her knees next to Devon. "Ouch." Her breath caught in her throat as she leaned over to peer at a piece of glass stuck in her knee. With a groan, she ripped it out and blood welled. She felt for Devon's neck.

His pulse was weak, and his eyes fluttered open. "Weird lasers. Get out. Get out right now."

Lasers? She looked around the room, seeing nothing out of the ordinary. "What are you talking about?"

The color returned to his face and he weakly pushed himself to a seated position. He pushed curly hair back from his forehead, his blue eyes bloodshot and a rueful smile sliding across his face. "Some weird red beam came from the camera and zapped me." He pointed to a camera in the far corner.

A laser in the camera? She frowned. They should probably get the heck out of the lab until she could figure out what happened. Blood, chemicals and broken vials littered the floor and caught Emma's gaze. Her knee already throbbed. "What in the hell are you doing in here?"

Devon sighed, struggling to his feet and holding out a hand to tug her up. "I'm sorry. Sandy screwed up with the protein results I gave you yesterday and she just panicked. Figured you'd fire her. So—"

"So you broke into a secured lab? Are you crazy?" Emma released his hand. "You know how secretive trade issues can become—we're dealing with drug patents that could earn billions of dollars."

"I know. But Sandy mixed up the ratio of protein to the antiviral agent, which would've really screwed up your research and rendered your samples moot."

Emma sucked in air. "I understand. But why not just call me? In the release you signed, you promised to follow all the rules as well as keep trade secrets." Damn but she hated lying to the man. She frowned. "How did you get in here, anyway?"

He rolled his eyes. "Do you have any idea the combined years of education a few of us have? It wasn't easy getting in here, but no system is perfect." He eyed the glass littering the floor and paled again. "I passed out against the counter and apparently made quite the mess. Please tell me we're not dealing with any type of airborne agents." Fear filled his voice.

"We're not," she guessed, glancing for the glass she'd removed. "Though we need to take a blood sample from you." As well as one from her. Hopefully the virus hadn't been on the glass that had cut her. The scent of bleach filled her nostrils. A beaker of the stuff had broken and spilled to the floor, where she'd tossed the glass. It'd be impossible to test what it had contained now. How many beakers down? At least five. And at least one of those had held the virus. Fear caught her breath in her throat.

The door slid open and two burly guards dodged inside, guns drawn. "Dr. Paulsen, are you all right?"

"Yes." She tugged Devon toward the door. "Please turn off the alarm, everything's fine." She wasn't sure what she'd do if the men stopped her, but they remained outside the lab. Seconds later the alarm thankfully cut off. All but running into the all access lab, she grabbed a syringe and turned toward Devon. "Roll up your sleeve."

Thirty minutes later she followed protocol after leaving the lab and emerged on the other side in a clean jumpsuit. Did she have a duty to tell Kane about Devon? Probably. Though she couldn't blame Devon for wanting to save his girlfriend's ass.

Emma rolled up her pant leg. A deep slash continued to bleed. Sharp pain attacked her nerves. What vial had nailed her, anyway? She surveyed the angry red flesh, tears burning her eyes. Okay. She could fix this. She took a deep breath and concentrated. Dage had the ability to heal himself, surely some of that had rubbed off on her.

She put all her energy into healing her skin, picturing the split ends mending together as Dage's chest had mended together in the forest. Nothing. Damn it.

With an irritated huff, she reached for the first aid kit under the table and sprayed antiseptic before covering her knee with a white bandage. What were the odds she'd been infected? Probably slim. Though certainly it was possible. She opened her mind to search for Dage, but his shields remained tightly in place. A chill of dread wound down her spine. Where was the king?

The king tapped his communicator. "Caleb, your men in place?"

"Yes. I took out the two guards on the south entry." His friend's deep voice came clearly across the line. "Waiting for your mark."

Dage gave a hand signal to Jordan. The shifter nodded, his entire body prepared to run for the building. He'd remain in human form unless werewolves or enemy shifters made an appearance.

"Talen, at your ready," Dage hissed.

He counted. One. Two. *Boom!* An explosion rent the peaceful night followed by two more as his brother opened the side of the main building. Bricks flew, dust billowed into the air along with fire, and the sound of gunfire pattered through the mess.

Grabbing his gun, he ran full bore into the smoke and through the gaping hole to immediately take one Kurjan soldier to the ground, ripping off his head. Blood sprayed across his face, burning like cigarette ashes. Two enemy soldiers rushed for him, one hit the floor when Talen leaped through the air, shooting green fire. Jase took out the other Kurjan by slashing a knife through the enemy's throat in a movement too fast to track.

Dage ran into the hallway, his back to the wall. Smoke

choked the oxygen and a high-pitched alarm began to trill through the compound. The steps and shouts from running men competed with the rhythmic warning.

He found his center and silence descended within his mind, within his soul. The soldier threw the king out of the way, and his intent focused with a razor's edge. Clarity of purpose calmed him as he ran into the murk.

"We're in the communication room," Conn said through the earpiece. "Prophet Milner is three floors down in a small cell. Two guards visible outside the door." A rapid typing could be heard. "Stairwell located in northeast corner." He typed again and swore. "Guiles isn't here."

Dage gave a short nod. "Good strategy. Find where they took Guiles." Thin smoke filtered through the air. "Team one to stairwell, teams two and three provide cover," he ordered. Green fire shot from ahead and he ducked and rolled, coming up firing. "Jase. Clear the path." Hopefully Jase had practiced using his gift to control the elements.

Dage's youngest brother emerged at his side in combat gear, his gaze toward the smoke, one hand outstretched. The smoke began to swirl, gathering speed and energy like a tornado. With a flick of Jase's wrist, the entire mass rushed down the hall, scattering bricks, dirt, and bodies.

One Kurjan soldier became caught up in the swirling mass and cried out when he hit the wall, bones breaking and blood spraying like rubies through the mist. He crumbled toward the hard-packed earth, and the walls trembled when he landed.

Jase grinned. "You want fire next?"

"Move now." Dage's boots echoed against the ground, leaping over bodies and debris.

Talen set a charge at a heavy metal door. "Fire in the hole."

Everyone ducked and protected their heads. A loud explosion rocked the building, and heat flashed across Dage's skin even through the protection. Battle sounds silenced for a moment as if the building itself drew a breath. Then cries, grunts, and gunfire echoed again in his earpiece.

Time slowed.

His vision sharpened.

Dage jumped into the gaping hole and cleared one flight of stairs, ducking when a sharp blade slashed at his neck. He pivoted and shot a roundhouse kick toward a Kurjan soldier, throwing him back against the cement block wall. Talen was on him within a second, knife flashing.

Three more Kurjans ran up the stairs, red hair flying, sharp incisors glimmering in the dim light. Talen froze one in place with a thought, and the Kurjan's purple eyes widened in shock and surprise.

"I never get tired of seeing you do that." Dage chuckled, then threw his shoulder into the gut of a soldier, and flipped him onto the floor. The bastard slashed a blade into Dage's calf. "Ouch." One plunge of Dage's knife ended the fight.

"Thank you." Talen threw the second soldier at Jase, who blocked a punch and kicked the laser gun out of the Kurjan's hand. The soldier aimed a punch at Jase's head, then howled in pain when his hand smacked into an invisible wall, the sound of bones breaking echoing over the blaring alarm.

Jase reached out and almost casually decapitated the monster with a clean slice of a double-edged knife.

Dage shifted his gaze to his brother. "How did you do that?"

Jase shrugged. "I just rearranged the oxygen molecules until they hardened to granite. No big deal."

No big deal? Kane was correct. Dage hadn't been using Jase's gifts. "Right." Dage focused on the still standing Kurjan, its muscles shaking with the need to break free of Talen's mental hold. "He's not very strong."

"No." Talen took a deep breath. "I can't kill him like this."

Dage shrugged. "So knock him out. I don't care."

The Kurjan hit the floor.

"You to the third level yet?" Conn said through the earpiece.

"No. We ran into resistance." Dage led the way down the steps, increasing his pace to a jog.

"Step on it. The Kurjans got a message out—reinforcements arrive within ten minutes." Conn swore, then the sound of a neck snapping filled the line. "Sorry. This one snuck up on me." The alarm abruptly cut off. "I'm going to blow the control room and go create a return path for you. Be clear in five. Conn out."

"I'll take lead," Dage said, jumping down a flight of stairs.

"No." Talen leapt over the railing, landing several cement steps ahead.

"I've got the rear," Jase muttered.

Dage began jogging behind his brother. "What the hell? You two are *flanking* me? I taught you both to fight."

Talen reached the landing and readied his stance. "It's a fine job you've done. But we're at war and losing our king would be, er, bad."

Dage reached the landing with Jase on his heels, hating when his brother was right. He yanked his gun from his waist to point at the industrial metal door. Checking to see Jase in position, the king nodded to Talen.

A swift kick had the door exploding open followed by green bursts of fire. Dage swiveled out of the way, shielding Talen whether he wished it or not. The man had a child on the way. Three bullets hit Dage's vest, knocking him back a step. A hazy wall instantly appeared before him to be punctured by green blasts which dropped to the floor with heavy pings.

Jesus. He eyed Jase out of the corner of his eye. "Quite the talent."

"I can't hold it." Jase leveled his gun. "Shoot now."

The wall disintegrated and Dage fired. A howl of pain

echoed through the underground space. "That's why you aim for the neck and not the vest, dumbass."

Talen dodged past him, throwing a Kurjan against the far wall while Jase took two soldiers on, wind whipping their hair into their faces.

Dage darted past the fight, boots pounding throughout the dim tunnel, his eyes scouting ahead. Why weren't there more guards?

Conn's voice echoed in his earpiece. "Reinforcements arrive in three minutes. Hurry, damn it."

Dage came to the end of the corridor and set his back against the wall before taking a deep breath, pivoting on one heel, and darting around the corner. His shot hit the first guard between the eyes. It went down, blood spraying. Not dead, but certainly unconscious for the duration.

The second guard lifted his weapon and failed to get off a shot before Dage was on him, knife sliding through cartilage and bone like scissors through silk. Another young soldier.

Standing, Dage studied the heavy metal door with industrial locks. A flick of his wrist had the locks disengaging with loud clicks. He yanked the door open, weapon at the ready.

The prophet sat bound and gagged on hard-packed earth, his back against the cement blocks of the wall, his eyes a bizarre mixture of yellow and blue. Dage had never seen Milner's vampire colors. He'd figured the guy had only metallic brown eyes.

Dage jumped inside, slashing through the ropes and helping Milner to his feet. The sour smell of anger mixed with fear in the small cell.

The prophet stumbled. "Sedatives." He clutched a bony hand into Dage's arm. "Lily?"

"She's secure." Dage helped the prophet through the doorway, stopping to survey the hall before dragging the man toward the stairwell to find Jase and Talen at ready. "Go," he ordered.

Talen took the lead while Dage half carried Milner up the stairs and through the deserted hallway, their boots thudding on the floor, smoke covering every surface.

The sun blasted down as they ran out of the building. The Kurjans couldn't follow them outside. Dage growled. "Casualties?"

"Several," Conn said through the earpiece, waving from outside an engaged Black Hawk. "We sent the severely injured to the Realm hospital in Canada, minor injuries went to Colorado."

"Caleb's forces?"

"Five to Canada, the rest home. They're good fighters." Conn helped Dage load Milner in the helicopter, jumping inside to flank the prophet. "Our troops and allies are clear."

Dage nodded, sliding the door shut after Jase and Talen had jumped inside. "Go."

The bird lifted into the sky and all eyes focused on the rapidly receding ground. "At your mark," Dage said.

Conn waited a moment, then pushed a button on the slim control in his hand. A rumble filled the air before the compound exploded. Bricks, bodies, and wood shattered into the sky to fall and litter the earth. Angry black smoke billowed into the air while fire ripped across the buildings, eating everything in a blaze of heat.

Prophet Milner gasped, his eyes wide and his hand at his throat. "You blew up the entire complex."

Dage smiled without any humor. "Welcome to the war, Prophet."

Chapter 17

Franco tipped his head back, allowing the fifty-year-old scotch to burn his throat. He gazed out the wall of windows in his office set into the cliffs of Baffin Island. The sea, cold and merciless, stared back. Calm, inscrutable but teeming with life he could only imagine. Life outside the walls.

Soon he'd lead his people to a destiny beyond their imaginations.

"Nunavut sucks," said a churlish voice from the doorway. "I'm not meant for Canada."

No. The boy was made for greatness. Franco inclined his head, inviting his nephew into the room. "Isolation suits me."

Kalin stalked inside and dropped into a chair on the other side of the marble desk. "Not me."

"No. Perhaps not." Franco settled into his leather chair and took another sip of scotch. His nephew had tied back his black hair, away from his not so pasty face. He'd find it easier than anyone in their race to pass for human—with makeup, and contacts to cover those purplish green eyes.

"I need to get the hell out of here."

Puberty did suck, if Franco remembered right. "The helicopter and planes are at your disposal."

Surprise flashed through Kalin's bizarre eyes. "They are?"

God. Who had green in their eyes, anyway? "Sure." Reaching for a gold coaster, Franco set the crystal down. "I understand your need to hunt. Please keep in mind I like it here, so I ask you to find women elsewhere. Take a weekend in Vegas, one in Omaha, and so on."

Kalin raised an eyebrow. "You don't mind?"

"Couldn't care less." So long as dead human females didn't pile up outside his door, of course. "Though you know this is a phase, right? The need to kill does abate." Well, maybe not abate. But it became honed, focused. Only truly worthy prey caught Franco's attention these days.

Kalin nodded. "Yes. Sometimes I'm already bored with the game. But then I think of the Kayrs family and the fun to come . . ." Sharp green dominated the purple through his eyes.

"The Kayrs and their prophesized child." Franco tapped long sharp nails on the desk. "I had looked forward to her aunt visiting. Before I killed her, of course."

"Of course." Kalin cocked his head to the side. "You have another long-term mate in mind, Uncle?"

"Yes." For years he'd dreamed about hair the color of sunshine and eyes the color of the darkest night. "Someday the prophet Lily will be mine." She'd bear him many fine sons.

Kalin threw back his head and laughed, the rumbling sound echoing off granite walls. "A Realm prophet as a Kurjan mate? Delicious."

Delicious—as was the moment when he'd slashed a knife through the throat of Lily's husband. The first Prophet Sotheby. The worthless spiritual leader had actually looked shocked when death arrived. As if prophets couldn't die.

"So if I visit Ohio, shall I stop in on Uncle Erik?" Kalin's eyes focused and his upper lip twisted.

Little prick. "Of course. My brother is the finest scientist alive today." As well as the absolute worst soldier. "Give him my regards."

Interest sizzled through Kalin's eyes and he sat forward.

"Erik's coming along on the virus, isn't he? I mean, we're that much closer to creating a werewolf slave class?"

Franco nodded. "Yes. He's still fine-tuning it, but I have complete confidence in his results. We already know the bug works on mates. Perfectly." His groin hardened as he thought of Lily. So fair. So defenseless. No longer mated.

"Excellent. How did the raid this afternoon go?"

"As planned." Thunder rumbled outside and Franco glanced toward the churning sea. "The king rescued Prophet Milner."

"Did Kayrs find the locating bug?" Kalin let loose with a grin.

Franco sighed. "Yes. All three of them, in fact." Lightning lit the sky over the ocean. "It was a long shot, to be sure."

"I told you so." Kalin sat back and crossed his arms. "We still have Prophet Guiles, right?"

"Of course." Well hidden, too. The Realm wouldn't find him. "Anything else?" He had a conference call and he held his contact within the Kayrs organization to himself.

Kalin shook his head and stood. "No. I'll take the plane tonight."

"Good." Franco grabbed his drink and took a healthy swallow. "Kalin? Stay away from the Kayrs family. We're not ready to take them yet. Your father will be avenged."

Sharp canines flashed in the parody of a smile. "No worries. I plan to avenge my father on my own time." He paused, gazing at the battle waging through the ocean. "Though Janie Belle has a new protector I'd like to hunt."

"Vampire?" Franco appreciated the boy's ventures into the dream world, even if they hadn't figured out how to use the ability to their advantage yet.

Kalin shrugged. "Maybe. I can't get a handle on him yet." He strode toward the door. "But I have a feeling killing him will be one of the greatest moments of my life."

Chapter 18

Emma tapped her foot against the tiled floor in the lab's communication room while Kane typed furiously on a keyboard, having returned nearly an hour ago. The soldiers had of course reported Devon's break-in to Kane the second he returned. Though she hadn't said a word about her injury.

"Devon was just trying to help a coworker, Kane." She brushed a curl off her face.

Kane shrugged. "I don't care. He broke protocol and is lucky I just fired him."

Temper swirled at the base of her skull. "Or what?"

Angry violet eyes met hers as Kane stopped typing. "Do you have any idea how many of our laws he broke in addition to breaching his contract? He's lucky he's still walking."

"Speaking of which, why in the hell do you have lasers that knock people out?" Of course no one had told her about the security measures.

"For this very reason I designed them to recognize faces . . . or attack."

Emma took a deep breath. She needed Kane's cooperation. "There's really no reason to tell Dage—"

Kane halted her with his palm in the air facing her. "No way. Don't even ask me to keep this from him." He turned back to the keyboard.

Butthead. Speaking of the king, where the heck was he?

She lowered her mental shields and sent out a call for Dage, careful to keep her injury away from her thoughts.

Hello love. Miss me? His deep voice filled her head.

Relief relaxed her shoulders. *Yes. Is the fight over?* This ability to communicate via thought was handy, and she wondered idly how the brain waves shifted into patterns to send out and receive messages. They'd have to conduct some tests when things slowed down.

Yes. We're on the way home. We didn't lose anyone but do have some casualties. I'll fill you in when I return in a few minutes. Shields rose again.

Emma nodded and shifted her focus to the screen covering the entire north wall of the room. She'd worked all afternoon on combining werewolf and vampire blood with the right protein, which had shown promise in attacking the catalyst. But something still protected the twenty-seventh chromosome and maybe Moira had the key.

A woman took shape, thick red hair rioting in curls around a face carved from pure alabaster. No sun for that gal. Green eyes narrowed on Emma, and a slow grin tipped generous lips. "So you're the king's mate. I'm Moira."

Emma gave a short nod. "Nice to meet you. Emma Paulsen here." Conn's mate was a beauty, no doubt about it.

Moira's grin turned to a full smile. "You haven't married Dage yet, then?" She rolled the *r*s like someone in a Celtic movie.

"No." Not that he'd asked. "Did you marry Conn?"

The witch lost her smile. "No. Not going to, either."

Kane's muted, "We'll see about that," was ignored by both women.

Emma cleared her throat. "So, you're probably wondering why we're contacting you."

Moira nodded. "Yes. I assume you need a witch for something."

How in the hell could Emma explain it? "Are you aware of Virus-27?"

"Yes. Conn sent word that vampire mates were in danger." Moira's lips tightened into a firm line. "I can take care of myself, Emma."

"I'm sure you can." Emma smiled. "But, well, we thought you could help with a cure."

"How?"

Emma shrugged. "I don't know. My niece Janie gets visions, and she thinks you can help with the science."

Moira tilted her head to the side. "I know about your niece. Some of our seers predicted her birth."

The breath caught in Emma's throat. Enough prophesying about a little girl. "Why?"

"Don't know. Apparently she's the key to the future—all our futures." Moira gave a half shrug. "No pressure there, poor darlin'."

No kidding. "I thought if we sent you all the data on the virus you might see a place to contribute."

Moira smiled again. "You're a scientist, right?"

"Geneticist."

A dimple flirted in Moira's flawless skin. "*Ceart go leor.* So you know any contribution I'd make would be in the form of magic?"

"Yes. I was marked by a vampire the other night, Moira. I'm willing to go on a bit of faith here."

Moira chuckled. "Good point." She stepped closer to the camera. "What makes you think magic was used to create this virus?"

Emma struggled for a moment. "I don't." She waited for the truth to piss off her new friend.

A genuine smile met her gaze. Moira gave a quick shake of her head. "Really? Ever study a virus like this?"

"No. But I've also never worried about a twenty-seventh chromosome." The virus fit the victims.

"Ah." Moira tilted her head to the side. "If magic is involved here, you're looking for a rather powerful witch who cast the spell."

"Like you?"

"*Ba mhaith liom.* Er, I mean, Yes."

Emma's mind calculated the new information. "If magic is somehow involved, how many people across the globe would have the necessary capability?"

"People?" Moira gave a nod to someone off camera. "You mean witches, my sister."

Inhaling deeply, Emma sought her inner reason. "Witches. And we're not sisters—neither of us married a Kayrs."

Moira's green eyes narrowed with a focus that could be felt across the globe. "There's a rather strong theory that potential vampire mates are descendants of the fey people, cousins to my people." She reached for a stack of papers. "Your information just came through—I'll look it over and get back to you."

Fey people? Unlikely. "You didn't answer my question." Would Moira help them?

Silence crackled across the space for a moment. "I have no idea how many people could pull something like this off." Moira stepped closer to the screen, her gaze running over Emma's form. "Exactly what do you think magic is, Emma?"

Uh, hocus pocus? "I don't know. Something about being naked under the moon, goddesses, and pretty spells?"

Moira threw back her head and laughed. "Not quite. What do you know about quantum physics?"

An unwilling curiosity welled up in Emma. "Not much except that it's a modern theory that explains the nature and behavior of energy and matter on the atomic and subatomic level." She raised an eyebrow. "You've studied quantum physics?"

Moira smiled. "I have several doctorates, one in quantum physics, and I teach at the University of Dublin as well as at a school you've never heard of. On a subatomic level, the right application of energy is able to alter matter, right?"

"Possibly." No one really knew. "So quantum theory explains magic?"

Moira shrugged. "What do you know about string theory?"

Emma coughed out a laugh. "String theory is a new theory that attempts to reconcile quantum physics with the general relativity theory." In a nutshell.

"Right. And there are five different string theories that all agree on one fact: that there are dimensions in space and time and everything's connected." Moira took another step closer to the camera. "These theories are from your scientists, Emma. The experts believe in dimensions—and the possibility of moving throughout them."

"So you're saying magic can be explained by quantum physics and string theory?"

"Well, those theories plus about nine more your people haven't figured out yet." Moira grinned. "What's important is that you believe. That's it. Start believing." She sighed, glancing at Kane and then back at Emma, her eyes darkening. "If you don't mind my asking, where did the king mark you?"

Quite the personal question. But a valid one, considering the witch also had been branded by a Kayrs brother. "On the upper right shoulder," Emma said, irritated. "You?"

"Front of my left hipbone." Moira rolled her eyes. "Bloody inconvenient if I want to wear a bikini."

Emma nodded in commiseration. "Yes. You'd think through the hundreds of years the Kayrs family could've devised a way to mate without branding anyone."

Moira shook her head. "Oh, Emma. They don't want another way. They *like* the marking." Her tone turned cutting by the end of the sentence.

"Men." Emma cleared her throat. She'd love to get a sample of Moira's blood. "So you're another immortal?"

Moira took a deep breath. "Well, mainly immortal. We can die from beheading and burning." She glanced off camera and then focused back on Emma. "I sent Kane a list of supplies you may need to counter a possible spell—have them ready. I'll read over your information and then work on a spell to counter the virus. Until then, *Slán go foil.*"

The screen went black.

"Good-bye for now." Emma repeated the one Gaelic phrase she knew. "Moira's beautiful. I can understand Conn's attraction." Pure spirit shone through those stunning eyes—the witch wouldn't go down easy. She wondered just how strong the greatest soldier claimed by the Realm would need to be if he thought to take Moira out of Ireland.

Kane rubbed a hand over his chin. "Yeah. You ever get the feeling all hell is about to break loose?"

Emma forced a grin. "In the last week I've been kidnapped by a monstrous vampire race, my sister has been knocked up by a vampire prince and I've been branded by a king, who also bites. I've discovered shifters and demons exist, and the niece I've protected since birth is somehow prophesized to do something important by these supernatural beings. I'm also seeking help from a century old witch who looks twenty." She exhaled loudly. "Hell already has broken loose and shattered reality."

Kane gathered papers and gestured her toward the door. "On that note, you might want to begin believing in magic. I think we're going to need it."

Once upon a time the same people who developed the scientific method also practiced magic. She'd have to keep her mind open to the idea of combining the two again. Where in the heck were her old college physics textbooks? In storage with the rest of her belongings, probably. She stepped into the hall and ran smack into Conn still in his combat gear, a rough purple bruise spread across his left cheekbone.

He righted her with gentle hands near the top of her biceps. His gaze met Kane's. "Prophet Guiles wasn't there. We found Prophet Milner and he's being seen to by the doctors right now—he seems fine to me."

"Any casualties?" Kane asked.

Conn nodded. "All being taken care of." He dropped his gaze to Emma. "You talked to Moira?" His eyes swirled a pure emerald, much darker than that of his mate.

Smoke and the odd scent of gun powder clung to the air around Conn. Emma stepped back and raised an eyebrow. "Just now. How did you know?"

The soldier gave a short shrug. "I always know where she is and what she's doing. Though I'd appreciate it if you wouldn't say anything." His smile would've melted a harder heart than Emma's. He turned toward his brother. "Is my mate in danger?"

"Yes."

"Because she's a mate?" Conn released Emma and stepped back.

Kane tapped his file against his leg. "Yes. Also, if magic helped create the virus, she's one of the few witches alive powerful enough to counteract it."

The smile sliding across Conn's broad face made Emma nervous and she couldn't help but intervene. "If Moira is that powerful, I'm sure she can handle any danger. Right?"

Conn's shoulders went back even further. "Wrong." He gave a short nod to his brother, pivoting to stride down the hall. "We find Prophet Guiles, and then I take Ireland," he called back.

Emma slapped her hands on her hips, rounding on Kane. "You're no help."

Humor filled his lavender eyes. "Because I agree with my brother?"

Damn it. How could they all be so dense? She tilted her head to the side. "I can't wait to meet your mate, Kane."

Kane shrugged. "Fate will plan well. My mate will be a logical woman, probably a scientist, who understands the rationale here. I'm not concerned."

Laughter bubbled up and Emma let it fly. "Oh Kane. If I've learned nothing else this past month, fate employs a wicked sense of humor." She wiped tears from her eyes.

"Now that's a beautiful sound." Dage rounded the corner and advanced like a man with purpose. One hand cupped her jaw, and he lowered his head to take.

A buzzing filled Emma's head and heat filled every pore while her tongue tangled with the king's. He backed her into the wall, the cool bricks contrasting with the heated vampire pressed against her front. Her knees began to tremble, and she clutched both hands into his bulletproof vest to keep from sliding to the floor.

The outside door slammed from Kane's rather quick exit.

Dage lifted his head, eyes swirling with sparks of color. "Miss me?"

For answer she stretched up on her tiptoes to run her tongue along the cord of muscle in his neck. Salt and power exploded on her taste buds and she sighed, rubbing her nose against his heated skin. "Yes." She relaxed and stepped back to survey him head to toe. "Any injuries?"

"No."

Copper scented the air and an odd twinge vibrated from the king's calve. "Then why is your leg bleeding?" She frowned, beginning to bend.

Strong hands at her elbows kept her in place. "'Tis nothing." He cocked his head to the side. "What's wrong?" Sucking in a breath, he centered them both in concentration.

Emma raised an eyebrow, her gaze meeting his. "Ah, nothing. In fact, we made excellent progress today. The scientific kind." Could he feel the vibrations from her stinging knee?

Sweet dimples flashed in a predatory face. "That's good news, love." He lost his smile and a frown descended between his eyes. "You're in pain."

"No. I'm fine." She took a step back. Oh this was so not going to be good.

Dage gave a low growl and bent at the waist, yanking up her pant leg. His lids lowered as he gazed at the blood seeping through the white gauze. "What the hell happened?"

Emma shrugged, trying to pull away. "Nothing. Really, I'm fine."

His shoulders tensed and he unwrapped the bandage with gentle hands to study the wound. "Ouch. How did you get hurt?" Burning silver eyes lifted to pin her with fury. "I'll kill Kane."

A trembling set up in her stomach. "No. He wasn't in the lab—he had gone to town for more supplies." She wouldn't let anyone else get blamed for this.

"You were cut in the lab? Which lab?" Dage's voice dropped to a hoarse rumble that had her back stiffening.

"The clean one." She glanced toward the door. "I need to get another bandage." And escape from what appeared to be a livid vampire.

Dage stood, put his wrist to his teeth and ripped open his skin. He pressed his vein to her mouth. She hesitated for a moment, then giving in, she closed her lips over his flesh, a low murmur of pleasure escaping as that loaded liquid slid down her throat. A buzzing set up in her ears. Stars swirled before her eyes. With a soft sigh, she released him, glancing down at her knee. The wound closed into healthy pink skin with no pain—almost as if the king's blood held a painkiller in its powerful depths.

She licked her lips. Maybe she was turning into a vampire.

Dage took her hand and strode into the office, where he punched in a series of code on the computer. An image of Lab Four came into view. Another series of code and the video reversed until she watched herself help Devon. Dage stilled to stone next to her.

He lifted his head to pin her with a gaze. "You ignored protocol?"

"Yes."

"Were you going to tell me about the human?"

The way he said the word *human* irritated her. "I was considering it."

Without a word, Dage grabbed her hand again and began

stalking down the hall. She could either jog along or fall on her ass. He pushed open the heavy metal door to the armory, shrugging out of his vest with a roll of strong shoulders, fury choking the room. Various knives and guns found their homes on different shelves.

"I should get back to work." She fought the urge to flee, channeling the adrenaline pumping through her veins into the will to remain still.

Night shot through the light silver of his eyes, turning them a pure blue closer to black. "You think you're going back to work?" His gaze pinned her in place as he awaited her answer, the muscles bunching under his skin. "What are the chances you're infected?"

She'd seen a myriad of color combinations in those eyes, but that one was new. Her rough swallow echoed in the deadly silent room. "They're slim. I mean, I have no idea what the beaker contained."

"How many beakers broke?"

She shrugged. "At least five." Worrying about it would accomplish nothing.

"Did any of those contain the virus?" Concern and anger swirled together in his deep voice.

"Yes." Saying the word out loud punched concern into her belly. She couldn't get sick. Who would find a cure for Cara? "I took tests. We'll know for sure in twenty-four hours." Her lungs inflated as she sucked in air. "I need to go—I have a virus to cure."

"To cure." He repeated her words without infliction, his face hardening to stone.

Dread pooled in her abdomen. His quiet calm was scaring the shit out of her. "Yes. I'm only doing what needs to be done here, Dage." Why couldn't he understand that?

"You. Putting yourself in danger." He studied her as if seeing her for the first time, his jaw clenched so tight it had to hurt. "It's all about you, isn't it? Finding a cure—facing any danger. All on your own."

As quick as that, her temper spiraled to life. "Yes. The man works for me—I had a duty to try and save him." Probably a serious miscalculation. It wasn't wise to piss off the king.

Awareness flashed across his hard face. "I've handled this entire situation poorly." He spoke mildly to himself as if she were no longer part of the conversation.

"Um, I don't understand." She certainly hadn't expected an apology.

His gaze refocused on her face and one broad hand manacled her arm. "No. You don't."

She had no choice but to follow him from the room and down the long hallway. "Care to explain?"

"Yes, that would be best," he agreed, opening the door and all but dragging her into the bright sunshine. For a moment his large body blocked out the sun. "I thought to ease you into this life, to prepare you for the battles to come."

Sunshine burned her eyes when he moved, and she shifted her gaze to the dark forest. "Yes, well. I should be prepared for this war." What the hell was he getting at?

He gave a sharp shake of his head, striding down the path toward the residence facility. "No. I thought you'd come to understand this life in a logical manner, one that makes sense." Birds chirped happily above and the wind rustled strong pine through the trees. "I was wrong."

Enough of this crap. She jerked her arm free and rounded on him, her tennis shoes kicking up dirt. "What in the hell are you talking about?"

No kindness or softness remained on the king's face. Determination settled hard across those unyielding features. "Our mates are the reason we breathe, the reason we live and fight."

Okay. He was pissed she'd ignored safety protocols. "I understand—"

"No." A dark flush worked its way across his high cheekbones. "I learned a long time ago when something or somebody threatens your family, you strike fast and you strike hard."

As did she. "Of course."

He clasped her arm again, stalking forward through the trees. "Your stubborn, willful, and untrusting actions continue to threaten my mate. My family. This need to court danger ends now."

He wouldn't allow her to jerk free, just kept striding toward the building emerging into sight. "Let me go."

He swung her around and pinned her against the rough wooden siding next to the door, once again blocking out the sun. "No." A flash of fury broke through his stone façade to be quickly smoothed out. "You're restricted to the family quarters."

Her anger rose to match his. "No way in hell. I need to continue to work in the lab." Her mind sought reason, a way to make him see logic. "You're the king—it's my duty and you damn well know it."

He lowered his face to within an inch of hers. "I have made it abundantly clear it's the man who claims you, not the king. You should've listened. Your sole duty is to me and me alone."

Butterflies winged through her stomach and temper threatened to explode out of her. "You arrogant ass."

His hand circled over her neck, effectively immobilizing her. "For a smart girl, your instinct for self-preservation is sorely lacking. Heed my warning, Highness. Don't push again."

Her eyes opened wide even as he tapped his earpiece, cocking his head to listen. "I'll be right there." He slowly straightened, his hand sliding down her neck to the center of her chest. "This discussion is over, love."

A haze pounded down over her vision as a fury she'd never known whipped through her. Her knee shot upward and only inhuman reflexes kept the king from having his balls rammed to his throat.

Quick as a whip he lashed out, grasping her arms and tossing her over his shoulder to stride inside the building, passing the guards and issuing orders. "I want two guards on the door to my quarters. My mate remains inside."

She lacked time to struggle before the doors opened and he maneuvered to the bedroom where she flew through the air and landed on the big bed. She bounced twice, too stunned to speak. Quick strides had him again through the living area, the doors sliding shut and the click of a lock snapping into place.

Emma ran forward and tugged on the doors. Son of a bitch. She'd kill him.

Chapter 19

Dage settled into the leather chair, getting damn tired of the conference room. His gaze focused on the prophet sitting across the slate oval table. Puffy wrinkled bags perched high on Milner's cheekbones and his bony shoulders slumped more than usual. A deep red gash marred his neck while his eyes had returned to their normal chocolate color. Dage cleared his throat. "When will his blood tests be finished?"

Kane glanced up from the printout in his hands. "A few more minutes."

Milner sat forward. "You think they injected me with the virus?"

Lily patted his spotted hand, her own pale and so small. "I'm sure you're fine, Samuel. The virus doesn't impact vampires."

Dage frowned. "Lily. You should be resting." He'd had it with women and their complete disregard for safety. For the love of Pete. Could the woman wear a pair of jeans once in a while? The long skirted dresses made her appear even more fragile and ill-equipped for this dangerous world.

Her narrowed onyx gaze pinned him. "I'm fine, King. You're not the only one with a duty to fulfill."

"Of course not." Dage did not fucking believe Emma had ignored all safety protocol. What if the virus had mingled with her blood? Fear at losing her nearly made his throat close. He struggled to keep focused. One of his duties was protecting the prophets and so far he was doing a piss-poor job. "Has Talen found Prophet Guiles yet?"

Conn shook his head. "No."

The chair creaked in protest when Dage sat forward. "Prophet Milner? Did the Kurjans who captured you say anything about Guiles?"

The prophet shook his head. "No. There was a pinch to my neck and I was out cold. I woke up bound in the room where you found me." Bound and gagged. Their spiritual leader treated like a prisoner.

Kane's cell buzzed and he lifted the phone to his ear for a short conversation. His gaze met Dage's and he snapped the phone shut. "The prophet's blood is clean. As is mine."

"No sign of the virus?" Lily asked.

"None. Though we need a full twenty-four hours to make sure."

"Well, I'm sure he hasn't been infected." Lily stood and assisted Milner to his feet. "Samuel has been debriefed and should probably get some rest." She escorted the prophet to the door where guards waited. "Please inform us if you hear anything about Prophet Guiles." The door shut quietly behind them.

Conn sat back, his gaze narrowing on the king. "What the fuck's your problem?"

Dage lifted an eyebrow as he faced two of his brothers across the table. "Excuse me?"

Sharp canines flashed in a parody of a smile. "Stop being the king for a minute. What's wrong?" Conn pushed his chair back.

"I need a workout." Dage flashed his own teeth. Apparently the battle hadn't been enough for him. He still needed to hit something.

Conn shot to his feet. "Excellent. I suggest you forget you're the king while we're sparring, because I already have." Two strides had him throwing open the doors. "I'll meet you in the gym." He didn't look back.

Dage cut his gaze to Kane. "Care to join in?"

"Hell no." Kane rubbed his chin. "You're both pissed, and I'm sure I'll need to be the voice of reason after you pummel the shit out of each other." He stood, his eyes narrowing. "Besides. I owe Talen a beating. We're meeting up in an hour. Clean up your blood when you're finished, please."

They rose and Dage reached the door first. "You're still mad at Talen?"

Kane shrugged. "No. But he needs to hit something and I need to train, so the gym seemed like a good idea."

"I may stick around to watch," Dage mused. Talen fought with heat and strategy while Kane owned cold logic. Both men were deadly. It'd be a good fight. "Ah, when Emma ignored protocol and entered the main lab without a protective suit, she got cut by a broken vial."

Kane stopped cold. "Excuse me?" Incredulous purple eyes flashed. "Did the vial initially hold the virus?"

"We couldn't tell. She's taken her blood and so far there's no sign of the virus, but the whole floor including the broken glass had been contaminated by bleach." Dage rubbed a hand over his chin, quelling fear. Damn but he couldn't lose her now. "I've issued orders she's not allowed out of the family quarters."

"That seems harsh. Plus it'll delay our research significantly." Kane shrugged and headed down the hallway, calling over his shoulder, "You might want to rethink that decision, King."

Dage was allowing emotion to cloud logic, and he knew it. He turned the other way, his mind spinning while he sprinted down the cement stairwell and past the pool to the sparring room with its thick black mats. He had no sooner entered the gym when a heavy body tackled him to the ground while plunging a fist into his jaw.

With a growl, Dage flipped Conn over his head and leaped

to his feet, wiping blood off his chin. "That how you want it?"

Conn rolled to his feet, his eyes narrowing and a dangerous grin lighting his face. "No rules."

"Agreed." The king lunged.

Emma paced back and forth, fury making breathing difficult.

"You need to settle down," Cara said from her perch on the broad leather sofa. "You're going to make yourself sick."

"Settle down?" Emma whirled toward her sister, her heart beating against her ribs. "He *locked* me inside here."

Cara glanced around the spacious suite decorated in early antiques. "We've been locked in much worse." Her voice came out breathy and weak, as if she had to struggle to force out sound.

Emma huffed out an irritated breath. "I wasn't thinking about the closet Daddy used to lock us in. The prick."

"Then what were you thinking about?" The dark circles marring her skin did nothing to detract from the intelligence in Cara's blue eyes.

"I trusted Dage. I trusted him to understand my job and look what happened." Emma swept an arm out. "I'm locked in."

"Well. He let me visit." Cara shivered and grabbed a blanket to cover her legs.

"Bully for him." Concern slid down Emma's spine. The room was plenty warm, but Cara must be chilled. Not good.

Cara bit her lip. "I'm mad at you, too."

Emma stopped pacing. "Why?"

"Why?" Cara jumped to her feet, letting the blanket slide to the floor. "Why? You dumbass. What if the glass that cut you had the virus on it? What if you've been infected now? Why would you put yourself in such danger?" Her voice rose to a shout at the end and she settled her hands on her hips.

Emma took a step back. "I had a duty to save Devon. It

would've taken twenty minutes minimum for the computer system to be reprogrammed to let anyone but me in." She refused to consider the possibility that she might be infected. The weakness in her limbs was from pure anger toward Dage. And exhaustion. She hadn't slept in much too long.

"Who the hell said that was your job?" Cara grabbed a sofa pillow in one hand.

Anger boiled through Emma's stomach, and she ruthlessly stamped the fury down. "I'm in charge of the lab. It is my job."

The pillow nailed her full in the face. Cara grabbed another one. "You could've called for the guards, or at least put on a protective suit. But no."

Emma tossed the chenille projectile to the floor. She would not throw something at a pregnant woman. "I did what I had to do. And curing this virus is the only consideration on my mind." But when her sister had recuperated after giving birth, they were going to spar.

Cara breathed deep. "You weren't just worried about Devon. You ran in there to make sure your data was safe."

"Of course." Did Cara not understand the fact that the virus was replicating itself, getting stronger, preparing to rip apart her DNA this very second?

Cara glared. "We're not kids anymore."

"I'm well aware of our ages."

"I do not need you to put yourself between me and danger any more, Emma."

Her sister could barely stand up she was so weak. "Yes, you do. We're family."

"You won't let Dage stand before you."

"The situation isn't the same."

"The hell it isn't. He wants to protect you the same way you want to protect me and Janie." Cara stomped her foot. She actually stomped her freakin' foot. "You're not letting him."

Emma sighed. "I can't."

"Why not?" Cara deflated like an old balloon and sat back down on the couch, her hand trembling as she grabbed the blanket.

Emma sank her teeth into her lip. "What if I get used to him and then he leaves? Or I leave him?" If death won the little battle coming up next spring, she'd be blown to bits.

Cara pinched her nose. "For someone so smart, you are so stupid. He isn't going to hurt you. Not all men are like Daddy."

"Jesus. I know that."

A soft gaze pinned her in place as Cara focused. "Do you? Or is this all about something else?"

Unease fluttered along Emma's skin. "No."

"Really? Maybe you're still blaming yourself. Maybe you think you shouldn't find happiness." Cara paled further even as she straightened her shoulders.

"I'm done discussing this."

"No, you're not. What happened wasn't your fault. Let go of the past."

"I don't know what you're talking about." Why did she have the sudden urge to lose her lunch?

Cara sighed. "Of course you do. You've shared your visions with me before, Em. I'm sure you had one about the day our parents died."

Emma sank to the floor, her hands clutching the oak coffee table and her gaze on Cara. "You knew?"

"I guessed. I'd thought you dealt with the situation, but maybe not."

Tears filled Emma's eyes. "I let them die." She shook her head. "Mama was supposed to be safe at the library—I had no idea she'd be in the car."

"It wouldn't have mattered if you told either of them, Em." Cara reached forward and clasped Emma's hands. "Mama would've told him, he would've beat the crap out of you, and then gone on his normal way. There was no way to save them." She squeezed. "Deep down you know the truth."

Emma squeezed back. "I was afraid to tell you."

"I should've brought up this issue, but I thought it was in the past." Cara brushed a curl off her face. "I think I understand what's going on here. So if you're not risking yourself, not being the front line of defense"—Cara tilted her head— "what good are you to any of us?"

Emma gasped. "What do you mean?"

Cara shook her head sadly. "You protected me. You've cared for and helped me protect Janie." Her lips trembled. "Emma. You matter all by yourself. You don't need to stand in front of danger to matter. I love you just for being the pain in the ass you naturally are."

"I know."

"So does Dage."

"He still had no right to lock me in here."

Cara nodded. "We're going to use some serious effort bringing those guys into the current century." She snuggled back into the sofa. "So, tell me about your current research."

"The virus binds itself to the chromosomes like it has glue all over it." Emma's shoulders slumped. "We can't get to it. At least we can't without using magic."

"Magic?" A small grin lit Cara's face. "So. Tell me about Moira."

Dage wiped blood off his face with his ripped shirt, his back against the cool wall. "I can't see out of my left eye." He blinked several times to make sure. Nope. Pure darkness. Closing his lid, he concentrated on sending healing cells to the tissue.

Conn grunted next to him. "I think you broke my jaw."

An attempt at a grin had Dage wincing when his lip split further in two. "Sorry." He'd had to throw more than one serious punch to impact Conn's stubborn jaw.

"No worries," his brother said cheerfully. "This was fun."

Dage shook his head and could actually hear his brain rattle against his skull. "You have an odd idea about fun." He closed both eyes and began to heal the concussions. Lights flashed behind his lids while pain ripped through his system. Healing hurt almost as much as sustaining the original injury. Conn hit hard.

Conn shrugged and then groaned when three loud pops pierced the silence. "Broken ribs." He exhaled loudly. "All better."

Dage had felt those shatter against his knuckles. "Good." He opened his one good eye, pleased it didn't fall out of his head. "Should we talk now?"

"Sure. You go first." Conn sucked in air with a whistling sound, no doubt repairing a fallen lung.

The shredded knuckles on Dage's right hand began to mend together. "Emma rushed into a destroyed lab to save a human scientist as well as her damn research without observing any safety measures. She was injured." And possibly infected with the damn virus. Fear clawed through Dage's gut.

Conn grabbed his nose and twisted the cartilage back into shape with a loud crack. "That sucks. Though she is trying to save her sister." Another pop reformed his eye socket.

"We could both save her sister."

"Yeah. I assume that's a learned behavior."

"Meaning?"

"From what Cara has said about their childhood, I'm thinking Emma's first instinct isn't to run for help. To trust anyone else to help." Conn straightened his legs and crossed them at the ankles. Blood soaked through the denim in several places. "She needs to learn to do so—to change brain patterns."

"Humph. I hadn't thought of her situation that way." Dage's shoulder popped back into the socket with a jar that had him clenching his jaw.

"Sure." Conn's collarbone snapped back into place. "We had mother, father, and each other. Someone always had our backs. Emma had a younger sister to protect—that's all. She's doing what she did to survive her childhood."

Conn understood Emma better than Dage did. "I am such an asshole."

"True. But you love the woman. It's okay not to think straight."

Dage set his other shoulder back in alignment. "Your turn. Why don't you get your ass to Ireland and bring back your witch?"

Conn grinned. "We're at war with two nations—I've been trying to avoid a third."

Ah, damn it. He should've known Conn would put the Realm before his own happiness. "When you're ready to go, we go." He still had his brother's back.

"I know. She just finished her final training last year. I thought perhaps she'd come to me at that time." Genuine surprise flashed across Conn's battered face.

Dage chuckled. "I'm pretty sure that's not how it works. You'll need to make the effort to bring her back—that much I know." Women were complicated and mates were that— times a hundred. There should be a guidebook.

Conn nodded. "Yeah. I had hoped to ease her into the thought, but now that she's in danger, well . . ."

Dage stood and tugged his brother up. They swayed for a moment. "We go when you're ready."

Talen loped inside the door and stopped cold with Kane right behind him. "Jesus. Who won?"

"Was a draw," they answered at once, then broke into chuckles of laughter.

Kane shook his head. "You're both concussed."

Jase darted through the door, his shoes squishing the thick mat. "Damn. I missed the fight." He handed Dage a grape energy drink.

"Thanks." Dage clapped an arm around Jase's shoulders. "No worries. We'll do it again. By the way, you're now appointed as liaison to the Realm."

Jase stepped back. "What?"

Dage wiped blood off his cheek. "Kane made it clear not

too long ago that I'm not using your talents. One of those talents is pure charm." Dage chuckled at Jase's frown. "We're at war with the Kurjans, possibly with the demons, we're going to be at war with the Irish coven soon, and the Bane's Council is going to be beyond pissed if they find out about Maggie." He limped toward the door, glancing over his shoulder at his youngest brother. "Our allies and our enemies need a face and a contact with the Realm. Congratulations brother. You're it."

"Damn," Jase breathed, even as first Conn, then Talen clapped him on the back with chuckled congratulations.

Kane remained off to the side. "Ah, well, I meant my comment in a good way. I didn't think—" The rest of his sentence was cut short when Jase body checked him and both men went sprawling across the mats.

"Hey. I'm supposed to kick Kane's ass," Talen grumbled.

"Me first," Jase said, punching Kane in the jaw.

Dage would like to stay and watch the brawl, but he had work to do.

Then he'd deal with his mate.

Chapter 20

A breath after midnight, Dage nudged the door to his suite open with one knuckle, fully expecting something to be thrown at his head. Nothing. He stepped inside the quiet room, his gaze dropping to the set of tea cups remaining on the sofa table. Good. Cara had visited.

He strode to the bedroom door and twisted, not surprised to find the lock engaged. The cocking of a pistol on the other side brought a wry grin to his face.

"Open the door and I shoot." While Emma's voice remained deadly calm, an underlying tremor lifted the consonants. His mate knew this was a bad idea.

No question he'd been an ass earlier. But he couldn't let the woman threaten him with a gun without some sort of repercussion. Would she really shoot? "Where'd you get the weapon, love?" He placed a palm against the door.

"In the armory earlier." A rustling sounded—the woman was readying her stance. "The gun's old-fashioned and not likely to kill a vampire, but I believe a bullet would sting."

"The gun had better not be in your hand when I enter the room, Emma." Enough of this. They needed to talk.

"Not only will the gun be in my hand, you'll be facing lead poisoning," she returned just as evenly.

He stepped back and put his boot to the door. The heavy

oak slammed open and he faced the barrel of a pistol, his mate's angry blue eyes shooting sparks.

She was perched on her knees in the middle of the big bed, wearing sweats and a faded shirt sporting Isaac Newton getting beamed by an apple. "I've always wanted to see somebody do that."

Leaning against the door jam, he crossed his arms. "The key is to plant your foot next to the doorknob." He could have those clothes off her in a matter of seconds.

"Good to know."

She looked healthy. Flushed skin, clear eyes. "Is the gun loaded?" A lead bullet would smart like a rubber band snap and not even pierce his skin.

"Yes." She raised an eyebrow. "Though I want to get myself one of those green laser shooting kinds."

"You may choose your own tomorrow." He wondered if she knew how to shoot. If not, they'd need to start practicing.

"I believe I told you not to come inside this room."

He smiled. She'd pulled her thick hair back into a ponytail and appeared as dangerous as a newborn kitten. "I didn't listen." His gaze focused on the gun and he heated the metal just enough . . .

"Damn." She dropped the gun to the bedspread and shook her hand. "That hurt."

"I barely warmed it." He flicked his glance to the weapon and the gun shot across the room to land near his feet. "Would you really have shot me?"

She crossed her arms. "You'll never know."

Two strides had him at the bed. "Lesson one with guns, love. If you're going to point it, shoot it." He reached out and tugged the band from her hair, appreciating when curls smelling like spiced peaches cascaded around her fragile shoulders.

She frowned. "Give me the gun back and I will."

He smiled. "You are such a pain in the ass." Damn but he loved her.

"Look who's talking. You overreacted earlier, King." She scooted back on the bed to rest against the headboard. A disgruntled frown settled between her pretty eyes, but she seemed more irritated than angry.

He inhaled deeply. Spiced peaches filled his head and made his cock throb worse than his healing ribs. "Yes, I did. I apologize."

Her dark eyelashes fluttered for a moment against her pale skin as she focused on the bedspread. "I probably should've called for help before rushing into the lab." She plucked a loose string. Her tone hinted that scientific discovery took some risks, but she lacked the energy to fight about it.

The mattress gave when Dage placed one knee in the center, reaching out and tugging her flat to be covered by his body. "We're still both finding our way here." He had no doubt she'd forget safety again in a heartbeat if there was science involved. She reminded him of Kane.

She smiled up at him. "True." Her nipples pebbled against his chest.

Forcing a smile, he brushed her hair away from her face. "We need to learn more about each other."

Sapphire eyes sparkled with laughter. "Really? Like what?"

"Like"—he ran his hand down the side of her body, enjoying the little catch in her breath—"are you ticklish?" Digging his fingers into her ribs, he easily held her in place when she bucked.

"No," she protested, a bubble of laughter escaping. "Okay, maybe a little." She yanked his head back with both hands. "Stop."

He paused as if considering. "For now." Tugging, he removed her shirt and then his own, fighting a groan as her soft skin met his. This was so much better than arguing with her. If she'd just allow him to keep her safe, life would be so much more peaceful.

"What else do you want to know?" She stretched against him like a satisfied cat.

Was she wet? "Favorite ice cream?" When she moved like that, he didn't give a shit about peace.

Her gaze dropped to his mouth. "Mint chocolate chip." She leaned up and nibbled on his bottom lip. "You?"

The sweats were ripped easily off her body by one of his large hands. "Chunky Monkey." Her scent filled his head, and he had to force himself not to pound into her, to slow down and enjoy this amazing creature.

She stilled, biting her bottom lip while laughter lightened her eyes. "Seriously? Chunky Monkey?"

He had to taste her neck. "What's wrong with my choice?" Canines retracted, his lips nipped her skin, filling his senses with ripe peaches.

Emma.

His.

"I don't know," she breathed, arching her silk covered mound against his ripped jeans. "You seem more of a French vanilla type to me."

Those panties snapped in two, and he flung them across the room. "Vanilla, huh?" Hmm. Not so sure he liked that.

"Yeah. It's more king-like."

Oh, he really didn't like that. He rose to his knees, straddling her nude body, both hands going to his leather belt to draw through the hoops. Her eyes darkened and her gaze ran over his chest in almost a physical caress. He breathed deep. "Open your mind."

She opened her eyes wide and lowered those powerful shields.

Ah. He let her seep into him, her incredible mind, her rioting emotions. She didn't know how to trust. So he didn't ask. He put pure male challenge in his eyes and sent her a mental whisper.

Her eyes widened further, her gaze flicking to the belt still in his hands and back again.

He waited, leaving the unspoken challenge hanging in the air between them.

She straightened her shoulders against the mattress and held out one wrist, dark sparking eyes that reminded him of the clearest sky over the purest part of the ocean.

The leather easily looped around her soft skin, and he jerked her to a seated position, grabbing her other wrist and securing her hands together behind her back. His strength so surpassed hers the belt was a silly prop—yet the representation of her extending her arm filled him with power. The blue-eyed minx trusted him, whether she'd admit it to herself or not.

Her lips parted and interest darkened her devastating eyes even as those damn shields began to rise.

"No." He tugged on her arms, leaning back on his haunches to appreciate her pretty breasts. "No shields."

She mentally dropped them and twisted her wrists, raising an eyebrow when the binding held tight. "You're kind of kinky for a king." Her husky voice slid over his skin like silk.

"You have no idea."

"Show me."

He smiled slowly, truly appreciating the hard nipples all but begging for his mouth. "With pleasure." A fluffed pillow cradled her head when propped against the headboard, her arms bound behind her back arching her chest. "You are comfortable?"

"I'm fine." She settled against the intricate wood, her eyes an intriguing combination of wariness and want. "What now?"

"Now we talk about your pointing a gun at me." He inhaled the intoxicating scent of her arousal. His mate.

Awareness flashed in those eyes. "You deserved it."

"No." He gave a low growl, nipping the underside of one breast. "Before we're finished tonight, you'll vow never to do it again."

She gave a half-hearted struggle. "I won't."

His chuckle echoed back from her soft skin and he levered up to engulf one nipple. She gasped, throwing her head back with a soft groan. He tweaked her with his tongue, his emotions melding with hers until he couldn't be certain which were his.

The king's emotions ripped into Emma with a force that left her breathless. The man really did love her, though a dark edge breathed inside him. For the first time she truly understood what a dangerous being she'd given herself to.

"I won't hurt you." He shifted his attention to her other nipple and she fought to keep her brain functioning.

"I know." She let herself navigate inside him, his heart bare, his soul laid wide open. Without question she sat in the middle of everything he was, everything he'd ever become. Her breath caught in her throat and tears burned her eyes. He'd do what it took to protect her . . . because she *mattered*.

He lifted his head to meet her gaze. "Yes, I will. And yes, you do. You're the one thing fate has given just to me. Without you"—balancing himself on his elbows, his wicked mouth wandered down her ribs to her navel—"nothing has meaning." He swirled his tongue inside and she pushed toward him, trying to loosen her hands to touch him. She needed to touch him.

He chuckled, going lower to bite her inner thigh. "I like you helpless."

She stilled, sparks of light shooting inside her eyelids as his heated breath brushed across her core. "Dage," she breathed. Her hands splayed against the small of her back, fighting the belt. The leather held firm.

"Now that's a lovely sound." He kissed her so softly, too softly right where she needed his mouth. He settled in with a low growl, his wide shoulders holding her open for him. "Say it again."

His fangs scraped her inner thigh and she stifled a scream. Oh God. Those dangerous canines were so close to her aching center. Heat flushed through her and a desire slammed home with a razor sharp edge of pain. "Dage."

The pleasure that filled him at her husky whisper of his name echoed throughout her own heart, along every inch of her skin.

"What, love?"

"Bite me."

She didn't need to ask twice. He struck fast and hard, sinking into her artery and pulling with sharp tugs. Warmth and energy sizzled through his veins, swirling into pure, raw power. Emma gasped, feeling from within Dage's skin. "Wow."

His fangs retracted, and he sealed the wound with his rough tongue. "You're telling me."

"My blood gave you energy." The scientist's mind fought against the woman's need. "Is it always so intense when you feed?

"God no." His tongue wandered north and found another place to play. Emma nearly slammed her thighs together, but his strong hands widened her further. "Only my mate packs a punch like that." He spoke against her clit, his breath heated more than a human's.

The scientist fell silent as Emma's thighs began to tremble. Dage slid both hands under her to cup her ass, tugging her further into his mouth. He moaned in appreciation and Emma cried out. He worked her for a while, his mouth relentless, his tongue wicked hot until she was a gasping, nearly pleading bundle of screaming nerves. If he moved just a little faster . . .

He chuckled again, the vibration nearly sending her over the edge. Nearly. "Dage," she moaned.

"Ah, love. Now we talk about the gun."

Irritation warred with need for a moment. "My hands hurt. Undo them."

He lifted up. A sharp eyebrow and shards of blue bisected the silver in his eyes. "I strongly suggest you never lie to me, love." The hands on her buttocks tightened.

She opened her mouth to protest, then fell silent.

"Oh yeah. I can feel what you feel. Your hands are just fine." He released her gaze and lowered his mouth to nip, sending her arching toward him. He rumbled against her core. "Now, promise you'll never point a gun at me again."

She rotated her hips, seeking the release he kept just out of her reach, the muscles in her neck stretching. "I promise I won't point a gun at you unless I intend to shoot," she moaned.

He stilled, then gave a short bark of laughter. "Fair enough." His mouth lowered, his tongue went to work and her world exploded.

He eased her down with soft licks and gentle kisses. She licked her lips, still needing something. More. Him. "Dage."

Quick movements had his clothes removed and tossed across the room. Strong arms flipped her over and she landed on her knees, pitching forward until he stabilized her with one hand curved over her shoulder, her wrists still bound against the small of her back. "Well now. Isn't this a sight." Dage leaned forward and ran his tongue along the marking on her shoulder.

Her entire body shuddered in reaction. "Undo my hands."

"Nope." His knee nudged hers farther apart and he paused before slowly entering her, one hand on her shoulder and the other clasping her hip. "We're not quite finished here." He slammed the rest of the way home with a low growl, tugging her back to meet his powerful thrust.

"I know that, damn it." He filled her, and she fought a keening that wanted loose. Oh God, start moving.

But he didn't. He waited, the hand at her hip sliding to her belly and up to her neck, his other hand dropping to the bed. Holding her in place, he placed a gentle kiss on her marking. The soft touch burned right through to where they remained joined.

Emma stiffened, her gaze on the headboard, her thoughts on the man behind her. Her mind rioted with need, and her bound hands clutched against his hard abs as he levered over her. She craved. Or was that him? The feelings rumbling from him were unfamiliar. Dark. Powerful. Dangerous. The need to take, to possess filled him, a raw instinctive demand he had no intention of quelling.

She whimpered and moved back against him.

"Emma?"

The harsh timbre of his voice nearly had her orgasming. "What?" She shut her eyes against the painful need whipping through her body.

"You will observe every safety protocol we have from now on." His breath brushed her earlobe. One fang clamped on, the pain a delicious hint of danger that almost had her orgasming. Almost.

She shivered. "Talk about safety later." Each word was gasped out with tremendous effort. Her mind spun. Her heart thumped. Every cell in her body focused away from their normal functions and on the vampire holding her captive.

He gave a low chuckle. "Now. I compromised on the gun, love. This is a promise you make now." Sweat dropped from him to sizzle against her shoulders.

She strained against him, her entire body vibrating with need. Helpless and restrained, she nevertheless felt her own power echoing throughout his strong body. "Later."

He pulled out and thrust back inside her, yanking her back into his thrust. "Now."

Nerves screamed in need and she groaned low. Oh God. He was killing her. Her mind fought reason. "Fine. But you don't do anything to hurt the geneticists who broke into the lab."

His sigh held frustration and amusement. "I won't hurt them. But the ones involved have been fired."

They'd probably been frightened within an inch of their lives as well. "That's fair. Now freakin' move."

His broad hand settled between her shoulder blades to

press her against the mattress, the side of her face cradled in the soft pillow, her body fully exposed to him. Both hands clenched into her hips and he began to move. Then he began to pound, faster and harder than humanly possible.

A spiraling echoed within her skin, shattering into a million nerve endings that had her shrieking his name when she exploded. She saw blackness for a moment even while he continued to pound, his teeth latching onto her neck. He came with a low growl of her name. Jerking inside her for several moments, his scent of sandalwood and power infused the room stronger than before.

He quickly released her wrists and flipped her around to cradle against him, his breath panting out of his chest. She struggled to gulp in air, her entire body melting into his heat. "Okay. I guess Chunky Monkey makes sense," she murmured drowsily.

He chuckled against her hair and followed her into sleep.

Chapter 21

"This is just silly," Emma muttered, searching under the large oak desk for the correct file. She found it in the makeshift cardboard filing system and stood, the chill of the small lab making her shiver. "I would like to study the werewolf, Kane." Sometimes risk was a necessary component of any scientific pursuit. Any promise made during sex shouldn't count. How unsafe could the werewolf be, anyway?

Kane grunted in response, peering into a microscope.

"Was that grunt in agreement?" Emma flipped open the correct file, squinting in irritation and wondering if they should buy a space heater. The scents of bleach and paper made her bite back a sneeze.

"No." Kane lifted his head. "The king rarely gives orders, Em. I suggest you follow them this time."

"I am so freakin' tired of taking orders from the Kayrs brothers." Nearly a week had passed since Dage had wrung a promise to be safe out of her. She needed to study the werewolf. All she'd learned so far was the beast ate raw meat and wanted to kill anything near it. "It seems like there's a way to trace the poor creature to its master. Somehow."

Kane scribbled some notes on a chart and nudged them toward Emma. "The b72 compound attacks the second dosage of the virus very nicely. But something's missing."

She'd noticed that about him. He easily ignored subjects he wished not to discuss. Like the werewolf. And designer shoes. Emma sighed, sitting on a rolling desk chair. "Yes. The compound attacks the proteins in a petri dish but if we apply the cure to a bound chromosome, nothing happens. There's something binding this savvy bug to the DNA strand." Regret for the fired doctoral students filled her for a moment. She needed everyone on this research, human or not.

A sharp bleep announced a caller on the large screen encompassing one wall. A woman took shape. Emma gave Kane a glare out the corner of her eye, wishing she'd put on some lipstick. A quick push rolled her close enough to kick him in the shin. Good thing she'd worn her cute pointy shoes today.

He cut her an irritated glance and stepped to the side, out of her range but still within camera view.

"Well now. Hello Kane." Simone's dark eyes flashed and she pouted her ruby-red lips.

"Hi Simone." Kane cleared his throat. "We might need some magical help and I thought to give you a ring."

Emma fought the urge to throw something at his stupid head. "We found help," she muttered quietly. A quick roll and her foot connected again.

Kane jumped and then nodded. "We contacted your cousin Moira, but I wanted to get a couple of opinions." Moving swiftly, he pivoted behind Emma's chair, holding it in place with the camera before them. Ass.

Simone threw back her head and issued a sexy laugh that belonged in a smoke-filled bar. "Little Moira, huh? Well, rumor has it she did all right during her last training—for a fledgling witch, of course."

Emma showed her teeth. "She's known as one of the best. Seventh sister of the seventh sister and such." She wished she knew a spell to give Simone a big old pimple on her pale nose. If she believed in spells, that is.

Simone's eyes darkened further. "Yet she hasn't secured a place on the Coven Nine, now has she?"

"What's the Coven Nine?" Emma glanced over her shoulder at Kane.

He cleared his throat. "The Nine is the ruling body for all covens. Only the most powerful witches are nominated. Simone has been a member for a hundred years." His raised eyebrow promised retribution for the kicks.

Would it be too childish if Emma rolled her eyes? Probably. "I'm sure Moira will take her place in due time." For some reason Emma felt compelled to defend her new sister-in-law. Or mate-in-law. Or whatever the hell the correct terminology was. "Give me science any day of the week," she whispered to Kane.

Simone sighed. "What do you need, Kane?"

"Have you heard of Virus 27?" He gave Emma's chair a push and moved them both closer to the screen.

"Of course. Though you should probably start organizing the information coming forth from the Realm." Simone leaned over to type on a keyboard, revealing ample breasts. "Rumors and innuendo are fine during peace time, but now we're at war."

"Good point." Kane nodded. "We think there's a magical component to the virus."

Simone frowned. "How so?"

"The virus is too strong to be without something extra," he said. He kept his hands firmly on the back of the chair so Emma couldn't turn around . . . and kick him again.

Hard black eyes focused on Emma. "Maybe you need better scientists."

Kane sighed. "If I send you the information, would you please take a look?"

"Of course." White teeth sparkled in a parody of a smile. "I'd do anything for a member of the Kayrs family. In fact, I believe I already have." Her voice lowered to a purr at the end.

Kane groaned quietly. "Thanks Simone."

Simone cleared her throat. "Um, I'm not sure how to say this, but there's a movement afoot to remove the Kayrs family from Realm leadership."

Kane stilled. "Is there, now?" His voice lowered to a softness that had Emma smiling. Those Kayrs men. Badasses all around.

Simone held her hands out placatingly. "Yes. I'm just reporting in, Kane. I support your family." She dropped her hands. "But the rumor is that you're working with humans—humans that have access to vampire DNA profiles."

"Who's leading the charge here, Simone?"

Her eyes darkened. "I don't know. I've only heard rumors."

Kane sighed. "The rumors are unfounded. Not one human has access to anything dealing with the Realm. You have my word on it."

Simone nodded. "I understand."

"Good. I'll speak with you soon. Bye." He cut off the feed and silence echoed around the room. "Sorry. I figured the more help we found, the better." He pushed Emma's chair forward and spun it until she faced him. "Kick me again and you'll regret it."

Her shoe made a loud thunk against his shin. She raised an eyebrow. "So?"

His grin reached his eyes. "I didn't say when, little sister."

Emma swallowed hard, then nodded. "Fine. Can Dage be removed as king?"

Kane sighed. "Yes. But it's a nearly impossible process, and no way it happens during a time of war."

Dread slid down her spine. "What is the process?"

"It doesn't matter. For now, we concentrate on the virus."

She'd have to corner Dage later to find out more. "Okay. Now let's call Moira."

*   *   *

Across the globe, Moira paced before the camera, wondering what the heck was taking so long. She had a bad feeling about this virus, and she need to talk to Kane and Emma.

She glanced around the communications room located in the basement of the large castle. The equipment was far superior to that at her cottage, and her father seemed pleased when she requested its use. Her boots echoed off the cement floor and bounced back toward her from the thick block walls. She'd shooed everyone else out. Who could she trust?

The screen bleeped and she frowned at the caller's identity. With a heartfelt sigh, she punched in a couple keys and waited until a woman took shape. "Cousin Simone. How nice to see you." The lie nearly caught in her throat.

Simone smiled. Always a dangerous sight. "Good day to you, cousin Moira."

"Thank you. How did you find me?"

Simone laughed. "I asked your mother."

Her mother served on the council with Simone. Moira fought a grimace. "What can I do for you?" Besides going back in time and not being born the seventh daughter of a seventh daughter. Simone may be on council of the Coven's Nine, but her powers wouldn't come close to Moira's once fully developed. A fact the older witch knew well.

Black eyes sparkled. "How kind of you to ask. The Kayrs family contacted me with a question regarding magic and some silly virus and Kane mentioned he'd spoken with you."

"Yes." Irritation battled reason. Of course a second opinion was often required when it came to science. Magic too, for that matter.

Simone arched a fine eyebrow. "What have you found? Is there any possibility magic is involved here?"

Moira nodded. "Anything is possible. But I don't know." Not true. She did know. Something perverse in her wanted to be the one to help the Realm. Simone would take all the credit if given the opportunity. Let the snotty witch reach her own conclusions. "I'm sure Kane sent you the same information. I'd appreciate it if you contact me once you've reviewed the documents." Simone would have to force herself away from shopping, parties, and pretending to rule on the council. "Of course, if magic is involved, the Coven Nine will need to be fully informed." So they could go after the perpetrator. *And Harm None* meant something to the Coven.

Simone's eyes darkened again. "Well, if you need help, of course I'll volunteer. So you've quit running from the Kayrs family?" Her voice lowered to a purr. "How is your mate?"

The smile Moira forced onto her face actually stung. "Conn is fine and fully understands I've been working on my craft . . . and not running." She moved closer to the camera. "I understand if you'd rather I communicated with the Kayrs family. With you and the king not working out and all." Petty. But satisfaction still raised its head.

Simon's smile belonged on a jaguar about to strike. "Yes, well. I've met the king's current interest. It'll never last."

An unwelcomed sympathy slid through Moira. She sighed. "Dage mated her, Simone. I'm sorry." For a moment she was.

Simone paled and pure fire lanced through those odd eyes before she gathered herself. "I see. A decision he will certainly regret, I'm afraid." She leaned forward and tapped the keyboard. "A pleasure as always, cousin." The screen went black.

Poor Simone. The woman was a complete bitch, but her feelings for the king had been real.

A loud bleep announced another call, and Moira punched in the appropriate code.

Emma took shape. "Hi Moira."

"Emma." Moira stepped closer to the camera. "I've spoken with Simone, and she'll look over the material you sent as well."

Emma rolled her eyes. "I didn't contact her. Kane did. I'd rather have my kidneys removed with a butter knife than work with that woman." Deep red rose to color the queen's flawless skin. "Oh. Er. Sorry. I know you're cousins."

"We're not close." Moira gave a grimace only another woman would understand. "Believe me."

Emma nodded. "I do. So, what do you think about the virus?"

Moira took a deep breath. "I've studied your material, and I believe someone cast an energy-altering spell allowing the catalyst to speed up the progression of the virus." Though why in the hell a witch would do something so destructive was beyond her.

Emma sat back in her chair. "You've been working on the catalyst?"

"Yes. I've identified a binding spell on the catalyst but haven't figured out the application of magic on the actual virus yet." Moira leafed through some papers. "I can create a spell to counteract the catalyst's energy, but you still need a scientific cure for the actual matter of the liquid."

"We think we're on to something." Kane shrugged. "We hope. We're not sure yet." He cut his eyes to Emma. "Don't even *think* of kicking me again."

Moira smiled. "I can wait if the Kayrs needs a kicking." They all did, as far as she was concerned. She eyed the queen with interest.

Emma shook her head. "I've done the best I can today. So what do we do about the virus now?"

Moira focused across the world at her new friend. "Give me some time to come up with a spell that won't backfire." Bugger. How many coven laws would she break by sharing this level of magic? She should seek permission, but she had enough problems right now. "Are those infected doing all right?"

Emma shook her head. "All are getting progressively worse."

Dread filled Moira. She needed time to do this right. A slow burn spiraled out from the front of her left hip, and she straightened her shoulders as two more Kayrs brothers came into view across the screen.

"Dailtín," Conn said, his emerald eyes hard.

"Connlan." Her voice came out a bit breathy. He looked good. Tall, broad, thick jaw, and long brown hair. He'd grown it out since she'd last seen him. No man should have eyes so pure. "Name calling, are we?"

He shrugged. "Stop acting like a brat, and I'll find something else to call you." His gaze warmed until her skin flushed. "As I recall, you enjoy sweet nothings whispered in your ear."

Those sweet nothings whispered in that deep voice had had her dropping her skirts for the vampire much too quickly. Her one and only time with a man. Heat slammed into her abdomen and only a true Irish will kept her from doubling over. She shifted her gaze to the soldier standing shoulder to shoulder with her mate. "King."

"Hi, Moira." Dage smiled at her, humor lightening his usually serious eyes.

Conn planted his feet. "I need the room." He kept his gaze pinned on her. The room quickly cleared, Dage shutting the door on his way out.

"Feeling dramatic, are we?" Moira lifted her chin. Damn but the marking on her hip was a bit too close to her core for comfort.

"I'm done waiting."

She'd known this day would come. Butterflies winged through her stomach and her heart sped up to a gallop. "You step foot on my continent and it's war, Connlan."

"You'd hide behind your soldiers, Dailtín? I'd thought more of you." He took another step closer to the camera, and she had to fight to keep from stepping back in reaction.

Anger rolled through her like the waves of the Northern Sea. "No. I don't need the soldiers, Conn."

"Ah." Promise swirled deep in those dangerous vampire

eyes. "War between us, then." A slow smile spread across his face more daunting than any battle cry.

She centered herself, drawing deep on power. "Come near Norcastle and I'll turn you into a toad." Okay, probably not. But she would inflict damage without question.

His smile didn't waver. "I gave you a hundred years to train for what you're meant to do. For what the damn treaty demanded." Moira's father had demanded the century of freedom for her and wanted Conn's and Dage's signature in order to prevent war. The Kayrs men had signed, but only after Moira insisted she needed the time. "You're done, as am I." He stepped closer and for a moment the air visibly crackled with his power.

Tossing her head, she sought calm. "Meant to do? No. I've trained for who I'm meant to be." He'd paid her no mind for a century. No way in hell was she traveling across the world to warm his bed.

Purpose flashed over his strong face, and his jaw set. "Wrong. Witchcraft is your calling, what you're meant to do. As for who and what—you're meant to be mine. Make peace with your destiny now."

"Think so?" A gust of wind tickled her neck. Damn. She needed to control her emotions. "You have no idea what I can do. What the right spell could . . ." Fire flashed in Conn's eyes and for a moment she lost her train of thought. Heat slashed through the cameras to slide through her veins. From him.

His voice lowered to a timbre that skittered awareness along her skin. "You thinking about removing my marking, *céadsearc*?"

Sweetheart. She'd taught him the word that night. "Yes." She'd been trying to remove the marking for several decades without success. "One night a century ago does not dictate my future, Kayrs." Though what a night. She still dreamed about his hard body covering her.

"The hell it doesn't." Shards of silver ripped through his emerald eyes. They had turned a deep liquid moonlight the night he'd taken her. Several times. "Fate made a choice, Moira. Prepare yourself. Because I've made mine."

The screen went black.

Bullocks. Moira grabbed the nearest files. First she'd deal with the virus. Then she'd erase Connlan's marking from her flesh. For good.

Chapter 22

Several hours after having deserted the conference room, Dage raised an eyebrow as Conn tossed a young vampire over his shoulder to land with a hard thud against the training field. The sun bleached the sky almost white while the dark forest promised coolness near the brutal field set several hundred yards away from the residential building. The vamp rose and swung at Conn only to be handed his ass again when he went down. Hard.

"Maybe we should purchase group insurance," Jase muttered from Dage's side. He tipped back his head and downed a bottle of water.

Dage grinned. "I take it training is going well?"

Jase wiped dirt and blood off his forehead. "Yeah." He pointed to a group sparring to the right, tossing up dust and small plants. "Caleb's men are showing the shifters new tactics against demons."

A prickle of irritation slid down Dage's spine. "We're not at war with the demons." He planned to call Suri again and negotiate a compromise. Until the first bullet or knife pierced skin, they remained at peace. He should probably sit down with Caleb later in the day to discuss terms. Surely the man had tired of his war by now.

"If you say so." Jase nodded toward the left where Talen

stood in the center of their most elite squad. "The team wants to find a couple werewolves to train with."

"No." They needed to keep the one contained in the lab sedated at all times in order to control the damn thing. While the animal may be able to communicate with its master telepathically, the beast had no idea of its current location.

"That's what Talen said you'd say. But if we find a couple during a raid we might want to consider capturing them instead of killing them." Jase stretched his neck and rolled his shoulders. "We haven't battled werewolves for centuries. Chances are we're going to come up against some soon, if the Kurjans are creating a fighting class like we suspect."

Made sense, as much as Dage hated the idea. "We might ask Terent to capture instead of kill his next hunt." At some point Dage needed to contact the Banes Council with new information regarding the virus, in addition to the fact that now he captured instead of ending werewolves. Such a discussion would screw up another one of his days.

"Terent might agree." Jase cracked his knuckles. "Are you going to train your mate to fight?"

Dage grinned. "Why? So she can kick my ass?"

His brother laughed. "She is a feisty one, isn't she?"

"That she is. I'd like to train all the humans to fight, especially Janie. They need to learn how to defend themselves." He made a mental note to schedule self-defense training. He'd also ask his brothers to teach classes with him in hand-to-hand, grappling, and weaponry.

Jase grinned as a large soldier knocked Conn down only to end up coughing out dirt with Conn standing over his prone and probably severely bruised body. "Ouch."

Dage nodded. "Conn's more dangerous on the ground than standing upright. Timothy should've remembered that fact." Blood and the scent of pine filled the air.

"Conn's dangerous right now, period." A slight wind picked up to brush dry pine needles across the field and Jase lifted his head into the breeze. "You should have him teach the grappling classes."

"He's going to Ireland soon." Dage narrowed his gaze on Conn, who had bent one knee to demonstrate a sweeping motion. The shadow he cast under the brutal sun spread far and wide.

"Yes."

Dage focused on his youngest brother. "What, no questions?"

Jase shrugged. "Questions? Like what?" His gaze remained on Conn.

"Like if I'll try to stop him? Like if we can survive yet another enemy declaring war on us?" Even with Dage's psychic abilities, Jase's head remained a closed vault. Maybe it was empty. He grinned to himself.

Jase whistled through his teeth when two lions charged Conn. "Nope."

"Why not?" Dage kept his gaze on the warriors, pride filling him when Conn took both cats to the ground, his hands snapping their powerful jaws closed.

"I already know the answer." Jase reached down and grabbed a second water bottle. "You won't stop him. In fact, you'll back him and declare war on Ireland if necessary." Copper eyes narrowed on Dage. "He's your brother."

All true. "I've kept in touch with Kellach." Dage waited for a reaction.

"Moira's favorite cousin, huh?" A wide grin split Jase's face. "How is the dangerous bastard?"

"Dangerous as ever." Dage narrowed his gaze on the men training in the field. "Though he's not the only one. Apparently Conn's witch has been learning more than magic the last century."

Humor filled Jase's copper eyes. "Do tell."

"She's been training. Combat, guns, swords . . . you name it."

Jase snorted. "She knows Conn is the greatest soldier ever born, right? Realm, Kurjan, Demon—nobody else has ever come close."

Dage smiled. "I assume she knows."

Jase sobered. "Conn will tear Ireland apart when he's ready. She knows that, right?" His voice lowered in doubt at the end.

"If not, she'll soon find out." Dage said a quick prayer for Ireland. He'd always liked the green isle. He cleared his throat. "Kane says you're more powerful than any of us realize."

Jase's deep chuckle reached across the field, and Conn glanced up with a frown. "I'm just what I'm supposed to be." Jase's eyes filled with anticipation while he dropped the bottle to the ground.

"What the hell does that mean?" Dage gave a short nod toward Conn. Yes. He would join the training session. At the moment he felt like kicking the crap out of both his brothers.

"Define power. We all enjoy different gifts, King. I own the elements."

Dage raised an eyebrow. "You own them, do you?" He flung a hard slap of arctic air into Jase's face.

Jase laughed and sent it spiraling back toward Dage's skin.

Damn, that burned. Dage smiled. "You want Conn or Talen?"

"Ah, I'll take Conn." Jase rubbed his hands together. "You get Talen. He's a mite pissed about his mate no longer wearing his mark."

Dage shrugged. "They're both pissed."

Emma nudged the door to Cara's suite open while balancing three jugs of fruit juice, a bottle of wine, and a corkscrew. Cara tiptoed out of Janie's bedroom. "She's asleep."

"Good." Emma eased into the kitchen to scrounge for glasses. "Before you ask, the virus hasn't shown up in my blood yet." Thank goodness her ignoring safety protocol didn't come back to bite her in the butt. So far anyway. Twelve more hours to go.

Prophet Sotheby's skirts rustled smooth silk as she exited the powder room and glided toward the table. "That is good news. I hope you don't mind if I join your game." She smiled with perfectly smooth teeth, her onyx eyes lighting up.

Hmm. Was the prophet a card shark? Emma smiled. "You know how to play poker, Prophet?"

"Lily." The woman pulled out a chair and sat. "I've tinkered with the game." She grabbed the cards and began to shuffle with the ease and smooth movement of an experienced Las Vegas dealer. "I appreciate the chance to act normal for a short time." She sighed. "We can't all just sit in our rooms waiting for this virus to ruin us."

"I agree." Emma grabbed four juice glasses to perch on the table before opening the Shiraz. Maybe pretending everything was all right would ease some of the tension they were all feeling. She nodded toward her sister. "You get juice."

Cara rolled her eyes, reaching in the cupboard for a tin of herbal tea. "I want tea."

Katie poked her head into the room. "We ready to play?" The lioness came inside with Maggie on her heels. "Maggie hasn't played before."

Maggie shrugged. "I may have played before, but I don't remember. So who the hell knows."

"Mags doesn't get to play tomorrow since it's a full moon, so let's have some fun tonight." Katie sat with a sigh. "The guys will be planning strategy for several hours, so we should have some peace and quiet."

"All of you get fruit juice with plenty of vitamins." They shouldn't be playing. Emma should be working, but there was nothing to do while the current tests ran. She poured four glasses of juice and passed them out, turning her focus to Maggie. "Do you feel any different with the full moon so close?" She sat and took a small sip of the wine.

Maggie shook her head. "Nope. But it'll be nice to shift

into wolf form again, if I can. I mean, if I don't turn into a freakin' werewolf." She worried her bottom lip with her teeth, her eyes on the table.

"You won't." Katie patted her friend's hand and tugged her down into a seat. "I wish I could shift—at least for a night." A frown marred her clear skin for a moment, and her tawny gaze met Emma's.

Emma gave a short nod—she'd remember her promise—if she failed to destroy the damn virus.

Cara took a seat, blowing on her tea. "Emma will find a cure, Katie. I promise."

Emma squelched rising panic. She hoped to find a cure. "We're doing our best. Kane thinks Moira will help." Even stacks of blue, red, and white poker chips clacked together as she slid them in front of each player. The bright colors contrasted with the pall hanging over them all. She shrugged, determined to put on a carefree face. Just for the night.

Katie tipped back her head and took a healthy swallow of fruit juice. "A witch, huh? Well better Moira than that bitch from New York."

"Simooone," Emma and Cara drawled together.

Lily snorted and dealt each player five cards, humming as she did so.

Katie grinned. "Yep. She flirted with Jordan all night at the ball. I'd like to turn her into a toad."

Lily tapped her cards on the table to straighten them, raising her eyebrow as she unfolded her hand. "I believe Simone and Moira are first cousins on their paternal side." She tossed two cards face down.

"Really?" Emma glanced at her cards. Three twos, an ace, and a seven. She cleared her mind. "Ouch." She frowned at her sister and reached down to rub her leg.

"No using psychic abilities," Cara sniffed.

Lily raised an eyebrow. "We can't use any?"

"Guess not." Emma narrowed her gaze on the prophet. "What's yours, anyway?"

Lily glanced at a stack of white chips and they floated through the air to land before her cards. "I'm a telekinetic, but once I married Sotheby, I ended up a decent empath as well." She smiled. "Katie likes the cards I dealt her."

Katie gave a soft groan. "Listen, I can't sense things like usual, so no using special gifts. Let's level the playing field for those of us fighting a virus." She tossed all five cards face down.

"Fair enough." Lily nodded. "Though everyone here but Emma is fighting the virus."

All gazes swung to Emma. She shrugged.

Cara paled. "Chances are they'll be coming for you next, Em."

Emma shook her head. "Don't kid yourself. They're coming for all of us—this is planned bioterrorism. Shifters might become werewolves and vampire mates become human." The idea of Dage's marking fading from her skin actually made her heart ache. She steeled her spine. They wouldn't get to her. She tossed the seven face down. "I need one card."

Lily dealt her a card and Emma lifted it, pleased to see an ace. She nudged a blue chip to the middle. "Bet twenty-five." She may be surrounded by shifters and empaths, but she'd supplemented her college job with poker winnings and figured she was due for some good luck. Everyone matched her bet and she forced a smile, laying down her cards. "Full house."

Chapter 23

Emma washed two more aspirin down with one of Dage's grape sodas in the spacious gym. She'd had a headache all day. You'd think she'd have received enough of Dage's healing abilities to cure a freakin' hangover. How much wine had she polished off last night during the poker game, anyway? She ignored Katie's knowing smirk.

Maggie rolled her eyes from her seated position on the thick mats. "No gloating." The industrial lights cut hard light through the air to illuminate the shadows in her pale face.

Katie flounced across the gym to sit by her friend. "I'm not gloating. Though even without my shifter senses, I schooled all of you last night." While the shifter was still pale, her features seemed more relaxed. Maybe having the poker game and escaping reality for a few hours had been good for all of them.

Dage stalked into the room followed by Jordan and two of his enforcers, Baye and Mac. Emma nodded at the lions, thinking once again their myriad of black, brown, and blond hair would have given her pause had she not known they were lions.

She reached up and gave Dage a peck on the cheek. His return smile appeared forced. "What's wrong, Dage?"

He shrugged. "We spent all day trying to locate Prophet

Guiles with no luck." Dage ran a rough hand through his hair. "Talen is still reaching out to our sources."

"Do you have sources in the Kurjan organization?"

"Yes." He glanced at his watch. "How was your day, love?"

"Productive. Kane and I worked in the lab most of the day. We created a new protein to test tomorrow." And she'd stayed away from the werewolf. She'd wait until Dage appeared in a better mood for discussing the tests she wanted to run on the beast.

"Good." Dage focused his gaze on Jordan. "Night falls in ten minutes."

Jordan nodded, leaning forward to tug Katie to her feet. "Okay. Everybody out of the gym."

Dage grasped Emma's arm. "Good luck, Maggie."

Maggie nodded, her face becoming more pale.

Jordan began to draw Katie toward the door, and the young woman yanked her arm back. "What are you doing? I'm staying."

"No, you're not." Jordan's tawny eyes flashed. "You can watch from the control room with Emma."

"But Jordan"—Katie glanced at the cameras set into the far corners and back—"her shift won't hurt other shifters."

A muscle began to pound in Jordan's jaw. Dead silence echoed around the room.

"Oh." Katie took a deep breath. "I see. I'm not a shifter." She turned and stormed for the doorway, only to give a startled yelp when Jordan jerked her back.

The lion lowered his head toward hers, a snarl curling his lip. "You *are* a shifter." He spun her and smacked her ass to propel her toward the door. "Until the virus runs its course, we're being careful."

Katie gave a startled gasp and hustled into the hallway.

Dage nodded to Jordan. "We'll lock the door from the outside. Guards are posted every few yards."

Jordan kept his gaze on the empty doorway. "I have a tranq in case we need it."

Maggie sighed. "Let's hope we don't." She flashed Emma a sad smile. "You need to go. I can feel the moon rising." Her eyes flicked a deep gray and back to brown again.

Dage swiveled Emma into the hall and engaged the lock. She followed him through the hallways and up two flights of stairs to the large conference room, passing several guards on the way. Cara and Katie already sat at the onyx table before the wall mounted screen.

Emma sat when Dage pulled out a chair for her. He leaned in. "Do you understand what happened to Maggie the last time there was a full moon?"

"Yes." Emma had read the reports as well as talked to Maggie earlier in the day. Basically, both werewolf and wolf shifter had battled to get out. The wolf shifter won. "I took several samples from Maggie earlier. Hopefully this time she won't be affected."

Dage placed a kiss on the top of Emma's head before stalking over to stand by the door. A sentinel, even now. "We can hope."

Considering Maggie had been infected the longest, if she beat the disease, there was hope for them all.

He glanced at Katie. "Kate? If you feel anything odd, anything . . ."

"To indicate I'm going to get hairy and bay at the moon?" Katie asked, a hint of a smile on her face.

He returned the grin. "Yes. You let me know."

Emma shook her head. "She won't. The virus hasn't been in her system long enough. No werewolfishness."

"Good." His eyes glimmered with amusement. "Apparently Cara isn't the only Paulsen who makes up her own words."

Emma opened her mouth to retort when the screen caught her eye as Baye and Mac shifted into mountain lions. One second they stood tall and then an odd sparkly shimmer washed over them until they perched on four legs, dangerous and predatory. Their clothes fell in ripped heaps to their paws. "Wow."

"I owe them clothes now," Dage said. "I told them not to arrive in the gym nude."

Katie gave Emma a sideways glance. "You're missing out. The enforcers are something to look at, let me tell you." She wiggled her eyebrows and pursed her lips.

"Kathrynne . . ." Dage warned, a smile playing on his lips.

Katie sobered. "I should be in there."

Emma patted her hand on the table, sympathy filling her for a moment. "Don't worry, Kate. We'll figure this out." They just had to. The woman's sorrow had a presence of its own in the small room. Cara shifted uncomfortably next to Emma, probably feeling Katie's pain and sorrow. Must suck to be an empath.

The lioness leaned forward. "Something's happening."

Emma zeroed in on the screen. Maggie had her eyes closed, leaning against the gym wall. She stretched her neck and lifted her head with her nostrils flaring. Then she looked down and focused on her right hand, which she held out with the fingers extended.

Sharp claws emerged.

Emma gasped.

The claws curled black and then elongated to yellow daggers. Maggie winced, dropping her chin to her chest and tightening her shoulders as if drawing in power. The claws narrowed and retracted into black wolf claws.

Jordan's low voice crooned through the space. "That's it, Mags. Concentrate. Search for the wolf—she needs you."

Katie began to tremble next to Emma. "Come on, Maggie," she whispered.

Maggie's eyes opened, shifting from light brown to yellow to dark brown to gray. Her face elongated and she let out an animalistic howl of pain. The shrill sound echoed throughout the room.

Sharp canines dropped low and fast, and she fell forward onto all fours. Hair emerged on her face, on her arms, shiny and brown. Then bristly and coarse. Her clothes ripped apart and she took the form of a wolf. The fur turned shiny and brown again. She lifted her head and yelped. The air shimmered with sparkles and suddenly a fully grown she-wolf rested on a pile of clothing.

She lowered her head and stretched out, a small whimper escaping.

Jordan crept forward and knelt, running a hand along her thick pelt. "Nice job, Mags." He drew in a deep breath and nodded toward the cameras. "Kane's going to come in and take some blood samples, and then we'll go for a run."

The wolf lifted her head and gave the equivalent of a canine smile. Apparently she wanted to run.

Emma muttered to herself, her handwriting no better than chicken scratches. The owl hooted outside, once again searching for something in the dead of night.

Lily swung her legs back and forth from her perch on the examination table. "Is there anything I can do to help?" Her scent of wild strawberries filled the air and competed against the medicinal smells of alcohol and pine-scented cleansers.

"No." Emma straightened her back and stretched her neck, her voice soft in the quiet lab. "Though maybe you should get some sleep. It's past midnight." She tossed the chart down on the table.

"You're not sleeping." The prophet stifled a yawn.

Dage was working with Talen, and settling down in a bed by herself had lost its appeal for Emma. "True. But I have this feeling I'm about to get a breakthrough, and I can't just go to sleep." She wanted to take another sample of Maggie's blood when she returned from her run as a wolf.

"I don't want to leave you all by yourself in this big old lab." Lily glanced around and gave an exaggerated shiver. "Plus, I, ah, wanted to ask you something."

"What's that?" Emma fought the urge to rub her tired eyes.

"The cure. If my body beats the virus, will I change back? I mean, will I be mated to Sotheby again?" A frown settled between Lily's finely arched brows.

Emma shrugged. "I doubt it. Truly, I don't believe that could happen. Even if you manage to reform the chromosomes, the individual aspects of each mating would be gone."

"Indeed." Lily's expression smoothed out.

"Damn it, Lily. You should be in bed." Caleb stormed into the room, a purple bruise spreading across one rugged cheekbone. Dust covered his dark training garb while his huge boots battered the tiled floor.

Lily raised an eyebrow. "I'm not the walking wounded here, Caleb." A pink blush slid under her skin and filled her face.

A low growl emitted from the soldier. "You should see the other guy. Besides, it's just training." He reached forward and tugged the prophet off the table. "You're going to rest."

Emma fought a grin as Lily jerked her arm away from the angry vampire. "Back off, Caleb. I'm a prophet with a job to do."

"A prophet?" Caleb threw back his head and laughed. "All you three do is wander around and enjoy free meals. When you're not banishing people, of course."

Lily perched her hands on her hips. "I didn't banish you and you damn well know it." She swished her skirts away and edged around the table with her head held high. "You have no idea what goes into being a spiritual leader for the Realm."

"A lot of nothing, if you ask me." Caleb's multi-colored eyes shifted to darker colors.

"Nobody asked you," Lily said.

"Well." Caleb's voice lowered to a softness that provided warning. "Then you need to get yourself some rest so you can save all those souls tomorrow. Move yourself, Prophet, or I'll move you."

Emma briefly considered intervening and decided against it. They were both adults.

"Touch me and I'll bring the force of the prophesy down on your derelict head," Lily spat, her hands clutching the table until her knuckles turned white.

Caleb smiled and settled his stance. "This is your last warning, Prophet."

Lily rolled her eyes, swishing her skirts in a hasty exit. "I'm leaving because I wish to go, you jackass." She held her head high as she swept out of the room.

Caleb pivoted and gave Emma a wink. "Good night, Highness." He followed the prophet into the hallway while whistling an Irish jig, giving a polite nod to Dage.

The king frowned, stepping inside the lab. "I wonder if I should do something about this."

Emma shrugged. "I say let them get it out of their systems." She stifled a yawn. "Have you noticed your race is a bit, well . . ."

"Neanderthalic?"

She frowned. "Is that a word?"

"According to your sister, that's a word."

Cara had always been fantastic about making up words that should be in the dictionary. "Vampires appear to be extremely behind the times when it comes to . . ." What was the correct expression?

"Being politically correct?" Dage ran a broad hand through his thick hair. "Granting equal rights?"

"Yes."

His gaze gentled on her face. "Do you think Caleb would do anything to hurt Lily?"

No. Not at all. "He doesn't have the right to boss her around. She's a prophet, for goodness sakes." What was the guy thinking? Surely the fates would be seriously pissed off to see one of their prophets treated in such a matter. Emma shook her head in exhaustion. The fates? God. When had reality taken a flying leap?

Dage nodded. "That's true. Keep in mind, most of us haven't been in a relationship for centuries. We may have some catching up to do."

Emma tilted her head to the side, focusing on the discussion at hand. "Will being granted more time even matter?"

Dage shrugged. "Probably not." His grin was lethal. Sexy. Tempting.

She huffed out a breath. If she chose to stay and have sons with the thick headed king, those boys would be modern, if it was the last thing she did. "Any luck finding Prophet Guiles?"

"We found a good lead and should have his location by tomorrow." Dage stalked forward, all grace, all muscle. "It'd be nice if he were in Ireland so we could capture two birds with one trip." He grinned.

Emma tapped her foot. So much for modern views. "Don't you start. Moira can make up her own mind."

A thoughtful smile flirted with Dage's full lips and that dangerous gaze narrowed in focus, pinning her in place. "Love? What do you think I'd do if you took off across the globe and refused to see me?" Curiosity melded with something darker, something intense in the deep tone.

She cleared her throat. "Respect my need for privacy, I assume." Like hell. "Don't threaten me, Dage." He was so lying if he claimed there wasn't a threat buried in that dark tone. And she'd be lying if she didn't admit his darkness pebbled her nipples and made her thighs clench. A need began to hum through her body—a craving only the vampire currently devouring her with his gaze could satisfy.

A smile flirted with his upper lip. "Just hinting at facts. I suggest you remain where I can touch you." He stepped forward and ran a gentle finger down the side of her face, reaching her chin to tilt her head up.

She sighed. "I've been wondering. What happens if you're dethroned?" This was the first chance she'd had to ask him.

He smiled. "Nobody's going to dethrone me, love. Your status as queen is safe."

"I don't care about being queen." She cared about the man whose gaze currently caressed her face. "What's the process?"

"The prophets, all three of them, must make a motion to the Realm to have me removed." He shrugged. "There's a vote, and seventy percent of the Realm has to agree. No worries. It won't happen." His lips brushed across hers, his breath heated. "Come to bed."

Ah. Something they agreed upon.

Chapter 24

The buzz of a cell phone woke Emma from a dream in which she tried to figure out how to ride a broom across a cloudy sky. Great. A couple discussions with a witch and she wanted to be one. Idly, she wondered about other scientific theories humans hadn't yet discovered. Did they use sound waves? Light waves? Some other type of waves humans hadn't discovered as of yet? She giggled in the darkness and placed a soft kiss on Dage's hard chest.

"What?" he barked into the phone, one broad hand sweeping down her body to cup her butt under the covers of the big bed. He stiffened. "Meet in the large conference room in ten minutes. Call Jordan and Caleb as well." The phone snapped shut with a click, and he rolled her onto her back and covered her with his warm body.

She brushed back a lock of his hair that had fallen forward. "What's going on?" Desire hummed to life when he settled his erection against her core. She licked her lips in anticipation.

His eyes flared at the action. "Talen found Prophet Guiles." Dage dropped his head and ran gentle kisses along her jaw, stopping with a sigh and rolling from the bed.

Emma sat up. "Where?" They were going off to fight again. She breathed deep, reminding herself the king knew how to fight. She needed to learn to trust his abilities, much as he needed to learn to trust hers. Damn two-way street.

"Nevada." Dage yanked on black cargo pants and a dark T-shirt. "The extraction team leaves in thirty minutes."

Dread slithered down her spine. "Do you have to go?"

"Yes." He tucked his earpiece into place and leaned over to plant a hard kiss on her lips, withdrawing to brush her hair off her face. He paused, his gaze searching hers. Finally he sighed. "You were right that I need action to give me focus and relief from my diplomatic duties. I don't do it just to show my leadership." Unease wandered across his hard face, and he rubbed his chin. With another deep breath, he exhaled. "I like it, and I need it."

Vulnerability was obviously a new emotion for the king, and one he didn't like. But he'd opened up to her. He'd admitted the truth, he'd trusted her.

Pleasure warmed her heart. She'd bet anything she was the only woman with whom Dage had ever let down his guard. "I appreciate you trusting me with the truth." Everything inside her softened. Maybe they had a chance. The king was willing to bend.

He nodded. "I do trust you, love. More than you could know."

"I trust you too." She shifted and kissed his palm. He was worth the risk.

His eyes heated. "I'll return safely and we'll pick up where we just left off."

"Promise?"

His smile warmed her skin. "I promise." He strode out of the room, shutting the door with a soft snap.

Emma snuggled back down into the covers, letting the scent of sandalwood and power ease her fears. He'd be all right. He had training, power, and his brothers. The king would return. The marking began to tingle on her shoulder, a constant soothing reminder of her connection with Dage.

Yet she couldn't sleep. Minutes passed. Then an hour.

Maybe she should get up and do some work. Sighing, she threw back the covers and slid from the bed, tugging on faded jeans and a ROLL TIDE, BABY sweatshirt.

She'd just clipped her hair back when a soft sound came from the living room. Tilting her head to listen, she hurried through the bedroom and gasped. Cara sagged against the doorjamb in a huge T-shirt, her face pale and her eyes wide with pain. "Emma." Her knuckles were white against the wood, her bare toes curled into the carpet.

Emma rushed forward and steadied her sister, holding her when Cara fumbled. "Car? What's wrong?" Panic rushed through her and she fought to keep her mind clear.

Cara winced, her hand going to her stomach. "It hurts. So bad." She sucked in air. "Fix this, Em."

Emma flashed back to a four-year-old Cara saying the same thing when she was stung by a bee. She gave the same answer. "I'll fix it, Cara." She pulled her sister into the room to sit on the couch, where she knelt to meet a blue-eyed gaze full of agony. "Tell me what hurts."

Tears filled Cara's eyes. "Something's wrong. The baby . . ." She bit her lip and paled even further. "Cramps. And I can't feel Talen. Something's wrong." A low moan escaped her.

Shit. Was it a progression of the virus or had Cara somehow been infected with the catalyst? "Where's Janie?"

Cara gasped in pain. "She and Katie had a slumber party to watch the new pony movie."

Good. Emma pulled Cara off the couch. "We need to go to the lab and call Kane."

"Kane went on the raid—they all did." Cara moaned.

Emma swung her sister around and cradled her strained face. Tears soaked her hands. "We're strong and we're smart. We'll fix this."

Cara nodded, bending at the waist and shifting toward the door.

Emma helped her down the hall and to the outside exit manned by an armed guard at least twice her size.

He shook his head. "You're to stay inside, Highness."

"No." Emma pushed open the door. "We have an emergency here. You can guard the lab, but we're going."

The man glanced in concern toward Cara and gave a short nod, tapping his earpiece. "I need the lab secured right now, full sweep and two guards at each entry." He held out his arms. "May I?"

"Yes," Cara moaned, doubling over again.

The guard lifted her gently. "We're not going inside the lab until the sweep is completed." He maneuvered out the door into the still dark night with Emma on his heels.

A full moon lit the path through the trees, crickets chirping in the distance and the scent of pine strong on the slight wind. They paused at the edge of the forest, and Emma made out the forms of several men scouting the perimeter of the building. Light cascaded out each window where more soldiers inspected each room.

Several minutes later the guard tapped his earpiece again. "Okay." He began to stride forward. "The building is clear." He nodded to the guards at the main entrance and one held the door open for them. "Which room?"

"The main clean lab." Emma rushed inside, her sandals clicking on the industrial tiles. She rapidly disengaged the key locks and gave her code, all but running through the clean rooms and showers.

The guard paused in the ultraviolet room, his deep voice echoing off the walls. "Are you sure, Highness?"

Emma kept moving, punching her code into the wall. "Yes. There's no need for further safety protocol." Cara was already in danger. What else could happen? Finally, she shoved open the large door and pointed to an examination table. "Put her there."

The guard lowered Cara to the bed and she immediately curled onto her side. He frowned. "Do you need me in here?"

"No." Emma switched on the computer system. "Thank you."

"Of course. I want to scout the outside again. Call me if you need me." He turned on his heel and hustled from the room, the door vacuuming shut with a suction of sound.

Cara gave a low moan from the bed. "I can't reach Talen. And this *hurts*."

Emma grabbed a needle and hurried toward her sister to draw blood. "Give me just a second to see what's going on."

She took the vial to the Prism and started the test, her foot tapping impatiently for the thirty seconds needed to spit out the results. She grabbed the paper to read, and fear cut into her heart like a sword. Schooling her face, she turned around.

"What?" Cara struggled to sit up on the bed, her hand clutching her stomach.

"The protein unique to the catalyst is in your blood."

"How?" Cara cried, pure panic rushing across her small features. "How did they get to me?"

Emma shrugged. "Not the time to deal with that. Right now we need to counter this progression." Oh God. The baby.

Realization dawned across Cara's face and she straightened, her lips turning white. "This will turn me human much faster."

"Yes."

"A human can't hold a vampire baby." Dead certainty colored each word.

"We don't know that for sure." Emma shifted toward the computer and tapped in keys with impatient fingers.

"You and Kane can counter the catalyst, right?" Tears flowed freely down Cara's face and her hands trembled in her lap.

"Kind of. But we think some sort of spell is needed to make it work." Relief filled Emma when Moira's face came into focus on the big screen.

"Hello." The witch stood in combat gear, a large sword at her side. "They called me in from the training field. Isn't it night there?"

"Yes." Emma straightened. "We need your help. Cara was infected with the catalyst, and we're worried about the baby."

Emerald green eyes flashed in concern. "Baby? Oh."

That one word said it all. The baby wouldn't be able to survive in a human body. "Have you figured out a spell?"

Moira shrugged out of her protective vest. "Kind of. It's not ready though." She whipped off a baseball cap and fiery curls rioted down. "You knowing this level of magic breaks several laws."

"I don't give a crap about laws." Cara swung her feet over the edge of the bed. "The spell has to be ready. I can feel this baby slipping away. We need to do this now."

"I'll deal with the legalities later." Moira's eyes widened and she gulped. "Do you have the supplies I told Kane to buy?"

Emma glanced around frantically and spotted a large box under the desk. She yanked it out and ripped open the top. "Yes."

Moira nodded. "Do you have the compound you and Kane have been working on for her to ingest?"

"Yes."

"Okay. Cara, lay back down. Emma, take out the three white candles and put one toward her head, the other two at her feet." Moira rifled through a stack of papers. "You'll have to do the spell since I'm not there."

Did she even believe in magic? Emma grabbed the candles and rushed forward to place one on the shelf by Cara's head and two on the table by her feet. A search in the drawers found matches, which she quickly used to light the candles. Soft vanilla wafted through the room.

"Do you have a bowl?" Moira squinted through the screen.

Emma grabbed a test beaker, steeling herself against Cara's low moan of pain. "How about this?"

Moira shrugged. "Close enough. Now cut a piece of Cara's hair to place in the bowl."

Her hair? Seriously? Emma located scissors and clipped off a curl. She brushed a kiss on Cara's forehead. "It'll be okay, Car. I promise." She put the hair in the glass beaker. "What now?"

"Find the lavender incense and crumple pieces into the pot and then add the golden rod seeds." Moira yanked her curls up into a band and out of her now pale face.

Emma read several labels on plastic bags until finding long rows of incense. She crumpled them up and ripped open the bag of seeds to toss in the beaker. "Okay."

"Now add the myrrh and dried boneset to the mixture."

The dried herbs joined the rest and Emma mixed the concoction with a spoon. "What now?"

Moira stepped to the side and the sound of keys tapping came across the line. "I just e-mailed you the spell. You'll have to say the words when everything is ready."

Emma's computer beeped and she opened the e-mail and pushed print. She said a quick prayer Moira knew what she was doing.

Moira sighed. "Okay. Do you have the dosage of your compound ready?"

"Just a minute." Emma shoved her way past the tables and desk to a small refrigerator, doubt filling her. They hadn't tested this on anyone yet. She grabbed a small vial and shut the door, turning back toward Cara.

Cara gave a shaky smile. "I want to do this, Em."

"But we haven't tested this. We don't know—"

"It doesn't matter." Cara placed her hand over the baby. "He'll die if we don't do something."

Emma nodded and trudged to the screen. "I have it." God. This had to work.

Moira glanced at the vial and then back to Emma's face.

"Light the contents of the beaker on fire, then prick Cara's finger with a needle. You'll have to put three drops of her blood into the mixture."

Blood? What in the hell was she doing? "So this spell only works one at a time with specific blood?"

Moira shook her head. "I'm not sure it works at all, Emma."

"I'm sure it does." If she believed in spells, that is. Emma slid a match along the match cover and the fire flared to life. She lowered the flame to the mixture which began to smolder. Emma grabbed a pin and pricked Cara's finger to hold over the smoking beaker. One, two, three drops of blood joined the flame. Smoke billowed an odd purple color into the room.

"Okay, Emma. Now listen to me. The actual words of a spell don't matter. What matters is that you believe. That you can visualize the energy swirling and changing the actual matter of the catalyst. It's all science. Choose quantum physics. Or string theory. Or chaos theory. Whichever theory you believe in—apply it. Use your innate ability to alter energy to do so."

Emma sucked in air, her mind spinning with what little she remembered about quantum physics. "Okay."

"Good. Now hold the vial over the beaker and say the spell." Moira's eyes darkened until green melded black. "I'll say the words in my head with you and send all the power I can your way."

Emma nodded and placed the beaker next to Cara on the table, grabbing the vial in one hand and the spell in the other. She focused on Cara. "Are you sure?"

"Yes." Cara's eyes filled with fear and hope in equal measure.

Emma took a deep breath and began to read.

With fire, herbs, and blood,
I seek to unbind an unnatural bond,

To use the candles as energy,
To set this affected virus free.

The candles flickered and an impossible breeze began to stir through the quiet lab. Emma shivered, the hair on her arms standing up. She pictured a bolt of energy ripping through the test tube, scattering atoms and molecules. Her hair curled and an electric current began to run just under her skin, while her heart settled into an ancient rhythm that felt like home. She dropped the paper and lifted her head, her eyes wide open as power slid through her bones. She felt the words to her very soul, and they came from her.

Reason, science, and chaos,
Separate the strings of the catalyst
Allow the virus to be free
As my will, so mote it be.

The air crackled and electrical flashes flew around the room. The liquid in the vial bubbled up, churning blue and green with white sparks. The candles swooshed out and the fire fell silent. Emma shifted wide eyes to Cara.

Cara sat up. "Give me the vial."

A fog had settled around Emma's brain and she struggled to surface. She handed the vial to Cara, who quickly tipped back her head and drank the midnight colored liquid. A red flush started at her hairline and swept down her face and neck.

"Cara?" Emma's feet remained rooted to the floor.

"Yum." Cara's eyes rolled back and she collapsed on the bed, out cold.

"She said, yum?" Moira asked, placing a shaky hand against her forehead.

"Yeah." Emma glanced in concern at her sister. "With the candles and seeds and everything, it smells like . . ." Panic swept through her blood to replace the power. "Oh God."

"Emma?" Moira stepped closer to the camera. "What does the room smell like?"

Emma shifted her gaze to Moira. "Tulips."

She sent Dage a shrieking call for help. With a soft cry, she leaped toward her unconscious sister.

Chapter 25

Dage studied the prophet across the aisle of the Black Hawk as the chopper blasted through the air. Jesus. The Kurjans had worked the man over and well. Deep purple and red bruises covered Guiles's face and his right arm sat in a sling with the vampire lacking the strength to repair the broken bone. For now. Unease whipped into Dage from his side and he glanced at Talen. "What?"

Talen shrugged, his golden eyes mutating to a pissed green. "The virus messes with my ability to reach Cara. I don't like it."

Dage nodded, sympathy tightening his throat. He kept his shields up for now, the residue of the battle still echoing through his brain. He'd killed hard and fast. His mate didn't need to see the blood in her dreams. "These soldiers were more advanced, more prepared for us." He nodded to where Conn concentrated to heal several knife wounds in his upper chest.

"Yes." Talen peered outside as the military helicopter touched down on the cement near the airplane hangars followed by three other choppers. He ripped open the door and jumped out, turning to assist with the wounded.

Dage exited last, stretching his neck as the moon split the night. The calm before dawn. His favorite time. He began to jog alongside Talen across the tarmac, musing he hadn't made love to Emma during dawn yet. He'd have to rectify that situation in about an hour.

A piercing scream in his head stopped him cold, shifting his gaze to the lab perched in the distance. Fear, Emma's view from inside the lab, and the strong scent of tulips flashed through him. Then two missiles shot from the sky and the building exploded.

He froze. His heart thumped hard. Opening his senses, he felt nothing. A coldness slithered under his skin. All warmth gone.

Emma.

Fire billowed into the air.

Pain shrieked through his bones. The king slammed to his knees. Rage and an unfathomable agony ripped into him. He lifted his head, howling to the universe. From his power, the earth rumbled. Clouds shot across the sky to bind the moon. Lightning attacked and thunder rose to an unholy pitch that pierced eardrums.

Several military helicopters dropped Kurjan soldiers to the ground.

Dage leapt to his feet, a feral growl erupting from his chest.

They'd all die.

He reached the enemy first and ripped off its head with one hand. His brothers flanked him but he was beyond caring. He roared his mate's name and set forth to destroy.

More Kurjans dropped and dark blurs of motion leaped out of the forest. A blaring alarm pierced the night. They were under attack.

Jordan and his enforcers ran full bore toward the tree line, shifting into cougars once far enough away not to impact the vampires. Shrill howls rent the air when the deadly cats met the werewolves.

Dage yanked his knife out of his vest and slashed into the nearest Kurjan, snarling when the bastard stabbed him in the knee. He welcomed the pain. "More." He sliced through the soldier's throat, running full out for his next target.

"Jesus, Dage, watch behind you," Jase shouted.

Dage ignored his brother, fighting like the minions of hell lived in his skin. Nothing mattered but getting to the lab. He vaguely heard Talen issue an order through the comm line for the secondary team to evacuate the women and prophets to the mountainous headquarters.

He reached the crackling pile of rubble, tossing glowing cement blocks out of the way, scalding his hands. Jase and Conn covered his back, grunting with the effort to fight back soldier after soldier who wanted the king dead.

If he didn't find her, they could have him.

She had to be there. Somewhere safe in the rubble.

A thick hand banded around his arm and jerked him around. He struggled in Jase's grasp.

"No. There's no life here, Dage." Jase's copper eyes swirled with a deep maroon Dage had never seen in them. "I can sense life. There's none here."

"No!" Dage roared, shoving his brother back three steps. He opened his mind, his heart again to find her.

He remained empty.

Emma was dead.

So was he.

But for now, he'd kill.

He glanced at the tarmac. Bodies were scattered across the cement, some moving to the side to repair themselves. Vampire guards. His men.

A knife slashed across his cheekbone and he pivoted, hissing at the Kurjan. "This is going to hurt."

The enemy's purple eyes widened and he lifted his arm again only to have Dage cut if off with a quick slice of his wrist. The soldier howled in pain. Dage waited until he closed cracked lips over those yellow fangs before stabbing him in the throat and twisting. The Kurjan's head beat the body to the ground, blood seeping into the cement.

The king in Dage was gone. The soldier in him craved more death. Slashing and gouging through enemy after enemy appeased his pain for a moment.

His fangs flashed, needing blood. Even his own. The sharp points pierced his lips and the taste of his blood, scented now with spiced peaches, threw him into a maelstrom of fire he'd never escape.

This one last taste of her was his undoing.

He growled low. Time stopped. Sound disappeared. An empty hole remained where his heart had beat; a gaping darkness swam where his soul had been. He regressed past human, past animal.

To death.

Maybe beyond.

The destruction he wreaked would be whispered about in fearful voices for centuries. He didn't care. Her image filled his head. An agonizing picture of her gentleness with Janie. A kindness his own sons would never know.

He slashed and diced and killed, spewing anger in an ancient tongue—in pure notes of pain. More than one Kurjan lost his head with a twist of the king's wrist. Desperate vengeance. Raw death. Undeniable power.

Until he came face to face with a werewolf.

Fangs glittered with blood as eyes the yellow of hell focused on him, the stench of death billowing out on its breath. The beast rose to at least a foot taller than Dage, coarse gray hair standing up and sharp claws extending.

The king settled into a fighting stance, more animalistic than the creature about to die, an image of Emma, eyes darkened, faced flushed with pleasure ripping through his thoughts. A sight he'd never see again.

The werewolf stretched and bunched thick back legs, leaping forward and taking Dage to the ground. He smashed into the cement, bones protesting as he flipped the animal over his head and rolled to his feet. Blood dripped down the back of his neck. Spiced peaches.

He grunted and took the putrid beast down with a tackle. They rolled end over end until he could lever his knife into its neck. It howled, trying to escape. Dage leaned on top of the hairy abomination and twisted the blade. The words he spewed while killing were even too ancient for him to recognize. The hellish eyes slowly closed. The warmth from Emma's last kiss against Dage's cheek faded away in unison.

A voice in his earpiece gave Dage pause. "Janie was loaded into the first helicopter. But the Kayrs women aren't here."

The words had a meaning he failed to grasp. Reason had fled. He fell off the dead werewolf to settle on his knees, blood soaking his clothes, pain ripping his skin. Conn and Jase stood above him, flanking their brother. Their king. If he'd had any energy left, he'd tell them it was too late.

Talen barked something through the line and someone answered that Cara had been with Emma. In the lab.

Her name was a needle sharp sword in his gut. Dage lifted his head as shock slammed across Talen's hard features. "No."

Leaping over smoldering wood, Talen landed in the middle of the fire and began tossing cement and debris out of his way. Kane stood guard, a desperate anger on his strong face. He and Jase shared a look the king couldn't decipher.

Jase raised his hands to the sky, muttered something under his breath and the skies opened to pour rain over the battlefield. The fire sputtered out. Black smoke billowed into the air.

Dage lowered his chin to his chest, unable to watch Talen dig. Nobody lived below the debris. His body hurt. Power and energy no longer pumped through his veins. Emma.

The clouds began to part and pinks and golds scattered across the sky to torture him with a new day. The remaining Kurjan soldiers ran for their helicopters, which quickly rose into the sky.

"Now," Conn ordered through the earpieces.

Missiles fired from the earth and blew all five Kurjan helicopters into sharp fiery pieces that pummeled to land with loud crashes against the ground. Metal rained down almost in slow motion, as if even time had given up.

Dage turned his head to survey the battlefield. Blood ran thick into the greedy earth; dead bodies littered the cement.

Vampire, Kurjan, and animal.

They'd all lost.

Chapter 26

Emma slowly opened one eye, pain radiating out of her ears. What the hell? Moist earth tickled her nose, and she rolled to her back on the wet ground to survey a clear blue sky. Trees surrounded her and birds chirped a happy tune. Where in the world was she?

Clarity came with a snap and she sat up, dizziness instantly swimming through her head. Oh yeah. She scrambled toward where Cara lay half in a prickle bush.

Emma pulled Cara away from the sharp points and propped her against the trunk of a pine tree. "Cara? Cara. Wake up." She gave her sister a little shake.

Cara groaned and slowly opened her eyes. She shook her head. "Emma?"

"Yeah." Emma glanced around the forest. It seemed familiar somehow.

"Um." Cara blinked several times, her gaze on her bare feet. She frowned. "What the hell happened?"

Emma fought a hysterical giggle. "I transported. I mean, we transported." Wow. She had Dage's powers now.

"Why?" Cara brushed pine needles off her legs.

"Why? Because the lab blew up." How in the heck would they get home?

"There was a bomb?"

Emma froze. "Um, er no. No bomb." This wasn't going to go well.

Blue eyes sparked with intelligence as Cara sat silent for moments. "No bomb? Then how did the lab blow up?" Her lips set in a white line.

"Um. Well. There probably was a bomb. But I didn't actually see it."

"Emma?"

Damn, she hated that tone of voice. Emma blinked twice. "Fine. I've had visions of the lab blowing up with me inside."

"What?" Cara gasped.

"Yes. But I didn't know you were there. Besides, the scent of tulips always filled the air, so I figured I was safe until next spring." The explanation sounded lame even to Emma's ears.

Cara shook her head, a frown bearing down between her eyes. She just stared.

"So I was wrong. I should've told you and Dage." Emma fought the urge to squirm. "Stop lecturing me."

"You think this is bad? Wait till Dage finds you." Cara eyed the forest around them. "Where the hell are we?"

"Dunno." Her feet slipped on moist pine needles when Emma tried to stand. She studied her sister's flushed face. "How are you feeling?"

Surprise widened Cara's eyes. "Oh. Yeah." She closed her eyes and her shoulders visibly relaxed. Her smile rivaled the sun's light. "Good. I feel good. I can sense the baby is all right." She stood to her feet and enveloped Emma in a hug. "You did it. You saved him."

Thank God. Emma bit her lip. "For now. We stopped the catalyst." The virus would meander slowly on its own damn path, and Cara's quick pregnancy was still unheard of. Would the virus stay at bay for nine months?

Cara sighed. "Good enough for today, Em. We'll worry about the virus tomorrow."

Emma nodded. "Good point. Um, do you have any sense of where we are?"

Cara peered around. "Oh."

"Oh what?" Unease whispered through Emma.

"Well . . ." Cara stepped onto the path. "I think we're in our forest. You know, back in Tennessee."

What? Oh crap. "You're right. I was so scared and only had a few seconds, so I must have teleported us somewhere we'd always fled for safety." Away from the bastard who'd raised them, the forest had always been a safe place to hide from their father during one of his drunken rages.

"So we're across the country from where we need to be." Cara lifted her hands and stretched her back. She closed her eyes and inhaled. Flashing blue eyes opened. "Nope. I still can't reach Talen. Damn it."

Emma took a deep breath. "Okay, let me try to find Dage. My brain is still kind of fuzzy." She opened her mind and a ball of rage slammed into her, dropping her to the ground.

"Emma!" Cara darted forward and dropped to her haunches. "Are you all right?"

"Yes. Wow. Dage is pissed." Emma pushed herself to a seated position and wiped slimy pine needles off her hands. "They must still be on the raid to rescue the prophet. I'll wait a couple minutes and try again." She let Cara tug her up.

Cara eyed the trail. "Come on. Let's check it out."

"Oh, ah, well . . ." Emma raised an eyebrow, glancing at the narrow path.

"Come on." Cara started forward, picking her way around prickle bushes and blackberry patches carefully with her bare feet. "I've always wanted to burn down the damn house. It's probably fallen to the ground by now anyway."

"Okay." Emma so did not need this trip down memory lane. She'd left Tennessee behind emotionally as well as physically years ago. But she couldn't let Cara go alone. When she reached the edge of the forest, she couldn't help but gasp in surprise.

Cara smiled. "Look at that."

Their crappy old house had been painted a soft white and

stood surrounded by carefully tended beds of geraniums and pansies. A small swing set and a myriad of softballs, footballs, and Frisbees dotted a lush green lawn.

A rumble of a truck sounded down the dirt road and Emma jumped, tugging Cara behind a tree. Clean but battered, the Chevy rolled to a stop and a man hopped out. He stood over six feet in dirty overalls, a thick thatch of sandy blond hair tucked partly under a St. Louis Cardinal cap.

Anxiety crept down Emma's spine. The guy was big.

The screen door tore open and a sandy-haired boy around six years old rushed out of the house, running full bore to leap at the man, who caught him and swung him in a wide arc.

"Mom burned dinner," the boy said with a shake of his head.

"What?" The man's shoulders shook with laughter and he eyed the doorway. "Are you sure?"

"Oh yeah." Solemn nod from the child. "Smoke, stinky stuff and"—he glanced behind him before refocusing on the man—"she said . . . damn."

"No," the man said, choking on a chuckle. "Really?"

The door opened quietly and a petite woman with brown curly hair firing in every direction put her hands on her hips. "I burned the heck out of the lasagna."

"I heard." The man upended the boy and began striding toward the house while holding his giggling bundle.

A girl about eight or nine peered around the woman. "Bobby Malone tried to kiss me again today."

The man stopped and clearly fought back another grin. "What did you do?"

The girl shrugged. "I said we should play kickball instead."

"Good choice. Let's celebrate such a wise decision." He threw the boy in the air and then landed him safely on his feet. "I'll shower and we can go to town for dinner."

The woman smiled. "I already found a coupon for Montey's Restaurant."

The door shut behind the man as he ushered his family inside.

Cara sighed next to her. "Wow. I guess the house has moved on."

Emma nodded, her shoulders slowly relaxing. "The house is happy."

Cara shut her eyes and inhaled. "So are the people in it."

"Good." Emma still didn't wish to have Cara's empathic abilities. "This isn't our life anymore, Car. Let's go home." She led her sister back down the quiet path, steeled herself, and opened her mind again, wincing when fury and raw pain sliced through her like a blade. *Dage, damn it. Knock it off.*

Quiet reigned for a moment. *Emma?*

Such pain, hope, and fear in the one tiny word. *Yes. I'm with Cara. Umm, in Tennessee. We're all right.*

The king materialized at her side, whisking her into his arms to drop his head to her neck. Birds scattered out of the trees, squawking in protest. His large body trembled around her and she fought to center her own breathing. "I'm okay," she whispered softly against his hair.

He lifted his head, tears swimming in those dangerous eyes. "I thought—"

"I'm fine. I teleported." She wrinkled her nose. "You smell like wet dog." Worse actually.

His deep chuckle echoed around the forest.

Raw cuts and bite marks marred every exposed surface of his skin. She frowned. "What happened?"

He lost his smile. "We were attacked." His gaze took in Cara standing quietly to the side. "Are you all right?"

She nodded. "Yes. Now I am. Emma and Moira saved my baby."

"Ah." Dage's face smoothed in understanding, and he held out his hand. "Come here, sweetheart. Your mate needs to touch you." He pulled Cara into his embrace, his entire body vibrating. "Everyone hold on."

Emma shut her eyes and nothingness filtered around her

again. Then they stood on a battlefield, bodies everywhere, the smell of burned flesh choking the air. Her eyes widened on the sight of Talen throwing huge chunks of concrete and wood into the air, digging into the demolished lab.

"Talen?" Cara called, pushing away from Dage and taking a step toward the smoldering mess.

Talen pivoted in slow motion, blood on his face, eyes a dangerous green. He leaped for her, grabbing her close and dropping to one knee. His roar filled the morning.

Tears choked Emma's vision and she turned her face into Dage's chest. "I was so scared."

Without a word, Dage lifted her in his arms and strode for the forest. Blood covered his clothing, transferring deep red to hers. Emma gasped, eyes widening on the deadly battle-field the soldiers were hurriedly cleaning up. No one met her gaze. Within seconds, darkness surrounded them, coolness in a heated day.

"What—" Emma started, then gasped as Dage's mouth de-voured hers. The smoothness, the diplomacy that was so much a part of him . . . was gone.

He took.

Hunger slashed through her. She craved. Now.

Shifting, he pressed her against a tree, his hands tearing the jeans and panties from her legs, ripping open his fly. He im-paled her in one sharp movement.

Without pausing, he began to pound, his fangs dropping into her jugular.

Shock held her immobile for a moment. Then a warmth began to hum inside her. A tingle started in her womb and exploded through her entire body, tightening every muscle as she came. She bit into his neck, and blood shot into her mouth, filling her with power. Raw energy. Need.

Waves pummeled through her. More than an orgasm. An affirmation of life.

He swelled inside her and then came in great, heated gusts, filling her beyond possible. Panting, he licked the wound on her jugular and dropped his head to be cradled between her neck and shoulder.

A low sob escaped him.

She stilled, and pure instinct had her clasping his head to her skin. His giant body trembled against her. Soft murmurings without meaning welled up and she whispered them into his dripping wet hair.

He lifted his head and she gasped. His eyes were the darkest of midnight. No color. Not even a hint of light.

His fangs retracted. "I thought I'd lost you." His jaw hardened. "I won't go through that again."

As she watched, a shard of silver swam to the surface in those deadly eyes. Then another. "I know. I had to go to the lab, Dage. Cara was losing the baby."

He released her, reaching down to yank her jeans up. She bit back a wince.

"I've covered you with blood. I'm sorry."

She glanced at the red marring her white sweatshirt. "At least it's not our blood." It needed to go in the garbage. Now.

He grabbed her hand. "We need to relocate. Somehow they found us. We'll figure out how later." Purposeful strides had them toward the edge of the forest way too soon.

Embarrassment caught in her throat and she tugged back. Everyone would know what had just happened.

Dage pivoted and lifted her without a word, tucking her head into his neck. Sandalwood filled her nostrils, and she relaxed. She kept her face hidden as he loped across the field until they were at the helicopter next to where Talen stood with Cara in his arms.

"Only family and our people to headquarters. Send the rest to the coastal facility," Dage ordered.

Talen nodded. "Already done. Caleb and Jordan are included as our people, right?"

Dage paused. "Jordan yes. Caleb? Perhaps. But have him come to Colorado anyway." He jumped inside and took a seat while Talen did the same, Cara still in his arms.

Emma looked around, trying to focus on anything but the dangerous mood that still gripped the king. Her mate. "Where's Janie?"

The door shut, and Talen nodded at the pilot. "I sent her with Max, Lily, and a full contingent of soldiers the second we were attacked." The chopper rose into the air. "They've already arrived at headquarters."

Emma shifted in Dage's arms. Her balance needed restoring—the king had scared the shit out of her. "The shifters?"

"Yes. They've arrived at headquarters as well." Talen sat back, extending his legs before him, his livid gaze not offering any reassurance. "Why in the hell were you two in the lab?"

Cara's hands began to tremble in her lap. "The baby . . ."

Emma struggled to get off Dage's lap and sit on the seat. He kept her in place, his muscles thick bands of unrelenting steel. Finally, she sighed and gave up the fight. "Cara was infected with the catalyst. She began to rapidly turn human again."

Dage stiffened, gripping her harder.

Fire shot through Talen's eyes. "Okay. Start from the beginning."

Janie snuggled down in her pink bed clutching Mr. Mullet to her nose. She was back underground with the earth who whispered secrets to her. The earth's heartbeat echoed softly through every rock wall along with peaceful warmth. Mama and Daddy slept in the next room, having shown up only a couple hours after Janie did. While she'd waited, the pretty prophet played Old Maid with her, and Janie even let Lily win twice.

Her eyes drifting closed, Janie let sleep come until she walked along the beach. She'd seen a picture of the ocean the day before and wanted to play alongside it. The water probably didn't smell like blueberries, but in her dream that was okay.

* * *

Zane wandered barefoot along the sand toward her, stopping to grab a white shell on the way. "You're dreaming about the ocean." A deep bruise covered the right side of his face.

"What happened to your face?" She'd really hurt anyone who dared hurt her Zane. Somehow.

He shrugged. "Training. I dodged when I should've ducked." His grin showed his dimples.

Boys. How dumb. "I've been thinking of calling Talen *Daddy*. What do you think?"

"I think he's your dad and you should call him that." Zane shifted his focus to the sparkling waves. "I'm sure he'd be proud if you did."

Warmth flushed through her. "Yeah, okay." She scrunched her toes in the gritty sand, wondering if that's how it really felt. "Have you seen Kalin again?"

"No. Not yet." Zane's jaw hardened. "But I will."

Janie nodded. They both would. "We got attacked by Kurjans and werewolves." She'd seen part of the fight as her helicopter lifted into the sky. "But I didn't see them coming. Why didn't I see them coming?"

Zane shrugged again. "You're not supposed to see everything, Janie Belle. You know that."

"What else don't I see?" And why did her friend seem kinda sad?

He sat on the warm sand and tugged her down next to him. "I don't know. Things are changing but everything will be all right in the end."

"You can see the end?"

"No. But I'll make sure it ends up okay. Trust me."

She did. He was her best friend. "We'll always be friends, right Zane?" She grabbed his hand to hold on tight.

"Absolutely." His big hand surrounded hers with warmth. "Even when we're really old."

"Like thirty?"

He smiled. "Even after that. Even if we don't talk for a while."

She clutched his hand harder. "Why wouldn't we talk for a while?"

He shifted his green gaze to her. "War has been declared and I need to train for my calling, Janie Belle. I may not be able to visit as often."

Wow he had pretty eyes. She sniffed. "But you'll try?"

"I promise."

Good. Zane would never break a promise to her. She'd seen him as a grown-up fighting. As a grown-up, as a soldier, a darkness surrounded her friend that she needed to fix.

That was *her* calling.

Chapter 27

Conn crossed his arms, leaning against the smooth rock wall of the communications room, Jordan at his side. While the king liked being underground, Conn hated it. He figured the enemy wouldn't come so far under the earth's surface, and he was more of a face-to-face kind of guy. The need to hit something made his fists clench against his ribs.

Before them, Jase stood in front of three cameras with a dark tarp behind him as camouflage, shielding the rocks. Their headquarters in the Colorado mountains needed to remain a secret—needed to be a haven.

Jase cleared his throat, continuing with his first press conference, for lack of a better term. "So the Realm dealt with the threat. The royal family is under lockdown for the time being."

Off camera, Chalton manned a console that looked like it belonged at NASA Space Center. He punched in a button and a face swam into focus on yet another screen. Vivienne Northcutt, head of council of the Coven Nine.

Deep black eyes set in a lined face still lovely sparked. "Where is the king?"

"The king is attending to business." Dage and Talen had locked themselves in a war room to plot strategy for the day. A wry grin lifted Jase's upper lip. "You're stuck with me from now on."

Conn fought his own grin. Jase had dressed in combat gear for his debut—nothing fancy, nothing formal. A silent message that they were at war. Nicely done.

The witch cleared her throat. "Rumors abound about the king . . . well, losing his mind."

Jase chuckled, all charm. "Vivienne. You know better than to listen to rumors." He moved closer to his camera. "The Kurjans attacked. The king is a soldier first and foremost, the ultimate soldier." The smile fled Jase's face, and his eyes glowed with determination. "He took care of the threat—as is his job."

Jordan ducked his head. "Your boy knows what he's doing. He just let every leader listening know to get on board or face the king's wrath."

Conn gave a short nod.

A male face came into view on camera. Deland, head of a shifting clan in Russia. "What about this virus we've been hearing about? Does the infection really turn shifters into werewolves?"

Jase shook his head. "Not at this point, though I'm sure the Kurjans are working on their scientific research as much as we are. I can assure you, our best people are on this."

"I see. And what about the rumors regarding humans researching vampire DNA? Human scientists being allowed to know about any of our species?" Deland asked.

"Absolutely not true." Jase took another step closer to the camera. "The king has not allowed one single human to know about us or to have access to our DNA. Those rumors are unfounded and simply untrue."

Conn inhaled through his nose, his mind calculating the issue. Someone was certainly spreading rumors, attempting to take down the king. He needed to discover who it was and take care of them. Permanently.

Conn's cell phone buzzed at his waist, and upon seeing the number he excused himself and dodged into the hallway.

Ducking into a smaller office, he connected the phone to a computer, punching in buttons. He smiled. "Hi."

Moira lifted an eyebrow, her pretty face filling the screen. "What the hell is going on, Connlan?"

"What?" Dark circles marred her creamy complexion and pinched the skin around her emerald eyes. Irritation swept him. She shouldn't be stressed.

Her jaw clenched. "Is the king's mate all right? We were on a call, she said something about tulips and then . . . nothing." Moira tossed an errant curl out of her eyes. "I'm hearing reports of the king going crazy, and now Jase is giving some asinine press conference to leaders of the Realm."

"Take a deep breath, Moira." The need to protect her had Conn dropping into a chair to keep from storming to Ireland. "Emma and Cara are both fine. Their building exploded but they reached safety first." He waited until relief filled Moira's eyes and she sat, leaning her face on her hands before continuing. "The king still has his mind. We were attacked and he kicked some ass. That's it." That wasn't it. Not even close.

Moira wasn't stupid. "The king thought his mate was dead?"

"Yes."

She leaned forward, fine lines wrinkling her normally smooth forehead. "Bugger. Is he all right now?"

Warmth flushed through Conn. His mate had a pure heart. "He will be." Probably. That type of anger took awhile to dissipate. "Dage will channel everything he's going through into beating the Kurjans."

Moira nodded, a small sigh escaping her. "Did the spell work? Is Cara okay? I mean, is the babe all right?"

"We think so. The contractions stopped and Cara said she feels better, though Emma is running more tests right now." He cleared his throat. "I'm sure they would've called, but we're under lockdown. Only a couple of us can send or receive calls."

"Good. I'm glad the babe is okay." Moira glanced down. "Tell Emma the spell needs more of a tweaking before she uses it again—especially with the infected shifters." She sighed. "I'm just not sure the spell is ready, you know? I'm not sure how it even worked on Cara."

Conn nodded. "Yes. Kane said the liquid antidote needs a couple more tests before Maggie can take it, although the woman is chomping at the bit."

"I would be, too." Moira's slender shoulders pressed inward.

"What kind of trouble are you in for sharing a spell like that, Moira?" He had plenty of enemies at the moment but would take on the Coven Nine if necessary. Damn witches thought everything had to be a secret.

"None at the moment. I mean, the Coven Nine doesn't know, and I'm trying to keep it that way." She wiped a hand across her eyes. "So, ah, thanks for answering my call."

He surveyed the room behind her. "Why are you at your father's castle?"

She shrugged, still avoiding his gaze. "Where else would I be?"

Really? She wanted to play that game? "At your pretty little cottage on the edge of town."

Surprise crossed her features. "How did you—"

"I'm aware of your location at all times, mate." He let the words sink in, disappointment surprising him when she didn't rise to the bait. He studied her for a moment. "What's going on, *dailtín?*"

Her sad smile twisted his heart. "I'm not a brat."

"Yes you are." He grinned. "One who looks like the world is falling onto her shoulders. What's up?" His were more than strong enough to shield her if necessary.

She leaned back, a rare moment of vulnerability lowering those shields she'd perfected for so long. "Magic. Someone used it to harm. To speed up the virus. Probably with the actual virus as well." Her pain slid along his own skin to bite.

Ah. Magic had made her and enriched her blood. His mate would take this attack personally. "We'll find them, Moira. I promise." Determination hardened his jaw. "You understand this puts you in even more danger, right?" Besides being a mate, her power as a witch painted a bull's-eye on her smooth forehead.

He expected fire to light her eyes. Her chin to rise. A declaration that she could handle anything. What he got was a small nod and a whispered, "I know."

Every protective instinct he owned bellowed through his formidable body. "I'll come and get you."

Her hesitation at refusing him solidified his intention as nothing else could have. "No. I have things to do, Connlan." Her surprisingly dark eyelashes fluttered against her pale skin.

He frowned. "You're worried about your chances to join the Nine? He'd heard the process could be dangerous, but she was the seventh daughter of a seventh daughter. Outsiders weren't privy to the rules of the Coven Nine, and he suddenly wished he'd tried harder to understand her world, rules be damned.

Fragile shoulders straightened before her gaze lifted. "There isn't a simple application and job interview, Conn. More is involved then just having been trained properly." She glanced away, hiding her eyes from him.

"What else?" He'd bet everything in his accounts there was something else. Something that turned his firebrand of a mate into someone who refused to meet his eyes.

She shrugged. "Nothing. Just a lot going on at once."

He inhaled, searching for the right words. "I'm a soldier, Moira."

Curls bobbed when she tilted her head to the side. "So I've

heard." Amusement sparkled her eyes into the clearest of lake bottoms.

Ah good. At least she'd quit avoiding his gaze. His chuckle released some of his tension. "If I were Dage I'd cajole you with kindness and reason; if I were Kane I'd use pure logic. But I'm not."

"Meaning?" Interest and something else lit her eyes. Desire? Need?

"Meaning, I'm coming to get you." The vow echoed through the room, filled with truth. Pure truth had its own ring.

There was that fire he loved to see in her eyes. Curls rioted when she tossed her head. "The hell you are. If you think a one night stand will dictate my life, you're bloody crazed."

Man, he loved her Gaelic accent. When he'd taken her, she'd cried out in Gaelic pleasure, a soft lilt to the words he still heard in his sleep. He was done waking alone. The marking on his hand began to burn. "Here's your kind reason. I need to be inside you so badly sometimes I think I'll go mad."

She swallowed hard, a sweet blush rising over those high cheekbones.

Pleasure filled him. "Here's your logic. Fate has given us a push, and a push only. I knew the second I tasted you that you were mine. Fate or not. Marking or not. We need to give this an honest shot, which is something we can't do living across the world from each other."

Her nostrils flared and her blush deepened. Those devastating eyes darkened to something that hardened his cock.

He stood, leaning down toward the webcam, all purpose. All danger. "That's all the reason or logic you're getting. From now on, it's the soldier. This is your one chance to negotiate terms for peace. For terms you can live with."

She stood, mimicking his stance and leaning forward. "Or what?"

"Or I'll take you, Moira." Regret lowered his voice. "On my terms."

Her hair crackled with energy, and her skin nearly glowed with power. "You think you can take me, Connlan?"

"Yes." He kept her gaze, not flinching, not moving an inch. She deserved fair warning. He could and would take her out of the danger edging closer to her. And he'd keep her whether she liked it or not. "Make your choice."

She flashed her teeth in a smile of pure challenge. "Come and get me."

Dage found Conn beating the hell out of a punching bag in the underground headquarters' impressive gym. The dark slate walls provided coolness and protection so far into the earth. Industrial lights angled down, bathing the area in harsh yellow. He rolled his shoulders, his mind calculating how in the hell the Kurjans had found their compound.

"I have the newest results on Emma. She hasn't been infected." The knot of fear he'd been living with had finally abated. He raised an eyebrow when his brother aimed a killing blow to the bag.

Conn nodded. "That's good news." Thick gouges and already healing cuts spread across his bare back from the battle earlier that morning.

Dage sighed. "You should get some rest."

"Don't need rest." Conn threw a roundhouse punch, sending the bag spiraling away and back again, where he shot a side-kick and tore off the bottom half that dropped on the mat. "Need to make sure our soldiers are prepared to fight exceptionally gifted werewolves."

Dage guessed werewolves were the last creatures on his brother's mind. He'd bet anything a little redheaded witch had put Conn in this killing mood. "Has Kane concluded his tests?"

"Yes. The werewolves that attacked us were all human

converts. No shifters." Conn's head butted the top of the bag, ripping the holdings loose from the ceiling. "Maybe the virus is unable to create werewolves out of shifters." He stepped back as the bag fell and rolled over.

"We should know more next time the full moon comes out." Dage cracked his neck, wondering if Maggie would be able to fight back the werewolf inside her for a third time. Although the third time signified the human victim becoming a werewolf for good, who knows how long it would take a shifter. He figured Kane was correct to wait after the next full moon before trying the spell on Maggie. If she beat the virus a third time with her natural immunities, there was a pretty good chance the virus needed some work.

"If she shifts into a werewolf?" Conn clapped both gloved hands together, his deep green gaze meeting Dage's. "Are you going to give the order?"

"No." Dage wouldn't order anyone to kill the shifter. "Even if she turns into a werewolf, there's a chance we might turn her back." If not, he'd be the one to take her out. He wouldn't ask anyone else to live with the deed.

"I see." Conn stepped back from the bag. "If the time comes, it's my job to take her out."

Not in a million years. They'd deal with the issue if the time came. Dage steeled his spine, his gaze direct on his brother. "I need to thank you for covering my back. When I—"

"Completely lost your mind? Completely forgot all your training?" Sweat ran in rivulets down Conn's strong face, his eyes an inscrutable green.

"Yes."

Conn nodded. "You're welcome."

Dage lifted both eyebrows. "That's it?" At the very least he had expected a punch to the face.

Conn shrugged. "What else is there?"

Hopefully Dage's talk with his other siblings would go as

well. "I guess Moira helped save our nephew's life." For now, anyway. Dage grabbed a towel off the rack to throw at his brother.

Conn snatched the thick cotton out of the air and wiped off his forehead and chest. "So I heard." He grinned. "My witch is a good woman, no question about that."

"Yes, she is." Dage narrowed his gaze. "Just let me know when you want to go and we'll go."

"I leave tomorrow." Conn tossed the towel into a nearby bin.

Dage stilled. "*We* leave tomorrow."

"No." Determination hardened Conn's square jaw. "I go. I'll call if I need help."

Dage shook his head. "No—"

"Yes." Conn set his stance. "Something's going on here. You need to stay." He reached out and clasped Dage's arm. "I promise I'll contact you if necessary." He let go, gesturing around the room. "We have a problem here, and I'll be back as soon as possible. But I have this weird tickle at the base of my neck . . ."

"Me too." Dage shifted his focus as Jase loped into the room.

"I've got a weird feeling," Jase said, a deep frown on his face. "Something's bugging me and I can't quite put my finger on it." He eyed the destroyed bag on the ground before shrugging.

Kane crossed into the room with a stack of papers in his hands, his eyes a sizzling purple. "Cara's orange juice was infected with the catalyst." He handed a printout to Dage. "We brought all the food and drink out of Talen's suite before blowing up the residence facility."

"What about my rooms?" Dage scanned the report.

"A bottle of soda in your fridge was infected with the virus, but no one had opened it yet." Kane shifted through his papers.

Dage growled. "Somebody managed to infect something in my private suite?" The idea of the enemy being so close to his mate clenched his gut and fired his spine. Did those damn humans who'd broken into the lab find a way into his private quarters? Maybe he should've killed them.

"Yes."

"Have you informed Talen about Cara's juice?" Dage asked.

"Yes, he did," Talen answered from the door, stalking inside with a furious scowl on his face. He handed Dage a computer printout. "Here are the names of anyone who had access to both of our suites. Family, friends, guards, and humans."

Dage smiled for the first time that day. Only five people knew he read minds, and four of them stood in the room with him. Emma was the fifth. "Apparently we need to meet one-on-one with some people." When he found the traitor, he'd rip off the bastard's head with his bare hands. "We need to speak with the scientists we fired."

"I've kept track of them." Talen nodded. "I've already scheduled the times to interview our people. We meet with the guards one at a time first."

"Good." Dage cleared his throat. "I wanted to thank all of you for covering my back when I thought—"

"And mine," Talen said solemnly.

Kane ran a hand through his thick hair, and Jase shuffled his feet. "No problem," they said in unison.

Jase grinned. "Though I am *never* getting mated. *Ever.*"

A vision swam into Dage's head where Jase stood at an altar with a woman in white. A veil shielded her face. "Don't be so sure." Dage chuckled and then left them to hash it out, striding down the hallway and up two flights of stairs.

The king quickly lost his smile as he remembered someone had been in his suite at the residency facility. Someone had been close enough to harm his mate. His thoughts shifted to Emma as he pushed open the door to their rooms.

His mate, dressed in jeans and a dark shirt, waited, stance set, hair pulled back. Spiced peaches filled his senses. He cocked his head to the side. "Emma?"

She lifted her chin. "A couple of things occurred to me earlier today, Dage."

Why did this not sound good? Without question he'd been rough with her in the forest. He deserved a tongue lashing. "Okay." His blood began to hum with the spirit of her challenge and the need to take her to the floor. Diplomacy squashed instinct inside him. For now.

"I don't take orders from you." She spoke slowly, clearly as if wanting to get each word exactly right. Her gaze focused hard on his jaw.

"I'm the king, love. Everyone takes orders from me." Only pure strength of will kept him from grinning. He waited to see how clear and calm she would stay.

"But that's just it." Triumph filled those stunning eyes when she lifted her gaze to meet his. Finally. "I'm with the man, not the king. The king can kiss my ass."

The king had every intention of kissing her ass, maybe biting it as well. "Frankly, you've done a piss-poor job of following my orders anyway."

Her gasp made him want to roar with laughter.

She put her hands on her hips. "I just wanted to make things clear."

His mate was on the offensive. A true sign of someone feeling defensive. Why? He narrowed his gaze. "It's always a good idea to strive for clarity." His mind flashed through the last twenty-four hours to seek the reason, and everything in him stilled. Ice pricked inside his veins. How did he not see this before? "Emma," he breathed.

She took the smallest step back, her blue eyes widening. "What?"

The blood rushing through his ears made it difficult to focus. Fury like he'd never known swept the breath from his chest. A crimson haze clouded his vision. "You knew."

She froze in place, a soft blush coloring her high cheekbones. "I don't know what you're—"

"Stop!"

His barked order had the color deserting her face. He was past giving a shit. "You knew." Her slight shrug sent a snarl bubbling up from his gut. "You fucking knew the lab would explode."

"Not until the spring," she whispered, clasping her hands. "In the vision the smell of tulips always preceded the explosion. I figured I had until next spring."

He'd assumed she'd been granted a vision seconds before the missiles fired. But she hadn't. "How long?"

"How long what?"

"How long have you known about the explosion?"

Emotions ran across her face as she considered lying. He waited her out. Finally, she sighed. "For years."

His blood heated and his veins began to burn. Anger whipped through him. Trust. They hadn't come close to trusting each other. The earth rumbled a warning. He stamped down on the need to explode and focused on the woman standing before him. His mate. "You've gone too far."

Emma readied her stance across the room from the king and gulped in air, searching for a logical way to diffuse the situation. She did what she had to do.

He cocked his head to the side, his rage slamming into her. "You managed to shield the information." His eyes flashed black. "From me."

Her own temper began to raise its head. "Why wouldn't I?" She lifted her chin. "You already had me banished from the lab once. I couldn't let that happen again." The focus of her entire life had been to protect Cara. No way would she stop now.

His nostrils flared. "I should've known. I should've guessed this." He took a step toward her. "You think I haven't noticed? The way relief fills your eyes when you see Talen taking care of Cara? In case you die?" Dage took another step and the air around Emma heated. "The way you study him for weaknesses. Just in case."

She frowned. "In case of what?"

"In case he hurts her and you need to take him out."

Emma wanted to deny the statement but couldn't. The king understood her better than she thought. "I don't want to hurt your brother."

"You think that's why I'm mad? Really?" Dage's voice lowered to a timber promising retribution. "I'm angry you don't trust me to take care of things. Don't trust me with the truth."

Furious was an understatement. If she'd ever believed Dage anything close to human, the thought was dispelled in that moment. Fire glinted through the silver in his eyes and a nearly amber energy crackled along his bare arms. Instinct set in, and she eyed the door. Time to run.

"You won't make it." The set of his chin and lift of his brow dared her to try. His expression promised louder than any words that he *wanted* to chase her down.

"You haven't trusted me, either." She spoke softly. While she'd rather toss something at his stubborn-ass head, survival instinct kicked in as she faced the animal inside the king. "I understand your anger."

He chuckled. Deep and without any humor. "You don't understand a damn thing. That ends this second."

Emma nodded, fighting a catch in her throat, in her heart. He'd leave now.

His head shot up and pure fire swirled through those immortal eyes. "Leave? You think this is over, love?" Anger punctuated each syllable. "No. This actually starts now."

She took a step backward, for the first time in her life lacking the right words. The force before her stole any logic she may own. "I don't understand."

His lids half closed, power filling the oxygen in the room. "You will."

Chapter 28

Emma's next step back put her flush against the cool rock wall. The pulse of the earth surrounded her in the underground haven. It was no longer soothing, as if mother earth was clearly on Dage's side.

A sudden thought occurred to Emma, and she focused her breathing.

"No." Dage waved a hand and the air began to swirl around her. "You teleported yesterday. It's too early to do it again." His jaw set into granite, a muscle ticked along the powerful cords of his neck.

What the hell did he know? Emma drew up power from inside herself and began to concentrate. Her feet stuck to the floor as if bound by weights. "Hey."

He lifted an eyebrow. "I said, no."

She struggled to move her feet but they remained in place. "Let me go."

"No."

Son of a bitch. She gave him her best glare and instantly yanked the shields up around her thoughts.

A piercing pain shot through her mind. Those shields shattered. She widened her eyes on Dage and gasped, fury ripping through her body. The brand on her shoulder began to burn.

"No more shields." He drew in a deep breath, lowering his chin, his gaze hard. "Any other new tricks you want to try?"

She set her shoulders, inhaling through her nose. Narrowing her gaze on those sparking eyes, she focused all her power into his mind. His rage and pain had her lifting her head, even as she attacked his mental shields.

He raised an eyebrow. "Be careful what you ask for, love." His shields disappeared. He laid bare his mind, his heart, his soul.

Agony and loss slammed into her as the lab exploded, as she experienced the raw pain that had ripped through the king when he'd thought her dead. The desperation, the destruction, and the thirst for vengeance. He let her feel it all.

A force within him sucked her deep—into his soul. She wasn't the only one who had been shielding. Raw, pure power lay at the center of the king's being. Untapped. Dangerous. Absolute. Not even his brothers knew of the competing forces within him.

Emma yanked free. "What are you?"

"Your mate."

Disbelief had her shaking her head. "You could've destroyed the entire world."

"What makes you think I wouldn't have?" He raised an eyebrow. "That I still won't?"

Because at the core of that incredible soul lay pure good. Dangerous. But good. "Because I know you." Complete certainty filled her for a moment. She did know him. In fact, her place existed right beside him.

"Yes. You give me a balance I've so far lacked."

A balance he needed. A trembling set up along her spine. He'd never let her go.

"Never." No question, no hesitation, no doubt. Politically as incorrect as possible. But the truth. His gaze met hers and held.

No one was going to dictate her life. Not even him. Lowering her chin, she focused every molecule of her thought into Dage. Into taking his power for her own.

He stepped forward, twisted one hand in the front of her shirt and tugged, ripping it down the back. "Keep trying." The soft cotton swished to the floor.

She focused harder, a tingling spreading across her skin as she met with success.

Her jeans disappeared. Not ripped, not removed, just . . . disappeared. "Careful, love. Take too much and it'll bite you." His fangs dropped low with the words.

More power burst into her, and she mentally tossed his shirt away. It flew across the room. Desire rose hard and fast, her breasts pebbling against her simple cotton bra. "More."

"Take all you want." He flicked open the bra's front clasp, his gaze heating her nipples to a degree that had her stifling a moan. He dropped to one knee, his fangs shredding the cotton panties into pieces to fall harmlessly to the floor.

She drew more power and then tried to use it. He'd frozen her more than once, and she tried to still the king's limbs. He placed one gentle kiss against her mound and then stood, cocking his head to the side. Both hands went to his jeans and he released the zipper, kicking out of them and standing hard and ready before her. "Try again?"

She set her jaw and focused hard. Let's see how the king liked being helpless.

His smile was more of a snarl. A gust of wind tossed her hair around her face. The rock wall warmed behind her. Lights flickered and spiced peaches filled the space. She shook her head. "How are you doing these things?"

"I'm within the earth, not on it." Dage flicked a glance to her left hand, which rose to rest against the rock wall next to her head.

Damn it. She struggled to lower her arm. It remained in place, her knuckles firm against the hard rock wall. Her other hand followed suit, palm out. "What are you doing?" Her voice came out way too husky. Vulnerability sped up her heart beat.

He shrugged, only the pounding vein in his neck showing he was still pissed. "I'm trying to put this into a framework you understand. Scientific experimentation, if you will."

"Let me go." Desire flushed through her.

He lifted his head to scent the air. "You don't want me to."

Her *mind* wanted him to.

He smiled. "I've tried logic and reason. I've tried understanding and patience. I'm done."

Soft flames began licking across her skin until every nerve ending screamed for release. Then cold air. She began to tremble with need and clutched her jaw shut to keep from begging.

"Oh, you'll beg." The arrogant vow accompanied more heat starting at her toes and spreading up her legs. "Soon you'll promise anything I want. Anything I demand."

A dark flush covered his high cheekbones, and his eyes swirled with too many colors to count. Dage focused on her neck until she could actually feel his mouth on her. But he stood a foot away. "Come."

The orgasm ripped through her with a force she couldn't have imagined. She cried out, her fingers curling to dig nails into her palms while her wrists remained captive against the wall. She closed her eyes against the intensity, the waves of pleasure tearing her away from reality for a moment.

Dazed, she opened her eyes on him. Temper roared through her again. "You'll pay for this." Even on the heels of the orgasm, she wanted him. A hollowness echoed through her only he could fill.

He raised an eyebrow. "Not ready to beg? Well . . ."

A sweep of his hand through harmless air had a stirring warmth begin under her skin, under her bones to sweep out through every pore. Her nipples pebbled into sharp points of pain. She fought to move. To leap forward and take him to the ground.

The wall turned to ice behind her, the contrast to her heated flesh forcing a whimper through her clenched lips.

"Ah, now that's a pretty sound." Dage stepped forward and dropped his mouth to her neck, running his tongue lightly down to her collarbone. His hands remained at his side. "Do it again." He nipped.

Another whimper escaped against her will. Sandalwood and power tempted her nostrils and she breathed in deep.

One fang flirted with her earlobe. "I love you, Emma. But I'll be damned if your actions will put you in danger again." He lifted his head, his gaze deadly serious, a rock hard erection pressed against her hip.

She struggled to focus. "You have no choice in my actions, Dage."

He smiled and her heart thumped hard. He inhaled deep. "Come."

The climax hummed at her core and exploded through her skin, through her nerves until she screamed his name. Pleasure edged with pain while her breath caught in her throat. She plateaued and her lungs expelled all oxygen.

And yet, she craved. "Damn you."

"Ready to beg?"

Not if the hounds of hell nipped at her ankles.

"We'll see about that."

His broad hands cupped her breasts and he tugged, rolling both nipples between his fingers. She gasped, her knees began to tremble, and a desperate ache set up in her womb. Her nails bit into her palms, and she fought to keep from moaning.

He lightly pinched and she lost the fight, a low moan escaping from deep within her. His smile combined arrogance and need. His gaze captured hers while his hand slowly slid down her body to tap three fingers against her clit. Hard.

Her knees buckled. He grasped her waist with one hand to keep her upright. He leaned in, his breath hot on her temple, two fingers slowly entering her. "Emma?"

"What?" she gasped, her eyes fluttering closed.

"Your hands have been free for several minutes."

Damn it. She dropped them to his shoulders, clutching into his heated skin with all of her might. She began to ride his fingers, no longer caring about anger. Or fear. There was only need.

She moaned, increasing the friction. So close.

"No." He released her, both hands going to her shoulders. He pressed down, applying pressure until her knees reached the floor. Her skin rested against hard stone as she knelt before the king, his muscles bunched, his hands clutching her hair to free her face.

His stance widened. "Open your mouth."

Her breath caught in her throat. The dark command sent a spark of intrigue through her she'd certainly deny later. His hands tightened and erotic sprinkles of pain cascaded along her scalp.

He wasn't playing.

His erection jutted out hard and demanding. She inhaled the musky scent of male. Licking her lips, she didn't protest when he pressed forward, pushing his cock past her lips, into the heat of her mouth.

They both groaned deep.

She smiled around him and hummed low, enjoying the power. They'd see who begged.

He chuckled deep. "Oh, you'll still be the one begging, Highness." Desire dropped his tone to a husky growl that made her clit ache even more.

She clutched one hand into the front of his muscled thigh, while the other cupped his balls. Her fingers playing, she increased her movements, slowly taking him deeper and increasing her speed.

His breath panted out and his hands began to direct her movements, encouraging her to take him even deeper. She breathed out through her nose, the king's pleasure wafting over her.

With a low growl, he jerked her to her feet.

"Wait," she protested, not even close to being finished.

"Later." His head descended and his mouth took hers, kissing her with a demand that echoed within her own heart. He grabbed her hands and put them beside her head just where they'd been earlier, his knee sliding between her legs to press up.

Oh God. His erection throbbed long and hard against her stomach and she wanted him inside her. Now.

His hard chest flattened her breasts, his mouth devouring her. He lifted her by the waist, carrying her to the kitchen table, his mouth still claiming. The hard oak slapped against her ass when he sat her down. He lifted his head.

A primitive desire lit his eyes, and his need slammed into her. She grabbed his hair and tugged him down to her, kissing him even as she lay back on the table with her legs dangling over the edge. "Now, Dage. Now."

He lifted his head and balanced on his elbows, those dangerous eyes holding hers. Slowly, ever so slowly, he slid inside her, giving a hard shove halfway to fill her completely. Then he stopped.

She clutched at his shoulders, wrapping her legs around his waist. He wasn't going anywhere.

He raised an eyebrow. "Come."

The orgasm whipped into her, waves beginning to cascade out through her skin.

"Stop."

The climax halted. "No." Her legs clutched him harder, her fingernails digging into his fierce biceps. "No. Please . . ." A frantic, desperate need had her seeing stars.

He leaned down, his breath hot against her ear. "Beg."

Tears filled her eyes and she struggled against him, struggled to get him moving. She *craved*.

Determined silver eyes met hers. She gulped in breath. "Please, Dage, please . . ."

He gave a short nod. "Feel this, Emma. Remember it." Digging his fingers into her hip, he pulled out, then thrust in, setting up a cadence that reached her soul. He pounded for several moments, sweat dripping off his chest, his body bound tight and keeping her on the edge. Finally, his fangs flashed bright and strong and he licked her neck. "Now."

The force that whipped through her had her back bowing and her voice shrieking his name, surpassing anything human. Her release cascaded through her, and his fangs pierced her neck.

Chapter 29

Emma slowly opened her eyes, her entire body loose and relaxed in the big bed. She inhaled the scent of sandalwood and snuggled her nose into Dage's hard chest. She felt totally relaxed.

Her wrist caught on the pillow. Or rather, the intricate golden cuff manacling her wrist caught on the pillow. Dage's cuff. She frowned, trying to yank the ancient jewelry off. When the hell had he put this on her? The band didn't move. With a sigh, she glanced at the king.

He breathed evenly next to her. Even kings needed rest. She fought a yawn and closed her eyes, letting peace waft over her. She'd argue about the cuff later.

Dage growled low.

Emma frowned, opening her mind to him. Pain. Agony. So much hurt. She gasped, fighting to draw in air, and anger surged. He'd held back. As devastated as she'd seen him while reliving the moment he thought she'd died, he'd held some of the pain back. Protecting her.

In his dreams, he failed to shield. She could feel every desperate thought to the second when he decided to die too.

Without her, life stopped.

The king ended.

The man perished.

Tears pricked her eyes. Responsibility straightened her

spine. She'd protect the king. She'd cherish the man. And if she needed to keep herself safe to do so, she would.

Cara and Janie had Talen now. Emma would always be there for them, but the king needed her more. She'd keep him safe.

She placed her hand flat against his heart. Hers.

The phone buzzed and he rumbled awake, flipping the lid open. "What?"

Emma smiled. What a grouch.

He sat up in bed, tugging her into his side. "What do you think? No. I can keep them here if I choose." Quiet reigned while he listened to the caller. "Okay. We'll be ready in thirty minutes." The phone snapped shut, and Dage rolled her onto her back to nip at her bottom lip. "I'd hoped to go for round two, love."

Emma stretched against him. "Not sure I'm up to more, King."

He smiled, his hair falling over his face and giving him a roguish look. "I bet I could change your mind."

"I'm sure you could." She cradled his enduring face in her hands. "I love you, Dage. I'll stay safe, I promise."

He gave a short nod, his eyes warming. "I love you, too, and I'll keep you safe as well."

She huffed out a breath. "Then I'll keep you safe, too."

"Deal." He rolled over and tugged her to straddle him, her bare butt perched on his hard abs. "Ah, I owe you an apology."

She stretched like a satisfied cat. "The sex was amazing, Dage. No apology."

A lethal grin lit his face. "Not for the sex, love. Trust goes both ways. If I'd given you mine, you wouldn't have hidden rather important information from me."

She warmed from her heart to her toes. "What are you saying?"

"I'm saying that I'm stronger with you by my side rather

than safely kept in a box." His silver eyes twinkled. "Not that you'd ever stay in a box."

"I won't let you down."

"I know. You're strong and smart, and frankly, I could use your support." He brushed a curl off her cheek. "So I was thinking."

She fought a snort. "Probably a frightening prospect for me." Her nails raked down the strong planes of his chest. Damn if she didn't love the way his eyes shot blue through the silver from her touch. His grin warmed her heart even as his body heated her thighs.

"True." He stretched a long arm and yanked open a drawer of the bed table to remove a worn velvet box. He placed it on his chest, flipping open the lid. "Marry me."

She gasped. At least four karats of sapphire sparkled, surrounded by the clearest of diamonds. "It's beautiful."

He removed the ring and clasped her left hand to slide the cool metal on her ring finger. The fit was perfect. Raising an eyebrow, the king waited.

Lifting her gaze from the amazing jewels, she met his pure blue gaze, which more than rivaled the beautiful ring. "Yes." Not that he'd actually phrased the proposal as a question. But still the correct response. The one she needed to say.

The most powerful being in existence grasped her head and lowered her to his mouth for a kiss sweet enough to taste like forever.

She straightened up, holding her hand out to admire the sparkle. "I didn't know vampires believed in marriage."

He shrugged, nearly knocking her off his large body. "We don't. But you do. Besides, the ring was my mother's. She'd like your wearing it."

Tears pricked Emma's eyes. "That's so nice." She cast a glare at the golden cuff on her arm. "The ring clashes with the cuff, Dage."

He tugged off the cuff. "We can't have that."

She flashed him a look of surprise.

He grinned. "I don't need the cuff to find you, love. I just like shackling you once in a while."

Her thighs clenched against his flesh in response. "Hmm. Well, who was on the phone?"

Rolling from the bed, he tugged her with him. "The prophets want to leave for their headquarters and we're having a quick send off breakfast."

She frowned. "Why would they leave?"

Dage shrugged, lifting her and striding into the attached bath, flipping on the shower and stepping inside. "They do have work, love. And their guards are usually top notch." He placed her on her feet.

"Oh." Emma rolled her neck, letting the warm water cascade down her back. "That's too bad. I wanted to get to know Lily better."

"Well," Dage poured shampoo into his hands and lathered up her hair. "I'll keep her here if you wish."

Emma fought a groan at his wicked fingers along her scalp. "Can you really tell the prophets what to do?"

Dage shrugged, rinsing the suds from her hair. "We're at war. I'm the military commander. I can do what I want."

Lots of power there. "Hmm. Sounds like a lot of responsibility." She reached down and took him in her hands, challenge sparking her smile. "So, about round two . . ."

Dage frowned at his mate across the long expanse of table. Whoever thought to put one long table in the underground executive dining room should be shot. She was all the way across the room from him, damn it. The sparkling smile she kept sending his way made his cock throb to be inside her, and the vixen knew it.

She looked at home surrounded by priceless oil paintings and gleaming antiques. Light glinted off the purest of crystal, still no match for her beauty. She spoke animatedly with

Guiles on one side of her and Milner on the other. The woman was surrounded by prophets.

Talen cleared his throat next to Cara, who sat on Dage's right. "Maybe you should stop scowling."

Caleb laughed, reaching to pour more champagne in his orange juice on the other side of Lily, who sat to Dage's left.

While Dage liked both Cara and Lily, he wanted Emma next to him. He'd arrange the seating much better next time they had an official meal.

Jordan, Katie, Kane, Jase, Conn, and Maggie took up the center sides of the sprawling table. Dage glanced again at the end of the table. Guiles still looked like somebody had thrown him through a meat grinder. Dage didn't blame the guy for wanting to heal at home. Kane had taken all the necessary blood samples and recorded the prophet's accounting of the kidnapping.

Basically the man was lucky to still be breathing. He'd been tortured for days, but vehemently denied giving up their former location. Dage was inclined to believe him.

Talen frowned and leaned forward until only those closest to him could hear. "I've excluded most of the guards from having access to both of our suites."

"I figured. We rotate them, so I doubted one would've had access to both." Dage finished his scrambled eggs. He placed his napkin on the table. Time to take his mate back to bed.

"So who would?" Talen huffed out a quiet breath. "I sent men to interview the humans last night. None of them came close to our suites."

"You're sure?"

"A few had to be taken to the hospital after the, ah, interviews."

"We'll pay the hospital bills." Unease began to trickle at Dage's neck. Who'd been invited into the rooms? Who did that possibly leave? Reality—so clean and simple slammed into him. No, his world couldn't be so screwed up. He smiled to his left. "Did you enjoy breakfast, Lily?"

She dabbed the corner of her mouth, her black eyes sparkling. "Very much, King."

He let his smile widen. "Rumor has it you're quite the poker player." It couldn't be.

Her twinkly laugh made his gut clench. "Well. I did all right but Katie was the big winner that night."

"I taught her to play years ago." Dage leaned back in his seat. "I wanted to thank you for keeping Emma company in our suite when I was busy." It was a long shot.

Lily nodded, her smile so sweet. "Of course. I enjoy spending time with the queen."

He shoved down a low growl. "She likes you, too." Smooth as a sigh, he began to reach into the prophet's head.

She lifted an eyebrow . . . and shoved him out. "You have something to ask me, Dage?"

The woman had some serious power. "That's quite the talent, Prophet." He kept his voice low and his face set in pleasant lines, ignoring Talen's sudden stillness next to him.

"Thank you, King." Irritation began to swirl through those otherworldly eyes. "May I ask why you thought to plumb my brain?" She kept her voice low and pleasant. So much so that conversations continued unhampered around them.

He narrowed his gaze. "You had access to my suite and Talen's. You're the only one who did."

Surprise flashed in her eyes followed by anger. And then hurt.

It was the hurt that gave him pause. "I'm sorry, Lily." What had he been thinking?

She frowned, her hands twisting the napkin in her lap. Her gaze dropped to her plate and disbelief filtered through her expression. Her breath hitched. Shock flashed across her pale face. "No. I wasn't the only one," she whispered, lifting her gaze to meet his.

He stiffened, every cell in his body standing to attention.

"What do you mean?" he whispered back, letting his words barely carry as conversations continued in the room.

She glanced down to the end of the table and back up. "Prophet Milner escorted me both times. On poker night, I used the facilities and came back out to find him gone. I didn't think anything of it." Her face paled more than normal. "And he retrieved ice water for the queen and me in your suite earlier that day when we dropped by for a visit. It was his idea to do so."

Talen sat forward, a pleasant smile on his face, his eyes hard as stone. "This raises a question about the Kurjan Idaho compound. They've been concentrating so hard on research, why have a complete compound without any labs? I mean, why take Milner to that place? It's almost as if . . ."

The back of Dage's neck prickled. "Almost as if the whole thing was staged?" His gaze narrowed on the prophet at the end of the table. Why were the soldiers at that compound so young and inexperienced?

Talen lowered his voice even further. "Yeah. Think about it. There was no research to gather, no prisoners to free besides Milner. He was rather easy to get to."

Compared to Guiles. They'd almost lost a couple soldiers rescuing him. Come to think of it, while Milner had a couple of scratches, the man certainly had avoided torture. Were the slight injuries just for show?

Anger ripped through Dage and he ruthlessly stamped it down. He slid a smooth smile on his face, winking at his mate. "Emma? How was breakfast?" He narrowed his focus while keeping his expression bland. *Get up from the table and walk this way, love.*

She started and pushed back her chair to rise. "It was wonderful, thank you." Her eyes lit with curiosity.

Damn but his mate couldn't lie worth shit. She began to move around the chair when Prophet Milner grabbed her arm.

He smiled. "I'm still a bit woozy, Highness. Help an old man up, would you?"

Dage fought the urge to leap across the table and take him down. Nobody touched his mate.

Emma faltered and tightened her wrist against her hip so he could hold on. "Of course, Prophet. Here you go." She gently helped him up.

Milner's muddy brown gaze met Dage's, and he stood. "King?"

"Yes, Prophet Milner?" He forced politeness into the words. Dage had to get the man away from Emma.

"I believe we have a problem." Swift as a snake, Milner yanked Emma in front of him and pressed a thick knife to her neck. "Sorry, Highness."

She began to struggle and stopped abruptly when the knife drew blood. Her wide-eyed gaze met Dage's across the room as red dripped down to stain her blouse.

The sight of her blood chilled him into a deadly focus.

Sound erupted around the table as warriors shoved back chairs and leaped to their feet. Jordan herded Maggie and Katie toward the door, reaching out a hand for Cara as well.

"No." Cara slapped him away. "I'm staying."

Jordan waited for Talen's nod before pushing the shifters out the door and shutting it, leaning his back against the thick oak. No one would get through the lion to escape that way.

Caleb edged to the left and rested against the only other exit. He smiled and crossed his arms.

Stay calm, love. Dage waited for her slight nod before focusing on Milner. "Prophet? If you release my mate right now, I promise I won't kill you." He used his most reasonable tone, while rage and fear battled in his gut. He began to ease around the table while Conn mirrored his moves on the other side.

Milner scowled. "I'm a prophet determined by the fates,

Kayrs. You can't kill me." The hand on the knife handle began to tremble.

Damn it. The blade was large enough to take her entire head off. Large enough to kill her. "You are threatening my mate. Last chance. Or you die." Dage took a couple more steps. If the bastard shook any more, he'd slice Emma's jugular by accident. She'd heal from that, but not from decapitation.

Milner's face paled and his eyes widened. "You don't understand. I've seen the prophesy. They must die."

"Who must die?" Talen drew the prophet's attention toward him, allowing Dage and Conn to draw nearer.

Milner flicked his gaze to Talen. "All of them. They can't live. The Paulsen women. They can't."

Talen growled low and flashed his fangs. "Why not?"

Dage maneuvered even closer, pausing when Lily darted forward and placed one pale hand on Milner's arm.

"Samuel? You're confused. Please release the queen." Lily reached her other hand to grasp Emma's arm.

Milner swung his swirling gaze to his fellow prophet. "You don't understand, you're nothing but a figurehead, Lily." Spittle formed at the corners of his mouth, and he yanked Emma harder against his trembling body. "I've *seen* the future. The child cannot live."

Dage gave Lily a subtle nod to step back. She released Milner and did so, the skin on her face so pale as to be nearly translucent.

Caleb spoke up from his vigil at the door. "What child?"

Milner shifted his stance so Emma stood directly between Dage and the prophet. "The child. The prophesy. They'll bring destruction upon us all. I've *seen* it." His eyes began to glow as madness swirled through them. "I have no choice. The women must die."

How had Dage missed this? The prophet was insane.

Emma drew in a shaky breath. "You infected them."

"Of course." Tears leaked from Milner's eyes as he focused on Lily. "I'm so sorry. You were not to be infected, Prophet Sotheby."

"But I was?" Cara shoved away from Talen, fury spinning red through her skin. "Twice?" He grabbed her arm and yanked her behind his large body until only her pale face was visible as she peered around his back.

"I had no choice. This must be stopped." Milner's mouth began to move in a barely audible chant.

Dage? Why don't I teleport? Emma drew in a shaky breath, the blood still dripping down her neck.

He had to fight his rage just to mentally answer her. *It's too soon since last time.*

She rolled her eyes.

In danger, a knife to her throat, the woman had the audacity to roll her eyes at him.

Freakin' trust me. I can draw on enough of your power to make it. Please trust me. And then she winked at her sister. Winked!

Dage drew air in through his nose. He could send her enough power to make it work and he did trust her. *Okay. But try to land close.*

Milner's hand tightened on the knife handle. "The queen must die."

"Now," Dage roared, shooting power through the air to Emma. She fizzled and disappeared to thinly materialize next to him. He reached for her and felt . . . nothing. He reached deeper, past oxygen, past space and grabbed her arm, ripping her through dimensions to land next to him.

Milner screamed a shrill cry and leaped for them, the blade extended, glinting in the soft light.

Dage shoved Emma behind his back, pivoting and letting Milner's momentum carry him near enough to grab the knife. Prophet or not, Milner had made Emma bleed. Life was no longer an option.

Dage yanked the weapon out of Milner's grip, spun the

blade and plunged it into the prophet's neck, twisting to the side while the man's eyes bulged out in pain and surprise. Blood sprayed across the room and the earth trembled. Lights flickered. Oxygen molecules popped through the air like bubble wrap.

Rage filled the king and he followed his prey to the floor, ripping through cartilage and bone until Milner's head rolled under the table.

Breathing heavily, Dage threw the knife to the ground and rose to clutch his mate close.

"Holy shit," Jase said from where he shielded Lily. "You killed a prophet."

Dage swung Emma around and propelled her toward the door, determined to get her away from death. A hard slap of freezing air stopped him. The earth roared. A gust of wind swept through the room, throwing plates and utensils to the ceiling and down to land hard on the table and floors. Chairs rose into the air to smack against each other, and Dage shoved Emma between his body and the wall.

A spark of neon light zipped through the space, clapping against furniture and rock walls before sliding over each occupant in the room. Electric static emanated from it, giving a small shock. It slithered around, crackling with a slight burn until consolidating once again and hovering for a moment in the very center of the table. The colors mutated from neon to bright blue to navy and finally back to an electric blue before shooting toward Caleb.

Dage pushed Emma back farther, his stance set to defend. What the hell? The light surrounded Caleb, visibly digging into the man's skin and bones. His mouth opened wide on a silent scream and electric light poured out, then rays shot from his eyes and ears.

A piercing whistle rent the air and everyone clapped hands over their eardrums in pain. The air lifted Caleb up to smash against the ceiling before smacking him into the wall. Caleb dropped to one knee, his hair billowing up behind him. He roared in anger, and a thick dark Celtic knot emerged along the back of his neck.

The room quieted.

Caleb struggled to stand, the breath heaving out of his chest with hard bursts. "What the fuck?"

Jordan stepped closer, his gaze on the tattoo. "The Mark of the Prophesy."

Caleb stilled, rushing over to shards of glass remaining from an antique mirror on the wall. He yanked his head to the side, eyeing the new marking. He lifted his head to the ceiling and bellowed out his displeasure. "Bloody hell."

Chapter 30

Emma smiled, hurrying along with her wrapped present. Dark stone walls made up the hallway and smooth rock lined her path in the underground haven. She'd piled her hair high on her head and the strapless dress she wore narrowed to a flared waist. Where in the world had Dage found an Xbox from deep within the earth's surface?

Kane and Conn flanked her on each side, and she fought the urge to roll her eyes. "You're aware the threat has passed, right boys? Milner is gone."

Conn shrugged. "The king said to guard you, so we guard you." He shortened his stride so she could keep up.

Kane nodded. "Not that we don't like spending time with you, of course." His sly smile reminded her he owed her a couple of good kicks.

She laughed. "You'd rather be in the lab, Kane, and you know it." Of course, so would she. "Speaking of which, when do I get to see the new lab?" Dage hadn't revealed the location to anyone. It was supposed to be ready in a week or so.

"When we move," Kane said, shifting his present from one arm to the other. He eyed the gift in her hands. "What did you guys get Janie?"

Emma shrugged. "An Xbox. What did you get her?"

Kane puffed out his chest. "A fifty-piece lab set complete with specimens, a microscope, and test tubes."

Conn snorted. "She's only five, nimrod."

Emma smiled. "I'm sure she'll love the lab set, Kane. What's in that pretty pink bag, Conn?"

Conn cleared his throat and stretched his neck. "I don't know much about little girls."

How sweet. Goodness, what had he purchased? "All you need to know is they love presents from people who love them." Emma lifted up on her toes to peek into the bag.

Conn yanked it away and to the side. "Okay. Geez. I bought her the newest Bond spy equipment set. It has listening devises, fake handcuffs, walkie-talkies, and even magic paper and disappearing ink." He slowed his pace even further. "Do you think she'll like it?"

Listening devices? "Yes. I think she'll love a spy set, Conn." Now they all had to be careful what they said with big ears listening. Not that the little protégée didn't already envision all of their futures.

The vampire smiled and relief filled his dangerous eyes. "Good. I want her to remember me while I'm gone."

Emma should find a secured line to call and warn Moira. The women needed to stick together in this new world, without a doubt.

Love? Where the hell are you? Dage's voice echoed throughout her head.

She rolled her eyes and pushed open the door to the cozy living room strewn with balloons and streamers. "Wow."

Lily took the gifts. "We had so much fun decorating. Katie and I have been taping streamers for hours." She hustled away to place the gifts on the table.

Emma pursed her lips. Lily's gaiety hadn't quite masked the dark circles under her eyes. The loss of a fellow prophet was probably difficult for her, even if Milner had been a crazy jackass. Emma rubbed her healed neck.

Janie gave a happy squeal and dashed across the room to

hug her aunt. "Hi Auntie Emma." She grabbed Emma's hand, sighing over the sparkling ring. "So he finally gave you his mama's ring, huh?"

"Hi sweet Janie." Emma leaned down to embrace the pretty girl. "I take it you knew I'd be wearing this?"

"Of course." She smiled, the gap in her teeth belying her intellectual age. "I dreamed about the sparkles years ago."

Emma rose up to take a good look. "That is a beautiful dress, Janie."

The little girl flounced twice, letting the bright pink ruffles fluff around her legs. Matching butterfly clips held back the rioting curls. "Thanks. Mama and I picked it out on the computer last week." She pointed a toe. "Do you like my big girl shoes?"

Emma nodded seriously, fighting a grin at the green sandals with bright white flowers. "Lovely. Why green?"

Janie hopped once. "They match Zane's eyes. He can't be here today, so I thought I'd wear his color on my feet."

Emma took a deep breath, figuring she'd worry about Janie's dream friend another day. She gave the child another kiss and made a beeline for her mate across the room.

He stood next to the hearth, a long necked beer bottle dangling between two fingers. His mouth on hers sent tendrils of need through her flesh. Waves of masculine pleasure wafted over her when he turned her around. "That's a pretty marking on your shoulder."

Man, she loved being inside his skin and feeling what he felt. She smiled and pivoted to focus on those silver eyes. "Thank you. The mark came with a vampire."

"I like that you're showing it off."

She bit her lip, fighting a laugh. "Well, so far I'm the only Kayrs mate who can show the marking without being arrested for indecent exposure."

Dage grinned. "I do think ahead, unlike my impetuous brothers."

"Well. You are the king." A dark edge still licked at the

king's emotions from the snapping of control when he'd thought she'd died, an edge she'd need to smooth. In time. She glanced over to where Talen stood with an arm wrapped securely around Cara. "What do you think Milner meant about the prophesy? About the child?"

Dage shrugged, running his fingers down Emma's arm to clasp her hand. "I think Milner had gone crazy. We're tracing his movements for the past hundred years to determine where he went off track, but it'll take a while."

"Did he actually work with the Kurjans?"

"Yes. We've found e-mails embedded in his computer." Dage sighed. "It's unthinkable really."

Emma fought against the fear of another attack. "Do you think he told them about the headquarters underground? I mean, could they be coming for us here?"

Dage tightened his grip. "It doesn't look like he got the chance. But we're still moving tomorrow." He lowered his head to press a gentle kiss on her ear. "To a place with a fantastic lab for my scientist."

Warmth slid through her from his whispering breath, and she cleared her throat when he rose back up to his full impressive height. "Speaking of which, so far the tests on Cara's blood are encouraging." She'd need to conduct more tests later. Emma surveyed the room. "Where's Caleb?"

"He left to escort Prophet Guiles home before heading to train his troops somewhere in the Midwest." Dage placed his beer on the mantle. "Caleb's determined to ignore the prophesy marking as long as possible."

"Do you think he'll succeed?"

"No. Fate wins every time. Our only choice is to claim it." The king dropped his head again to run his heated mouth along her bare shoulder.

Emma shivered, her gaze wandering around the room. The shifters laughed over by the pool table while Kane and Jase jockeyed for position next to Janie on the sofa. Conn handed

Lily a glass of what looked like punch by a table sporting a huge cake decorated with horses.

"What are you looking at, love?" Dage whispered into her ear.

Warmth slid through her heart. "Family."

He chuckled. "We'll stay until Janie opens her presents. Then I have plans for my mouth and your body."

Emma settled back into his hard chest. Now that was a plan she could certainly embrace.

Chapter 31

Sound asleep, cuddled in her bed in the underground Colorado headquarters, Janie sighed. She wondered if Zane remembered her birthday.

He jogged out from behind a wall of rock, a bunch of pink balloons in his hand. She took them with a happy squeal. "You remembered."

"Of course." He rolled his pretty green eyes. "You reminded me every time I saw you last month."

Well. Boys sometimes forgot important stuff. "I've missed you." She released the balloons to float into the sky.

He watched the balloons rise with a grin and nodded, yanking a small black box out of his jeans. "I've missed you too. Happy birthday."

Janie took the smooth velvet box and slowly opened the lid. A fragile silver chain held a sparkling horseshoe at the end. "It's beautiful," she whispered.

Zane smiled. "I know you like horses, and we need good luck, so . . ." He took the box from her and unclasped the necklace, motioning for her to turn around.

She reached for the horseshoe when he placed the chain around her neck and secured the fastening. "Thank you, Zane."

He maneuvered her around to face him. "The necklace

looks pretty on you. You're welcome." A frown settled between his eyes. "I wish you could take your present with you, but this is just a dream."

She smiled up the several inches to his strong face. "I'll keep the sparkles in my memory."

"Good idea." He brushed his thick hair back from his forehead. "I'd send your present to you, but I don't know where you are."

Janie shrugged. "We're moving tomorrow to somewhere new, and they won't tell me where." Not that she didn't have a good idea, but she wasn't completely sure.

Zane frowned. "Why are you moving?"

Janie cocked her head to the side. "No one will tell me."

"Oh. Well, I'm sure the king is doing his best to keep you safe." Zane glanced toward the rocks and back again. "I must go, Janie Belle. I'll leave you for the king to protect for now."

Janie grinned. "He thinks that's his job."

Zane's dimples flashed at her. "Your safety is the king's duty right now. Someday it'll be mine."

Janie nodded, watching Zane walk away until he faded into the mist. Boys. She wasn't sure how or why, but the safety of them all would end on her shoulders.

She awoke from the dream with a start, her gaze wandering around her pretty room inside the earth, softly lit by a night-light in the corner. Her clothes lay packed in boxes near the door. Mr. Mullet had fallen to the floor, and she reached down to grab him by the hair.

A sparkle caught her eye.

Sitting up in bed, she perched Mr. Mullet on her lap and clasped the horseshoe necklace around her neck. She smiled.

Zane.

If you liked this book, try Kathy Love's
DEVILISHLY HOT!—in stores now!

"Couldn't you just have fired her?" Tristan looked down at the motionless body of yet another of Finola's personal assistants.

Finola lifted her herbal relaxation mask from her eyes and made a rueful face. "I suppose. But if you had seen what she'd done," she sighed deeply, "Well, you'd have had a hard time thinking rationally too."

Tristan, still contemplating the body, raised a dubious eyebrow. "I highly doubt it."

Finola sighed again. "That's true. You are so much more judicial than I am."

Was that what she was going to call it? Tristan would have gone with sane, but tomato/tomahto.

Finola retrieved her crystal champagne flute from the glass end table beside her massage chair. She sipped her Dom Perignon White Gold Jeroboam. A sure sign Finola wasn't pleased. The champagne always came out when she was feeling stressed. He'd call it petulant, but there was no point mentioning that to Finola. Best to just let her soothe herself with her $40,000 bottle bubbly.

"Honestly though, Tristan," she said once she'd drained her glass and poured herself another glass, "she was utterly in competent. I mean, she couldn't do a single thing right. And it wasn't like I was asking for the moon. I just expect that when I ask for something to be done, it be done on time."

Tristan, only half-listening, made a sympathetic noise. What the hell was he going to do with *this* one? Getting a grown woman down from the fifteenth floor of a busy building out to the even busier streets of Manhattan wasn't easy, even for a demon.

Really, he was the one who deserved the damned champagne.

"I simply asked her to get me the fabrics that an artist in Milan was creating specifically for the Alber Elbaz photo shoot. This was not an unreasonable request."

"When is the photo shoot?" Tristan asked, considering the white hand woven Persian carpet in Finola's office. It was big enough to wrap the body in, but Finola would have a conniption that he was using her handmade, original flown in directly from Nain, Iran. But then again, this was her doing. He couldn't help if her damned rug was another casualty of her temper.

"It's tomorrow," Finola said, a hint of peevishness making her tone a little defensive. "I didn't say it wouldn't be easy. But it was absolutely doable."

Tristan looked from the carpet to the body then back to the carpet. "What time did you tell her about this absolutely doable feat?"

Out of the corner of his eye, he saw her wave her hand, "Oh, I don't know. Probably one-ish."

His gaze shifted from the rug to the cabinet behind Finola's desk. That would be heavy all on its own, and with a body in it . . . he returned his attention back to the carpet—also heavy, the best bet.

"When is the photo shoot?"

"Eleven," she answered, topping off her glass again, the golden liquid, sparkling, bubbles dancing.

Tristan didn't feel like dancing, he was furious, but he

pushed it aside, remaining cool. Giving in to his own emotions wouldn't help the situation.

He returned to the body, crouching down to slide an arm under its neck and under its knees. With only a slight grunt, he hefted it up. Thank Lucifer and his many minions, this one was thin. The last one had been a good twenty-five pounds overweight, which hadn't helped her with Finola's wrath and ultimately was a large part (no pun intended) of her . . . early retirement.

"You do realize that gave her less than twenty-four hours to get the material for you, don't you?" he said, his tone breathy as he struggled to carry the body over to the rug.

"Well it can't be impossible. It could have been flown on the Concorde or something."

Tristan dropped the body rather unceremoniously onto the one side of the carpet. "The Concorde stopped flying about five years ago."

"Oh," Finola sighed, clearly weary of their conversation, "well whatever, she was a terrible assistant."

She settled back in her lounger, replacing her mask over her eyes. Tristan arranged the body so the limbs were straight, then he lifted the edge of the carpet and started to ease the carpet and body over, rolling the body up like the filling of a jelly roll. A very complicated, costly jelly roll.

Finola lifted the edge of her mask and peered at him. "What are you doing?"

Saving your ass.

"Playing it safe," he said, with a grunt, shoving with both arms to finish rolling the carpet. "You should really require height and weight to be included on all your employee résumés."

"You are so right," she agreed, but not for the reason he wanted the measurements on there.

He rose, running his hands down the front of his Armani trousers, smoothing any wrinkles. Ah, there was an analogy there.

"I quite like that carpet, you know," Finola said, but then released her mask back over her eyes.

Well, at least she accepted that better than he'd expected.

"I'm going to have to go get one of the moving vans to dispose of this," he told her.

She made a noise of acknowledgment, disinterested acknowledgment. But why would she care? Finola just made the messes, he cleaned them up.

He strode across her office, heading out to get the van and get this done.

"Wait," Finola said, sitting up, her voice suddenly panicked, "I don't have a personal assistant."

"No," Tristan agreed, his voice wry, "this is true."

"I need an assistant. I mean, look." She took off her eye mask and waved it in his direction. "My mask is absolutely cool now. A cool mask is not going to help this wretched headache behind my eyes. I need someone to warm my mask."

Tristan fought back the urge to roll his eyes. Instead he walked over the cabinet he had considered using for the body disposal. He opened the bottom drawer and pulled out a thick manila folder. Then he went to Finola and placed it onto her lap.

"Pick one."

She considered the file for a moment, then opened it. She flipped through several of the résumés, scanning them very briefly.

Finally she sighed, and randomly tugged one out of the dozens. "Hire this one."

She held the page out to him without even glancing at the person's education, abilities or experience.

"This could be why your assistants never work out," he said dryly, but accepted the résumé.

He raised an eyebrow as he perused the information there, but he walked over to Finola's desk and picked up her phone. After punching in the numbers, he waited as the phone rang.

Finally, just when he would have hung up, a woman answered, her voice breathless, and heavily laced with a Southern drawl.

Tristan cringed. Not a good start. Finola wasn't fond of the South.

"Hello," he glanced back to the page in front of him, "I'm trying to reach Annie—Lou," *Lou?* Really? "Riddle."

Oh yeah, this was *not* going to go well.

The woman on the other end excitedly told him that was she.

"My name is Tristan McIntyre and I'm calling from *HOT!* magazine. I'm pleased to tell you that Ms. Finola White has decided to hire you as her personal assistant."

Tristan nodded impatiently as Annie Lou thanked him profusely—and lengthily.

"Great," he said, finally cutting off her sweet, golly-gee gratitude. "We'll see you tomorrow morning. Eight o'clock sharp."

Annie Lou Riddle was still drawling away as he hung up the phone.

"Done," he said.

"You are the best, Tristan."

Yes, he was. But he didn't say anything, he just left the office. As he strolled past the large, ultra-modern assistant's desk, he made note to himself that he had to get rid of all of the last assistant's personal items that were still there.

Annie Lou Riddle. She had no idea that by accepting this job, she'd just sold her soul to the devil. Literally.

And catch ANGEL OF DARKNESS
by Cynthia Eden, coming next month . . .

He'd been created for one purpose—death. He was not there to comfort or to enlighten.

Keenan's only job was to bring death to those unlucky enough to know his touch.

And on the cold, windy New Orleans night, his latest victim was in sight. He watched her from his perch high atop the St. Louis Cathedral. Mortal eyes wouldn't find him. Only those preparing to leave the earthly realm could ever glimpse his face so he didn't worry about shocking those few humans who straggled through the nearby square.

No, he worried about nothing. No one. He never had. He simply touched and he killed and he waited for his next victim.

The woman he watched tonight was small, with long, black hair, and skin a pale cream. The wind whipped her hair back, jerking it away from her face as she hurried down the stone cathedral steps. The doors had been locked. She hadn't made it inside. No chance to pray.

Pity.

He slipped to the side of the cathedral, still watching her as she edged down the narrow alley way. Pirate Alley. He'd taken others from this place before. The path seemed to scream with the memories of the past.

"No!"

That wasn't the past screaming. His body stiffened. His wings beat at the air around him. It was *her.*

Nicole St. James. School teacher. Age twenty-nine. A woman who avoided the party streets. Who tutored children on the weekends. A woman who'd tried to live her life just right . . .

A woman who was dying tonight.

His eyes narrowed as he leapt from his perch. Time to go in closer.

Nicole's attacker had her against the wall. One of the man's hands was over her mouth, the better to make sure she didn't scream again. His other hand slammed against the front of her chest and held her pinned against the cold stone wall.

She was fighting harder than Keenan had really expected. Struggling. Kicking.

Her attacker just laughed.

And Keenan watched—as he'd always watched. So many years . . .

Tears streamed down Nicole's cheeks.

The man holding her leaned in and licked them away.

Keenan's gut clenched. Knowing that her time was at hand, he'd watched Nicole for a few weeks now. He'd slipped into her classroom and listened to the soft drawl of her voice. He'd watched as her lips curled into a smile and a dimple winked in her right cheek.

He'd seen laughter in her eyes. Seen longing. Seen . . . life.

Now, her green eyes were filled with the stark, wild terror that only the helpless can truly know.

He didn't like that look in her eyes. His hands clenched.

Don't look if you don't like it. His gaze jerked away from her face. The job wasn't about what he liked. It never had been.

There'd never been a choice.

They have the choices. I only have orders to follow.

That was way it had always been. So why did it bother

him, now? Because it was her? Because he'd watched too much? Slipped beside her too much?

Temptation.

"This is gonna hurt . . ."

The man's grating whisper scratched through Keenan's mind. Neither the attacker nor Nicole could see him. Not yet.

One touch, that was all it would take.

But the time hadn't come for her yet.

"The wind's so loud . . ." The man lifted his hand off Nicole's mouth. "No one's gonna hear you scream anyway."

But she still screamed—a loud, long, desperate scream—and she kept fighting.

Keenan truly hadn't realized she'd struggle so much against death. Some didn't fight at all when the time came. Others fought until he had to drag them away.

Fabric ripped. Tore. The guy had jerked her shirt, rending the material. Keenan glimpsed the soft ivory of her bra and the firm mounds of her breasts.

Help her. The urge came from deep within, but it was an urge he couldn't heed.

"Don't!" Nicole yelled. "Please—no! Just let me go!"

Her attacker lifted his head. Keenan stared at him, noting the gaunt features, the black hair, and the eyes that were too dark for a normal man. "No, baby. I'm not lettin' you go." The guy licked his lips. "I'm too damn hungry." Then he smiled and revealed sharpened teeth that no human could possess.

Vampire. Figured. Keenan had been cleaning up their messes for centuries. *A mistake.* That's what all those parasites were. An experiment gone wrong.

Nicole opened her mouth to scream again and the vamp sank his teeth into her throat. Then he started drinking from her, gulping and growling and Nicole's fingernails raked against his face as she struggled against him.

*   *   *

But it was too late to fight. She'd never be strong enough to break away from the vampire. She was five feet six inches tall. Maybe one hundred thirty five-pounds.

The vamp was over six feet. He was lean, but muscle mass and weight didn't really matter—not when you were talking about a vamp's strength.

Keenan stared at the narrow opening of the alley. Soon, he'd be able to touch her and her nightmare would end. *Soon.*

"*You're just going to stand there?*" Her voice cracked.

His head whipped back toward her. Those green eyes— fury and fear—and those eyes were locked on *him*.

Impossible.

She shouldn't see me yet. It wasn't time. The vamp hadn't taken enough blood from her.

Nicole slammed her hands into the vampire's chest, but he kept his teeth in her throat and didn't so much as stumble. Her neck was tilted back, her head angled, and her stare was on—

Me.

"Help me." She mouthed the words as tears slipped down her cheeks. "Please."

By the fire, she could *see* him. Every muscle in Keenan's body went tight. "I will." The words felt rusty and he couldn't remember the last time he'd talked to a human. No need for talk, not really. Not when you were just carting souls. "Soon . . ."

The vamp's head lifted. Her blood stained his mouth and chin. "Baby, you taste so good."

Her body slumped as her knees buckled. Kenton's wings stretched behind him even as his muscles tensed.

"Grade Fucking A," the vamp muttered and he eased back. *Why?* The vamp planned to kill her. Keenan knew that. Nicole St. James was dying tonight.

Nicole's hand rose to her throat. Her fingers were shaking.

Her whole body trembled. "Y-you're not real . . ." Her eyes never left Keenan.

"Oh, I'm damn real." The vamp swiped the back of his hand over his chin. "Guess what, sweet thing? All those stories you heard? About the vamps and this city? Every damn one of 'em tales is true."

Nicole didn't look at the vamp. She kept her eyes on Keenan as she inched her way down the alley. With every slow move, she kept her hands pressed against the wall.

"You gonna run?" The vamp asked. "Oh, damn, I love it when they run."

Yes, he did. Most vamps did. They liked the thrill of the hunt.

"*Why don't you help me?*" She yelled at Keenan and the wind took the words, making them into a whisper as they left the alley.

That was the way of Pirates Alley. Sometimes, no one could ever hear the screams.

The vamp seemed to finally realize his prey wasn't focused on him. The vamp spun around, turning so that he nearly brushed against Keenan. "What the fuck?" The vamp demanded. "Bitch, no one's—"

Nicole's footsteps pounded down the alley. *Smart.* Keenan almost smiled. Had she ever even seen him? Or had her words all been a trick to escape?

The vampire laughed, then he lunged after her. Four steps and the parasite leapt at her, tackling Nicole to the ground, and keeping her trapped in the alley. Glass shattered when she fell—a beer bottle that had been tossed aside to litter the ground. She crashed into it and the bottle smashed beneath her weight.

"You're gonna beg for death," the vamp promised her.

Perhaps. Keenan slowly stalked toward them. He lifted his hand, aware of the growing cold in the air. The stories about death's cold touch were true. Nicole's time was at hand.

"Please, God, no!" Nicole cried.

God had other plans. That was why an Angel of Death had been sent to collect her.

The vamp's hands were at her throat. His claws dug into her skin. The scent of decay and cigarettes swirled in the air around Keenan.

"Flowers," Nicole whispered. "I smell . . ."

Him. Angels often carried a floral scent. Humans caught a trace of that scent all the time, but never realized they weren't alone.

The vamp sank his teeth into Sarah's throat again. She didn't even have the voice to scream now. Tears leaked from her eyes.

Keenan knelt beside her. The first time he'd seen her, he'd thought . . .

Beautiful.

Now . . . covered in garbage and blood, still fighting a vampire, still struggling to live . . .

Beautiful.

It was time. His hand lifted toward her and hovered over her tangled hair. His fingers were so close to touching her. Just an inch, maybe two, separated them. But . . .

He hesitated.

Why couldn't someone else have come in the alley this night? A cop? A college kid? Someone *to help* her.

And not someone who was just supposed to watch her suffer.

A fire burned in his gut. She didn't deserve this brutal end to her human life. From what he'd seen, Nicole had been *good.* She'd tried to help others. His jaw ached and he realized he'd been clenching his teeth.

His gaze drifted to the vampire. It would be so easy to stop him and to take one less monster from the world.

Forbidden. The order burned into his mind. He wasn't supposed to interfere. That wasn't the way. Wasn't allowed.

He was to collect his charge and move on. Those were the rules.

He'd take Nicole St. James this night, and someone else would wait on him tomorrow. There were always more humans. More souls. More death.

Her hands fell limply to her sides as the vampire drank from her and her head turned toward Keenan.

There was gold buried in her eyes. He'd thought her eyes were solid emerald, but now, he could see the gold glinting in her eyes. Angels had strong vision—in darkness or light—but he'd never noticed that gold before.

Her eyes locked right on him. She was so close to passing. He had no doubt that she saw him then.

"Don't worry," he told her. The vampire wouldn't hear him. No one but Nicole would hear his voice. "The pain is already ending for you." His hand still reached for her. He'd wanted to touch her before. To see if her skin was as soft as it looked. But he knew just how dangerous such a touch would be—to both of them.

Keenan well understand what happened to those of his kind when they did not obey their orders.

Despite popular belief, angels were not the favored ones. They did not have choices like the humans. Angels had only duty.

"I don't . . ." Her words were barely a whisper. Had the vamp savaged her neck too much? "D-don't . . . want to . . . die . . ."

The vamp gulped down her blood, growling as he drank.

"Don't . . . let me . . ." Her lashes began to fall. The fingers of her right hand began to curl inward, and her wrist brushed against the jagged glass. "Die . . ."

There was so much desperation in her voice, but he'd heard desperation before. Heard fear. Heard lies. Promises.

But he'd never heard them from *her.*

Keenan didn't touch her. His hand eased back as he hesitated.

Hesitated.

He'd taken a thousand souls. No, far more. But her . . .

Why her? Why tonight? She's barely lived. The vamp should be the one to go, not—

Nicole let out a guttural groan. Keenan blinked and his wings rustled behind him. No, he had a job to do. He would do it—

Nicole grabbed a thick shard of broken glass and wrenched it up. She shoved it into the vampire's neck and caught him right in the jugular. His blood spilled over her as the vamp wrenched back, howling in pain and fury.

Her throat was a mess, ripped flesh, blood—so much blood. Hers. The vamp's. Nicole grabbed another chunk of glass and swung again with a slice to the vamp's neck.

Fighting.

She was fighting desperately for every second of life that she had left. And he was supposed to just stop her? Supposed to take her away when she struggled so hard to live?

You've done it before. Do it again.

So many humans. So little life. So much death.

"Bitch! I'll cut you open—"

The vamp would. In that instant, Keenan could see everything the vamp had planned for Nicole. Her death would be ten times more brutal now. The future had already altered for her. *Because I hesitated.*

"I'll rip your heart out—"

Yes, in the end, he'd do that, too.

She'd die with her eyes open, with fear and blood choking her.

"I'll shred that pretty face—"

Her coffin would be closed.

A fire began to burn inside Keenan. Burning hotter, brighter with every slow second that passed. *Why her?* She'd . . . soothed him before. When he'd heard her voice, it had seemed to flow through him. And when she'd laughed . . .

He'd liked the sound of her laughter. Sweet, free.

"*Help . . . me . . .*" Her broken voice.

Keenan squared his shoulders. What did she see when she looked at him? A monster just like the vamp? Or a savior?

"No one fuckin' cares about you . . ." The vamp yanked the glass out of his neck. More blood sprayed on Nicole. "You'll die alone and no one will even notice you're gone."

I will notice. Because she wouldn't be there for him to watch anymore. She'd be far beyond Keenan's reach. He didn't know paradise, only death.

She tried to push off the ground, but couldn't move. The blood loss had gotten to her and made her the perfect prey.

The vamp's claws were up. "I'm gonna start with that face."

Nicole shook her head and swiped out with the glass. The wounds didn't stop the vampire. Nothing was going to stop him. No one. Nicole would scream and suffer and then finally—*die*.

And Keenan would watch. Every moment.

No.

His hand lifted, rising in that last, final touch. His touch could steal life and rip the soul right of a body.

He reached out—and locked his fingers around the vampire's shoulder.

The vampire jerked and shuddered as if an electric charge had blasted through him. Keenan didn't try to soften his power. He wanted the vampire to hurt. Wanted him to suffer.

And that was wrong. Angels weren't supposed to want vengeance. They weren't supposed to get angry. They weren't supposed to care.

Killing the vampire was wrong. Against orders. But . . .

She will suffer no more.